Through Thick and Thin

By

Mark Barber

ZMOK
BOOKS

Some people do a ton for the Kings of War community, quietly and without fanfare. The risk is that they do not get the recognition they deserve. This book is for Mat Green, Mark Cunningham, Eldon Krosch Jnr and Michael C Carter.

Tales of Pannithor: Through Thick and Thin
By Mark Barber
Cover image by Mantic Games
This edition published in 2025

Zmok Books is an imprint of

Winged Hussar Publishing, LLC
1525 Hulse Rd, Unit 1
Point Pleasant, NJ 08742

Bibliographical References and Index
1. Fantasy. 2. Epic Fantasy. 3. Action & Adventure

For more information
visit us at www.whpsupplyroom.com
Twitter: WingHusPubLLC
Facebook: Winged Hussar Publishing LLC

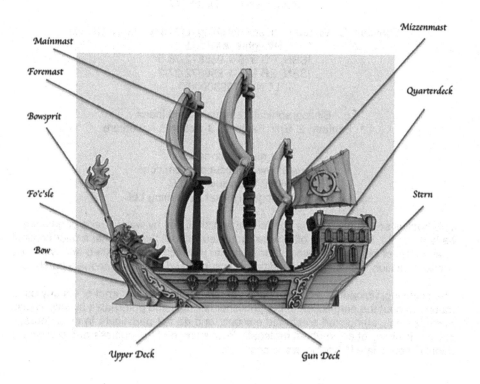

Mainmast

Foremast

Bowsprit

Fo'c'sle

Bow

Mizzenmast

Quarterdeck

Stern

Upper Deck

Gun Deck

Elohi-Class Frigate (Batch Two) – Basilean
Navy

An Introduction to Pannithor

The world of Pannithor is a place of magic and adventure, but it is also beset by danger in this, the Age of Conflict. Legions of evil cast their shadow across the lands while the forces of good strive to hold back the darkness. Between both, the armies of nature fight to maintain the balance of the world, led by a demi-god from another time.

Humanity is split into numerous provinces and kingdoms, each with their own allegiances and vendettas. Amongst the most powerful of all is the Hegemony of Basilea, with its devout army that marches to war with hymns in their hearts and the blessings of the Shining Ones, ready to smite those they deem as followers of the Wicked Ones.

Meanwhile, the Wicked Ones themselves toil endlessly in the depths of the Abyss to bring the lands of men to their knees. Demons, monsters, and other unspeakable creatures spill forth from its fiery pits to wreak havoc throughout Pannithor.

To the north of the Abyss, the Northern Alliance holds back the forces of evil in the icy depths of the Winterlands. Led by the mysterious Talannar, this alliance of races guards a great power to stop it from being grasped by the followers of the Wicked Ones. For if it ever did, Pannithor would fall under into darkness.

In the south, the secretive Ophidians remain neutral in the battles against the Abyss but work toward their own shadowy agenda. Their agents are always on-hand to make sure they whisper into the right ear or slit the right throat.

Amongst all this chaos, the other noble races – dwarfs, elves, salamanders and other ancient peoples – fight their own pitched battles against goblins, orcs, and chittering hordes of rat-men, while the terrifying Nightstalkers flit in and out of existence, preying on the nightmares of any foolish enough to face them.

The world shakes as the armies of Pannithor march to war…

Chapter One

Red Skull
Infantosian Islands
East Infant Sea

The waves gently but audibly rolled up the sands of the beach, paused for the briefest of moments, and then retreated back silently. Back home, across the shingles of very different beaches, it was the retreat that generated more sound; out here in the tropics, across the sunbaked white sands, there was next to nothing. The smell of the salty water – that remained the same. The pounding headache that came with a night of excess; that too was all too familiar.

Tem Mosso let out a groan, the gritty texture of sand seeping past his lips and grating against his gums as he stirred. Then the pain of a black eye flared up, reminding him that he was hurt as well as hungover, but not permeating his alcohol-flooded body with enough presence of mind to pluck the memories to the fore. His fingers sank into the wet sand. He opened his uninjured eye and saw bright, blue skies. Agonizingly bright.

"Tem. Get up."

Somebody was kicking him. He knew the voice. It was the second time he had been addressed.

"Just a minute..." Tem slurred, closed his eyes, and sank back to lie face down in the sand to resume his slumber.

A booted foot whacked him in the ribs.

"Last time, Tem. Get up."

Grunting in protest, Tem struggled up to his hands and knees, spitting out a grog-infused mouthful of sand. He opened his good eye again. His head swam. The curative benefits of the fresh air went to war with the nauseating effects of a spinning horizon, worsened by the ebb and flow of the tide against the beach. Broken bottles, wooden planks, and small stone circle firepits littered the once idyllic beach.

Tem managed to claw his way up to one knee. Then, in an instant, he realized who was standing over him and what had happened last night. He looked up at the older, taller pirate. Black hair, recently cut short, framed a charming face dominated by a thin, pristine mustache.

"Oh f..."

"Forget about it," Cerri Denayo muttered, his handsome features showing a frustration that contrasted the charity of his words as he offered a hand. "Get up. We need to talk."

Tem stumbled to his feet, the horizon still maliciously refusing to stay steady and in focus. A flood of foulness attempted to rush up from his gut to his mouth. But Tem, at the age of twenty-three, was an experienced sailor and a veteran drinker. He swallowed it back down with ease. Cerri turned and walked slowly back up the beach toward the improvised, shanty town of Red Skull. Sea water dripped down Tem's soaked, brown breeches and boots to form a puddle in the sand before he stepped unsteadily forward to follow the notorious pirate captain.

The independent town of Red Skull was built upon the shattered hulls of thirteen ships, ranging in size from the smallest sloops to the vessel the town took its name from. The *Red Skull*, originally the *Windfall*, was a century old Genezan caravel that was taken up from trade and converted for privateering duties until, as the story went, the first mate led a mutiny, killed the captain, and renamed the ship. The desperate mutiny was driven by a lack of success as privateers, and the new crew turned to piracy against merchantmen of their own nation before sailing east to the Infantosian Islands. The ship was dashed against this very beach – either by a storm, while fleeing a sea serpent, or deliberately by the captain to kill off his crew and increase the survivors' shares of their treasure, depending on which version of the story was to be believed. Rumors of the lost treasure of the *Red Skull* spread far and wide, and the next half-dozen wrecks on the same beach came from would-be treasure hunters who lacked the local area expertise to navigate the notoriously treacherous shallows surrounding the island chain; the same shallows that formed the most effective part of the pirate settlement's defense against the Basilean Navy to the north and the Salamander fleets to the south.

Now, decades later, and with no sign of the legendary treasure of the Red Skull ever being found – having probably been taken and spent on drink and women by the original crew, anyway – a thriving community now existed around that old, original wreck. Ladders and walkways connected the thirteen wrecked ship hulls and the additional huts built over and around them, each converted for accommodation, more than enough taverns of unvarying quality, general goods stores and their storehouses, defensive cannon emplacements, and a basic shipyard. Those later ships were deliberately driven up the beach by their captains once their hulls succumbed to the ravenous woodworm that the warm waters of the east Infant Sea were legendary for; an infestation that could only be remedied with proper dry dock facilities or, rather uselessly, by crashing a ship into a beach, turning it upside-down, and letting the blazing tropical sun of the region burn the infestation out.

"You remember much about last night?" Cerri asked as the two reached the top of the debris-littered beach and met the entrance to the settlement's main street.

"Aye," Tem replied quietly, running a hand across his blond-stub-bled jaw as he recalled his conduct during the previous evening. The pain in both his black eye and his grog-addled gut flared up again. It was the events of the afternoon just before, whilst stone-cold sober, that were more troubling.

Cerri turned to the left and paced up onto the boardwalk skirting around the front of the upturned brig-shipyard office. Tem just about recognized two of the three passed out pirates slumped by the barrels in front of the ship's office as crew members of the schooner *Attacker*.

"I voted against you yesterday for a good reason," Cerri con-tinued as a refreshing blast of sea breeze swept across the wooden boards, half-buried in the light sand.

"I know, Captain," Tem replied.

Only three days before, Cerri had captained one of his four ships – the brigantine *Cutlass* – just off the Sand Lane, a densely populated merchant shipping lane running east to west, north of the Infantosian Islands. Rich pickings, but high risk due to the frequency of Basilean naval patrols. They fell foul of a frigate – the *Veneration* – and before managing to escape, a salvo of chain shot from the *Veneration's* bow chasers aimed high at the *Cutlass's* rigging ended up falling low and cutting across the deck. It also cut the quartermaster – Deadeye Skans-mari – cleanly in half at the waist. In accordance with the rules ratified and signed by Red Skull's three leading pirate captains, of which Cerri was one, a new quartermaster would be voted in democratically by the crew. The captain's vote counted as double. The captain's vote tipped the balance, just, and Tem lost that vote to Mari DuLane, a fearsome red-headed woman from the Port of Lantor.

So, Captain Cerri Denayo voted against him for good reason. Because he favored Mari, as she was one of his many, many lovers.

"What's the reason, then?" Cerri demanded as they approached Red Skull's western berth and the multitude of small vessels tied up alongside there. "If you know, what is it?"

"Because I'm not ready, Captain," Tem replied resentfully, and dishonestly.

Cerri stopped and turned to face him. The thin lips beneath his black, obsessively pruned mustache twitched with something between amusement and suspicion.

"I voted you out for two reasons. First, it's not that you're not ready. It's that you are capable of better things. Second, it's because there's two types of pirate in this world. You're one type. I'm the other. Mari DuLane? She's also the other. Brutal, lacking any morals or prin-ciples. Quartermaster is second only to the captain and needs to be trusted to keep the crew in line. One way or the other, Mari has a way of keeping men in line. You? You're an idealist. You're out here for the romance and legend of adventure on the high seas. All that nonsense. You don't really belong in my crew. You never have."

Tem's eyes immediately snapped into focus. Bile forced its way up toward his throat for a second time. His pulse quickened as he looked around the deserted jetty and the long shadows cast by the early morning sun.

"I've been loyal, Captain!" Tem protested. "Yes, I made an arse out of myself last night by landing one on Whes's fat face, but he pushed me! I was pissed off after losing the vote, and that belter pushed me! That doesn't mean I'm any less of a sailor and a fighter this morning as I was this time yesterday!"

Cerri laughed lightly and shook his head.

"Calm down, princess, I haven't brought you out here to kill you. Follow me."

Exhaling slowly, Tem took a moment before following the taller man further along the boardwalk, up a trio of battered wooden steps, and then along the jetty. Tem stopped momentarily between a white-hulled pinnace and a small, battered barque with an almost Varanguran feel to her lines, fearing the dreaded hangover had finally won the war in his gut. After a failed attempt to stifle a large belch, he considered himself the victor and carried on to catch up with the slim pirate chief.

"There," Cerri gestured to his right as he turned back to face Tem, "this is what I've dragged you here to see. And why I voted against you yesterday."

Tem looked across to see a slender, race-built sloop with a low freeboard and aggressive cut to her bows. The hull, immaculate in condition, was varnished a deep, almost maroon brown, while the decking was a contrasting pale yellow-white. Four light cannons – perhaps four-pounders – sat on red gun carriages, two on each side of the vessel.

"I grabbed this little beauty last week." Cerri beamed. "What do you think?"

Tem walked along the jetty, eyeing the modern-looking sloop and her speedy, decidedly Nyssian lines.

"She looks fast," he remarked, confident in his knowledge of lighter vessels such as the fifty-tonner in front of him. "Pretty. What's the word... cutesy?"

Cerri folded his arms and shook his head.

"Come on, have you learned nothing? You getting your head kicked in last night for shooting your mouth off, that's funny. Not knowing the perfect small raider when you see it? That's disappointing."

Tem narrowed his eyes suspiciously.

"Is this a test, Captain? I mean... you do own a frigate."

"A *light* frigate," Cerri corrected, "and she's the largest of all my ships. And I never use her. You know why? Because it's little belters like this that capture prizes *and* get away with it. The only thing keeping us safe here is the local geography, and the guns we've got positioned to take advantage of it. The largest vessel you'd ever even hope to get into that bay out there is a medium brig, and that would take intimate knowledge of the lanes and exceptional skill. Sloops, cutters, pinnaces, it's these that can skip in and out of here without a problem. And that's your way home to safety. Specifically, this ship is *your* way home to safety, Tem. I'm making you her captain. That's why I voted against you."

Tem's eyes opened wide. His vision swam again. A few seconds later, embarrassment kicked in as he realized he was stammering like a child. Cerri held his hands up.

"Just... just... yes. I get it. You're welcome. I've got another pair of four-pounders for her. I'd recommend putting them up front as bow chasers, but if you want them all in the sides, that's up to you. And I'll send twenty sea dogs your way to crew her. She'll take four times that, if you make enough of a reputation for yourself to get the volunteers."

Tem looked at the beautiful sloop, running a hand affectionately along her taffrail but still not daring to step aboard her, lest this moment reveal itself to be a dream or a prank of exceedingly poor taste.

"Captain, I..."

"Cerri," the older man corrected. "Captains don't call captains 'captain' around these parts."

"I'm a captain already? Don't I need to... I don't know, isn't there some sort of..."

Cerri narrowed his eyes.

"What? You want some sort of ceremony? I can wave my hands around a bit and make sorcerer noises if you want? Or you can just accept that the biggest moment in your life so far just passed by a few seconds ago while you stood there, three sheets to the wind like death warmed up, dripping sea water, and with a black eye. But remember, this isn't charity. You still work for me. I expect a full share in every, *every,* coin you pilfer. And I'll know, shipmate. I'll know. You understand me?"

Tem met Cerri's stare and nodded slowly. The veteran sailor's expression eased.

"Let me give you some advice," he continued, "before you go sailing off to chase your plunder and glory. One – don't get caught busking in the Sand Lane. Nibble away at the southern edge and be ready to cut and run, by all means, but don't sit in there all fat, dumb, and happy. The Basilean Navy will fill you in quicker than they can look at you, so if you see any of their lot, sling your hook and scarper. Don't believe any of these salty old dogs here who swing the lamp with their tales of taking on the mob. It's all bollocks. You see 'em, you cut and run. Got it?"

"Got it."

"Two – steer clear of Ax Island. You think facing the navy is bad, you think scurvy pirates like me are bastards, imagine combining the two. That's orcs. We've mixed with 'em before, I know. But in an eight-gun sloop, you'll not even be able to stand up to their rabble boats. Don't try."

"Understood."

"Three – stow away any of these foolish notions of gentleman piracy. I've heard you spinning dits for the past two years. I know you think you're one of the good ones. There are no good ones out here. We're not here for the dream of independence from the Hegemony and liberty for all. We're here to kill people and take their money. The sooner you accept that, shippers, the better."

Tem nodded, folded his arms, considered his response, and then gave it.

"No."

"No?"

"No. Black Davey Krax, Ginny Morrs, and Black Bob Reynault all made a fortune without killing anybody who didn't resist them. I can do that, too."

Cerri's face twisted into a scowl.

"Now you listen here, me bloody hearty! Black Davey Krax was caught and sunk by a salamander pirate hunter, Ginny Moors got the short drop up in Keretia, and Black Bob disappeared four years ago. I think Ginny is still in Keretia somewhere, in a gibbet. That reminds me. Four – this is a great life, but the navy has more guns than us, and at some point, either the sea or those bastards will get you. Enjoy it whilst you can. If you have any success as a pirate captain, you'll very likely be dead within a year."

"Oh? Oh. Is there a five?"

Cerri took a few paces back toward his exquisite rooms in the old captain's cabin of the *Red Skull* itself. He turned around for one last time as Tem pondered on why so many pirates had chosen the precursor 'black' in an attempt to make themselves sound even more intimidating. Certainly in the stories they were always described as wearing black. Which in this heat was possibly why they were now dead.

"Aye, there's a five. You're a captain now, but remember that captains still have a pecking order. I'm at the very top. You're at the very bottom. We're on first name terms, but just remember who calls the shots."

"Aye. Got it."

Tem watched Cerri stride boldly back up the jetty, his expensive leather boots thudding on the creaking boards. A thought forced its way to the fore of his mind.

"Who's my quartermaster?" he called after the pirate chief.

Cerri did not slow down or even look over his shoulder.

"I thought you'd figured that out by now, shippers! You need to vote one in!"

Tem let out a chuckle, it became a hiccup, and then the grog finally won the war, and he projectile vomited all over his new sloop.

***

Thatraskos Harbor
Keretia
Northeast Infant Sea

The night always added color to the coastal town of Thatraskos. During the day, the picturesque, deep water harbor boasted rows of sparkling white buildings with neat, terracotta roofs cascading gently down the slopes toward the shimmering turquoise waters. Within the mouth of the harbor lay fishing boats and merchant ships of myriad shapes, sizes, and designs, as well as the Keratin Fleet of the Basilean Navy, led by its famous Elohi-class frigates. Two powerful forts flanked the harbor, somewhat ruining the beautiful scenery of the town, the negativity of their presence more than diffused by the sun-kissed waters of the River Thatras to the northeast.

But at night, strings of colored lamps lined the town, transforming the cobbled streets from uniform white to flickering reds, greens, blues, and yellows. Music flooded from a dozen taverns, ranging from the bawdy sea shanties of the fishermen and naval ratings; through the elegant arrangements imported from the mainland capital of the City of the Golden Horn; right through to the upbeat, eternally happy, and optimistic strings and drums of the descendents of the island's natives.

It was nearing midnight as Jaymes Ellias and Karnon Senne reached the winding path leading up to the entrance of the 'Palm Spring,' a late night bar just outside the town center with smooth walls painted in shimmering scarlet and emerald green by the rows of paper lights strung around its grounds. From inside the bar, an upbeat ditty sung quickly in the island's native tongue was accompanied by the happy music of the ukiola, a tiny stringed instrument favored by sailors, and the thumping of hand drums.

"They'll be annoyed," Karnon grumbled as the two men walked up the path, weaving between the colorful flowers of the venue's ornamental gardens to either side. "I've paid through the nose to move Sabine out here, and at the rate you work, she'll end up divorcing me before she's even been here for a month."

Jaymes looked across at the muscular man, flashing a brief and exaggerated smile as they reached the doors.

"To spend a life on Keretia?" He beamed. "For that, any woman would willingly put up with a miserable bugger like you! Come on, a rum'll cheer you up."

The cheerful music flooded out of the bar as Jaymes opened the doors. The flickering lights of the low-ceilinged bar, seemingly animated all the more by the fifty men and women – mainly human but interspersed with some hulking but happy salamanders – crowded on the dancing floor to the side of the tables and chairs still did not possess enough collective color to undo the aesthetic offense inflicted by Karnon's brazen, violet pantaloons. Jaymes wore much more subdued breeches and a silk shirt of plain white, contrasting his dark, short ponytail.

As he walked into the bar, he was greeted with smiles, waves, and even a few whistles from the regular patrons, girlfriends of some of his acquaintances, and the crooning singer of the band, hunched over his turquoise ukiola. Tarance, the barman, looked up at the two new arrivals and jabbed a thumb over at the bottles on the shelf behind him, his brow raised questioningly. Jaymes grinned and nodded to confirm their normal order of dark rum before walking down the short set of steps leading down to the bar.

A short, red-headed woman eased her way through the packed room toward them.

"You took your time!" Sabine shouted over the music and the din of conversation. "Has this idiot been keeping you back late with pointless paperwork?"

"As always," Karnon grumbled, "he's always bloody..."

"I was talking to Jaymes," Sabine smirked at her husband.

"Yeah, same as always," Jaymes shrugged, "I wanted to get here hours ago, but this grumpy sod insisted we finish the entire week's returns in one go before we came here to have any fun."

Karnon turned to stare incredulously at Jaymes.

"*I* insisted! *I?*"

"You said it," Jaymes blinked before easing past the couple to grab the two shots of rum.

His eyes were immediately drawn to the young woman of incomparable beauty at the bar, her tanned skin standing out against a short, white dress of elven style and long, blonde hair. Two rums were slid across the bar to Jaymes as the woman looked up at him, her face lit up with a coy, but genuine smile as she flicked a coin and caught it repetitively with one hand.

"Crowns say I let the sailor buy me a drink," the woman said in her sing-song, Genezan accent. "Dragons say I tell him that he and his bootneck sidekick need to stop leaving Sabine and I waiting at bars for so long."

Jaymes wrapped his arms around Caithlin's waist and pulled her in to kiss her.

"I'm so sorry. It was all Karnon's fault."

Caithlin snatched Jaymes's rum from his hand, sank it in one, slammed the empty glass on the bar, and led him off to the dancing floor.

"Was it?" she queried.

"Erm... no. Not remotely. Entirely my fault, actually. This whole promotion thing, it turns out there's an awful lot more paperwork required being a captain than I thought."

Caithlin leaned against Jaymes as the two danced amidst the crowd, adopting the dancing style of the islanders that was so tame here on Keretia, but would be considered scandalous even in the cosmopolitan City of the Golden Horn.

"Haven't you got some lackey lieutenant you can get to do that for you?" Caithlin suggested. "The great captain of the warship *Pious*, the legend, the man who has hunted down three pirate ships in the last two weeks?"

"Well," Jaymes smiled, "I had a frigate – just out of a refit to reinforce her hull after that scrap with the orc smasher – and they had sloops and schooners. Little bit like using a dragon to hunt a duck, really. Still, keeps the Sand Lane safe. Keeps the trade routes open. Keeps the rum coming in. Speaking of which..."

"Dance first. Rum later." Caithlin frowned.

Jaymes held his fellow sea captain and pirate-hunter close, casting his eyes around the room of friends and friendly strangers alike. Four nights ago, he was clinging to the mizzenmast as his battered frigate plowed through the peaks and troughs of the Infant Sea in one of her notorious, unannounced storms. The night before, he stood high on the fighting tops, yelling for the royals and the stud sails to fly to coax every last knot out of his ship as they frantically ran from the jaws of a raging giant narwhal. The night before that, he yelled orders down from the quarterdeck to his officers, his frigate's guns pounding as his ears rang and the blue skies above were obscured by the choking, gray fumes of the ship's weapons.

On the deck of a warship, one lived or one died; sometimes through skill but often sheer providence. One thing that was certain was that it was never worth dwelling on. Every moment for the taking, every minute of happiness, was worth enjoying to the fullest. Jaymes smiled down at Caithlin as the two danced in the center of the small crowd, oblivious to all save the look of despair on Karnon's dour face as his wife forced him onto the dance floor.

***

Their feet crunched across the graveled parade square in front of the naval administration building as the two frigate captains walked briskly toward the main entrance. A trio of sloop lieutenants struck up salutes as they walked past, their downturned hands snapping up to touch the brims of their black, bicorn hats. Marcellus Dio, the senior of the two captains, brought his own arm up to acknowledge and return the salutes.

"I nearly had him!" Marcellus winced, wafting away a midge that incessantly buzzed near his sweat-soaked face in the late morning sun. "I was so bloody close! Had the weather gauge, fresh wind on the port quarter, good visibility... the one thing I didn't have was light. I only had a half hour, and it just wasn't enough. The bastards got away."

Jaymes looked up at the impressive building ahead. A central, broad cylinder led up to a narrower, glass-paned office some one hundred feet up, not dissimilar in appearance to the top of a lighthouse. All around the center block were tall, graceful marble pillars imported from the capital, their styling showing that even down on the south coast of the island of Keretia, this was Basilea. Two long wings, each four stories high, led east and west out of the central hub of the building. On the far side, a line of thick battlements looked out over the bay and the town, complete with twenty heavy cannons. And those cannons were merely there as a light support element to the guns in the two naval forts.

"I even saw him through my telescope!" Marcellus continued. "Standing on the quarterdeck of that brigantine. I mean... I think it was him. Two hundred ton brigantine, twenty guns – although some were fairly small. I'm pretty sure it was the *Cutlass*."

Jaymes looked across at the older captain and offered a sympathetic smile. The world was changing. Relations between Basilea and her neighbors – particularly the dwarfs – seemed worse than ever, and every week it seemed that more and more squadrons were being assembled to disappear off over the horizon as a show of force. That left less warships to ensure security of the vital shipping lanes that were the lifeblood of the capital, the City of the Golden Horn. And with less security came a rise in piracy. And with that, all of a sudden, the same warships were frequently encountering the same pirate vessels to exchange blows. The names of successful captains on both sides of the conflict were well known to each other. But while these encounters almost invariably ended up with either a naval victory or at least a fleeing pirate, the number of small pirate vessels slipping through the increasingly stretched nodes of the naval net was growing.

The two marine guards at the main entrance to the administration building, complete in their newly colored red jackets, stood stiffly to attention and brought their pikes up straight. Marcellus again returned the salute, stepped inside the cool building, and took off his hat to reveal his prematurely receding hairline. Jaymes followed him in and removed his own hat. Both the captains were all but identically attired, but to the expert observer, the differences in their careers and attitudes were demonstrated in their dress.

Both officers wore white uniform shirts and blue trousers. Marcellus, being more traditionally minded, wore blue leggings tucked into white stockings and black shoes. Jaymes wore looser fitting blue trousers – the regulation issue for non-commissioned rating sailors – normally only worn by officers commissioned from the lower ranks. Jaymes was, however, from a relatively affluent family and joined as a boy sailor destined for a commission; his choice in wearing loose trousers was twofold – it was popular among officers in the coastguard sloop force where he had spent much of his career, and as a sailor who still insisted on spending much time atop rigging, despite his rank, they were more comfortable and practical. Jaymes also wore boots rather than shoes – again, a uniform item more common amongst ratings, but since his promotion to captain, he had at least invested in more ostentatious boots of black leather which Samus, his perpetually grumpy steward, had insisted in polishing to a near mirror finish, in clear contravention to Jaymes's instructions.

Both officers carried straight, single-edged sabers attached to their belts by two long strips of leather, rather than wearing them at the hip – as had been the fashion for gentlemen for the past decade. Both wore dark blue neckerchiefs under their shirts. Jaymes's was a simple issue neckerchief which he was quick to doff as soon as he was at sea and out of sight of anybody of a higher rank. Marcellus's neckerchief was decorated with thin lines of sky blue; a design he adopted for all the crew of his frigate, the *Veneration*, a sign of his success in battle as outfitting a crew of over two hundred sailors and marines with custom-order neckerchiefs was not inexpensive. Perhaps a little showy, but not as ostentatious as some – Jaymes had heard of one outrageously extravagant commodore in the capital who had ordered red and yellow checkered sails for every ship in his squadron. Marcellus and Jaymes's uniforms were finished with heavy jackets of dark blue, decorated with the gold epaulets of captains. Again, Jaymes was very quick to discard the jacket once at sea, much to the chagrin of his former captain, Shining Ones above rest his soul.

The two officers walked across the plush, blue carpet of the ground floor, their echoing footsteps momentarily dulled, before they clipped their way up the spiral staircase toward the Vice Admiral's office in the glazed building top colloquially known as 'The Spy Glass.' As they reached the second floor, they were intercepted by Mauriss, the admiral's flag-lieutenant.

"Good morning, sirs!" the breathless, red-faced staff officer greeted Marcellus and Jaymes. "If you'll follow me, the admiral is waiting for you."

"We had instructions to report to Vice Admiral Horton," Marcellus explained.

"The vice admiral has taken leave of absence at short notice, sir," Mauriss explained. "Admiral Pattia is waiting for you."

Marcellus and Jaymes exchanged brief glances of relief as they followed the flag-lieutenant through the wood-paneled corridors to the building's west wing and the admiral's office.

"I wonder where the vice admiral is?" Jaymes muttered quietly.

"I dunno," Marcellus suppressed a yawn as he stopped briefly to straighten a framed painting of an Elohi class fifth-rate on the wall. "Given his temper, he's probably taken a few days off to go and punch small children repetitively in the face."

Jaymes choked on a failed attempt to suppress a laugh as Mauriss hurried his pace and flushed an even deeper red, failing in his own attempt to pretend he did not hear the insubordinate remark. The trio of officers passed more stylized, nautical paintings before they finally reached the admiral's outer office. The door to the admiral's main office was open, with sunlight pouring through the bay windows overlooking the sparkling turquoise waters of the harbor.

"Straight in here, gents," a curt order came from within.

Leaving Mauriss at his desk in the outer office, Jaymes followed Marcellus through the polished door and shut it behind him. Jaymes had always thought that Admiral Sir Jerris Pattia's office exhumed success. Yet more maritime paintings, now accompanied by highly detailed wooden models of warships old and modern in glass display cases. A highly polished desk wider than one man could ever need, particularly one of such short stature. A grand balcony overlooking the bay and the frigates tied up alongside; a beautiful view, functional, but not the intrusive and overbearing office and view of the vice admiral's 'Spy Glass.'

The admiral looked up from an impressive drinks cabinet in the corner of his office, where he emptied a decanter of dark liquid into three copper-bottomed glasses atop a mirrored, fold out cabinet door.

"Don't stand on ceremony," the short, middle-aged man beamed as Jaymes moved to stand to attention before the desk, "pull up a couple of chairs."

The two captains did as instructed as Jerris placed a glass down in front of each of them. The wiry little admiral then took a seat on the other side of the desk and drained half of his glass.

"Marcellus!" He beamed. "Good to see the *Veneration* is looking as fine as ever! I hear you chased away that bastard Cerri Denayo a couple of days ago! Grand job, old man! Grand job!"

"Nearly had him, sir," Marcellus winced bitterly. "We put a shot through his gaff from the bow chasers, but it wasn't enough to slow him."

"Saved the convoy, though," Jerris shrugged, "and protecting the Lane, that was your objective. So let's call that one a minor victory, keep our chins up, and just sink the bastard next time you see him, eh?"

"Right you are, sir."

The short admiral turned to grin at Jaymes.

"And Captain Jaymes Ellias! Now, what was it I told you last time I saw you in this very office?"

Jaymes paused to recollect.

"That I'd never make admiral, sir."

"Time before that."

"Can't recall, sir."

"I distinctly... *distinctly* remember telling you that less than a year from then, you'd be a famous and heroic frigate captain, romantically embroiled with a beautiful pirate captain! Didn't I? Well? Jaymes?"

Jaymes offered a thin and uncomfortable smile, took a small mouthful of the brandy poured for him, raised an approving eyebrow as the interior of his chest burned faintly and pleasantly as a result, and then looked back at the admiral. Yes, the promotion to captain had changed his life remarkably – much to the distress of Jaymes's parents, who he had previously told of his resignation of his lieutenancy and his plan to return home to join some old friends in a business venture.

"Well, I certainly wouldn't describe myself as famous, sir. And she's a privateer captain, not a pirate. And we're barely acquainted."

Jerris narrowed his eyes in something between amused suspicion and patronized disappointment before finishing his brandy and standing to return his glass to the drinks cabinet for a top up.

"Regardless," the admiral continued, "pirates are the precise reason I've brought you here. Marcellus, you're my... what do they call them in the theater? Star turn. That's the phrase. You're my anti-piracy star turn. Jaymes, you're off to a good start, and with a thirty-six gun, Batch Two – now upgraded with the toughest hull in the frigate force at my expense, I think it's worth me reminding you – so I'm sure you'll catch up. I've got the *Worship* and her squadron off east, keeping the dwarfs as grumpy as ever. I've got the *Encounter* and the *Devotion* heading south to investigate reports of Ahmunite bone ships making a nuisance of themselves. With the *Loyalty* and the *Reverence* both in refit, we're as thin on the ground as ever, and those pirate bastards basing themselves out of the Infantosians are getting bolder than ever. I need you both back out on the Sand Lane."

Jaymes took another mouthful of the expensive brandy and found his glass being topped up again before he had even returned it to the desk. He paused to spare a thought for his previous captain, Charn Ferrus. In his mind, as abrasive as he was, Ferrus would always be the star turn of Keretia's frigate fleet.

"We'll slip and proceed at first light, sir," Marcellus nodded.

"Likewise, sir," Jaymes added.

"We've had an unseasonably mild spring," the admiral continued, "fair westerlies, smooth seas. The Lane is getting busier than ever. If I had two dozen brigs with captains skilled enough to get in amongst the Infantosians, past their bloody fort, and able to land a detachment of marines, then this would be over. If I could spare even half of that to lay anchor around the islands and starve them out, I would. But right now we're stuck with a dozen different commitments, and you're all I can spare. Get yourself stacked to the gunwales with everything you need to stay out there for a while. I'll have your orders formalized and signed by this evening."

"Understood, sir," Marcellus said as he finished his brandy. "How many sloops are out there at the moment?"

"Twelve," Jerris replied, "paired up, but stretched thin across the entire route. You know the vulnerable points. Get yourselves out there and make some bloody noise."

***

Jaymes gave a brief wave of the hand as Marcellus peeled away, striding along the footpath leading to the steps down to the naval docks and his frigate. Gulls cawed in the clear sky above; more colorful birds chirped and sang from the branches of thick, drooping palm trees dotted around the perimeter of the naval base. Cannons lay idle at their emplacements along the stone walls, their duty crews remaining indoors, at the ready but clear of the blazing rays of the fierce, morning sun. Jaymes made his way over to one of the silent cannons and leaned on the wall, looking down at the harbor. He tapped an open envelope thoughtfully against one hand; given to him by the flag lieutenant just as he was leaving. It was a warning order that a newly appointed third lieutenant was finally being sent to him from the capital. Jaymes let out a derisive breath. From the capital. So, some rich boy with family influence was jumping the queue of perfectly capable midshipmen already at Thatraskos who could give a good account of themselves at the lieutenant's board.

Below the clifftop base, the hustle and bustle of morning activity in the harbor continued. A handful of fishing boats who were late to slip made their way out of the harbor walls to head south. Controlling and directing shouts drifted up from below as petty officers took charge of the lines of sailors passing crates across the jetty and up to the frigates to store ship. A new cannon was hoisted onto a merchant barque via a pulley. Hammering and banging could be heard as craftsmen and artificers repaired the damage to a small sloop.

"I thought I might find you here."

Jaymes looked up to see Caithlin walking across from the white gravel path to the cannon. The smiles and laughter of the previous evening were replaced with the stern, stoic face of the professional sea captain. As a privateer in the employment of the Basilean Navy and holding an auxiliary commission as a captain, Caithlin wore a jacket of dark blue with gold epaulets, similar enough to the jacket of a true Basilean naval captain to be confused by an observer who did not know better, but dissimilar enough so that any naval officer or rating could immediately tell the difference and recognize her for what she was. The white shirt and polished black boots were similar to Jaymes's, but Caithlin wore a black neckerchief and white breeches which were more common in the navies of the Successor Kingdoms as a nod to her Genezan origins. Atop her blonde hair, tied back in a broad black bow, she wore a black tricorn hat. A red sash made of orc sailcloth was tied around her waist, adding a piratical touch to her otherwise severe uniform.

Jaymes turned to face Caithlin and offered a smile. The privateer returned the greeting with a barely perceptible smirk before running a hand over the cannon and, determining it was clean enough to risk with a white uniform, hopped up to sit near the priming vent.

"Orders?" she asked.

Jaymes nodded.

"When are you heading out?"

"Tomorrow," he replied.

"Me too."

"How long have you known that?"

Caithlin looked down at the town square clock tower.

"Oh, about five seconds ago," she replied coolly.

Jaymes let out a mutter of disagreement and paced over to lean back against the gun, next to her.

"You can't go out just because I am. You've got a hundred sailors on that brig. You can't base your entire ship's program around what I'm doing."

"Why not?" Caithlin countered evenly, her beautiful face still serious, business-like. "It's my ship. I can do what I want. Look... there's two things keeping me here. I owe your government so much money that unless I capture a serious prize, I'll be indebted and unable to go home for nearly a decade. That's first. Second, and no less important... well, that's you."

Jaymes looked up at where she sat, her stony exterior at odds with the compassion behind her words. The Genezan captain looked past him, at the horizon.

"I sit here," she continued, "wearing a rank that is incredibly difficult to achieve. Yet I find myself incredibly saddened by the consequences, sometimes. It would be considered an absolute outrage and deeply inappropriate for the two of us to merely hold hands while we're in uniform. What I wouldn't give to trade it in for a dress so that we could do something as simple as go for a walk, arm in arm."

"Well... we can... and we do, from time to time."

"In secrecy, with caveats on our freedom. I promised you that every time you put to sea, I'd be there with you. That at least gives us something."

Jaymes span around to face her, his face contorted in a wince.

"We spoke about this. You'll never pay that debt off this way. If you take the *Queen* out in company with a frigate, you'll never get prizes of your own. *Pious* has twice the guns and over twice the crew. I don't want to compete with you. I want you to earn enough to buy back your independence."

Caithlin hopped down from her perch on the gun and looked up at him, closer to him than she should have been. She narrowed her dark eyes and nodded.

"I know. You're right. But it doesn't mean I have to like it. Look... do you know Linidi? It's a rather lovely coastal village about an hour west of here."

Jaymes nodded.

"I know it. From the sea, at least. I've never visited."

Caithlin looked back at him and began to step backward away, toward the gravel path.

"Meet me there, this evening. Eight bells, in the village square. We'll dine, go for a walk along the coast in peace, get a room together for the night. We can come back in the morning in separate carriages, slip and proceed to sea, and then go our separate ways to blow things up until we meet back here."

Jaymes flashed a smile, still feeling hollow inside from the sadness of her tone, and raised his hand to the brim of his hat.

"Eight bells. I promise I'll be there."

Caithlin returned the salute with an almost mocking smile and one raised eyebrow before turning to walk away.

***

The top of an orange-red sun peered over the hazy horizon, reflected almost perfectly in the still, blue waters below. Gulls circled and cawed noisily above in the dark blue of dawn, their cries audible over the rush of water streaming past the hull of the slender sloop. The *Adventure Prize* – the name carved into the stern of the ship and the name that Tem was too superstitious to change – cut easily through the gentle waves, the morning breeze billowing out her mainsail and headsail to starboard.

"Mainsail made!" Flyde called from aft.

"Heads'l made!" Ash repeated from forward.

Tem glanced along the deck at his twenty sailors as the deck began to heave gently beneath him. His first command. A pretty little race-built ship that looked to be made for comfortably transporting rich folk on simple, coastal excursions; but now fitted with six light cannon, she was a ship ready to fight.

"Heads'l! Haul in the heads'l sheets!"

Ash, a small sailor from Nyseena, immediately obeyed the command and dragged in the sheet to pull the sail taunt. Tem folded his arms and nodded. If they intended to capture any prizes, they could not afford to lose a single knot of speed with poor standards of seamanship. And then there was what was expected of them once they boarded. Tem had already given his new crew 'the talk' on the jetty; his first time stating the expectations and rules rather than mutely listening and absorbing. There would be dissenters. That much he was sure of. But he had his own ideas about how things would run, and any bilge rat who dared stand in his way would wish they had not.

The lithe sloop dipped at the prow and slid down into a trough as the seas began to pick up in intensity, the relative comforts of Red Skull receding toward the southern horizon in the dawn light. Tem looked ahead, past his crew on the fo'c'sle, and further still past the bowsprit. The northern horizon beckoned, his pathway to fame and a name of his own, leading for the first time instead of following. A chance to prove himself to the father of the girl – there was always a girl – who thought a poor, out of work sailor to be not good enough for his daughter. And the girl herself, the one who should have had the courage to stand up for their promise to each other instead of backing down in fear at the first sign of anger and opposition from her overbearing father.

Tem would show them all.

***

Up ahead, the first of the bow chasers on *Veneration's* fo'c'sle snapped out a staccato bang as the frigate rounded the edge of the harbor's west mole. With one second intervals, the firing continued down the warship's starboard side until seventeen guns had fired – the very specific number required to salute a full admiral. The gun's salute was answered a second later by a corresponding bang from the long balcony on the east wing of the naval administration building, signifying the admiral's staff returning the salute – an excessive courtesy in some eyes, and certainly not mandated. The great, twin-masted Elohi frigate plunged through the turquoise waters, propelled southward by the fresh winds caught on her topsails and staysails.

Three ship's lengths astern, the larger, three-masted Batch Two Elohi, *Pious*, followed the lead ship out of the harbor. Over two hundred sailors stood rigidly to attention in their neatly pressed uniforms of Basilean naval blue, punctuated at regular intervals by marines in their newly issued red jackets, formed up in a neat line that ran around the perimeter of the upper deck. Jaymes stood central on the quarterdeck with Danne Estrayia, the ship's master, and Mayhew Knox, his first lieutenant; both of them relatively new to the ship's company. Sweat trickled down both sides of his face as he stood to attention, the midday sun burning down and practically igniting the thick material of his fore-and-aft, bicorn hat, and dark blue jacket.

Pious's bowsprit drew level with the end of the mole.

"Mister Knox," Jaymes called, "pipe the salute."

"Bosun!" Mayhew Knox yelled. "Pipe the salute!"

The ship's bosun raised his metal whistle to his lips and let out a long blast of a single note.

Karnon Senne, the captain of marines, braced up in response to the ceremonial call.

"Starboard guns! Seventeen gun salute!" Karnon bellowed. "Fire!"

The first gun barked out a boom, and white-gray smoke wafted across the quarterdeck. With well-drilled precision and perfect interval timing, the firing rippled down the side of the large frigate. Again, the salute was replied promptly from ashore. The stench of expended gunpowder wafting through his nostrils to replace the salt of the warm waters below, Jaymes risked a glance out of the corner of his eye and saw the day-to-day activity along the jetty and seawall continue as normal. Sailors loaded and unloaded stores from ships. Carpenters and shipwrights continued with repairs and refurbishments. Gunners and marines checked over their cannons. As the two frigates set out to sea and their possible destruction along the Sand Lane, life carried on.

A final series of guns blasted away from behind the *Pious*, as the smaller nine-pounder cannons from the privateer brig, *Martolian Queen,* sounded her own salute. Not officially commissioned into the Basilean Navy, there was no formal requirement for the *Martolian*

Queen to salute the admiral on exiting his harbor, but her captain chose to do so nonetheless. As a return courtesy, the admiral's gun replied in acknowledgment.

Satisfied that the *Pious* was clear and his ceremonial duties were complete, Jaymes turned to face his first lieutenant.

"Mister Knox, fall the men out and to their watch stations. Mister Estrayia, topsl's and headsl's, station us off *Veneration's* port quarter."

"Bosun!" Mayhew shouted. "Pipe the carry on!"

The shrill, two-tone note sounded. Immediately on its abrupt end, the sailors and marines turned smartly in place and then quickly set about returning to their positions as the buzz of conversation swept across the deck.

"Loose the topsails!" Danne Estrayia bellowed up to the top-men positioned on the three masts. "Set the headsails! Helmsman! Two points to port! And... thus!"

The powerful frigate heaved into life underfoot, listing gently with the turn as the great, pale gray sails above were unfurled with precision and discipline by the veteran crew. Jaymes paced back to the stern of his ship and looked down as the brig in tow loosed her own sails, aggressively setting studding sails to catch every iota of the seabreeze as she peeled off to starboard to turn away for the west. Jaymes saw Caithlin stood with her hulking salamander first mate on the quarterdeck, quickly removing her jacket and hat now she was out of visual range of the admiral's offices. She hopped up onto the taffrail before nimbly climbing up the ratlines sloping up to the mainmast, and then waved one hand, slow and high above her head. Jaymes held his own hat up high, issued one wave, and then brought it down low before bowing his head to her. Caithlin blew him a kiss, formal and rigid in its delivery, but perhaps as romantic as she could manage in front of the potential gaze of three hundred sailors, then leapt back down to her ship as it sped away.

Jaymes looked forward to the great, bronze angel figurehead leaning back into the bow of his frigate and offered a silent prayer for Caithlin and her crew as the wind took them away. And that was that. No time to dawdle in self-pity or dwell on better days. To work.

"Samus?" Jaymes called as he removed his jacket, hat, and neckerchief.

His steward stomped over from the foot of the mizzenmast, grunted something under his breath, and then took Jaymes's effects before pacing away again. Jaymes allowed himself a brief laugh. There was no effort whatsoever from his steward to even begin to hide the disdain he had for the lack of formality in his captain. Jaymes's smile faded as he recalled that same disgust from the *Pious's* previous captain.

The bold lines of the harbor and town of Thatraskos softened and faded to smears as the summer heat haze melted home away on the northern horizon. *Pious* took station to the port of *Veneration*. The two frigates headed south. After an hour, a sailor on the main course yard began belting out a sea shanty.

"Aloft there! Shackle the ditties!" Danne, the gray-haired ship's master thundered.

"No!" Jaymes called, pacing over toward the front of the quarter-deck. "Let them sing if they want to. Up top! Give us a song, you tone deaf bastard!"

The topman high on the yard above shouted down a song, quickly taken up by the majority of the crew on the masts and deck alike as the frigate picked up speed.

> *"To fight! To fight we go!*
> *Out to face both sea and foe!*
> *To fight! To fight we go!*
> *Sails above, and oak below;*
>
> *But if fire and storm await,*
> *We still answer Basilea's call!*
> *Steady are us tars 'gainst all,*
> *The faith in our hearts ne'er abate!"*

Jaymes leaned back against the quarterdeck's port taffrail and looked forward at his ship and crew. Samus shook his head slowly and grimaced in disapproval as the sailors belted out the familiar song. Mayhew Knox, Jaymes's first lieutenant and a youthful, red-bearded man of twenty-three years, stood by the helmsman and shouted out along with the song. Francis Turnio, a pale-faced midshipman who had been with *Pious* longer than Jaymes, fidgeted uncomfortably and tried unsuccessfully to join in with a song he still somehow only knew a quarter of the words to.

"Singing, then," Karnon grumbled as he appeared silently next to Jaymes, making the latter jump with a start. "You intend to carry on permitting this?"

Jaymes flashed a smile to his captain of marines.

"Lighten up, me hearty!" he beamed, slapping the muscular man on the shoulder and eliciting a frown in response. "Soldiers sing on their way to action, too!"

"Do they?" Karnon narrowed his eyes. "Wouldn't know. I'm a marine, not a soldier."

"Oh, here we go," Jaymes hung his head despondently. "This again. You spent years in the legion. The marines have existed as a separate entity for... about five minutes in the grand scheme of things. Stop being such an elitist prick and sing the bloody song!"

Karnon folded his broad arms.

"I don't know the words."

"You don't need to."

"Of course I bloody well need to! How do I sing if I don't know the words?"

Jaymes looked forward again and cast an eye over the sails, nodding in satisfaction at the trim of his ship.

"Lesson one of sea shanties," he replied, "to get stuck in, you only need 'Hey' and 'Ho'! But, shipmate, here's the thing. They're different, you see? 'Ho,' you can shout out at any point. Any point you want to! But 'Hey'? That requires a bit more skill. Needs to be at a logical time of the song, normally crammed in between lines when people who know the words are drawing breath."

Karnon twisted up his face in fury.

"Well, I can't do that! I'm no musician! I don't know about timing and all of that bollocks!"

"Yes, I know that." Jaymes nodded sympathetically. "I've seen you try to dance. So I rather suppose that leaves you as a 'Ho' man rather than a 'Hey' sort of fellow. Now stop taking yourself so seriously and start shouting 'Ho' at random intervals!"

Veneration and *Pious* continued onward to the south, one more voice awkwardly joining in the din of sea shanties that drifted across the breeze from the latter warship.

Chapter Two

Adventure Prize
Six-gun Sloop, taken up from trade
Thirty leagues northwest of the Infantosian Islands

"Two points to starboard!" Tem yelled. "Two points, roundly, now! Give me everything she's got!"

Gunnta flung the helm sharply, and the nimble sloop responded beautifully, her bowsprit swinging about to line up ahead of the cutter. Both small vessels rose and fell gracefully with the turquoise waves beneath the emerging stars of the clear evening, the boards of the *Adventure Prize* creaking as the gap closed.

The white-hulled cutter continued to run regardless, her captain no doubt hoping and praying that they could hold off for long enough until the darkness of the night enveloped the seas and they could slip away from their rapid pursuer. One foot up on the taffrail just forward of the port guns, Tem leaned forward eagerly and brought his brass-rimmed telescope up to his right eye again. The cutter had altered course to starboard, desperate to place the wind at the optimal angle to increase her speed. But that cut her just a little across the *Adventure Prize's* bows; yes, she was faster, but now Tem was not giving chase from directly astern – he was cutting the corner of a triangle. It was a foolish move.

"Heave to!" Ash yelled over the wind as it whipped across the sloop's sails, banging a loose sheet against the boom. "Heave to, you bastards!"

Skordak, a hulking, bearded Varangurian sailor a long way from home, let out a long whistle and shouted out something decidedly more predatory and threatening. The rest of the crew roared and bellowed in laughter. His eyes narrowed in concentration, Tem looked up at the black flag fluttering atop his sloop's mast, then forward again. Cerri was right. He should have positioned those two guns up forward as bow chasers. It was not beyond the realms of possibility to move them now, but with the swell picking up and the deck heaving, there was a fair chance he would injure one of his crew. No, he need not do that. The captain of the cutter was panicking. It would not need much to push him over the edge.

"Stand by the port guns!" Tem roared. "By your guns, you bilge rats! Move!"

A trio of sailors rushed across to each gun, the cannons already loaded and run out.

"On my mark!" Tem held up one arm.

The elegant, white cutter continued on. The dark of the night drew closer.

"Helm," Tem yelled, "hard a' starboard!"

Gunnta dragged the ship's wheel around. The *Adventure Prize* swung about in response, the hull dropping to starboard and leaning into the turn. Tem wrapped one fist around the shrouds connecting the hull to the top of the mast, a smile forcing its way across his lips momentarily as the severity of the situation was lost on him and he escaped the moment to remember why he first fell in love with sailing. Then the ship was in position and he needed to act again.

"Midships!" Tem shouted. "Thus! Midships, thus!"

Gunnta centered the wheel. The *Adventure Prize* eased instantly out of the turn, her deck straight and level. The guns lined up.

"Port guns, fire!"

The triplet of guns barked out in response, jumping back on their small, knee-high carriages until held taunt at the end of their restraining lines. In quick succession, a fountain of water blossomed up just ahead of the cutter's stem; a ragged hole was torn through her staysail and a loud thud cracked out across the waves as wooden splinters flew up from her bow. Tem's crew cheered as one. Almost instantly, the flag atop the cutter's mast was hauled down in defeat.

Tem had stood by as one of the jeering crew over a dozen times before as ships surrendered to a pirate attack. But, since his first action, this was the first time he remembered his heart hammering against his chest so intensely. He leaned forward over the rail again as his vessel drew closer to the cutter.

"Shorten your sail!" he bellowed out to the crew of the cutter. "Heave to wind! Look lively, now!"

The cutter's crew responded. The sails shortened, and the vessel slowed as the stem came about to point into wind. Tem's crew did not need another order. Two of his men took position at the port waist and threw grapple lines across to attach the *Adventure Prize* to its first victim. The two vessels came together with a thud. Ash and Skordak were the first across to the slightly smaller vessel's deck, their cutlasses drawn. Another five pirates followed before Tem hopped across, his flintlock pistol held at the ready.

A short man of perhaps thirty years of age – rotund, balding, and white-faced – walked hesitantly out to the pirates from the cutter's quarterdeck. The remaining sailors, only eight of which could be seen, remained at their positions as they watched the pirates with a mixture of fear and loathing.

"Who's the captain here?" the bald man asked. "Who have I surrendered to?"

Ash immediately raised his cutlass, ready to smash down the basket hilt into the mariner's face. Tem whistled to stop Ash in his paces. The wiry sailor looked over his tattooed shoulder. Tem glared at him and shook his head before pacing out to meet the other captain.

"I'm in command here," he announced, "and you should have stopped dead in the water the moment you saw us raise the black flag. That's what the black means! We'll give you quarter! You've wasted two hours of my time, me bloody hearty, and for that, I'm royally pissed off! Now, what's your cargo?"

"Passengers!" the older captain exclaimed in desperation. "Just passengers! None of them are even wealthy! Look... I'm not criticizing what you're doing here. I've done my years in the merchant fleets. I've heard from dozens of sailors that the navy is just as bad! I understand why you've chosen to do this and I'm not against you! But you've got the wrong ship! There's nothing here for you to take!"

For a moment – just a brief moment – the short captain's words had Tem convinced. Yes, Tem himself was an ex-merchant fleet sailor. From a boy sailor at the age of nine to a topman by his late teens, Tem had served his time from the Endless Sea to the Garric Gulf and everything in between. He still had the scars on his back to prove he knew the harsh discipline of a merchant captain tyrant firsthand. But any brief connection that was established between the two captains was instantly severed when Tem's attention was dragged to the open companionway behind the captain and the terrified shrieking that echoed up from the deck below.

A young woman with auburn hair, not even out of her teens, rushed up onto the deck. Blood drizzled down from a cut by the side of her eye. Her simple dress was torn, and her face was pale with panic as she screamed out in terror. The hulking figure of Skordak lumbered out of the hatchway after her, a grin plastered across his crooked, scarred face. Practically dragging on one of the Varangarian sailor's treetrunk-like arms was a thin man of perhaps forty years, one of his eyes already closed from heavy bruising, and blood dribbling from his mouth and forehead. Yet, despite the laughable difference in size between the two men and the smaller man's bleeding wounds, he valiantly continued to try to stop Skordak from pursuing the girl.

A trio of Tem's pirates burst into laughter and encouraged their towering shipmate with lewd shouts and bawdy calls. Skordak laughed and half turned to slam a fist into the small man, knocking him senseless before grabbing the girl by her hair. She screamed louder in a mixture of pain and panic as the Varangarian dragged her by her long locks across the deck, kicking uselessly with her small, bare feet as she was forced back toward the hatchway leading down below the deck.

Tem was not even aware that he was acting before it was done. He had not stopped to consider his responsibilities as captain, the long term effects of allowing this ogre of a man to act in any way he pleased, the weakness it would show if he did not insist immediately on his rules of conduct being followed to the letter. Somehow, in an instantly forgotten blur of a moment, the world fell silent as Tem held a cocked pistol to Skordak's head. He had seen Skordak fight. He knew he did not stand a chance against the immense mountain man. But he also knew that pistols were rare enough in human hands, he had one, and all the muscle in the world would not stop a bullet.

"Which part of my damn rules didn't you understand, shipmate?" Tem spat venomously. "Because I made it clear as day that on my ship, on *my* crew, quarter will always be given to those who surrender. Always. So you explain to me exactly what's going on with that wench, or as the demons of the damn Abyss are my witness, I'm gonna blow your brains out."

Skordak looked down at his new captain with no attempt to veil his disgust. The girl fell silent. Both crews stood frozen in place, silently watching the confrontation.

"Just having a bit of fun, *Captain*," the huge man sneered, "nothing more."

Tem narrowed his eyes. He nodded slowly. He kept the pistol in place.

"A bit of fun?" he repeated in contempt. "Getting shitfaced on grog is a bit of fun. Losing an entire month's pay on a roll of the die is a bit of fun. This? This ain't fun, shippers. Not for her."

Skordak grunted in his native tongue, clearly a bitter insult.

Tem pulled the trigger and blew the contents of the big man's head out of the back of his skull. The girl, now covered in her attacker's blood, began screaming again. The bald captain rushed to kneel beside her, pulling her away from the corpse of the giant Varangarian. Tem span in place to face his crew, knowing full well that the old friends of Skordak – Gunnta in particular – would likely already be reaching for their weapons.

"Did I not make myself clear?" Tem yelled as he paced toward his crew. "The rules are that a new captain gives the Talk! I gave you the Talk, and I made it clear *exactly* what my thoughts are on giving quarter! If any of you dogs act like animals, then I'll put you down like animals!"

Footsteps creaked on the boards next to Tem. A shadow fell across him. He looked up and saw Halladai, his dark-skinned Ophidian quartermaster, stood side by side with him.

"You heard the captain!" the older sailor snarled. "You heard him on the Talk, and you're hearing him now! Any sea dog here before me that has a problem with obeying his captain's orders at sea? I'll rip your throat out with my damn teeth! You hear me?"

"Aye!" Ash shouted, loud and enthusiastic.

Good old Ash. He had jumped from that merchant ship with Tem years ago, back in Keretia. Tem nodded his gratitude to Halladai and then held up his pistol to commence reloading the weapon before turning to look down at the cutter's captain. He dropped to one knee next to the older sailor.

"Now listen in, and listen in good," he whispered. "I'm going to let you go. I'm going to let your crew go, and your passengers. I'm not going to harm so much as a hair on one head. I'm going to let you take your ship and all of your food and water. But you've got five minutes – and not a second longer, shipmate – to make every last ounce of anything valuable appear on this deck. Everything. Absolutely everything of value that you don't need to survive. Then I'll check this ship to see if you've held anything back from me. If you have? I'll set my dogs on you. Do we have an agreement?"

The bald captain swallowed and nodded immediately.

"Aye. We have an agreement."

***

Hegemon's Warship Pious (36)
278 souls on board
The Sand Lane

A thin layer of low, overcast cloud painted the skies in a dreary white as drizzle sprinkled down in the light winds. A weather front had passed through; its strong winds now abated, but their effects were still clear with heavy, uneven waves of turquoise topped with white foam crashing into the ships along the traffic lane.

"Watch him!" Jaymes shouted across the frigate's quarterdeck, pointing a hand at the second enemy vessel to the south. "Mister Innes, do not take your eyes off that damn sail!"

Three ponderous merchantmen heaved and fell in the heavy seas ahead, formed up in line astern as if sailing to battle. A pair of Basilean naval sloops had peeled off and were already altering starboard to move out to intercept the two red-sailed vessels to the south. Jaymes raised his telescope to his eye again. Both orc vessels were something that he could deal with well enough – the hammerfist would be problematic, and if it came to a full fight, he knew he would be limping home with significant damage and a list of dead. The blood runner, that was less of a problem. In isolation, at least. Together, if they worked well as a team – something orcs were not prone to demonstrating – even an upgraded Elohi Batch Two with a slick, highly experienced crew might be overcome.

"Mister Turnio!" Jaymes shouted across the quarterdeck at his senior midshipman. "Tell those two sloops to get back on station and form up to either side of us before those orcs cut them up for bloody firewood!"

The teenaged junior officer who was stood by the pennant locker tapped one hand to his forehead.

"Aye, sir!"

Jaymes snapped his telescope shut. Beat to quarters had been called, and the ship's company was closed up for action and ready. Kaeso Innes, his second lieutenant, stood on the quarterdeck with him along with Danne Estrayia, the ship's sailing master. Mayhew Knox, the first lieutenant, paced the upper deck below alongside Karnon Senne, the captain of marines, as the two inspected the readiness of the gun crews.

"They've got the weather gauge, the bastards," Danne murmured, "whether they realize that or know what to do with it is another matter."

Jaymes exhaled and shook his head as the deck lurched beneath them, the drizzle thickening as mist rolled in.

"I've underestimated orcs before," he replied quietly, "never again. These two know exactly what they're doing. They're not positioned upwind of a convoy's defense with the wind off their starboard quarters by chance."

Jaymes noticed the middle-aged sailing master scowl and mutter something under his breath, but he chose not to challenge it. Not now, at least. As a twenty-six year old lieutenant, life was generally easier as age and seniority married up rather well in the eyes of the crew. But, as a twenty-six year old frigate captain? For those who did not know his past, it was the obvious and incorrect assumption that he was born to privilege, from a family with that golden word in the naval service – influence.

"They're going for it! They're bloody well going for it!" Kaeso shouted excitedly as he stared through his brass telescope. "Sir! Look at this!"

Jaymes looked through his own telescope. Off to the south, visible as faded lines in the thickening mist, the orc blood runner heaved and fell with the waves as the crude, almost comical metal drill on its prow span up into life. The red-sailed, fore-and-aft rigged hulk of a vessel caught the wind and shot forward in an ungainly fashion, heading just to the west of north. Abeam of the blood runner, the stockier and infinitely more dangerous hammerfist had also set sails but shorter than the blood runner, leaving her wallowing off the starboard quarter as the lighter vessel took the lead.

"Mister Turnio," Jaymes shouted across to his signals midshipman, "signal the convoy! Tell them to reduce speed! Mister Estrayia – get us just upwind of the convoy, right in the middle, beam on to those bastards!"

Colored signaling flags shot up the halyard on the side of Pious's mainmast as the sailing master rushed down to the forward end of the quarterdeck, bellowing orders up to the topmen on each of the three masts to set the sails for overtaking the convoy up ahead. Heavy footsteps thunked quickly across as Karnon Senne made his way over to the huddle of officers on the quarterdeck. He positioned himself to Jaymes's side, out of earshot of the others.

"What's going on?" the marine officer asked quietly.

"Those two orcs are sniffing us out," Jaymes replied, pointing his telescope to the red-sailed hulks approaching from starboard. "The blood runner is taking the lead to draw us out and take fire. That'll leave the hammerfist to slip past and engage the convoy."

"But we can take 'em?" Karnon asked. "A Batch Two Elohi against those? We can take 'em, right?"

"We can take a hammerfist and win, with casualties," Jaymes replied grimly. "We can absolutely shatter a blood runner. Both, together? I'm not sure, shipmate. Too close for my comfort. And I guarantee you that they're both thinking exactly the same thing. That's why they're being uncharacteristically cautious for orcs. They're aggressive, they throw caution to the wind... but they won't kill themselves for nothing. Not when there's an easier target tomorrow."

"And our sloops?" the burly marine pointed to the southeast. "They'll give us an edge?"

Jaymes's eyes widened as he saw the two light sloops practically skipping across the foamy waves as they tacked through the winds to meet the orcs.

"Mister Turnio! Signal those bloody sloops again! What in the seven circles of the Abyss are those stupid bastards doing?! Get them on my flanks, now!"

Jaymes swore and shook his head as he watched Francis and an assisting petty officer quickly reattach the line of signals that had been hauled down for the communique to the merchantmen.

"About there," Jaymes continued his explanation to his captain of marines, pointing to an area of sea just to the south of the trio of merchant ships, "those two will have to come straight for us, initially at least. The blood runner is positioned to absorb the hits. Fine. I'll bite. We'll smash her in the face and rake her bow on her way in. I don't think she'll make it to us intact. That leaves us with the hammerfist and, one on one, I fancy our chances. Turnio! The signals for the sloops! Hurry up, man!"

The two orc ships drew nearer. If the two sloop captains had seen the orders from the frigate or not, Jaymes had no idea. Adjusting for the conditions and skillfully tacking and jibing through the headwind, the sloops shot on toward the orc raiders.

"Jaymes, if that hammerfist gets through your fire and boards us..." Karnon warned quietly.

"I know. I know."

The three large merchant ships reefed their sails and slowed to allow *Pious* to take up a better position. The orc ships drew closer, the less sea-worthy blood runner rising and falling in an almost exaggerated fashion with the increasing ferocity of the sea state, the forward end of her keel just aft of the churning drill even visible as the ship was thrown upward at the peaks of the waves. Jaymes raised his telescope again.

"'Bout six hundred tons," he nodded to Karnon, Danne, and Kaeso, "that's what I'd reckon at. Fairly light for a blood runner."

"Oh?" Karnon queried.

"They're not like ours, you see," Kaeso explained. "Our shipyards built our ships to very exacting specifications. The orcs? They're ship classes are more... ideas. Common ideas agreed on by their mob. An orc krudger with enough clout to build a ship will point at something he wants and tell his crowd to copy it. But no two are ever the same."

"Reef the courses!" Danne hollered up to the sailors along the yards above, ordering them to bring in more sail to slow the frigate again now that she was in position. "Handsomely there on the mizzen! Watch your bloody footing, lad!"

Clearing his throat as a claw of concern grasped at his chest, Jaymes watched as the two orc vessels increased to full sail. They were not sniffing out a potential fight. They were committed now. He turned to Samus.

"Sword and jacket, if you please," Jaymes ordered, pulling his dark neckerchief out of his pocket and tying it neatly before buttoning up his shirt.

"And your hat, sir?" the steward enquired gruffly.

"No. I shan't need that to kill orcs."

Wincing as if his entire family history had been mortally insulted, Samus headed down below to the captain's day cabin to recover his jacket and saber. Jaymes paced over to the forward end of the quarterdeck, looking down at the sailors and marines stood ready by the starboard cannons along the upper deck.

"Be ready on the eighteen pounders!" Jaymes called down to his first lieutenant. "They're nearly in range now!"

"Aye, sir!" Mayhew Knox called back up.

Jaymes saw yellow flashes through his telescope briefly light up the decks of the two sloops – now too far away to stand any chance of reading signal flags in the mist – as their light cannons fired on the blood runner. A moment later, downwind of the action, the crack of the cannons drifted back across the drizzle-soaked, salt-laden breeze. Jaymes swore again and shook his head as the pair of one-hundred-ton sloops stood between him and the blood runner, their light cannons barking out again as their decks were swallowed up by the white smoke from their guns.

"Come on!" Jaymes urged as he watched through his telescope. "Out of the way! You're too close!"

As if taking his whispered advice, the blood runner suddenly swerved violently like a shark darting out to bite at a fish. The orc vessel's drill plowed straight into the first sloop a'midships, the metal bit biting deep into the wood and physically flinging the entire ship fully around in an arc that plunged her inverted and beneath the waves. She appeared again a second later, dismasted, then split in two to sink beneath the waves. A sickening in his gut as he helplessly watched the carnage, Jaymes saw the second sloop react quickly but not fast enough, swerving in an attempt to clear from the dark-hulled orc vessel. The blood runner, the wind astern and free to maneuver with ease, altered course aggressively to port and smashed into the back of the sloop, knocking off a good ten feet of the ship's length from the very stern and flinging it to one side.

"Engage the blood runner!" Jaymes yelled angrily.

"Starboard guns! Target, starboard abeam! Fire!" Mayhew bellowed.

The frigate shook and rolled as the heavy eighteen-pound cannons roared as one, Jaymes's hearing instantly switching from the deafening blasts to a dull, high-pitched whine as his ears failed to keep up with the cacophony. Smoke streamed back over the deck, hiding the gun crews as they responded to muffled yells of commands from their gun captains to reload the cannons. The smoke had barely cleared from the deck before the last gun captain stood by his gun, arm raised to signal his team were ready to fire again.

"Fire!"

Again, the frigate shook and heaved. Jaymes coughed in the smoke, his eyes streaming from the acidic, stinging gray clouds. In a gap between salvos, he managed to catch a glimpse of the blood runner through his telescope – the spinning drill on the ship's prow was dented and worked itself around at an angle, black smoke pouring back from the damaged mechanism. The vessel continued to plunge straight toward *Pious* regardless as the hammerfist proceeded at full sail to her starboard; the badly wounded Basilean sloop limped away and altered course for the west.

Jaymes paced across the quarterdeck to the starboard quarter, away from much of the gunsmoke. Nothing else to do but monitor now; the ship was in position, and the gunners were laying down accurate fire at a rate commensurate with their skill and experience. The blood runner reeled from another salvo, her mizzenmast half-severed and falling to port at an unhealthy angle. The ship was close enough for Jaymes to see goblins dangling from the yards of the damaged mizzenmast, some losing their footing and falling the long, fatal drop to the deck and the sea below.

"That hammerfist is coming ahead of us," Danne warned his captain.

"I know," Jaymes replied.

"If we don't counter her, she'll be the one raking us."

"I know!" Jaymes repeated.

He rushed off to bellow an order to the fo'c'sle guns.

"Nine pounders! Open fire!"

The lighter nines joined their heavier brethren in flinging out round shot at the approaching blood runner, catching the damaged orc ship just forward of port midships and sending huge splints of wood twirling up into the air. Not far now, nearly close enough for the stumpy, guttural close range thirty-twos on the quarterdeck. Jaymes turned to Danne.

"Loose some sail! Catch the wind and get us right on the bastard's nose for a bow rake! Right up close!"

"Aye, sir!"

"Gunners! Stand to, port and starboard!" Jaymes called down. "Be ready for that hammerfist, port side!"

Each eight-man gun team divided in two, with a quartet of sailors leaving each gun to rush to port and be ready to fire from both broadsides simultaneously.

Under the sailing master's commands, *Pious* leaned away from the convoy and cut across the waves to intercept the blood runner's approach, closing the gap before a curt command to the helmsman swung her about to port again to position directly ahead of the orc vessel. To the orc captain's credit, he clearly saw what the powerful frigate was trying to achieve; the blood runner began a turn back away from the wind. But too late. Drifting into range of *Pious's* entire, thunderous broadside, Jaymes yelled an order across the crowded deck of his frigate.

"Fire!"

The order was echoed from stem to stern along the frigate's quarterdeck, upper deck, and fo'c'sle as the combined might of the heavy, light, and stubby close in cannons blasted out their deafening song. The entire ship seemed to jump as the full broadside erupted as one, nine, eighteen, and thirty-two pounder guns leaped back on their carriages to stop dead against their restraining ropes. Even before the next wave of smoke covered the frigate's quarterdeck, Jaymes saw that the angle was perfect. Cannonballs flew out to smash into the blood runner's prow, cutting across the upper deck from stem to stern in a bloodbath of carnage and destruction. Coughing and leaning forward out of the smoke, Jaymes rubbed his eyes as his streamed vision slowly cleared, orders to reload each weapon screaming out from his left. Cheers echoed from somewhere up forward, on the fo'c'sle where the smoke of battle was always quickest to clear. He knew what it meant.

Then he saw it for himself. In a gap amidst the white smoke, he saw the flickering yellow of flames. For a brief moment, he thought his eyes were deceiving him, an optical illusion where the sea was somehow on its side next to the stricken orc vessel. Then his brain made sense of the jumbled images and he realized that the blood runner had capsized and lay to port, her masts and sails dragging through the water as waves crashed up over her deck.

"Gunners! Port side! Stand ready!" Jaymes shouted out, fumbling his way across the smoke-filled quarterdeck to reposition on the opposite side of the frigate.

The vision that greeted him seemed to permit him to breathe evenly again, confirming his ship's victory. The hammerfist had already broken away, altering to starboard to open up and away from *Pious's* crippling broadside, the orc and goblin sailors in the complicated mess of the ship's rigging frantically trimming her sails and setting her up to tack through the wind. Another cheer erupted from *Pious's* crowded upper deck. Jaymes did not silence his men.

***

Martolian Queen (18)
Privateer (Converted Trade Brig)
110 souls on board
Twenty Leagues South of the Sand Lane

Five days. Five days of nothing more than the seemingly endless lines of Sand Lane traffic – sometimes just a trade galleon on the horizon; other times two entire trade fleets passing each other by on reciprocal courses – with not a threat in sight. It had seemed to be a fair idea from X'And, the ship's salamander first mate, to leave the lanes and head south to cut across the 'rat runs' leading up from the pirate-infested Infantosian Islands toward the trade lanes, but even they were empty from horizon to horizon.

The boards creaked beneath Captain Caithlin Viconti's feet as she paced the quarterdeck. Now out of sight of the stuffy Basilean naval authorities, she had changed her uniform of an auxiliary officer for simple and practical tan-colored breeches, softer boots, and a silk shirt with slits cut along the entire length of the sleeves – the only real aesthetic indulgence she allowed herself at sea. Her crew set about their work in the rigging above and across the deck ahead – almost exclusively human, with only a handful of salamanders, half-elves, and even a couple of Free Dwarfs who were masterful with the cannons, but really not much use up on the yards.

"It'll be alright," X'And said quietly from next to her, the gruff voice of his species eased by the kind tone he normally adopted when addressing his younger, less-experienced captain. Caithlin looked up at the hulking, muscular salamander.

"Yes. I'm perfectly content."

"Well, you're not. You have that concerned look. But this is just one slow cruise. That Valentican brig we brought in has kept us in credit for paying this lot for a little while, at least."

Caithlin tightened the bow on her ponytail and walked across to the port taffrail, her hands clasped formally at the small of her back.

"That brig we took was nearly a month ago. The only reason we're in credit with paying the crew is because nearly a third of them were killed in that engagement, and their replacements are still serving on little more than hope and good will. And as for capturing a Valentican naval vessel... well, Basilea is not at war with Valentica, and we risked a significant diplomatic incident."

The salamander sailor threw back his scaly head and let out a chittering noise that Caithlin knew well was a sign of disagreement.

"*We* risked no diplomatic occurrence!" X'And countered. "*They* fired on us! They were in a Basilean shipping lane, we were flying the Basilean flag, and we legitimately challenged them to stand down and prepare to be boarded to have their ship inspected... They fired on us, we engaged them. We captured them and, to the surprise and amazement of nobody, they were smuggling contraband! On a military vessel! So, we did our jobs and they..."

Caithlin's attention wandered off, away from that bloody and terrifying encounter and back to her current woes. Her father, a successful trader from Geneza, had raised her on the ocean waves. She grew up with a respect for the sea, a mastery of sail, and the discipline and drive required to captain her own trading ship in her father's company by her mid-twenties. Then came the incident – only a few weeks before – where orc pirates had forced her to dump her cargo and guns, and then run. She and her crew nursed her battered and broken brig into the Basilean port of Thatraskos, where the true extent of her debts were made clear to her.

A long story, summed up in a simple choice – prison and the potential ruin of her father's company, or… accept a conveniently timed offer from the Basilean Navy to repair and refit her brig as a ship of war, and accept a commission as a privateer. And, depending on her success in her newfound role as a fighting captain rather than a trader, perhaps she could pay off her debt and buy back her freedom in as little as ten years. At least her participation in a noteworthy sea battle resulting in the sinking of a hulking, orc smasher had been acknowledged by the Basilean authorities, resulting in one-tenth of her debt being written off. So, only nine years to go, then. And it very nearly killed her and her entire crew.

"Sail ho!"

Caithlin and X'And both looked up at the crow's nest – no, 'fighting top;' now that she was a woman of war, terminology was everything – and saw one of her lookouts pointing just to the east of south. Caithlin raised her telescope to her eye and scanned the horizon, as her first mate – who vehemently insisted on retaining his merchant shipping title, despite his new role – extended his own brass telescope and did the same. There, beneath a near cloudless, blue sky was a smudge on the horizon, just as indicated. Caithlin waited for her eye to adjust, but the smudge was merely recognizable as a sail at this range and not much more. A few seconds later, Caithlin allowed herself the smallest of smiles as a hint of color seeped into the speck on the horizon. A vivid, attractive emerald green.

"I think that's one of yours," Caithlin remarked to her salamander first mate.

"Yes, I should think so," X'And replied, "navy. A J'Koor'uk frigate."

Caithlin lowered her telescope and turned to look up at the huge figure next to her incredulously.

"You can tell that from here?"

X'And blinked down at her.

"Well… of course. Look at the lines of the sails, Cathy. Stands out from miles away. Very distinctive vessel, the J'Koor'uk."

Caithlin raised her telescope again.

"She's a long way from the Three Kings. A long way from home, this far north."

"Probably acting as part of the Koronai Accord."

Caithlin nodded. Whilst she certainly was not party to the finer detail of the Koronai Accord – and given recent events now perhaps should have been – she knew enough to know that the agreement between the Hegemony of Basilea and the Salamanders of the Three

Kings was a show of force to combat piracy in the Infant Sea. Basilean vessels would venture south to support the salamander warships in their operations and here, most likely, was a J'Koor'uk – a wide-beamed vessel of about nine hundred tons – sailing north into Basilea's area of responsibility to support its sometimes-ally.

Caithlin opened her mouth to ask something she had always wondered about the J'Koor'uk, but then stopped dead. Her brow lowered. The deck beneath her rose and fell out of time, just a little, but with enough of a change that it was simply too much for the current sea state to generate. Caithlin knew the *Martolian Queen* too well; certainly well enough to sense that something was not right. A second later, X'And's head tilted to one side, his long face frowning in concentration. Caithlin turned and rushed over to the front of the short quarterdeck.

"Beat to quarters!"

The naval terminology was symbolic – she had no drummer on board – but the result was the same. The cry of "Quarters!" was echoed up to the fighting tops and down the hatches to the very depths of the hold. Off-watch crewmen rushed up from below, dragging on their shirts as they sprinted to run out the guns. Then, just a moment later, the waters to starboard darkened. A huge shape, disc-like and black, appeared beneath the light blue waters, gliding in place next to the brig. A wave erupted in a spray of white foam over the shape which then blossomed and sprouted outward in all directions as a cream, rocky structure plunged up from the depths.

Looking back at the Basilean flag flying from her ship, Caithlin fought through her fear to make a rapid assessment of the wind and formulate her options to face whatever monster of the deep was rising to the surface. The rocks continued to climb up, forming into neat, clinical lines of smooth coral fashioned into angular, precise shapes. A structure the size of a small shore fort now towered over the brig, followed mere moments later by the huge shell of a massive turtle. The creature, the size of a fifth-rate frigate, swam alongside the brig, its massive flippers sweeping gracefully forward and then hauling the waves back behind it as the huge animal propelled itself forth in short bursts. Panicked cries and shouts issued from one end of the brig to the other until X'And rushed to the foot of the mainmast and yelled out a single command.

"Silence!"

The helmsman looked at Caithlin expectantly. X'And paced back over to her.

"Cathy? Your orders? We need to open up away from that thing!"

Caithlin held up a hand to silence her trusted second-in-command. She looked up in sheer awe at the giant creature serenely paddling alongside them and the almost fairy tale-magical fortress of cream-gold coral built upon its beautiful shell. The turtle's dark eyes sparkled as it looked forward, almost dopily, its toothless mouth curled up into what could be confused for a gentle smile.

"Double up on the starboard guns," Caithlin ordered curtly, "quoin them high. Look lively now. Nobody fire without my command."

"Captain," X'And murmured, "the wind is forward of the starboard beam. We can turn to port and outrun this thing. It's a giant turtle. We can open up and get away from it."

Caithlin shook her head.

"No. If they wanted to attack us, they would have done so by now. They had the element of surprise. Let's hear what they have to say."

X'And looked up at the shimmering, coral fortress looming over them to starboard. His face twisted into a mask of anger and resentment. Figures – humanoid in size and shape, were now appearing from holes cut into the walls of the fortress to line the balcony-like protrusions on its flanks.

"You want to listen to *them*?" the salamander spat. "I know where this is going, Cathy! These bastards are just here to tell us to get out of *their* sea! If we alter to port now, we can set every sail we have, and we'll be out of range of half of those harpoon launchers sticking out of the coral monstrosity sat on that poor thing's back before they even know what we're doing!"

Caithlin looked up at the figures moving nimbly across the coral fortress' battlements; some moving forward to take position by the array of barnacle-encrusted launchers facing forward, others forming up into units armed with spears and tridents. An array of races; some that Caithlin had seen only once or twice before during an entire life spent on or near the sea. Most prevalent were the naiads – lithe, blue-skinned females clad in crustacean-shell armor with long, flowing hair of darker indigo. Interspersed amongst them were their larger, more muscular placoderm cousins and a handful of purple-skinned, tentacle-headed thuul.

Conversation rippled across the deck of the *Martolian Queen* as older sailors eyed the Neriticans warily, while a handful of the adolescent crewmen stared wide-eyed at the graceful, feminine naiads. One of the blue-skinned figures – her armor trimmed in gold – jumped down from a balcony on the side of the coral fortress to a lower platform. She stepped forward, flanked by two huge placoderms, and still notably and no doubt deliberately higher than the quarterdeck of the Genezan brig, to plant her fists on her hips and stare down at the privateer crew.

"Which one of you is in command here?" she demanded, her words heavily accented.

Caithlin stepped forward.

"I am."

The naiad sailor looked down at Caithlin – both literally from the platform above, and figuratively with a raised eyebrow and a sneer.

"You're trespassing."

"Not according to my chart," Caithlin folded her arms. "This region is the responsibility of the Basilean Navy. We're flying a Basilean flag. We're here to…"

"This region is the sea," the naiad captain cut her off, "and none of it belongs to you. Every ship that passes safely across it does so because Trident Realm allows it."

Caithlin paused. She raised one fist to her chin thoughtfully, analyzing the naiad's words.

"You own the seas? All of them? Well… by that logic, you belong down there and we belong up here. So… I rather suppose that means *you* are trespassing. And you need to stop using our air. Because you're not allowed up here because I say so. I've decided that this is my air. Do you see how ridiculous your argument is?"

Laughter broke out along the deck of the *Martolian Queen*. One of the placoderm guards snapped out something in a language Caithlin did not understand. The naiad captain held up one hand to silence her subordinate.

"Don't play the fool, you stupid girl!" the tall Neritican snapped. "You think that your people can lay claim to our home because you've got a colored bit of cloth on the back of your silly, little boat! There are things going on leagues beneath your feet, right now, that you have no right to know about. What you do need to know is that this area is significant, you are trespassing, and as a courtesy I have elected to give you fair warning rather than kill you outright!"

"By playing the fool, do you mean delivering a demonstration of superior intellect to dismiss your argument and claims as sheer folly?" Caithlin shrugged.

"You really wish to keep pushing?!" the Neritican captain shouted down. "While you stand there outgunned and outmatched on your pathetic, wooden boat? Have you seen what a gun turtle is capable of?"

X'And stepped forward and glowered up at the naiad and her guards.

"I ask you instead – have you ever seen one of these magnificent creatures left to live its life in peace, before you utter, utter pieces of shit captured it, beat it into submission, and then built a fortress on its back?"

Fighting to keep her expression neutral, Caithlin held up a single finger to signify to her adversary that a moment was required, and then turned her back on the sea turtle and its fortress to address her first mate.

"X'And. What in the Abyss was that?"

"I told you, Cathy! Isn't this *exactly* what I said would happen?"

"I appreciate that. But I was dealing with it."

"What, by ridiculing their captain in front of her entire crew? I was just following your lead! Now look, we've got this! Look at the wind! We've got the weather gauge here! Let fly with the starboard broadside and cut back around to rake them! By then..."

Caithlin's eyes opened wide. She gestured up to the towering sea creature and its launcher-lined, coral fortress.

"You want us to go head to head with *that*? And why? Because you're angry that they've been cruel to a turtle? Now, X'And, you know that I love animals as much as the next person, but my crew did not sign on to come out here to die for a turtle!"

"No!" the salamander growled, leaning in aggressively. "They signed on to enforce the political will of the Hegemony of Basilea! And some bitch on a turtle has just challenged that will to your face! *That*, they did sign on to die for! You expect us to skulk off because the fish people want their pond back? Shoot them, cut across to port to reposition, and by then, that J'Koor'uk will be here!"

Caithlin risked a glance in the direction of the salamander frigate, quickly looking away again so as not to alert the Neritican crew of its presence.

"It's still leagues away!" she gasped beneath her breath. "Besides, what use are they? Do you really think they're looking through their telescopes right now at a Genezan brig next to a giant sea turtle and thinking, 'I wonder if there's one rogue salamander on that human brig! Let's go and help them!'"

A whistle was issued from the balcony built into the coral fortress atop the giant turtle. Caithlin span back around.

"As much as I hate to interrupt the conversation between you and your pet gecko," the naiad captain hissed, "but could I trouble you for compliance with my orders? Before I sink you and drown your entire crew?"

"Just wait a minute!" Caithlin snapped before turning back to X'And.

The salamander looked down at her with a confident smirk.

"Break away and get range!" X'And urged. "We're faster, and once we're outside of the range of some of their launchers, there's not much between our firepower. That'll give me time to get the signal flags up for the J'Koor'uk."

Caithlin shook her head.

"It's not just about speed and firepower! It's about sustaining the damage! We can't last against that thing! I'm not having my crew die over an argument!"

"It's not an argument, it's doing our job! This is open water, which Basilea has publicly declared its intent to patrol! If we back off, we've failed! And that J'Koor'uk *will* come to our aid, I assure you! It's been three years since you fished me out of the water and saved my life. In three years, when have I ever let you down?"

"Well," Caithlin mused, "you've been really hostile to my sweetheart. I felt rather let down over that."

"That's because he's a dick!" X'And exploded. "I've seen his type a thousand times, the world over! Do we really have to have this conversation here and now, Cathy?"

Gasps and cries of alarm broke out across the upper deck of the brig. Caithlin turned to see the sea turtle listing over to starboard, its face twisted into an expression that could have been pain or anger. An immense, swept-back flipper was dragged up into the air, raining water down on the deck of the brig and drenching the sailors on the fo'c'sle. The appendage paused at the apex of its climb to the heavens, then crashed down to tear through the ratlines attached to the *Martolian Queen's* foremast, ripping through the ropes with ease before clipping the starboard taffrail to tear a length of it off. Wood splintered up into the air as the entire ship lurched and shook, knocking Caithlin and X'And to their knees.

"Do I have your attention now?" the naiad captain shouted down.

Caithlin shot back up to her feet. She looked across X'And. The salamander gave her a determined nod. She turned to face her crew.

"Starboard guns! Fire! Helm, hard to port!"

Chapter Three

Martolian Queen (18)
Privateer (Converted Trade Brig)
110 souls on board
Twenty Leagues South of the Sand Lane

"Brace!"

Caithlin flung herself down to the deck, curling up and wrapping her hands over the back of her head as another salvo of projectiles whooshed through the air. Her eyes closed, her heart thumping in her chest with terror, she heard something zoom over her head. Whether it was momentarily before or after that whoosh she could not tell; a deep thud sounded as heavy harpoons smashed into the brig. The ship shook and lurched; screams sounded from over the shouts of commands, an acidic taste lingered in her mouth, and the accompanying stench of smoke from the guns clung to her smoke-stained clothes. Opening her streaming eyes again, Caithlin staggered back to her feet, her legs weak beneath her. She looked quickly around at her ship.

The main mast was splintered but holding, although some of the sheets and braces were cut, leaving the main topsail flapping in the wind. Up forward, the starboard side of the fo'c'sle was battered and broken, with a hole gouged through the hull and two of the cannons knocked back; one clean off its carriage. Four sailors lay in pools of blood at the point of impact; two motionless, the other pair writhing and screaming. Caithlin looked up at her topmen on the main mast.

"Secure the sheets!" she shouted up. "Take charge of that topsail! Reef it in!"

Some fifty sailors stood by their stations on the upper deck, hurriedly reloading the broadside nine-pound cannons, dragging the wounded away from the action and down below deck, or rushing up through the hatches from down below with bags of gunpowder and more shot. A few paces away, X'And hurriedly hauled on the rope attached to the signaling flags, finally sending his colored pennants shooting up the side of the damaged main mast, seemingly oblivious to the half dozen wooden splinters protruding from his left arm.

"This'll do it!" he smiled unconvincingly, breathing heavily. "This'll fix everything! It'll all be alright now!"

Caithlin looked forward again. The two dwarfs – Oswalt and Nudd – shifted one of the forward cannons back into a firing position with an almost superhuman show of strength before loading the gun at the same pace as the four-human crew next to them. Off to starboard, the gun turtle continued to close with them as it shifted in place to keep its forward firing launchers lined up with the brig, no matter what course the *Martolian Queen* was altered to. Caithlin smiled grimly. The fishy bastards were keeping those forward firing guns pointed at her, always. They were keeping the front of the ship pointed right at her broadsides.

"Hold fire!" she yelled above the din of orders, from gun commanders and topmen. "Wait for the shot! We'll rake them!"

Her order was repeated along the bloody upper deck as gun captains raised their hands in turn to signify the readiness of their individual cannons. Off to the south, the salamander frigate continued to close, its emerald green sails set to full as it made a direct course for the battle between the brig and the giant sea turtle.

"How close do you want to get to that thing?" X'And asked as he returned to Caithlin's side, grabbing handfuls of wooden splinters and yanking them out of the armored scales along his thick arm.

"Not close," Caithlin replied, one fist nervously clenched around the handle of her saber. "I'm not trading a close in bow rake for getting within range of all of their weapons. Let's stay back here, but place our shots well."

X'And raised his telescope and let out what sounded like a curse in his own tongue. Caithlin looked across, her chest aching with anxiety and her mind bombarded with a longing for the simpler, safer days of captaining a trading vessel.

"What? What is it?"

"Signals!" X'And hissed. "The J'Koor'uk is signaling us! I need to reply!"

The salamander sprinted off again to the main mast and began hauling down the linked row of signal flags.

"Captain!" Oswalt yelled from one of the forward guns. "I reckon half a cable to run for the shot!"

Caithlin looked out at the sea turtle. From this range, she hoped and prayed that every last shot from her ship would tear through the fortress atop its shell and, by a miracle, not a single cannonball would strike the hapless, enslaved creature below. As for the shot... well, Caithlin knew sailing well. She knew the sea, the weather above, trade routes, ship handling, how to climb and leap through rigging with the agility of an elf. She was a competent sailing commander. But with only a handful of weeks under her belt as a war fighter, she still did not know gunnery.

"On your command!" she shouted back across the deck to the black-bearded dwarf. "Fire on your command!"

The short, stocky dwarf grinned and raised a thumb before twisting to look back to the south. Again, X'And frantically hauled on the rope leading up the side of the main mast and propelled another line of signaling flags high up toward the main topsail as a quartet of sailors edged out along the yard to splice the damaged sheets. Caithlin raised her telescope to survey the seascape around her. The salamander frigate continued to close at full sail. She shifted off to the right. Her eyes widened. The sea turtle's captain had anticipated the brig positioning to rake and was altering course to change the relative angle. The shot was now.

"Starboard guns! Fire!" Caithlin yelled.

The ship leaned over with the combined force of the cannons, the deafening blast sending the now familiar shrill-whistle through Caithlin's ears as they were temporarily damaged by the noise. Smoke from the guns billowed out and engulfed the deck, hiding everything in a bitter tasting fog. The smoke cleared in seconds and, coughing and wiping at her streaming eyes, Caithlin raised her telescope again.

Holes were cut into the magically reinforced coral of the turtle-top fortress; something akin to a tower leaned slowly over, broke, and detached to fall down, bouncing off the turtle's near impervious shell and slipping over into the waves. Caithlin narrowed her eyes and smiled. That would give them something to think about.

"Load!" she shouted forward across the upper deck. "Roundly now! Helm, bring her two points to starboard! Up top! Altering to starboard! Keep her trimmed for battle sail!"

The crack-bang of the harpoon launchers on the gun turtle blasted again, and with a combination of near unbearable weariness and failing nerves, Caithlin again dropped to the deck. A series of lethal-tipped harpoons nearly as long as small sloops rocketed just behind the brig's boom before the projectiles plowed into the waves and sank. Caithlin staggered back to her feet, her hands shaking and bile in her throat. She looked across and saw the gun turtle altering course to starboard in an attempt to keep its front-mounted weapons pointed at the brig. One more broadside. One more broadside from the *Martolian Queen's* guns, and then full sail to get away from the coral fortress and its devastating harpoon launchers.

Along the upper deck, gun captains reported their firing positions ready. X'And rushed back over to Caithlin's side. The salamander J'Koor'uk was closer now, close enough to make out its distinctive fan sails and ornate, low hull. Caithlin checked her foe. The angle was wrong.

"Helm! One point to starboard! Up top! Ready for full sail, on my command!"

"Full sail?" X'And's dark eyes opened wide. "We're not running, surely?"

Biting back an angry retort, Caithlin stared out to starboard again and watched impatiently as the sea turtle paddled around after the brig to line up its launchers while simultaneously the brig swung her prow about to bring her own broadside to bear.

"Starboard guns! Fire!" Caithlin shouted.

Again, the deafening roar and shaking of the boards beneath her feet, the insufferable ringing in the ears and choking sense of claustrophobia from the bitter smoke and heat. As the smoke wafted away, Caithlin saw more damage amongst the coral fortress, with an entire pseudo-tower now detached and gone. The thumping of return fire sounded. She hung her head and let out a breath, praying to the Shining Ones that this one-sided duel would end. She heard cheering. Her eyes widened in surprise as she looked up.

Cannonballs slammed into the fortress atop the turtle, plunging through the coral and battering the barnacle-encrusted superstructure. Debris fell down in clumps, smashing on top of the turtle's skull before falling down into the water to either side. Downwind of the giant turtle, the salamander frigate's hull was enveloped in gray smoke from its guns. Caithlin let out a gasp of optimism. She turned to her first mate with a smile.

"You did it! You... you did it!"

"You seem surprised that I did what I said I would do." X'And smirked.

The sea turtle turned away from the brig, desperately trying to bring its forward facing launchers to bear on this newly arrived, far greater threat. The J'Koor'uk's guns blasted out again, pelting the sea turtle with another devastating broadside. Again, the crew of the *Martolian Queen* cheered.

"Don't just watch them save your souls for you, you idle dogs!" X'And shouted. "Load the guns! Load!"

The sea turtle, caught between the persistent and accurate fire of the brig and the heavy, hard hitting broadside of the salamander frigate, was destined for only one fate. With smoke rising from the decimated fortress atop the turtle's back, Caithlin watched with grim satisfaction as naiad, placoderm, and thuul crew members dived from the giant sea creature to abandon their posts, swimming down to the safety of the deep below.

***

"She's sitting low in the water, sir," Kaeso remarked eagerly as he leaned over the edge of the quarterdeck taffrail to look down at the wounded sloop.

Jaymes glanced down momentarily before returning his attention to the sailors of his crew as they secured the lines connecting the two vessels together, line abreast.

"She'll hold," he said calmly, "they're tougher than they look."

Karnon looked down at the *HW Scout*, the comparatively tiny sloop, gently bumping and banging against the starboard side of the towering frigate. Whether the little ship was sat low in the water or was tougher than she looked, he had absolutely no idea. Even with a couple of months as one of the first officers in the newly formed Basilean marines – of which only a handful of weeks had been spent actually embarked and at sea – the maritime world felt alien to him. At least now that he had found his sea legs, the few boarding actions he had been involved in were not as much of a gulf from the battlefields he had known for years, having soldiered from the age of sixteen until his transfer to the marines six years later.

The upper deck of the sloop below had minimal crew visible. A few sailors helped secure the lines across from *Pious*, and only a solitary lieutenant stood watch on the quarterdeck. Karnon looked across at Jaymes. The frigate captain was an ex-sloop officer himself, having spent the early years of his career in coast guarding and anti-smuggling duties to the west of the capital, along the beautiful and often serene southern coast of the Solios province of Basilea. That much, Jaymes had told Karnon before. Perhaps it went some way to explaining Jaymes's laid back, sometimes even lackadaisical, approach to leadership – an attitude that would never have passed muster in the legion. That being said, Karnon mused, Jaymes had noticeably changed since promotion and taking command of *Pious*. Karnon had found himself surprised with just how quickly Jaymes's relaxed demeanor had hardened.

"Captain Senne, Mister Innes," Jaymes turned to Karnon and Kaeso, "take a party of men across to the *Scout*. Get down below deck and see if we can lend a hand."

"Aye, sir," Kaeso nodded enthusiastically before rushing down to the upper deck to begin rounding up sailors to take across.

Karnon walked across to Jaymes.

"You reckon they'll be alright?" he asked his friend quietly.

Jaymes nodded.

"Should be. They took a hell of a hit from that blood runner. Not as bad as *Skimmer*, granted. That was no way for Davey to go. He should have known better than to get so close."

Karnon let out a sigh. The sight of the *Skimmer* being ripped apart for matchwood by the orc vessel had been harrowing, especially when left at a range where it was impossible to even lend aid. After sinking the blood runner, they had at least recovered some twenty survivors from the water. But their captain, Daviff Gren – a man they both knew from lunches at the Thatraskos Wardroom, and a handful of memorable nights out on the town – was now dead and gone with well over half of his crew.

"I'll head across now," Karnon remarked. "We had an afternoon's tuition in ship damage control when they converted us across as marines. I've forgotten practically every word of it, but I can shift lumber if it helps them."

"Sloop crews are king when it comes to damage control," Jaymes answered, his eyes still scanning the horizon in every direction as they spoke. "We – rather, they – are trained to lend assistance to larger vessels even under fire. *Scout* is Josh Azur's ship. He's a good egg. He'll talk you through it all. Tell him to send every spare hand he's got up here to us for a rest and a tot of rum. We'll send him all the hands he needs until his ship is stable, then we'll tow him home."

"Got it."

Karnon walked briskly down from the quarterdeck to the upper deck and then to midships where a ladder – it no doubt had a proper naval name, but he still had not learned it – was built into the side of the frigate. Kaeso Innes led a party of ten sailors down to jump onto the sloop's deck; the second lieutenant still observed the formality of standing to attention and saluting as soon as his feet were onboard the sloop, despite the fact that she may well have been sinking. With the example in formality set, each and every sailor from *Pious* followed Kaeso's lead.

"Hello Mister Innes!" shouted the blond-bearded lieutenant from the sloop's quarterdeck. "The captain's down below, on the orlop deck."

"Right oh!" Kaeso beamed before turning to his men. "Follow me! You too, Captain Senne, if you please."

Karnon followed the short procession down to the orlop deck where his senses were instantly bombarded with the familiar but certainly less than pleasant stench of a warship's living quarters. With only a single hatchway at each end of the deck leading up to the clear air above, the smells of everyday life were trapped amidst the triple slung hammocks. The deck itself was relatively clear, with a group of perhaps half a dozen sailors crowded around the next hatchway leading down to the hold. Kaeso led his way through the men and called down the open hatchway.

"Below! It's Mister Innes, second of the *Pious*!"

"Down here, Kaeso!" a familiar voice called up from the darkness. "Have you brought fresh hands?"

"Aye, sir!"

Karnon followed the sailors down into the near darkness of the lowest deck of the sloop, where shadows danced along the wooden walls from the flickering flames of closed lamps. Before he had even reached the bottom of the ladder, Karnon found himself up to his knees in warm seawater. Apples and oranges from smashed crates in the hold floated past him, alongside what looked in the darkness to be a dead rat. Some twenty sailors were crowded around the ship's bilge pumps, stripped to the waist and sweating profusely as they desperately pumped the sea water out of the dark deck.

"In you go!" Kaeso beamed at the *Pious* sailors. "Let's give 'em a rest!"

The sailors from *Pious* waded over to the pumps and took over, the pace of the pumping immediately increasing as fresh arms replaced tired, aching limbs.

"Hello Kaeso, Karnon," Karnon heard the voice of Joshua Azer, a lieutenant he knew from the officers' rather busy social scene back at Thatraskos.

"Hello, mate," Karnon winced, "what can we do to help?"

Kaeso immediately grabbed Karnon by the arm with a force that the marine thought the young naval officer incapable of. He leaned in closely in the darkness.

"It's 'sir,' here, Karnon. This is Lieutenant Azer's ship."

"He's a lieutenant," Karnon screwed up his face in confusion. "Same rank as a marine captain. We're equal, just like you and me."

"No, we're not. Sloops are commanded by lieutenants. The lieutenant in command of a sloop is referred to as 'captain' onboard. They might not hold the rank of captain, but they fulfill the role. They are 'sir,' especially in front of subordinates. You'd better apologize."

Muttering under his breath and shaking his head in bewilderment at the never-ending procession of patternless naval traditions and bullshit, Karnon took a step through the water towards Azer.

"Apologies, sir. Very improper of me. How can we help?"

The tall, bulky lieutenant waded over.

"That bastard hit us hard. Knocked off a chunk of my quarterdeck and split the hull. We're taking on water faster than we can pump it out. Petty Officer Manni has already got a party stuck in with shoring up with wedges and props, but we need to check it all over, now things have calmed down a bit, and slow down the rate of flooding. We saw what happened to the Skimmer. Did anybody survive?"

"We recovered some twenty of her crew," Kaeso replied. "I'm afraid Lieutenant Gren was lost with his ship."

"Damn. Poor old Davey."

Karnon's eyes suddenly widened.

"Hang on a minute. Did you just say that we're taking on water faster than we can pump it out? Doesn't that mean we're sinking?"

Joshua flashed an almost amused smile.

"Well, technically, yes."

Karnon stared incredulously at the two lieutenants, stood in the sinking ship in the dark and exchanging pleasantries as if out for a stroll through Thatraskos's market street.

"Well, shouldn't we be getting everybody up to the upper deck and getting the hell off this thing? Before it drops like a stone and we all drown?"

Kaeso turned slowly to look at the tall marine, confusion distorting his normally smooth features in the flickering torch light. Joshua tilted his head and paused before answering.

"You see... the thing is... there's a chance we can save the ship. You know, decent damage control and all that. Traditionally, we don't all panic and jump off the thing as soon as things look a bit bad. It's not really the naval way. Now, how long can you hold your breath for?"

Karnon stared at the older officer, still utterly confused by the situation he found himself plunged into.

"What?"

"How long can you hold your breath for?"

"Pretty much indefinitely. Breathing is for the weak. What do you need?"

"Come with me, shippers. Grab a hammer and a bag of wooden wedges. That rate of water we're taking on that you're so concerned about. You're going to fix it."

***

Caithlin could not help but feel sympathy for the giant turtle as it paddled groggily onward, maintaining the same course and speed as its dazed, half-closed eyes focused on the horizon ahead. As the *Martolian Queen* approached from the great animal's left side, she was presented with a clearer view of the damage inflicted by her ship's guns. Great holes were blasted through the coral on the turtle's back; dead bodies of naiads, thuul, and placoderms littered the ruins and the turtle's huge, smooth shell. Some twenty of Caithlin's crew crowded along the starboard waist of the brig, eager to see the damage they had caused and the rare glimpse of the gentle sea giant up close. A boarding party of twenty sailors had already armed themselves with cutlasses and hatchets – the sailors all selected for their ability to swim rather than fight, given the unpredictability of the platform they were boarding.

"Grapeshot!" X'And shouted out. "Starboard guns, load grapeshot! There may still be some of those bastards in there!"

It was a sensible precaution, but Caithlin highly doubted anybody was still onboard the ruined fortress. As the combined onslaught of the guns of the fighting brig and the salamander frigate had caught the fortress in the crossfire, Caithlin had seen scores of Neriticans diving overboard to evacuate, some carrying wounded with them. That was their privilege – the ability to simply dive off their equivalent of a sinking ship and then slip beneath the waves, to safety rather than the death that awaited land-dwellers.

Downwind of the dazed sea turtle, the salamander J'Koor'uk frigate came about to approach the creature from the right of its shell, leaving both vessels the room to board from either side. Caithlin raised her telescope, identified a few hard points on the shattered coral fortress, and then turned to the crowd of sailors on the brig's waist.

"Back to work! Grapple lines and hooks! There – there's three points just above the port aft quarter – secure us alongside. Don't tie the lines, just in case that thing dives."

Caithlin turned to check her pistol and buckle her sword belt around her waist. X'And was back by her side in moments.

"I can handle this," he smiled, "you can stay here and keep an eye on things. It's best I deal with the crew from the J'Koor'uk, and..."

Caithlin shot the broad salamander a warning glare.

"X'And. Whilst I appreciate you bringing in that frigate to save our souls, let us just pause for a moment and remember who is in command here. I'm the captain. I'm going across to meet them. I know *exactly* what our boarding party will want to do. And quite frankly, we're not nearly at the point where I'm going to allow my crew to loot dead bodies for valuables."

X'And took a pace back and bowed his head respectfully.

"Of course. I'm sorry, I allowed myself to get carried away. I would like to accompany you, though, in case their boarding officer is not so familiar with your language. And as for the looting, well, your principles are one of the reasons that have kept me by your side for these past years."

Caithlin returned her pistol to the brace slung around her shoulder. She noticed that her hands were still shaking, and she quickly clasped them at the small of her back.

"It is my principles that have stopped this ship going on the offensive and getting decent amounts of prize money. It is my principles that leave us lacking in pay for the crew and put us in the position where they're considering looting the dead in the first place."

X'And tilted his head to one side.

"Still. Please do not compromise them."

The brig moved gently into position to nudge against the giant sea turtle, lines thrown across to secure to the hard points on the ruined coral fortress. Recovering her pistol from its brace, her other hand resting on the handle of the saber at her waist, Caithlin was the first to step across onto the turtle's huge shell. She immediately stopped dead in her tracks, caught by the beautiful patterns in the dull hexagons of the shell. She crouched down and carefully placed one hand on the shell, taking a moment to appreciate the rarity of the situation she found herself in. Then she looked up and saw five dead bodies strewn amidst the wreckage inflicted by her ship's gun, scattered and dismembered in pools of blood.

The boarding party moved past Caithlin as she stared, transfixed by the macabre scene before her. Again, she found herself pining for the more simple, honest dangers of braving the seas for trade rather than battle. X'And patted a friendly hand on her shoulder as he passed before he rushed across to the far side of the sloping shell to assist the J'Koor'uk with its own lines. Raising herself back to her feet, Caithlin made the conscious effort to concentrate on the exotic majesty of the salamander frigate rather than the torn corpses left amidst the shattered coral walls.

The J'Koor'uk frigate's hull was crafted out of the crimson-hued timber that was so common in the stout, Dawn Redwood trees of the Three Kings islands. The superstructure atop the low, broad hull was beautiful enough to put most human ships to shame – a series of sweeping, square-topped decks that replicated the styles of the more modern salamander settlements blended perfectly into the hull. The aft end of the ship rose up into powerful lines that seemed almost feathered, painted in a dazzling gold.

Rather than the lines of guns that frequented human fighting ships, the salamanders relied on a smaller number of much larger cannons, some of which towered above even the tall crew members, leaving Caithlin wondering how they could possibly be loaded. The eye-catching ship was finished with the most distinctive features of any salamander vessel – the fan sails; in this case, dyed in a splendid emerald green. The salamanders, like the Basileans, insisted on classifying their ships based on size and role rather than rigging, and so, like the Elohi Batch One frigate, the J'Koor'Uk had only two masts – contravening the widely accepted convention that Caithlin had grown up understanding, that frigates were ship-rigged with three masts.

A group of ten salamanders stepped down from the upper deck of their frigate and onto the sea turtle, led by a figure in a blue greatcoat. From her previous encounters with their navy, the only thing that Caithlin had discerned was that a standardized approach to uniform and symbols of rank was completely absent. Looking up at the figures on the deck of the frigate, Caithlin saw an almost even mix of the tall, muscular salamanders and their thinner, smoother-skinned arkosaur cousins. Arkosaurs she had encountered before – in fact, on her first trading expedition with her father when she was fourteen, it was an arkosaur ship that they met at the City of the Golden Horn.

Predictably, given the reluctance of arkosaurs to deal with other races, the boarding party from the frigate consisted solely of salamanders. Caithlin walked briskly across, noticing with interest that half of the salamanders were carrying large, heavy looking barrels from their ship. X'And paced over to greet the blue-coated salamander, and they had exchanged a few words by the time Caithlin arrived. She took in a better view of the blue-coated salamander as she approached; darker and craggier of skin than X'And, notifying he was older — possibly not far from middle age. He was taller and broader than X'And, walking with a slight limp, with a longer snout and a more vibrant range of reds in the skin which Caithlin had learned was considered handsome in the reptilian culture. He turned to glare down at Caithlin as she approached, with a fearsome stare from his narrowed eyes. X'And chittered something in their language and the salamander braced up, struck a fist against his chest, and bowed his head respectfully.

"Captain," he said, his voice deep and gruff, "I am Zu'Max, senior lieutenant of the *Deliver's Flame*. My captain sends his compliments. We responded as soon as we saw your signal."

Caithlin uncocked her pistol and returned it to its brace.

"Thank you for your assistance. Suffice to say, without X'And's input, my knowledge of your customs and culture would have left me in the dark regarding how to communicate with you."

"Not a worry, Captain," Zu'Max replied, his words heavily accented. "We saw a Genezan brig alongside these bastards. We were on the way anyway."

Caithlin looked around at the salamander sailors dragging the barrels up to the coral fortress.

"If I may," she ventured, "what are your crew doing?"

"Setting explosives."

Caithlin's eyes widened.

"What? You can't do that! You'd blow this poor creature up for..."

X'And stepped in with his hands held up.

"No, Captain. Quite the opposite."

"Yes, yes," Zu'Max agreed, "this is standard for how we deal with one of these creatures. The link between their captain and the turtle is broken, leaving it dazed. We only have a few minutes until it dives. That gives us time to blow as much of this infernal fortress off its back as we can, to give it the chance of a normal life. Unless these Neritican bastards recapture it, that is."

Caithlin looked across at the ruined fortress and the salamander team quickly and efficiently laying the barrels and setting fuses.

"You're...you're sure this won't hurt it?"

"Yes, yes. We've all done it before. It works. Best thing for the turtle. But it will dive soon. Respectfully, Captain, you should return to your ship. Are you bound for Keretia or Geneza?"

Caithlin turned to look up again at the two salamanders.

"Keretia," she replied hesitantly, "for repairs."

"I only ask because I was confused," the salamander naval officer continued. "I recognized the racing bow and the low quarterdeck of your brig as Genezan. But you fly a Basilean naval flag. You are a privateer, then?"

Caithlin nodded.

"Yes."

The salamander smiled.

"Either way. Geneza and Basilea are both friends of ours. I will report back to my captain. We, too, are bound for Thatraskos. Should I suggest we sail in company? Safety in numbers."

"Yes," Caithlin replied uneasily, still in a daze from the fear of combat followed by the unlikely encounter with salamanders atop a giant turtle, "please. Please do suggest that to your captain. The escort home would be much appreciated."

There was a shout from one of the salamanders setting the fuses in the fortress ruins, followed by the indecipherable clicks of their native tongue.

"We need to go now, Captain," Zu'Max said, saluting with clenched fist against chest, "the fuses are set and ready."

Caithlin returned the salute by bringing her right hand up to level with her eye, immediately chastised herself for breaking regulations by saluting without headgear, and then realized how little it mattered. Within minutes, she was back on the quarterdeck of the *Martolian Queen* with her crew, the lines cut as the brig and its frigate escort broke away from the turtle. Caithlin watched, an uncommon tear in her eye as moments later the charges exploded with a dull crump, and more pieces of coral masonry tumbled down off the turtle's back. The giant creature let out a hoarse croak, blinked, and then slipped down beneath the waves, free of the vast majority of the unnatural burden that had been attached to its shell. X'And smiled broadly as he watched the freed creature disappear.

***

To the uninitiated, the lopsided sloop sat unhappily on the sandbank off the beach no doubt looked like a minor disaster; a wreck, evidence of a storm or poor seamanship. However, to those privy to the technicalities of a life nautical – those such as Tem, the three comrades he sat with, and the five sailors working on the sloop's lower hull and keel – the beached ship was actually evidence to the contrary.

Tem had carefully beached the *Adventure Prize* some three hours after morning high tide in the tiny but stunningly picturesque Ferla Bay – named after the notorious pirate who was marooned by his mutinous crew there nearly one hundred years before. The *Adventure*

Prize had been deliberately beached, allowing the seas to roll away as the tides turned to force the ship to lean over. This exposed her hull and gave her crew a few precious hours to chip and carve away the barnacles from her underside, streamlining her to add an extra, precious turn of speed. It was certainly needed. In his first week as captain, Tem had attempted to intercept three merchant vessels. His first resulted in him executing one of his own crew for minimal plunder, the second was a little more successful, although he now faced the task of finding a suitable contact to fence the crates of sugar and cotton he had stolen, and the third... the third outran him with ease.

"You know," Flyde mused from where he sat next to Tem on the white, sandy beach, chewing thoughtfully on the stem of his smoking pipe, "there's not many things I actually envy the navies over. But this? We've got no dry docks and we have to go through all of this to keep our ships in one piece, whilst those bastards just sail into a dock to have some other buggers do it for them."

"Scrape barnacles off in dry dock?" Halladai scoffed as he took a swig from a green, glass bottle of rum. "What decade are you living in? Naval ships are all copper-bottomed these days. From the smallest cutters to their first-rate ships of the line. The copper stops the barnacles attaching, and even more importantly, it stops the woodworm from getting in. In these waters, we'll only get a couple of years out of each ship. The navy? They'll get half a century out of their hulls."

Ash grabbed the offered bottle of rum from Halladai and took a long draw before wiping his whiskered mouth on the back of his sleeve.

"We ain't got it that bad," he grimaced, watching the other sailors sweating in the morning sun over the backbreaking work. "I mean... we're sitting here with rum and baccy, as idle as landsmen, watching other people do the digging out. I wouldn't trade this in for one cruise in a navy ship. That's not the dream. This? This is the dream. This is freedom."

Tem jumped as Flyde burst into laughter at his friend's words. Halladai's stern exterior broke, and his deep chortles joined the younger man.

"What?" Ash demanded. "What are you two buggers so amused about?"

Flyde drew from his pipe again and blew out a smoke ring.

"You, you daft shite! 'Freedom!' Come on, shippers, you've known the deal for long enough! We're out here for money. Plain and simple. Nothing noble, no idealism. We're here to rob helpless people of their cargo and hard earned valuables, so we can live a short and happy life with enough means for sun, rum, and whores before our short lives end – hopefully – with the short drop rather than the long one."

Tem glanced over his shoulder at the lush jungle behind him. The island was relatively small – perhaps five miles from north to south – but there was a freshwater creek about a mile inland, and a plentiful supply of edible fruit. He had sent half his crew for food and water, while the other half was split between working on the ship's hull and, for his trio of closest friends, idling in the sun. There had to be some perks to being the captain's closest confidants.

"Forgive me for dreaming of something bigger, you miserable sod!" Ash continued. "Shame on both of you buggers! That's really your lot? Your aim is to... survive for a bit? No. Not me. There's three pirate chiefs who've brought us all together for something bigger. Something worthwhile. No fighting and dying so that the captain can get twenty shares for every one of ours for our spilt blood. No being confined onboard in every port, lest we do a runner. No lashes to split our backs open for not saluting some sodding officer! No! We're free men, we're equal, we vote on our destiny, and we live in the sun with rum, beer, and women. That's why I'm doing this."

Flyde began laughing again. Halladai did not join him. The dark-skinned quartermaster looked across at Tem.

"You're quiet. Not like you."

Tem took his turn with the bottle of rum as a pair of gulls squawked noisily from the gentle surf at the end of the beach, eyeing a group of scuttering crabs curiously.

"Just thinking," Tem shrugged.

"You don't want to do that. That's dangerous. First thinking, next thing you'll be dreaming, and you'll sound as stupid as this ugly bastard here."

Tem let out a brief laugh at Ash's misfortune. He shook his head as he watched the crabs siddle quickly into the warm water.

"I shouldn't have shot Skordak," he admitted after another pause. "I shouldn't have done it."

"Bollocks," Ash snapped, "he deserved it. You told us how you were running this crew before we even stepped onboard the *Adventure Prize*. He knew what the expectation was. He tried it on, you called him out, he insulted you, so you shot him in the face. Fair's fair."

Tem shook his head.

"No. Not that. I'm not shying away from killing a man. I'd be in the wrong trade if that were the case, shipmate. No. Skordak had friends. Friends on this crew."

"Aye," Halladai nodded as he took his turn with what was left of the rum, "aye, he did. Him and Gunnta went back some. But we were at sea, and he had his orders. Yes, we vote on our plans. We vote our captains and our quartermasters. That's our way. But once the guns are run out and the cutlasses are drawn, we follow our captain's orders. That's the way it has to be. No time for some damn committee then! Skordak knew that. He disobeyed your order. Even his friends understand. I know, because I've spoken to 'em. No, Captain. You did the right thing. They all needed to see who was running things."

Tem considered for a moment whether it was worth telling the other three that he valued their loyalty. He appreciated the way they stood by him when others in the small crew grimaced, muttered, and spat their disapproval of his plans. But they – his detractors – had not voted him down yet. Not even suggested it.

Flyde stood up and dusted the sand off his ragged, striped, and holed leggings.

"Right. The guilt has got me. I'm going to go do my time scrapping the hull."

Ash wordlessly stood, dusted himself off, and followed the other pirate to join in on the work on the ship's hull. Halladai finished the last of the rum.

"Jeffi's lot have been a while looking for fresh water," he observed, producing his own tobacco pipe from his shirt pocket.

"No rush," Tem said, looking out at the horizon, "let's stay here for the night. Let these buggers get blind drunk. We'll go out again at high tide tomorrow evening."

"Out again?" Halladai asked. "You don't want to head back to the Skull and sell these crates?"

Tem stood up and kicked one foot thoughtfully through the sand.

"No. Not yet. The hold is only half full. We're out here now. We've got powder and ammunition, and we'll soon have food and water. Let's go out again. That's what I reckon. But we'll put it to the vote. See what these sea dogs think."

Halladai stood, patted a hand against Tem's shoulder, and drew from his pipe.

"Aye, Captain," he said with a grin, and then walked off to join the work party at the sand bank.

Tem stood motionless and alone for a few moments, staring out across the shallow bay as he thought through his options for the next cruise. Still, four years later, thoughts of Jess and their failed romance forced their way to the fore. Jess, the girl he had grown up with, the girl who said she would never even look twice at a man who could not provide, and a year later was somehow horrified at him when he returned home affluent and self-sufficient after becoming a pirate.

Those memories were quashed again as quickly as they had intruded his thoughts when Tem suddenly noticed a trio of small sails on the horizon.

Chapter Four

In the seas north of the treacherous lands of the rebels of Ophidia
Dedicated to the worship of Shobik, True God of the Afterlife
That worship carried out onboard 'Purification of Ul'Astia', a galley of war of one hundred and twenty cubits

When he lived and walked as a mortal, High Priest T'mork would notice the smallest changes upon returning to the Great Temple to Shokbik that dominated the center of the city of Nehkesharr. After a mere few days' travel, changes were subtle; after the long journeys to the north and leaving his home for upward of a year, he would return to see entire new streets built while old ones were gone in the ever-morphing, living city that existed to honor the True God of the Dead. Yet all of that wonder paled to insignificance when, stood atop the bone prow of the war galley *Purification of Ul'Astia*, he marveled at what was now known as the Infant Sea. When T'mork lived, thousands of years before, this was a long succession of green pastures and plains, part of the Grand Republic of Primovantor. T'mork smiled slightly. How times had changed.

The broad, powerful ship continued on to the northwest beneath a clear, cloudless sky. Two decks below, row after row of oarsmen – some three hundred tireless, fleshless bodies, animated into being by T'mok's own arcane mastery – continued to propel the ship forward into wind. The ship's captain, Demelecles, stood amidships on the upper deck. He looked skyward at the squat, broad yards positioned atop the two masts. With the ship into wind and reliant on the oarsmen, the sails were taken in completely. That was about the extent of T'mork's knowledge of sail handling, and it was all he needed to know. He commanded the ship; Demelecles was the one who transformed the intent into orders.

Of far more interest to T'mork were the nine dwarf captives on their knees before him, at the forward end of the upper deck. The nine sailors were all that was left of the curious, metal ship T'mork's small fleet had encountered and, after a costly battle, destroyed. Wounded and half-drowned, the fearless dwarfs had still fought and resisted as T'mork's undead crew recovered them from the water in two of the galley's boats. They had even managed to defeat three skeletal sailors with their bare hands before they were beaten senseless, into submission. Now with their hands bound behind their backs, all nine bloodied dwarfs stared at T'mork as he paced the deck, his still broad arms folded across the bare, dead flesh of his chest. The curved khopesh blades of a troop of ten revenants were held at the dwarf's throats, ready to instantly put down any further attempt at resistance.

T'mork turned to face... the woman. The... scholar. He had forgotten her name. It did not matter. What did matter is that she possessed enough knowledge of, in her eyes, an ancient culture that she could understand T'mork's words and put together a passable attempt at a response to him when she translated to those who did not speak the tongue of the Ahmunites.

"Ask them who their leader is," T'mork demanded, his voice dry and raspy in his dead throat. "Ask them now."

The short, dark-haired woman stared down at her feet, her hands shaking. Her mouth opened and closed a few times, but no words were issued. Tutting to himself behind his lipless mouth, T'mork walked over to tower over the scholar. He had been tall in life, taller than any man he knew, but in undeath, he had returned perhaps another half cubit taller still. The bookish young woman, meanwhile, was short and unremarkable, with her black hair cut in a neat, severe fringe that ended just above her thick eyebrows. T'mork looked down at her. Tears rolled down her cheeks.

"You... still haven't grasped how this works." The high priest smiled thinly. "You see, I was important in life. The high priest of the most sacred of all temples in the Ahmunite empire. At a time when the world... made more sense than it does now. A time of real importance, as opposed to these trivial days in which you now live out your meaningless existence. That was before. And now? I have been chosen to come back. Purified. The importance of my task is unparalleled. Do you see?"

The tearful woman swallowed and nodded.

"Y... yes. Highness."

"Master," T'mork corrected, "I appreciate the mark of respect, but the correct form of address from a commoner to a high priest is 'master.' And your pronunciation and accent needs much work. But we have time for that. Now, I shall continue with my patience and lenience, and you do what I have kept you alive for, and translate my words. Ask them who is in command. I shan't ask again."

The scholar wiped away a tear, took a moment to compose herself, and then spoke to the restrained dwarfs. Instantly, a gray-bearded sailor barked out a response. One of the revenants stood by him – T'mork did not bother to learn their names in life, so he certainly had no intention of doing so now they were brought back to unlife – raised his curved blade. T'mork held up his shriveled hand. The elite warrior instantly obeyed and lowered his weapon.

T'mork walked over to the dwarf, the ends of the folds of his blue skirts sweeping across the wooden deck. The aging dwarf stared back up at him, typically fearless and defiant. T'mork had seen it in his foes a thousand times before, both in life and in undeath. The dwarf spat out a few words in a modern language that T'mork could not understand. He turned to the scholar and raised an eyebrow. The woman looked down at her feet.

"I... I could not repeat it to you, Master."

"An insult, then?"

"Yes, Master."

T'mork turned away from the indignant dwarf sailor and looked out over the bows of his war galley at the small fleet of ships that sailed in company with him. Three sleek, high-prowed Khopeshiis cut through the water to either side of the war galley; behind them were two smaller, single-masted Dust Chasers. A squadron of four comparatively tiny slave galleys plowed through the waves ahead of the Ahmunite fleet. But it was the lone Soul Hunter that T'mork was interested in right now. A small vessel, modified from a design he remembered well when he lived, with the single mast removed to make room on the deck for a pyramid shaped construct that supported a convex pentagon-shaped armillary. Within the large arms of the armillary, a blue energy field crackled and thrummed with unnatural power – the prison of an enslaved djinn.

T'mork looked back to the raised after deck and signaled for Demelecles, the war galley's captain, to report to him. The powerfully built revenant sailor made his way over immediately and stopped to bow.

"Yes, Master?"

"Signal for the Soul Hunter to close up to the starboard bow. Have this captive taken on one of our boats and rowed across to it."

"Yes, Master," the dour captain acknowledged with another bow.

Within minutes, the proud dwarf was shoved unceremoniously onto one of the ship's boats and lowered, along with a crew of skeletal oarsmen, off the after end of the war galley as the bone-prowed, oar-driven Soul Hunter closed to position off to starboard. T'mork watched with no small amount of satisfaction from above as his ten skeletal sailors rowed the small boat across, their timing perfectly as one, with the sole dwarf captive stood between two revenant guards at the back of the boat.

T'mork felt it before he could see it. The tingle, like lightning dancing across his cold, dry, dead flesh. Then the pulsating, thrumming of power wafting across from the rotating armillary that dominated the upper deck of the Soul Hunter. The imprisoned djinn sucked in the life force as it approached, and in turn, T'mork extracted it from the shimmering blue, portal-like prison set atop the smaller ship to starboard. Thin lines of azure energy drifted slowly across from the Soul Hunter and directly into T'mork's outstretched palm, revitalizing his very core. His brown-hued, skinless flesh twitched, and a smile spread slowly across the yellow-toothed, lipless mouth set beneath his nostril holes.

On the boat now halfway between the war galley and the Soul Hunter, the effects of the imprisoned djinn's parasitic powers were beginning to make themselves manifest. The gray-bearded dwarf was now hunched and bent over, visibly thinning as hair lost its color and faded to white. Within a few more strokes of the oars, the now decrepit dwarf had fallen to one knee, bald head hung wearily. The valiant, proud dwarf did not let out even a whimper to acknowledge the immense pain that was no doubt tearing through his failing body. Resolute to the last, completely silent in defiance, the withered and wrinkled dwarf dropped dead in the boat.

Standing taller, feeling the life-force seeping down through limbs to his very fingertips, T'mork turned to face the surviving dwarfs stood in chains on his deck.

"Ask them if any more of them wish to insult me," he demanded of the tear-streaked academic.

The woman dutifully translated the high priest's message. Instantly, one of the dwarfs spat out a challenge. Then another. Then all of them, in turn, barked out a few words each that could only be the most bitter and malicious of insults in their own language. The captives looked at each other and then all burst out laughing. T'mork tutted and shook his head in response to the dwarf's bitter mirth. Yes, he had invited that response, he realized that much now. He should have expected no less from their kind.

"Alright," he smiled, with genuine amusement, "I appreciate that. Honestly, I do. But, please do relay onto them that they must understand that I am a man of my principles. Were this a dwarven tale of heroism, no doubt the great, evil high priest would grant them their freedom as a sign of respect for their most uncommon display of bravery. However... this is the real world, and I must adhere to these principles of mine. So, with that in mind... row these filth across to the Soul Hunter. All of them. Slower, this time."

***

The early evening breeze had slackened considerably, leaving little more than a gentle push from the southeast to billow out the frigate's sails. Up ahead, the familiar port of Thatraskos sat at the foot of the hills to the north, its picturesque white buildings with their red-brown roofs spanning around the sheltered harbor like a warm embrace. Already, flickering rows of lanterns were just about visible as the townsfolk set about lighting their evening candles.

Down on the upper deck, below the quarterdeck, one of the topmen scratched a melancholy sounding tune on a fiddle, from where he sat at the foot of the mainmast. Kaeso Innes kept watch by the helmsman and the master, leaving Karnon at the stern taffrail with Jaymes, Joshua Azur, Mayhew Knox, and a bottle of rum. Joshua looked back, perhaps a little forlornly at his crippled sloop, towed behind *Pious* by stout lines secured to the frigate. Less than a mile to go now, and the sloop would safely be alongside for repairs.

"I left her behind, she wept freely as I sailed
The horizon parted us, for how long we would not know;
The dangers of the deep lay ahead of me, no matter how far we sailed,
And if she still lived when I returned, liberty is where we'd go."

"Well, this one is bloody miserable," Mayhew remarked dryly from behind his rum tumbler, scratching thoughtfully at his neat, ginger beard as four or five sailors on the upper deck joined in singing to the fiddler's tune.

Karnon exchanged knowing glances with both the frigate and the sloop captains as they leaned back against the rail in the evening glow. With only a handful of weeks as a marine officer, Karnon very much still considered himself an infantryman first and a nautical man by little more than title. However, even he knew the words to the infamous song 'Liberty Torn.'

"Can't you get 'em to play something happier, sir?" Mayhew asked Jaymes. "Perhaps a song that, for once, isn't about some bloody doomed romance to the girl back home?"

Jaymes issued a slight smile.

"The song's not about a girl, Mayhew."

His eyes still locked on the damaged sloop towed behind the majestic frigate, Joshua finished his glass of rum.

"It's a rebel song, Mister Knox. 'She' is not a girl. She's a nation."

"Specifically, Valentica," Karnon added quietly.

"Well, all the more reason for a different song," Knox grumbled. "I'm not so sure it's best practice to be singing songs of rebellion on a naval..."

"Perhaps you leave worrying about musical best practice on my ship to me," Jaymes interrupted, his tone soft but certainly not without a threatening edge. "I'm no politician – I'll be the first to admit that I have no interest in politics whatsoever. But from what I do know about Lord

Darvled and Valentica, I'm fairly confident that if that was my homeland, I'd not be so quick to judge the rebel movement there."

"Yes, sir. Sorry, sir."

The song continued as the last light of the day lingered on the horizon, the breaks between verses punctuated by the creaking of wooden boards and the slap of water against the metal-covered prow of the frigate. Jaymes raised his telescope to one eye and scanned across the harbor ahead. He lowered it seconds later, his face set grimly. Karnon knew little about matters nautical but knew enough about people to know exactly what ship Jaymes was looking for, and that his expression confirmed her absence. A few seconds later, he raised the telescope again, but this time stopped facing just west of the harbor.

"Hullo, there's something you don't see everyday out here."

Joshua and Mayhew both raised their own telescopes, and Karnon accepted Jaymes's. He raised the instrument to his eye, but a slow scan past the harbor revealed only the two forts, the beautiful town, and the normal bewildering array of masts from a hundred different types of sailing vessel.

"Bit further left, shipmate," Jaymes said quietly.

"Don't you mean, alter a point to port, or some bollocks?" Karnon grumbled quietly.

There – just a little further to the west. A huge warship, two full gundecks, laying at anchor perhaps half a mile from the shore.

"Is that a Dictator?" Karnon mused.

Joshua and Mayhew immediately burst into laughter. Jaymes shot them both a warning glance.

"A Dictator is a lot bigger than that!" Mayhew grinned. "My last job was on one of those."

"Thirty-eighth lieutenant, were you?" Joshua beamed.

"Very funny. No, what you see there is a Defender-class, third-rate battleship. A ship of the line, in old speak. She's a seventy-four, based on the Sisterhood's Abbess-class. A handful more guns, though."

Karnon raised the telescope again. He noted the arrangement of the masts and long yards.

"So... a sort of super-brig, then."

Mayhew's lips curled into another patronizing smile before yet another warning glare from Jaymes transformed his features to solemnity.

"No," Jaymes explained, "you see... you were right the first time. She is a very large fighting ship. Much bigger than us. We're only a fifth-rate. A brig, well, you remember Caithlin's ship? That's a brig. It's the distance, you see, from all the way out here size can be..."

"She's got two masts. Square-rigged," Karnon sniffed

dismissively, "so by definition, she's a brig. Just like any Batch One Elohi-class, come to think of it."

Mayhew's face dropped in horror. Jaymes's brow lowered and his jaw clenched. Joshua burst into laughter again.

"That's good! That's a good one, marine! Come on, gentlemen, that's more than fair!" the sloop captain beamed.

"An Elohi-class is *not* a brig," Jaymes said, slowly and deliberately. "She's a frigate. Even the Batch One hulls with two masts. This is the Basilean Navy, and we classify ships by role, not by rigging."

"Which is a bit odd, sir," Karnon suppressed a malevolent grin, "because I bought a book – it's down below, in my cabin, I can get it if you want – and it says that every human navy in the world, with the exception of Basilea, classifies ships by rigging. And by that definition, an Elohi is a brig and not a frigate. As is an Abbess. And that… Defender, is it? All brigs. And then there's the origins of the term 'frigate-built' – which means a raised quarterdeck and fo'c'sle – and, well, Elohi-class vessels don't have a raised fo'c'sle…"

"Of course they bloody do!" Jaymes snapped. "Look at it! Look for'ard! It's raised!"

"Not clear of the main deck…"

"*Upper* deck, and yes, it is! Besides, that's merely the *origin* of the term because otherwise nine out of ten vessels these days would be 'frigate-built'! It's a legacy term! These days, frigate-built means built for speed and agility. Which Elohi-class frigates are. Even the Batch Ones!"

Karnon eyed Jaymes with suspicion, in the manner of a man weighing up the integrity of his intellectual opponent. Jaymes met his stare, wracking his brain for further evidence as all eyes on the quarterdeck fell on them both.

"The salamander J'Koor'uk is a frigate," Jaymes offered a sinister smile, "and they have only two masts. The salamanders are, to the best of my knowledge, the undisputed masters of sailing in this part of the world. Standfast our navy, of course. Perhaps you'd like to tell them that the bloody Valenticans have got it right, and they're wrong?"

"The picture in my book shows that a J'Koor'uk isn't even square-rigged, if I remember it correctly," Karnon shrugged, "so it's neither a brig nor a frigate, sir."

The conversation was interrupted as Samus, the captain's steward, appeared at the edge of the quarterdeck. He walked briskly over and offered Jaymes his blue jacket and black, bicorn hat.

"We're close enough to be seen from the Spyglass now, sir," the steward grunted.

"Yes," Jaymes accepted the jacket and pulled it on over his white shirt, "thank you. Go and tell the chaps to pipe down with the fiddling and the shanties, too. We'll pipe for harbor stations."

The tall captain pulled on his bicorn hat and fished his dark neckerchief out of his pocket before tying it smartly around his throat.

"'I bought a book'," he grumbled, shaking his head. "Bloody hell, man, I didn't think you could read."

Karnon's smile spread.

"I'm getting my head around all of this boaty shit. It's pretty simple, really. But I pray to the Ones above that you'll never need to learn about my world and what we do. Sir."

Jaymes offered a genuine grin as the frigate's bosun let out a shrill series of whistles, ordering the crew to their stations to enter harbor and bring the warship to her berth.

"Alright. You've read a book and you know what a brig is. Don't push it, or I'll put you in charge of bringing us alongside."

***

His throat dry and his vision just a little unsteady, Jaymes sat at the end of the bench seat and massaged his temples. Piercing sunlight poured in through the gaps in the curtains pulled across the great cabin's stern windows. A few paces away was the entrance to his bedchamber which, well after midnight when he returned to the ship, for some ludicrous reason seemed to be a poor place to sleep. Instead, he had chosen the cushioned bench seat running along the after end of the captain's great cabin, below the fresh air of the open stern windows and quarter galleries. He cursed his lack of mental discipline for allowing 'popping into town for one or two quick drinks' to become a late night session with Karnon Senne, his wife Sabine, and Joshua Azur.

After finishing the water in his metal tankard that, no matter how heavy a night and how severe the memory loss, Drunk Jaymes always somehow managed to lovingly pre-place for Hungover Jaymes in the morning as part of his almost guaranteed hangover cure, Jaymes washed, shaved, and pulled on his uniform. Dragging the curtains back to allow the morning sunlight into the frigate's great cabin, Jaymes allowed himself a smile as he saw the Martolian Queen safely alongside the north jetty. Curiously enough, a salamander frigate was tied alongside just forward of her. A little further down, the sorry sight of Joshua's wounded sloop was already subject to repair work. But safely home, at least.

Leaving behind the positive decadence of the great cabin's long, polished table and chairs, white carpeted flooring, and wall-mounted artwork, Jaymes made his way to Pious's upper deck, forcing smiles and returning morning pleasantries to the greetings from his crew. As the mere second lieutenant he had joined Pious as, it was far easier to stop and talk to his sailors about their evenings – particularly given his background serving aboard the far smaller, more close-knit and intimate sloops. Jaymes mentally chastised himself for the distance that he had allowed to grow between himself and his subordinates since assuming command.

Pious, although secured to the jetty, was still alive with activity as fresh stores were loaded and the ship's carpenter and his team banged away with tools to rectify minor issues. Jaymes saw Karnon taking morning tea on the quarterdeck with Kaeso Innes – the former looking, as he always did after a night out, suspiciously sober, well-turned out, and soldierly in appearance. Jaymes stopped at the scuttlebutt to refill his tankard with drinking water and then made his way up the steps leading to the quarterdeck.

"Morning," he smiled to the two officers, wincing as the blazing sun beat mercilessly down on the harbor without a single cloud in the sky to lessen the blow.

"Morning, sir!" Kaeso beamed, the short man's grin punctuated with what always appeared to be more teeth than most people had, just far smaller. Still, somehow, it was a look that the young lieutenant wore well.

"Morning, sir," Karnon repeated, his red uniform jacket standing out against the naval officers' blues. "Captain Viconti of the *Martolian Queen* was here about half an hour ago. I told her that you would be available after your meeting with the admiral."

Jaymes failed to suppress his smile. He thought himself a confident man in a handful of areas, but certainly not in the company of ladies. Yet here he was, in a semi-clandestine relationship with a woman universally regarded to be the most beautiful, daring, and quick-witted in the entire East Infant Sea. Seeing her ship safely returned was a great relief, yet part of him often wondered at what point she would realize that she could do better than him. But she had tried to visit him, nonetheless. So she had not realized that just yet.

Jaymes's smile instantly faded as the second half of Karnon's greeting sunk in.

"Samus!" he yelled as he looked up at the clock tower of the naval administration building and calculated how fast he would need to cross the dockyard to meet the admiral on time. "Sword and hat! Quickly, now!"

It was with a sweat-soaked brow that reminded Jaymes to redouble his efforts to maintain his levels of fitness that he arrived, with a few minutes to spare, in the admiral's outer office. Mauriss, the flag lieutenant, showed Jaymes into the office as the clocktower above them struck on the hour. Admiral Sir Jerris Pattia stood by his bay windows with another officer, both of them laughing out loud into their tumblers as Mauriss opened the office doors.

"Captain Ellias of *HW Pious*, sir," he announced to the admiral.

The doors shut behind Jaymes as he strode forward to the desk, stood to attention, and then was interrupted before he could salute.

"Never mind that bollocks!" the short admiral beamed. "Get rid of your hat! By the Ones, man! You look like you've gone a whole watch against a man o'war! Did you run here?"

Jaymes removed his hat and wiped his sweating brow again.

"Yes, sir."

"Running late because you lost track of time? Woke up late after a heavy night?"

"Yes, sir."

"Good man! Well, you're here on time. Let's fight that hangover the proper way. Gin? Whisky? No, you're a rum man, if I recall?"

Jaymes took a deep breath. Yes, he considered himself a rum man. But not halfway through the forenoon, with his stomach still turning from the previous night. But he knew what was expected.

"That's right, sir. Rum, if you please."

The admiral let out a strange sort of growl which Jaymes assumed roughly translated as 'good lad' as he fetched a third tumbler from his drinks cabinet and poured out a dark rum. That gave him a second to glance across at the room's other occupant.

The other officer wore the epaulets of a captain, but the sheer richness of the gold dangling from his shoulders spoke of wealth. The captain was in his early thirties, tall and perhaps just a touch overweight, with a neat wig of white curls surrounding a stern looking face. He regarded Jaymes in turn and offered a courteous nod with a not-unfriendly smile.

"Zakery Uwell, this is Jaymes Ellias of the *Pious*," Jerris introduced. "He's one of the fellows you'll be taking out with you. But we'll get onto that in a moment. Jaymes, you're back early."

Jaymes stopped dead, his glass halfway to his lips.

"I... yes. Sir. Escorting the *Scout* back home, sir, after she took damage."

"Yes, I read your report. What confused me was that you very quickly managed to get alongside and save her entire crew... but then elected to leave the merchant ships you were charged with escorting. All three of them. Each of which, individually, was worth as much as ten sloops with what they were carrying."

Jaymes slowly returned his glass to the admiral's desk.

"Well, sir," he began hesitantly, "after the action, I regrouped with the *Veneration*. I signaled my intentions to get the *Scout* safely home, and Captain Dio seemed perfectly content to continue the patrol alone. I'd also stress that my orders were to patrol the Sand Lane, not specifically escort that group of merchantmen. I left them with Captain Dio and the *Veneration*. There's a very small chance that they might be destroyed before they get there, but they'll most likely reach their destination. If I left the *Scout*, she would definitely be destroyed."

The short admiral narrowed his eyes and took a gulp from whatever fiery liquid was in his neatly etched glass.

"Then let's hope Marcellus returns from patrol shortly, with news of the safe departure of those ships from the Sand Lane. Because if you're right, then you made a good choice. If you're wrong, and we've lost valuable merchantmen to save a single sloop whose crew were already safely recovered... well... it wouldn't look good. Would it?"

The admiral's normally jovial exterior was replaced by something Jaymes was yet to witness. He tried to meet the older officer's piercing stare and failed.

"No, sir. It wouldn't," he agreed submissively.

Jaymes looked up again. The admiral was refilling his glass. The extravagantly dressed, portly captain – Zakery – flashed an encouraging smile at Jaymes and issued a curt, supportive nod.

"Well," Jerris spoke again, his tone returning to its normal lively level, "to business! We've got a bit of a pickle, gents! Bit of a pickle. As you already know, Zakery, we've had reports of an Ahmunite fleet straying north of the Infantosians. Undead, this close to us! Unbelievable. This is normally a problem that our salamander chums deal with down south, but some bastard of a walking corpse has decided to stray all the way up into our playground. So the two of you, and Marcellus when he gets back, are going out there to shove a proverbial boat hook up his arse."

His eyes half closed in confusion as he wracked his brain for the proverb the admiral was referring to, Jaymes took a sip from his glass. He then immediately remembered his hangover.

"Sightings have come from civilian vessels," the admiral continued, "so it might be a load of bollocks, gents, might be a load of bollocks. But four individual reports are enough for Zakery and the Shield Royal to be sent down here from the Grand Fleet at best speed."

"I've read through the reports, sir," Zakery said, "they do all agree on a large flagship. Two of them gave enough detail to indicate that it was a sailing vessel, so most likely we're looking at one of their old war galleys rather than a Monolith. Accounts do disagree on the number of vessels. Anything between three and twenty."

"As I said," Jerris smiled, "civilian accounts. Your average civilian mariner tends to panic a bit when faced with a ship that shoots at him, so I doubt very much there's twenty of them out there. But, with a Defender, two Elohis and as many smaller vessels as I can spare, I think you'll be able to give a bloody nose to whatever you find."

"Normal procedures for their lot is for a couple of Khopeshii to escort a war galley," Zakery continued, "they're about the size of a frigate, faster than an Elohi, and built tough. Not as much of a broadside, though – certainly not compared to a Batch Two. Depending on how many of the smaller vessels are in support – for both us and for them – will determine the balance."

Jaymes frantically thought of something intelligent to add. He had never seen an Ahmunite ship in his life, let alone positioned alongside one to trade broadsides. With no experience or opinion to add, best to fall back on the old reliable – chunter on with some nonsense that sounded determined and keen to fight.

"*Pious* is ready to go as soon as you like, sir," Jaymes said formally.

Jerris beamed.

"Good! Good! We need to wait for *Veneration* to return, and for stores for the lot of you. It'll be a few days yet. That'll give us a chance to get some eyes and ears put out to sea to find out a little more of what's going on. I'm not particularly keen on assembling a sizable force to go looking for the proverbial badger in a forest."

Jaymes again found himself wincing as he frantically searched for what proverb the admiral was referring to.

"Well, that's all for now. Come on, Zakery, it's about stand easy time, and I get priority on pastries downstairs. Check back in with me in a couple of days, Jaymes."

It was with his mind whirring and second guessing that Jaymes made his way out of the office, back down to the ground floor, and across the cavernous entrance hall to exit the administration building. Was leaving the patrol early the wrong decision? Had he even stopped to really think it over? Was he subconsciously finding an excuse to head back to port? Why? Ultimately, the sole responsibility for any failure lay with the captain, and that was something he had still not managed to normalize. Was he shirking that responsibility at the first opportunity? Was he jeopardizing all to save a sloop out of some misplaced loyalty to his former fleet? Did he just want to come back to port for another reason entirely?

As if that final thought somehow manifested itself into reality before his very eyes, Jaymes saw Caithlin waiting by the same cannon they had met at before they both left on their last cruises. A weight lifting from his shoulders and the knots in his gut easing, he walked briskly over to her. She saw him approaching and offered a slight smile – the small, cool smiles she gave when in uniform that seemed reserved, almost cold, when compared to the joy-filled smiles she allowed herself when away from work.

"It's good to see you," Jaymes greeted.

"And you," Caithlin replied. "I bumped into Karnon this morning. He said you'd run into orcs only a few days out. I'm glad you are all safe. Mainly, I'm glad that you are safe."

"If they'd worked together properly, they could have given us some real problems," Jaymes admitted, standing next to Caithlin and leaning against the cannon, "but... well, we didn't suffer so much as a scratch on this one. What about you? I saw your mast. What happened?"

Leaning back against the cannon, her back to the crenulated fort perimeter wall and the sheer drop down to the harbor, Caithlin stared straight ahead but risked reaching down to hold one of Jaymes's hands.

"A giant turtle, would you believe? Just... came to the surface right next to us. I had a particularly spiky naiad deliver some contrived speech about being in her ocean. There was a J'Koor'uk racing over to see what was happening. Between us, we forced the crew to abandon the poor creature."

Jaymes glanced across, eyes wide.

"You... that's... well! It seems everybody is making a play for the north at the moment. Trident Realm coming into our part of the world, and from what I've just heard, possibly the Ahmunites, too. How bad was it? Did you lose anybody?"

Caithlin nodded slowly.

"Yes. A few. Two of my old crew among them. Men who had sailed with me for nearly two years."

Jaymes gave her hand what he hoped was a reassuring squeeze.

"I'm sorry. I'm truly glad that you're safe. But I'm sorry for your loss."

Caithlin shrugged in what Jaymes assumed was supposed to be a gesture of stern nonchalance. The gesture failed.

"Thank you. I'll need to go and talk to Kassia. The pay coming in from the navy for the patrols is just about paying my crews' wages enough to keep them retained. Just. But it doesn't leave anything for damages. And a new mainmast isn't cheap, without even factoring in the costs of fitting the thing."

Jaymes turned to face her.

"Surely you can bill the admiralty? You took damage flying our flag. You should be getting logistical support from here, not paying for it for yourself."

Caithlin shook her head.

"Not the way my orders are written. Not under these signatures. I'll see what I can work out with Kassia, she's had my back since I first arrived. After you, she's the only person I trust out here. But... enough of that. We've both been out and had some fool shoot at us. We're both back in one piece. Let's not talk about this anymore. If that's alright with you. I'd rather concentrate on something entirely happier. When do you get away today?"

Jaymes turned to face her. He offered an encouraging smile. What he hoped was one, at least.

"We're waiting now. We're off out with that Defender class at anchor over there, once Marcellus gets back. I've got a few days to myself. I... was actually thinking about going to look at houses, I don't know if you remember me mentioning that a couple of weeks ago. Now I've decided to stick this out, I..."

Jaymes stopped himself from finishing the sentence. Now that the increased pay from his promotion to captain was coming through. That was insensitive. He had already offered to support Caithlin by helping to pay her crew's wages, but she had politely declined.

"Where were you thinking of buying?" Caithlin asked.

"I was thinking something along the coastal road south of here. When we met at Linidi before we last went out. Not quite as far away as that, but maybe halfway."

Jaymes took off his hat for a moment to wipe his brow before returning it. Below them, a Sisterhood Gur Panther brig made its way into the harbor as a trio of brigantines proceeded southward past it.

"I'm sorry this didn't turn out the way we wanted," Caithlin said quietly.

Jaymes turned to look at her again, wistful thoughts of a house with a balcony and a sea view suddenly replaced by the darker turn in the conversation.

"In what way?"

"I... I had this rather foolish, naive, and romantic idea. That we would both sail out together to do battle against evil. Pirates, slavers... we'd be side by side. But... I have a crew to pay. I have a debt to pay off. I can't put an eighteen-gun brig in company with a thirty-six-gun frigate, not when I need to capture prizes. That ends in one of two ways. Either I get the scraps of what's left after a fifth-rate has torn any potential prize to pieces or, more likely, you'll do something foolish like soften a prize up for me to take. And then you'd have a mutiny on your hands, in the name of love."

Jaymes swallowed, sympathetic to her plight and respectful of the realistic appraisal of the situation. But also suddenly uplifted in an almost dreamlike euphoria over the first time she had used that word to describe their relationship.

"We'll work it out!" he offered. "I have no idea how just yet, but between you and I, we'll come up with something! This isn't ideal, I know, but it's still good. I'd prefer it if we saw each other more. But I wouldn't trade what we have for the world."

Caithlin smiled – not one of the subdued ones, but something far more cheerful and carefree. She took a step back.

"I've got to go and speak to Kassia about the repairs. I'll see you this afternoon? If you want company in your search for a lair of your own away from this harbor?"

Jaymes beamed.

"I wouldn't miss it for the world."

***

Her footsteps echoing along the cobbles of the narrow alleyway and her shoulders slumped, Caithlin made her way from the naval dockyard toward the civilian harbor to the east of Thatraskos. She had stopped off at her ship to leave her military-styled jacket and hat, but for the first time in her career as a privateer, had elected to keep her saber by her side. She looked down at the weapon as she emerged from the alleyway and onto the main street running alongside the piers crammed with trading ships busily loading and unloading goods. Her old world; a happier one. The sword, which she carried on two short lengths of leather attached to her belt – as was the naval fashion, rather than to wear it hanging from the waist – represented her new life.

Yet, even though she barely knew how to use the sword, and in her few boarding actions had found herself strangely more comfortable with a pistol, carrying it now seemed almost like a statement. Proof that, even without the jacket and hat of an auxiliary naval captain, the saber proved that she was a fighting woman, and to be taken seriously as such. She tutted and shook her head. If one had to make an obvious statement to prove anything, then there was a good chance it was not true.

Threading her way through the busy street running along the edge of the sparkling water, Caithlin finally arrived at the harbor master's office. Making her way down the thin corridor to the stairs leading up to the first floor, she knocked at a familiar door and then made her way into the small, fastidious tidy office that weeks before had been the first step in this new chapter of her life. The harbormaster, a short woman of fifty years with a severe, gray ponytail, looked up angrily from behind her desk. Recognition immediately registered in her eyes, and a friendly smile spread across her wrinkled face.

"Cathy! Come and sit down! I saw your brig limp in last night – glad to see you're not hurt."

Caithlin unclipped her sword and propped it up against a small anchor by the door, clipped the two dangling straps from her sword belt together to make a loop by her hip, and then sat down by Kassia's desk.

"Well," she shrugged, "that's what brings me here. Main mast needs replacing. Who would you recommend, and what deal can you secure for me?"

Kassia narrowed her eyes and passed a piece of paper across the desk. The numbers were already drawn up.

"I made some enquiries earlier this morning. As soon as I saw that mast. JD Talcio and Sons is your best bet. That's the best price I managed. I've worked with them for years, so they agreed to knock one tenth off their normal rate."

Caithlin sighed as she scanned her eyes over the quote. It was a good rate. But still expensive. She recalled the charity Kassia first extended to her when she arrived in Thatraskos, having narrowly survived being attacked by orc pirates. That charity quickly changed to support being provided 'at cost,' which was still very much appreciated. At cost was now replaced with a one tenth price reduction. Caithlin could not hold that against Kassia. The harbormaster's office was still accountable to a contracted, profit-making organization.

"I can't afford this. It's a good deal, but I can't keep delaying the payment of my crew to deal with repairs."

Kassia nodded sympathetically.

"Well... you could take out a loan. There are a good few..."

"I can't take out a loan," Caithlin interjected, "I already owe too much to the Basilean government. I... it all started well. But word has spread south to the pirate nests now. They all know to keep an eye out for the Genezan brig. None of them are fooled anymore, none of them will come in close. No more easy prizes for me."

Kassia grimaced and linked her fingers together atop her tidy but battered desk.

"Cathy, you're a privateer. You're supposed to be making money by taking merchant ships from enemies of Basilea. Instead, you're going out and conducting yourself like a pirate-hunter. You need to be a privateer."

"Then be a good shipmate and tell your government to declare war on somebody, would you?" Caithlin snapped. "Because right now, I don't have anything to do other than defend the Sand Lane against pirates, orcs, and bloody giant turtles! And there's no money in any of that!"

Kassia leaned back in her chair, her features hardening.

"I'm sorry," Caithlin offered immediately, "that wasn't fair. You've done nothing other than support me since the day we met."

The older woman smiled softly.

"Answer me this. If Basilea did declare war on another nation tomorrow, would you go attacking their civilian merchant shipping to make money to pay off your debt? Would you kill civilian mariners for that?"

Caithlin looked away for a moment, resumed eye contact, and then shook her head.

"Look... some advice, if I may be so patronizing," Kassia continued.

"Please. Go on."

The harbormaster paused momentarily before speaking again.

"You were... fortunate enough to be born into a fairly affluent family. I appreciate that you had a major event push your life here, to Thatraskos, and this wasn't part of the plan. But still, down on your luck in comparative terms only, you find yourself captain of a ship. You might be struggling to pay off your debts, but you are slowly paying them off. You are surviving, day by day, better than most. Perhaps it's time to just accept that this is your life now, and life isn't easy."

Caithlin bit back her first response. She took a moment to compose herself with a few long breaths. She carefully selected her words. They were interrupted when the door behind her flew open. She turned. A thin man in his mid-fifties, balding, and wearing a long coat of brown, entered the room. Physically shaking, bile rising in her throat, Caithlin shot to her feet.

"Excuse me!" Kassia thundered, slowly rising. "This is my office, and I'll..."

"Would you give us a moment, please?" the aging man asked, his harsh tone at dissonance with his polite words.

"I'll be damned if..."

Caithlin looked over at her friend and shook her head.

"Just a few minutes," she pleaded, "please, Kassia."

Kassia looked incredulously at the younger woman for a few awkward moments of silence, before shaking her head and walking briskly past the thin man. He slammed the door shut and paced over to Caithlin.

"Sit down."

"I..."

"I told you to sit down!"

Caithlin nodded.

"Yes, father."

Chapter Five

Adventure Prize
Six-gun sloop, taken up from trade
Ten leagues north of Ferla Bay, East Infant Sea

The sleek hull of the sloop fell down into the trough with an audible slam, salt-laden foam shooting across the forward end of the deck before the prow lifted again for the next wave. The distance was closing. Like sharks closing in on a wounded whale, the four pirate sloops shot across the blue-green sea toward the twin-masted trade schooner. The fast merchant ship suddenly swung about to port, bringing its beam to line up with one pair of the smaller pirate ships. A volley of fire rippled out of its small, port broadside, and a quartet of cannonballs whooshed through the hot, summer air to plough through the closest of the sloops.

"Well!" Ash shouted above the rushing wind on the second sloop. "I guess they're fighting now!"

"Keep closing!" Tem yelled back to where Gunnta hunkered over the helm. "Get us right alongside! Half a point starboard! Close the gap!"

The nimble sloop eased to starboard, her bows lined up with the black and white hulled schooner. Tem looked ahead to the pirate squadron commander's sloop – Wez's dramatically renamed *Ranger's Revenge* – and saw a trio of sailors scramble up into the rigging to hurriedly begin affecting repairs from the damage sustained from the schooner's defensive fire. Tem grinned. They were slowing down. He looked off to starboard and saw the other two sloops – the *Anne-Marie* and the *Blue Rise* – closing from the schooner's other side, but not closing as fast as the *Adventure Prize*.

"Hooks!" Tem shouted to his crew. "Straight through the guns and on 'em, lads!"

Even without a telescope, Tem could see the handful of sailors on the schooner's deck frantically trying to reload the four cannons pointing to port, their gesticulations showing their panic even from this range. Tem grimaced. If they loaded again in time – and, Ones above forbid, if they for some reason had grapeshot – he and his crew would be torn limb from limb once alongside.

"Come on!" Flyde screamed, a belaying pin in one hand and a short hatchet in the other as he stared wild-eyed at the schooner.

"Come on, you bastards!"

The *Adventure Prize* surged across the waves, approaching the schooner from its port quarter, wind dead astern and perfectly positioned for both vessels. The *Ranger's Revenge* turned back in to catch up but was lost behind now, as were the two sloops approaching the schooner from starboard with the wind on their beam. No, this was Tem's prize. If those guns were not loaded in time, he would be first aboard.

Halladai flung a hook and line across from the sloop's fo'c'sle, slamming it down on the schooner's quarterdeck. It dragged back and caught firm. Tem's crew cheered as, beaming, the burly quartermaster heaved in the rope to keep the line taught. Predictably, one of the schooner's crewmen raced back aft and set about hacking through the attached rope with a dirk. Tem raised his pistol and fired an ineffectual shot in the sailor's direction in an attempt to dissuade him, but at this range only succeeded in making the desperate mariner flinch for a moment.

Reloading his pistol, Tem stared straight ahead. Another hook and line was thrown across by Jeffi, similarly accurate and quickly pulled tight. Halladai and Jeffi quickly hauled in their lines as the range closed.

"Straight into their port quarter!" Tem shouted back to Gunnta at the helm, "hold back from their broadside! Just get us next to the bastards and we'll jump!"

The guns were run out on the side of the schooner. Only just over a ship's length dividing them, the schooner turned hard to port in an attempt to bring the cannons around. As she did so, the wind came about to her beam, and the sails on her two tall masts flapped noisily as they lost that perfect bearing. The ship slowed. Tem's sloop crashed into her port quarter.

With a roar and his pistol and cutlass held high, Tem led the charge across. Taking a run across the fo'c'sle, he jumped up to plant a foot on the taffrail of his own sloop before propelling himself up and onto the quarterdeck of the schooner. Ten sailors stood by the four port cannons, armed with a motley assortment of improvised weapons. One of them, a wrinkled man with long white hair who looked old enough to be Tem's grandfather, walked out hesitantly and drew a cutlass. Tem brought up his pistol and shot him in the belly. The old man dropped his weapon, clutched at the growing patch of dark red spreading across his shirt, and crumpled down to the deck.

"Get away from those guns and drop your weapons!" Tem yelled as Halladai and Flyde jumped across to join him on the schooner. "I won't say it twice!"

More of Tem's pirates piled across from the sloop. The merchant mariners wordlessly dropped their weapons and raised their hands. Tem looked up into the rigging above.

"Up top! Bring in the sails and heave to!"

Halladai led a handful of the pirates across to shove their prisoners down to their knees, pulling the dying old man with them and dumping him in front of his comrades. The other three sloops were already rapidly closing. Time was short.

"Ash! With me!" Tem shouted and turned to head back aft to the captain's cabin.

The cabin below the quarterdeck was plush enough, extravagantly furnished with a mauve rug and two matching sofas. Papers were scattered haphazardly across a desk. One of the stern windows was open, silhouetting a small figure against the morning sunlight. The sailor – who could only be a halfling, given his build and height – leaned out of the window and flung armfulls of letters and scrolls out into the sea.

"Stop right there, or you're going out next!" Tem growled as he paced across.

The halfling continued regardless, quickly grabbing envelopes from the desk and throwing them out of the window.

Tem grabbed the small man by the arm and dragged him back into the cabin, holding his cutlass to the halfling's throat. The short sailor was young, probably no older than Tem, with a neat green jacket with tails and a head topped with voluminous curls of brown hair. A mischievous, victorious glint in his eyes seemed to fight for control with the panicked frown pulling down on his thin, pale lips.

"What was in those letters?" Tem demanded.

"It d-doesn't matter now!" the halfling captain managed. "They're gone!"

"If you're ditching them, then they're secret. If they're secret, then they're worth something!" Tem dragged the captain back toward the door leading to the upper deck.

"They're not worth anything to you," the halfling muttered, "they're not worth gold. But they're worth something to somebody, and a promise is a..."

Tem slammed his fist into the halfling's gut, bending the little man over double in pain. He picked him up and threw him through the door to crash out into the open air of the upper deck.

"What in the Abyss is that?" Halladai asked as he emerged from a hatchway leading beneath the fo'c'sle.

"The captain, I think," Tem replied, kicking the prone halfling in the gut for good measure. "Caught the little bastard throwing documents overboard."

"Well, never mind that now, Captain," Halladai replied, grinning broadly. "The hold is stacked to the gunwales with silk, spices, wine... there's a fair penny in this for all of us."

As if the mention of plunder had somehow summoned him, Captain Wez Polleri's *Ranger's Revenge* nudged alongside the *Adventure Prize*, and Tem saw the captain hop from from sloop to sloop, and then across to the captured schooner.

"Grand job, mate!" the red-headed pirate grinned. "Grand job! What's the haul?"

"Go down and take a look, Captain," Halladai gestured to the hatchway, "but there's enough to split four ways for four crews and still call this a good day."

"Champion!" Wez grinned, sneering down at the kneeling captives as he strode past them, his long coat seemingly out of place in the relentless heat. "Come on. Kill these bastards and we'll get the crates up here to split."

Tem looked across at Halladai. The burly quartermaster folded his dark arms.

"No," Tem spat, "we're not killing them. We agreed that any cargo and valuables would be split equally. But this is my prize and my prisoners. They surrendered, so they live."

A metal hook slammed into the deck not far from Tem's feet before it was dragged across the deck to dig into the starboard taffrail. A single line secured the sloop *Anne-Marie* to the schooner, and a trio of pirates jumped across from the third sloop.

"Ahoy!" grinned Captain Yordan Iale, his near toothless smile matching his scared face. "What have we here?"

Wez pointed downward.

"A hold full of cargo. And a captain who won't kill his prisoners."

Yordan let out a belly laugh and cocked his pistol.

"Don't be wet, boy! Now you kill these sods, or I'll tie 'em to the masts and they'll wish you'd killed 'em!"

Tem's feet slammed into the deck as he rushed over to meet the two captains face-to-face, his jaw set and his fists clenched.

"Am I talking to myself here?" he growled. "This is my prize! My prisoners! You'll each get your quarter share, but you'll damn well shut your face-holes when it comes to me deciding what I do with my prisoners!"

Wez raised an interested eyebrow. Yordan's smile faded, replaced with a bitter sneer as he stared across at the younger pirate captain.

"Well," Wez mused, turning to face Tem's crew, "you're right about the agreement. We only talked about the cargo. But... you, like the rest of us, are part of Cerri Denayo's lot. So you follow his rules, or you sling your hook and piss off. And that means that once the fighting stops, any decisions are put to the vote of the crew. So... not your decision on what happens to this here schooner and her crew. It's up to your boyos, here."

Tem looked across at the terrified prisoners, the dying old man he had gunned down, the bruised halfling captain, and then his own sailors. Yordan laughed again. Tem turned back to Wez and Yordan, his voice hushed so that only his two fellow pirate captains could hear.

"Look here," he grunted, "we all know I'm new at playing captain. But I'm not new at this pirate game. So I can see from a dozen cables away when a pair of arseholes are trying to play a round of who's the double hard bastard of the Infant Sea at my expense. So do us a favor, stop acting like pricks and stop testing me to see if I'll snap. Because I'm about one second away from breaking your noses with my pistol butt. We clear, mateys?"

It was Wez's turn to laugh. He clapped a hand against Tem's shoulder.

"Alright, Tem. You're alright, mate."

Tem turned away and spat on the deck.

"Oi."

He turned back. Yordan grinned across at him.

"I want this ship," he narrowed his eyes, "the *Marie-Anne* is rotten with woodworm. The boys are sick of spending all night on the pumps. I want this schooner."

Tem scratched at his stubbled jaw and nodded slowly. He ran a few figures through his blond hair.

"Alright, mate. Fair enough. She's yours. Your quarter of the plunder is forfeit to me. That'll cover one fifth of the price of this ship."

The older pirate's eyes opened wide.

"Are you taking the piss?"

"You don't even know what's in the cargo hold yet."

"Doesn't bloody well matter! I know what a schooner's worth, and unless each of our shares down there are a crate of piss-vinegared wine, you're... you're *insulting* me with that price!"

Tem shrugged.

"Couldn't give two shits, mate. It's my ship. Yours is leaking and sinking. I've got you over a barrel. You're a captive buyer. You and me, we ain't bezzy oppos. We don't go back years, and I don't owe you a good deal. This is business. So if you want this fast schooner with eight guns and a good hull, you're paying my price."

Yordan swore and turned on his heel, muttering a string of barely audible obscenities before turning back. His response was cut off when Halladai tapped Tem on the shoulder.

"What is it?" he asked quietly, stepping out of earshot of the two captains.

The quartermaster winced.

"The lads... they've voted. They want to kill the schooner's crew."

Tem's eyes opened wide.

"What? Why? Tell them to f..."

Halladai held his hands up passively.

"It was a close vote. Not much in it. But they don't want witnesses getting back up north. They're worried that we're making a name for ourselves already."

"You've offered the crew the deal?" Tem asked.

Halladai nodded.

"Yes. Six out of fifteen of them are joining us. The others are, I think, hoping that this is all a bluff and we'll let them go."

"Oi!" Yordan growled. "Tem! We're still haggling here!"

"Shut up and wait, Lofty!" Tem snapped before turning back to his quartermaster. "Halladai, you need to grip this. I'm making more money for us here, a lot more. I need you to get this sorted. That bag of bastards knew my rules before we came out here! We kill who we need to kill! Nobody else!"

"You gonna overrule a crew vote?" Halladai's eyes widened.

"If I have to, yeah! Nobody is killing prisoners, not while I'm calling the shots! Remind those pricks who just beat three veteran captains to this prize, and who is getting a bucket load of money for selling this schooner to a bloody idiot! Keep the six new hands, they've agreed to it now. The others are going free – in the *Anne-Marie* or in their own seaboat. I don't care which."

Tem turned back to the two captains.

"Trouble with your boys?" Wez smiled slyly. "This all 'bout you not wanting to kill these poor sailors, here? C'mon, Tem! Think! One of them is bleeding out because you shot him, and the captain is broken and sobbing after you beat him! But now yer gonna piss off every last man-jack on your ship by telling them they have to play nice?"

"A man runs at me with a sword, I kill him. I give a prisoner an order and he disobeys, I give the bastard a shoeing," Tem shrugged, "that's my moral compass. But this lot? They've surrendered. I'm taking what I want, but I'm no murderer. I'm certainly no murderer when it comes to sailors who brave the same storms and seas full of kraken, serpents, and fish-women bastards as we do! Now, Yordan, my offer. It ain't budging. It has an expiry. Five seconds. Take it or get back onto your sinking ship."

***

Only minutes before, Caithlin had walked these very streets

with her head held high and her saber carried as a proclamation of her fighting prowess. Now she followed Stefano, her father, back through the same streets in silence, her shoulders slumped and her head hung low, her sword carried awkwardly like a toy she felt she no longer deserved. Two paces behind the master merchant, whilst his eyes were fixed forward away from her, Caithlin took the opportunity to quickly button her shirt all the way up to the neck and pull her dark neckerchief out of her pocket and tie it in place. A more prim and proper appearance might not help things, but it was one thing less for him to criticize her for.

The father and daughter walked briskly and silently back to the naval dockyard, where Caithlin was admitted without hesitation, and her father's papers of identification and status as a military-approved trader caused only a slight delay. The two walked to where the *Martolian Queen* lay alongside a low jetty in the sun, resplendent and holding her own against the dedicated military vessels around her, save her broken main mast which drooped down pathetically at a slight angle. Caithlin recognized a figure waiting by the gangway leading up to the upper deck. Jense Kalloway, a passing acquaintance from her childhood who later came to work for her father and was now a junior partner in the company. The short, already balding man smiled sympathetically to her as they approached.

"Hello, Cathy."

"Jense. How are Tia and the children?"

"Well, thank you. They..."

"Not now!" Stefano snapped, storming past the younger man and striding up the gangway.

Caithlin followed her father up to her ship. The tall man stopped the moment his feet touched the upper deck. He let out a breath as he scanned his eyes across the eighteen guns neatly gleaming on their carriages in the sunlight.

"By the Ones," he swore under his breath.

Two of Caithlin's crew saw the man – a stranger to them – and paced over purposefully. Caithlin held up a hand and shot them a warning glance to come no closer. Stefano turned to glare at his daughter.

"How... how in the Abyss have you ended up in this mess?"

Caithlin failed to meet his withering stare.

"It was the run for the South Mantica Trading Company. I had Owynne with me. We were..."

"I know all of that!" Stefano growled. "I read the report from their company. I read the insurance report. I read all three letters you've managed to find the time to send to your mother and I since you disappeared, and..."

"Six!" Caithlin snapped. "Six letters! And you haven't replied to a single one of them! You…"

"I'll let you know when it's your turn to talk!" Stefano boomed. "And I'll have you know that I wrote to you on multiple occasions! Three of your letters don't make it to me in Geneza – how many of my letters to you do you think have disappeared for the same reasons? Now! You were attacked by orc pirates. You dumped your cargo and your guns to save your crew. Good. You led them on a merry chase into shallow waters and shook them off. Excellent. That's the daughter I know. Resourceful, quick thinking, intelligent. You nursed your vessel to a port for assistance. Good. All good. All the way I taught you. Then… then! Then you completely lost your head and panicked the first time some Basilean bully mentioned a few legal words, and signed your life away as a bloody pirate! What were you thinking?!"

"What I was thinking was the ten year prison sentence they threatened me with for the money I owed!"

"Prison? Prison! You were never going to prison! Ten years? They made up some nonsense to panic you into doing what they wanted, and you fell for it!"

"I owed them for repairs! I owed the company for the lost cargo! I couldn't even afford the harbor fees! They doubled back and recovered half of the cargo, and said it was salvage and I still owed them for…"

"I know! I know all of that! And it's all nonsense! The ship was insured for the damage! And you took on assistance from the Basilean Navy and invalidated the entire policy! If the South Mantica Company recovered half their lost cargo, then the law says half of your debt is gone! But you're ignorant of the law, and you buckled as soon as they tried to pin this on you! Now they're laughing with half their cargo back and a full reimbursement from a debt that doesn't exist, which the Basilean Navy have paid and pinned on you! And prison? You're a legitimate captain of a well-respected trading company, and victim of a pirate attack in a shipping lane protected by Basilea! They would have put you up in a perfectly pleasant townhouse until this was resolved, not prison!"

A shaking hand pressed to her brow, Caithlin turned away. The nausea was the same, taking her right back to that day when she limped into this very harbor, her ship shattered and dead crewmen piled in the orlop deck. She took a breath and looked up again.

"That's not what they told me. None of them. You could have…"

"Could have what, Caithlin? Could have what? You tell me what more I could have done. You're my daughter. As soon as I found out, I dropped everything! I've spent a fortune on the finest maritime law company in the region to fight this! I've personally visited the Chief Trading Officer of the South Mantica company to fight this! And now look. Look at these guns. I've never, *never,* in forty years at sea seen so much firepower crammed into such a small amount of deck space. There's enough here to sink a frigate!"

"Father, they're only nine pounders! It would have to be a stern rake, and a pretty small frigate!"

Stefano's eyes opened wide.

"You shouldn't even know what a stern rake is! Look at this poor ship!"

"Poor ship?!" Caithlin exploded. "Has the fate of your poor daughter entered your stubborn head at any point? I'm the one committed to another nine years of battle here, not you!"

Her father stopped for a moment. It was his turn to take a few breaths. He looked up at the split main mast and tutted.

"Nine years. Thought it was ten."

"I received a substantial reward for services to the Hegemony in my first week."

"Was it dangerous? No. Don't answer that. That mast... I know somebody who can get that sorted. I'll pay for that. But until this is sorted, I'm taking you home. I'll arrange that with the Admiral of the Keretian Fleet."

Caithlin looked down the gangway at where Jense was pretending not to listen to the argument. She looked across at the naval administration building and the imposing Spyglass tower above it. Then across at the beautiful port and surrounding hills that had been her home for nearly a quarter of a year now. If her father was right... this would all be over. She could go home. There would be a bill to pay off, no doubt, but if her father's company could shoulder that financial burden, Caithlin could be home with her family in only a couple of weeks. The *Martolian Queen* could return to her trading fit. She could travel the world again, seeing the nice parts. The safer parts. The crisp beauty of the snowy Winterlands to the serenity and exotic beauty of Elvenhome. For a moment, she felt relief. Then that crutch fell away again.

"Father... which letters did you get?"

"Well... I don't know. I don't know what was in the letters I didn't receive."

Caithlin paused. A seagull landed on the taffrail near them and eyed the father and daughter suspiciously.

"Did you get the letter where I told you that I'd met somebody here?"

Stefano's brow furrowed instantly. The seagull hopped closer.

"What? No! No, I didn't get that letter! What do you mean, you've met somebody? Here? In Thatraskos? A Basilean port! That means you've met a Basilean, or a sailor, because that's all that is here! Either way, that's even more of a bloody disaster than this whole business with the South Mantica lot!"

"He's, umm… he's both."

"You've shacked up with a Basilean sailor?! You've become a bloody pirate, in my ship, and shacked up with a Basilean sailor! Oh, Ones! Caithlin! Please at least tell me he's a trader or a fisherman and not… Caithlin! A naval man! What have I told you about the navy? Did you learn nothing from me? You're a prize, Caithlin! Look at you! You're a pretty prize to men like that, to show off and then discard! Nothing more! Do you honestly think he cares for you or respects you for who you are? You…"

Caithlin looked across at the cannons. Her grip tightened around her sword. Instruments of war. Fights she had been forced into and come out alive, and as the victor. Warfare her father had never experienced. She looked up at him.

"Enough!"

"I beg your pardon?"

"You mentioned there being a time I'd speak. Well, it's now! You're on my ship, and…"

"A ship I had commissioned and still own a share of!" Stefano growled.

"A ship the Basilean Navy owns a nine-tenth share of! And they've commissioned me as her captain, which means I'm in command here, you're on my ship, and you'll shut your damned mouth while I talk! You lecturing me on company business is one thing, but don't strut your way up here and start judging my personal life! I'm twenty-six, not sixteen! You dare lecture me on my sweetheart treating me disrespectfully? The bloody irony! He's treated me with more respect than you have!"

Stefano rolled his eyes and opened his mouth again.

"I'm still talking!" Caithlin snapped with enough force to make her father jump. "And quite frankly, I've had enough of you! So take your preaching and your judging, and get off my ship! Get out of this dockyard, or I'll have you arrested! Some idiot once told me that they'll only put you up in a townhouse until things blows over, but I can't guarantee that! Go on, sod off!"

Caithlin glowered at her father as the wide-eyed, pale-faced mariner stepped away from her, and then silently walked down the gangway and toward the dockyard gates, his junior partner in tow.

***

The flaming projectile reached the zenith of its arc before falling back down toward the sea, trailing wisps of smoke behind the unnaturally bright fire. The blazing rock narrowly missed its target – a broad ship of dark wood with two masts – and plummeted into the foam-topped waves, the magical fire still burning as it dropped down toward the sea bed. From his command platform in front of the marble temple built atop the after deck of the war galley, T'mork allowed himself a thin smile. That was hopefully enough to cause panic. He needed them to surrender. He needed them alive, for now.

"Again, I think," he said calmly to Demelecles. "I will give them another warning shot. If they do not surrender then, I may well sink one of them."

The revenant captain stared ahead but said nothing. The Ahmunite fleet surged north, fanned out in a symmetrical formation as the eleven ships sailed headlong toward the human trading fleet. T'mork's war galley loomed tall and powerful in the center; either side it was flanked by the rapid, knife-like hulls of the escorting Khopeshiis with a third guarding the rear. Outboard of those were the smaller, single-masted Dust Chasers, their oars digging into the waves with otherworldly discipline to assist the speed generated by the winds. Outboard again, forming the flanks of T'mork's fleet, were his tiny slave galleys – a pair on each side of the formation. Finally, struggling to keep up with the war galley was the fleet's solitary Soul Hunter, oar-driven and dominated by the crackling energies of the djinn prison atop its ancient hull.

T'mork looked forward to the very stem of his ship where a large, circular platform was built as an extension above the bow. Atop the platform which, like the bows themselves were encased in magically reformed bone, sat a solitary catapult of immense proportions. T'mork concentrated, sending a series of simple commands to the skeletal crew of the catapult to order them to reset the arm and then load another heavy rock into the weapon's bucket. He sensed a spark, just a hint of feedback through his magical connection with the catapult crew, as a sliver of individuality – perhaps kindled by a distant memory still clinging to the dead bones – flared up from one of the skeletons. With a wave of one hand, T'mork killed the unnatural energy. As much as he loved the sensation of that feedback, and was truly fascinated by what might cause it, he needed blind and instant obedience.

The catapult was reloaded. Hidden from view in the bowels of the war galley, row after row of three hundred undead oarsmen mindlessly powered the near two thousand ton vessel forward, assisted by what little wind was caught in the two low, wide sails hanging from the masts above. Ahead, the four trade ships continued to run, tacking out of the headwind in a frantic attempt to open up away from their Ahmunite attackers.

"Four of them," T'mork nodded, folding his arms across his bare, shriveled chest, "four. Back in our world, that would be many lives to serve our purpose. But now? Here?"

The high priest turned to where his captive scholar stood by his left side.

"What is the crew of a ship of that size?" he gestured toward the quartet of twin-masted sailing ships ahead.

The young woman swallowed and shook her head.

"I... I do not know, Master. Please... my apologies..."

T'mork sucked through his broken teeth and dismissed her groveling with a wave of one hand. It was fair, he supposed, the woman was an academic, not a sailor. She had no way of knowing such things.

On the prow platform, six skeletal sailors finished loading a huge rock into the catapult. T'mork concentrated again – a miniscule effort, compared to many things he simultaneously used his powers for – and great sheets of amber, magical fire roared up to envelop the stone projectile. He looked out at the smooth seas ahead and picked a spot between two of the ships – close to the bows of the nearest merchantman. That would do for his last warning. He issued a command, a brief thought, and the training that served the skeletons in life immediately came to the fore in undeath as they turned the catapult in place to line up for the shot.

With a creaking of timber, the arm of the catapult was flung forward, and the blazing rock was propelled into the cloudless sky. It reached the apex of its flight and then drifted down to the sea, plummeting into the waves and leaving a great pillar of water in its wake. T'mork narrowed his milky, pupiless eyes. He had made his intentions clear, and even with a fair few cannons protruding from their hulls, four merchantmen stood no chance against an eleven-ship Ahmunite fleet. Now it was a waiting game. They would either surrender to him or face a long, drawn out chase with one inevitable conclusion. T'mork allowed himself a brief, silent laugh. If the merchant sailors ahead knew what was in store for them, he fancied they would find the energy to run to the very ends of Pannithor in their ignorance to avoid the blessing he would bestow upon them.

***

Jaymes finished scanning his eyes across the neatly written letter and placed it down on the desk. A letter from a captain of a Dictator-class, first-rate battleship, somehow addressing Jaymes as if they were on equal terms. Was it possible to feel like an imposter, even after several weeks in post? Jaymes placed the letter down and looked across his desk at where the fresh-faced youth in the immaculate uniform and the new lieutenant's epaulets stared across expectantly.

"Well," Jaymes said, "your previous captain speaks highly of you. Very highly, in fact. And you passing your lieutenant's board at the youngest eligible age is also commendable."

"Thank you, sir," Benn Orellio nodded eagerly.

"Welcome to the *Pious*." Jaymes smiled. "Given your service record, I'm guessing you've done no time on frigates before?"

"No, sir, I'm afraid not."

"Not a problem. Neither had I before a couple of years ago. You'll be straight into the watch system as soon as we leave the wall. Come to think of it, we'll need you as officer of the day alongside, but take a couple of days to find your way around first. I run a fairly relaxed ship, up until one of two things. First, we beat to quarters. As soon as we're in action, whatever it may be, I expect nothing less than total commitment from every sailor on board. Second, if a line is crossed. I'll back anybody here if things go wrong, and I want this ship to be a comfortable place to live and work. But if anybody takes the piss, and that includes officers, I'll go for the jugular. But I'm sure it won't come to that."

"No, sir," the young lieutenant continued to nod, wide-eyed.

Jaymes stood up and offered his hand across the desk.

"Again, welcome to the *Pious*, Benn. We've been without a third lieutenant for some time, so you are a very welcome addition to this crew. Get your belongings onboard and get settled in. I'll see you tomorrow."

The newly commissioned lieutenant shot to his feet and shook his captain's hand – not as firmly as Jaymes would have liked, but he tried not to judge.

"Thank you, sir."

"Officers cabins are the deck below, on the gun deck. Not too dissimilar to what you've been used to on a Dictator. Samus, the steward, is preparing your cabin for you now. We've been using it as a store room whilst we've been gapped a third lieutenant. Oh, and Lieutenant Knox – that's the first lieutenant, the one who met you when you first came onboard. Go and send him here to me, would you?"

Benn backed away to the great cabin's door, somehow still nodding.

"Aye, sir."

"At the rush, Benn. Tell him to drop what he's doing and come here right away."

"Aye, sir."

Jaymes waited until the door was shut and then walked back to the stern windows and sat on the sill below them, folding his arms and looking out across the still waters of the harbor as the sun slowly set. Small glints reflected off the shimmering water around frigates, brigs, and sloops. The strings of lights that characterized Thatraskos after dark were already illuminating around the residential districts and the bars and taverns which readied themselves for a night of trade. Jaymes glanced back at his desk. Next to Benn's letter of introduction was a letter from his parents, and a quote for the house he had viewed that afternoon. Without Caithlin. She had never showed up.

A knock at the door brought him back to the present. He remained seated at the sill.

"Yes?"

Mayhew Knox appeared at the door.

"You sent for me..."

"Shut the door. Don't sit down."

The young lieutenant ambled in and stood before the desk, something halfway between standing to attention and casually that managed to look more untidy than both.

"I've just had a new joiner to the ship report to me. Lieutenant Ben Orellio. Nice fellow. What confused me is that upon reporting to this ship and asking where the captain was, from what he tells me, the first lieutenant – remember, that's you, Mayhew – told him that he didn't need to see the captain. That reporting to the first lieutenant was ample enough."

Mayhew's eyes flickered from corner to corner of the cabin.

"Well, sir, you see, I thought..."

"Did you, Mayhew?" Jaymes grinned venomously. "Did you think? Because this fellow is the third lieutenant. You know, the chap who, when the quarterdeck is hit in battle and both the captain and the first lieutenant are killed, and moments later, the second lieutenant gets cut in half, is then left in command of the entire warship. You know, *that* third lieutenant. So, just run past me precisely why you, in all of your years of experience and seemingly infinite wisdom, saw fit to cut me out of the loop of meeting my own third?"

Mayhew took a breath.

"Y'see, sir, I thought it was something I could deal with. So not to trouble you. I thought you'd be busy with all you're doing, and this was something within my..."

"You were concerned with my workload?" Jaymes smiled. "Lieutenant Mayhew Knox, the renowned team player! The same man who, only yesterday, asked for two days off work to go on a coastal walk, when I had asked *three-bloody-times* to update our stock of admiralty charts... which still had not been done. I mean, it's not a big job, is it? Yet, still not completed, you told me that it could wait another two days whilst you went pissing up a string of coastal taverns for two days with your mates! *That* Mayhew Knox, the all round good egg and hard worker?"

The first lieutenant looked down at the deck.

"Sorry, sir. I was trying to make up for that by doing more. I got it wrong."

Jaymes shook his head. The answer was reasonable enough. The man trying to help was more plausible than him trying to undermine his captain. Jaymes shifted his stare from his subordinate. His eyes flicked past his own reflection in the glass pane of his drinks cabinet. For just a moment, the derisive, contemptuous face of the frigate's previous captain stared back at him. Jaymes closed his eyes and paused for a moment.

"Alright, Mayhew, alright. I see what you were trying to do. My apologies, I jumped to the wrong conclusion. Just... keep me informed on anything important. And a new officer arriving at this ship is important."

"Aye, sir."

"Alright, off you go."

Jaymes remained sat at the window sill for some time, watching the skies grow darker and more lights illuminate along the coast. After only another few minutes, there was another knock on the door.

"Yes?" Jaymes exhaled wearily.

The door opened to reveal Karnon Senne, wearing a patterned brown shirt that clashed offensively with a set of eye-catching lilac, silk pantaloons.

"Do you have a moment, sir?" the marine officer asked, his tone formal and respectful.

"Yeah."

Karnon closed the door.

"Come on, mate," he urged, his entire demeanor changing once the door was shut. "You said you'd be ready an age ago. The missus is waiting for us at the Palm Spring, and if I don't turn up on time one of these days..."

Jaymes waved a hand.

"Go on without me. I'll give it a miss tonight."

"Bollocks. Come on. Get changed."

Jaymes looked out of the window at the *Martolian Queen*, across at his friend, momentarily considered being the first man to finally challenge the marine on his endless procession of offensively colored trousers, but buckled on both that and the thought of a quiet, early night.

"Alright, then," Jaymes shrugged.

Chapter Six

Red Skull
Infantosian Islands
East Infant Sea

The sun hung low in the sky, its tip touching the horizon to paint a beautiful and impressive picture of shimmering, orange lines against the blues of the seas and skies. Stood on the verandah of the 'Final Grapeshot' tavern with the first of what he hoped were many, many tankards of ale for the night, Cerri Denayo watched the quartet of masts far out to sea as they slowly drew closer. Sprawled out lazily in rickety chairs next to him, likewise armed with metal tankards and staring down at their shanty but independent island empire were Andars Taithe and Hector Dunn. The trio of veteran captains formed the nucleus of the pirate island at Red Skull; they had not adopted any formal titles, but it was their signatures on the island's... sort of constitution that laid down the rules for everybody else. Some called them governors. They did not like that. Others referred to them as chiefs. That was a little better.

Two of the tavern's working girls walked up the sandy path from the tumbledown huts and shacks that formed part of the settlement's accommodation. Cerri raised his tankard in greeting and was rewarded with smiles and waves. Further down, at the water's edge, a dozen pirates were boarding their sloop – one of Hector's crews, by the look of it – to slip and proceed for a cruise in search of plunder. They were waved off by another crew who were sprawled out across the beach, two fires already underway for an evening of fine food and foul grog before passing out in the sand.

"What I was saying," Andars continued, eliciting rolled eyes from Cerri as he buried his face in his tankard, "was that there has to be more to it than this. Yes, this is a measure of success. But I don't think we should stop here."

Cerri rested his tankard on the wooden rail running around the verandah.

"Where would you stop, then?" he sighed. "Where? Seaborne invasion of Keretia? By the Abyss, why not go for old Goldie Horn, shipmate?"

"Don't be a dick!" Hector laughed, his hands rested across his slightly corpulent belly. "He's just saying that his ambitions take him past what we've got here."

"I can speak for myself, old man." Andars eyed the gray-haired mariner with a warning glance, his dark eyes narrowed beneath his ogre-like brow. "But yeah, that is what I'm saying. You two really want to stop here? This is your life? Prisoner on an island made up of ninety-nine parts jungle, one part shitty, rundown village inhabited by pissed pirates and whores?"

"Well, you're one of the two types of what you reckon this place is inhabited by." Hector winked.

"I thought he was both." Cerri grinned.

Andars shot up and slammed an open hand into Cerri's shoulder, spinning him around to face him.

"You wind your neck in, lofty!" the blazing eyed, dark-haired pirate growled. "Or I'll..."

"You'll what?" Cerri sneered at the notorious killer. "Who d'ye think you're talking to? I'm not some sniveling landsmen who's afraid of your reputation! We're equals here, boyo, the three of us! You think you're above a bit of piss taking, do you? Sling your hook, you b..."

"Alright, alright!" Hector shouted across from his seat. "Enough! Come on, avast and all that bollocks."

Andars stepped away, his hands held up in mock surrender, before slowly walking a brief lap of their end of the verandah in silence. Cerri returned to his drink. He watched the single sloop cast away and the four small ships return toward the jetty from the north.

"What I'm saying," he started quietly after a pensive pause, "is that this is enough. We're not prisoners here. We're free to follow the rules we made for everybody. Tell me where an ordinary crewman can vote for what his ship does next? Tell me where a ship's captain gets two shares of a prize instead of twenty? Here. Only here, in what we've created in the last few years. Yeah, the place looks like shit. But that's its charm. To me, at least. This is enough for me. Sun, drink, women. I have no need to take over the world. To prove a point. To lash out at any sovereign state. I'm a pirate, not a politician."

Andars flashed a devilish grin.

"Could have fooled me, shipmate. What, with you being thick as thieves with the orcs on Ax Island. That's not comradeship, is it? That's politics if ever I saw it."

"Well, you know me. You, Andars, you're a demon from the fires of the Abyss, feared by all. Me? I've got a thousand plans and schemes, and a finger in every pie. What about you, Hector?"

The oldest of the trio grinned.

"Me? I'm happy to just dine out of my reputation as a fearsome scallywag of yesteryear, growing fat and old as I think about retirement. But look, Andars, I'm with Cerri on this. We – or more accurately, *you* – shouldn't go rocking the boat! You'll balls things up for all of us, and we've got a good thing here!"

The stone-faced mariner glowered at his two fellows. His dark eyes darted from man to man.

"Black Davey Krax and Huck Farelee both made more money sacking settlements than they ever did capturing prize vessels and their cargo."

"I knew both of them, and both of them died when you were still a boy." Hector shrugged. "What's your point?"

"My point is that the real money is in the colonies, not at sea!"

"And my point," Cerri stepped in, "as I tried to explain to that moronic orc who got himself killed a couple of months back, is that we don't upset the balance. Just as I'm no politician, I'm also no scholar. I'm not amazing with numbers, but you're even worse, so I'll keep it simple. Pirates are a pain in the arse. Let's say that the number of monies that we steal from... Basilea in a year is... ten."

"Ten what?"

"It doesn't matter! Ten bananas! Just call it ten. Now... the Basilean Navy is split between a dozen different commitments. Holding the line against the dwarfs, patrolling further south in case of anything from the Ahmunites, diplomatic missions way off west to Elvenhome. They haven't got the resources to do all of these tasks to the level that the Senate is demanding from them. Anyway, they form an anti-piracy squadron and send it after us, patrolling the Sand Lane."

Andars folded his broad arms and grunted. Cerri continued regardless.

"We're worth ten to them, it's a simple game of numbers, and if they spare eleven, then one of their other commitments suffers needlessly. We're only worth ten. No more. As soon as you sack a colony, we're now costing them twenty. Or thirty. So, we're a lot more of a pain now. We move up the priority list. There's uproar in the capital. Pirates are a worse problem than Abyssals, orcs... take your pick. Either way, all of a sudden we're facing third-rates instead of frigates. Or, worse still, they decide they'll accept the casualties and they plan a full blown assault against Red Skull, lose a handful of small ships and dozens, if not hundreds, of marines and sailors to our guns on the way in... but they get ashore and then they wipe us out. All because you made us a bigger problem than ten. If we stay at ten, they leave us alone because we're not worth it, not when there's bigger problems to deal with. D'ye follow, shipmate?"

The taller pirate swore and spat.

"I follow. I follow that you don't want me to make a fortune for myself, so that you can live safe like a coward, here in this pigswill!"

Cerri grinned and slammed an open hand against Andar's upper arm.

"Good! You *do* get it!"

Hector let out a laugh and slowly clambered to his feet. The aging pirate looked out to the beach and the rickety jetty as the four ships positioned to come alongside. Cerri looked out, recognizing three of them.

"Looks like your new boy is back." Hector nodded, stuffing a measure of tobacco into the end of his pipe.

"Let's hope he fares better than your last protege," Andars laughed venomously, "I hear they gave Pearl the long drop, up at Thatraskos. Courtesy for a woman, even if she was a pirate captain."

Cerri flashed a dangerous smile.

"The three of us run this show. We might not always see eye to eye, but it's worked for three years. If Pearl had wound her neck in, done what she was told and not tried to muscle in on what the three of us do, maybe nobody would have tipped off the Basilean Navy about where she was operating from."

Leaving Hector and Andars on the verandah, Cerri walked briskly down the sandy path toward the beach and accompanying jetties. The sun set ever lower, painting a band of light blue across the horizon below a now twinkling starscape sprinkling across the dark azure above, reminding him of the clear nights from his youth near Primantor.

The revelry from the pirate gathering on the beach hushed as Cerri walked past, the closest few mariners calling out respectful greetings in the twilight which Cerri acknowledged with a brisk wave of one hand. His booted feet thumped along the dry planks as he hopped up onto the jetty, pacing out to meet the *Adventure Prize* as the sloop came alongside, one of her crew jumping across to secure a forespring around a rusted, iron bollard. Cerri watched the crew quickly and efficiently secure the sloop to the jetty, noting with interest that she now carried eight guns rather than the six she went to sea with several days earlier.

Tem Mosso stepped ashore, striding confidently out to meet Cerri.

"I see you've found a couple of four-pounders for a bit more punch," Cerri greeted.

"A few more deckhands, too," Tem issued a slight smile.

"Good," Cerri nodded, "good."

"I've got your share of what we've made put to one side. As we agreed."

Cerri waved a hand.

"Alright, shippers, I know you're good for it. D'ye lose anybody?"

Tem nodded.

"Skordak."

Cerri grimaced.

"What happened? A fight or a storm?"

Tem folded his arms, his brow darkening.

"He didn't do what I told him to do. So I shot him."

Cerri's brow raised. That, he had not expected. Not after all the talk of altruistic adventures on the high seas, with the minimal possible spilt blood.

"I reckon there's more to that story, Tem. Come on, leave your boys to secure the ship. I'll buy you a drink."

***

"You'll never see arkosaurs with them," Sabine remarked from where she leaned against the bar, nodding in the direction of the four terrifying-looking salamander sailors who politely picked their way through the crowd toward their booth seats. "Well... rarely. Not never. My father was a diplomat, so I grew up in the capital until I was ten. Funny bunch, the arkosaurs. Very polite. Very proper. But not at all social."

Jaymes managed a polite, and genuinely appreciative smile. He had known Karnon's wife long enough to deduce that she was well capable of being a formidable woman – she had to be to keep her husband in line – but was also very quick with her acts of kindness. Such as now, working hard to keep the conversation going despite Jaymes's miserable demeanor. The trio stood with their backs to the bar, looking out across the dance floor at the row of tables behind, and the bay windows overlooking the brightly lit verandah that in turn overlooked the bright, ornamental garden, the harbor, and the bay.

"Good fighters," Karnon added, sliding a few coins across the bar to pay for the next round of drinks, "the salamanders, I mean, not the arkosaurs. I take it these four are from that brig tied up in the harbor?"

"Frigate," Jaymes corrected.

Karnon narrowed his eyes mischievously and grinned. Jaymes shook his head in disappointment at his own gullibility.

"So anyway, this book I've got..."

"The childrens' book about ships?" Jaymes asked.

"Yeah. That's the one. It says pretty clearly that a brig is a square-rigged sailing vessel with two masts..."

"In civilian service, unless defined by its role..."

"In every nation in Upper Mantica, navies and all. Except Basilea. So... those ships we've got with the big mortars. Given that they're sloops, why do we call them gunbrigs?"

Jaymes's eyes widened, and a sudden feeling of elation wiped away his melancholy as he shot up, slamming an open palm down into the bar victoriously.

"Ha! Ha ha! It's *not* a sloop, you landlubber bastard! It can't be a sloop! Sloops are fore-and-aft rigged, with a mainsail and jib! Basilean naval gunbrigs are square-rigged with a main course, topsail, and spanker! Will you two stop laughing every time anybody says 'spanker'?!"

Karnon and Sabine continued giggling mirthfully before the marine finally asked a follow up question.

"If they're not a brig and they're not a sloop, what are they?"

Jaymes paused. He looked up at the ceiling of the busy bar, fighting conflicting definitions and facts in his head until he finally stammered out an approximation of an answer.

"A... ship... rigged... sloop?"

"Ha! So it is a sloop! A gunbrig isn't a brig, an Elohi frigate *is* a brig and not a frigate, and an Abbess is also a brig which is absolutely farcical for a ship of its size! Everybody else in the world goes for full, ship-rigged three masts for a third-rate! Ha! My children's book has taught me enough, fishhead! I'm a bloody *master* of how much bollocks all of your terminology is! Or, at least, how little whoever designed all of our ships knows about..."

Karnon's gleeful rant tailed off. His smile faded as he looked over Jaymes's shoulder. Jaymes turned around and saw Caithlin stood a few paces from him. In notable contrast to every night they had visited the Palm Spring, she still wore the breeches, boots, and shirt linked with her vocation, rather than one of the elegant dresses she preferred to sport on evenings. Her eyes, whilst still holding their characteristic focus and resolute determination, were red-rimmed.

"Can we talk for a moment?"

Jaymes lowered his rum glass onto the bar. His stomach suddenly ached, and his throat felt tight. It was to be expected, sooner or later. He nodded silently. Caithlin walked out of the bar, past the verandah to the right of the main entrance and into the small flower gardens flanking the path leading up from the street below. The sound of laughter continued from inside the bar. The upbeat, cheerful tones of a ukiola rang out as the evening's music began. Caithlin checked there was nobody near them and then looked up at him uncomfortably.

"I need to apologize to you. About a few things, in fact."

Jaymes nodded and looked down at his feet. Yes, inevitable. But what now? Go out with a bang? Get the first broadside in and break it up himself? No, that was decidedly ungentlemanly. Best to walk away with his head held high, having done morally the right thing. Best to make it easy for her.

"It's alright," he forced a smile, "I know. I understand."

"It's just that... avast there a moment. You know *what*, exactly?"

Jaymes's brow furrowed.

"That... that you didn't meet me today to look at the house, like you said you would."

"I know, and I'm truly sorry. It's just that..."

"No," Jaymes interrupted, "it's my fault entirely. I was clumsy with my words and I can see how it looked like... well... I put pressure on you and I didn't mean to imply..."

Caithlin stared back at him, her perfect face twisted in confusion.

"Jaymes, what in the world are you babbling about?"

Jaymes stopped. He looked around for inspiration, found none, and then stared at her blankly. Her face morphed from confusion to despair.

"You... you think I deliberately did not meet you today because you accidently pressured me into moving in with you? That you rushed me and now I'm breaking things off with you?"

Jaymes leaned a touch closer, one eye narrowed.

"No... Yes?... No?"

Caithlin's lips turned up into a sympathetic but not unpatronising smile.

"Jaymes. It's been nine hours. We haven't seen each other in nine hours and you've come to this conclusion? Do you think that maybe you've overthought this and come to a rather silly deduction? I think that you buying your own house is a fine plan and a sensible use of your assets. And, if one were to be so callous as to completely remove the romance from our nocturnal meetings, it's also infinitely more practical for me to stay at your house from time to time rather than some of the rather silly measures we have in place at the moment. Now look, I'm trying to apologize to you here, and this idiocy is making it rather difficult."

Jaymes did not even bother to try to hide his relief. Air flowed into his lungs once more. The pains of anxiety in his gut almost instantly dissipated. A smile tugged at his lips.

"Right. Sorry. Do go on."

Caithlin turned, her hands on her hips. She looked down across the harbor and took in a breath before turning back to face him.

"I'm sorry I let you down today. Something happened, and I completely lost track of time. I... I ended up in a bit of a whirlpool, so to speak. My... father appeared. He's here, in Thatraskos."

Jaymes took a step forward, his enthusiasm still driven by his relief of the misunderstanding that had plagued him for most of the day.

"Well, that's excellent news! Fantastic! You must be delighted! Would it be too forward for me to meet him?"

Caithlin waved her hands slightly between them.

"No, no you don't understand. He's not happy. It appears I

signed on with your naval auxiliary somewhat hastily. That's actually something of an understatement. A large understatement. There are legal proceedings going on as we speak to ascertain whether the authorities here at Thatraskos have, alongside the South Mantica Trading Company, intentionally strong-armed me into agreeing to something that I did not have the knowledge available to decline. In short, my father thinks he can cancel the majority of my debts."

"Well, that's fantastic news, too!"

"In a way. Also, no. First off, he might fail, and I'll have to go on, knowing that not only have I lost my freedom for the better part of a decade, but also that it's unjust. Second, if he is successful, well... I don't want to go home. I want to stay here. With you."

Deciding that this was one of those moments that it was probably best just to keep his mouth shut, Jaymes stepped forward to embrace her. She returned the gesture and rested a head on his shoulder.

"And also... my father... sort of... hates naval men. And Basileans. And you're both. And he's just found out about you."

The moment well and truly destroyed, Jaymes felt himself tense up.

"Ah."

"Ah indeed."

"Why does he hate Basileans? I mean, all of us?"

"Well," Caithlin mused, "you know how the Successor Kingdoms see Genezans as emotional, gregarious, heart-on-sleeve sort of people? I'm afraid we all see your lot as cold, arrogant, aloof types."

"So...which one of us is Genezan and which one of us is Basilean again?" Jaymes risked.

Caithlin laughed. It was rare to hear, which he thought was a great shame. She stepped away but held both of his hands.

"I'm afraid things are something of a mess. I don't know what will happen legally, and I became rather angry at my father when he insulted you. I may have even threatened to have him arrested, which I'm fairly sure I don't have the authority to do. I certainly threw him off my ship. Which should really be his ship. Anyhow, I'm rambling. But I did have one more apology."

Jaymes smiled, feeling a little alarmed by the news but still relieved after the disaster he had spent the afternoon convincing himself was coming was now proved to be a falsity.

"Things aren't so bad," Caithlin said, "it took Kassia to point it out to me. Nobody ever promised anyone an easy life. I've decided to stop moping and sulking about my ill providence and being unbearable to be around. It's not fair on everybody else, but mainly you. Things aren't easy, but they could be a lot worse. I'm sorry I've been so dour."

Jaymes pulled her in for another embrace.

"You haven't," he said, "we all have our bad days. We're all allowed them. There's nothing to apologize for. We'll work all of this out."

The two remained in the garden in silence for a few minutes as the music continued inside the bar. Jaymes looked up at the stars in the clear night, wondering how he was possibly going to convince Caithlin's father that he was indeed a good man. That he was not the arrogant, cold-hearted and formulaic Basilean that the man had already convinced himself was using his daughter.

"Are you coming in for a drink?" he finally asked her.

She stepped away again.

"No. Not dressed like this. I'll head back to my cabin. I need to sort a few things out."

Caithlin threw him a smile and walked away to the path leading down to the street and the harbor. She turned again.

"Thank you for listening."

"Any time."

Jaymes offered her a smile in return and watched her walk away before heading back to the bar.

***

When T'mork had walked amongst the living as one of their kind, this sandy island had once been a peak, part of a range of mountains to the west of Abkhazla, not too far from Difetth. He neither remembered nor cared to recall the name of the mountain range, it did not matter. What did matter was the site's significance, as was so often the way with necromancy. Necromancy, whilst certainly surging to popularity in those early days of conflict between the rebels of Ophidia and the Ahmunites, still had a long and rich past with a multitude of unanswered questions for those with a mind and an inclination for the scholastics.

T'mork walked slowly up the beach, his bare feet kicking gently through the soft sands as his impressive fleet lay at anchor in the bay behind him. Had he been here before? Purification did not completely restore one's memories, and those days from centuries before felt like another lifetime entirely, even discounting the near eternal slumber he was raised from in between. It was merely a point of interest, it mattered not whether this was his first time here or a return to something significant from mortal life. The point was that Shobik himself had guided T'mork and his fleet here, so here was where worship must be conducted.

The ancient high priest reached the top of the beach, his dead feet now walking on smooth rocks. He turned to look back. The *Purification of Ul'Astia* lay at anchor some way out to sea, the shelving sea bottom severely restricting his options regarding where the great war galley could operate. The three escorting Khopeshii flanked the flagship, with the smaller ships spaced out like wood and bone stepping stones leading to the shore. A trio of boats were beached at the water's edge, used to transport T'mork and his entourage. A guard formed up of revenants clad in gold and blue; three of his sea captains and, of course, his now indispensable mortal translator.

Demelecles, the captain of the *Purification of Ul'Astia*, barked out a series of hoarse orders to the revenants. Two groups formed up to secure either end of the beach whilst a third group jogged over to guard T'mork. Demelecles walked over with the three Khopeshii captains; Henneus, Serriass, and M'orbb. Demelecles bowed as he approached the high priest.

"You are content this is the correct location, Master? You wish us to start bringing the workers ashore?"

T'mork turned away again and looked inland. The dry, rocky ground led up into lush vegetation, and in turn, a series of jagged peaks that could barely be called hills now, but were once impressive mountains. If he had the time and resources, he could send out scouting parties into the jungle in the hope of finding the remains of previous temples. T'mork laughed briefly. It would be like trying to find a knife buried in the desert. No, better to start afresh. He closed his eyes and concentrated, tapping into the reserve of arcane energy that swirled and fluctuated within his very core. Like plunging a hand into a dark but orderly draw, he grabbed at the energy source he needed to form a connection with the arcane vortices flowing invisibly across the island. He nodded.

"Yes. This is the one. We build here."

***

"Consider it a compliment," Caithlin flashed a grin to her salamander first mate as the two walked up toward the naval administration building.

"A compliment?" X'And scowled, eyeing a young midshipman who walked past the unlikely pair, failing in his attempt to avert his gaze from the beautiful privateer captain and her imposing salamander comrade. "This isn't my world, Cathy. For that matter, it isn't *your* world, either. We shouldn't be here."

A rogue patch of cloud drifted in front of the blazing morning sun to provide a moment's respite from the fierce heat. A succession of naval officers came and went from the tall, impressive building ahead, ranging in rank from midshipmen barely into their teens, to captains of warships in the bay below. Caithlin noticed a horse-drawn carriage pull up near the administration building's main entrance. Marcellus Dio, captain of the *Veneration* and a man who had treated her respectfully since they first met, clambered down before adjusting his sword belt and hat. A moment later, a small girl in a green dress, perhaps ten years of age, dashed after him and wrapped both of her arms around his legs. Marcellus looked around uncomfortably before prizing her arms off and then dropping to one knee, looking at her on her own level and smiling broadly at her as he spoke soothing words. Seconds later, a middle-aged woman, no doubt the child's governess, dashed out of the carriage. Marcellus held a hand up to stop her and pulled his daughter into an embrace.

For a moment, Caithlin was transported back to her childhood and running after her father on a jetty, tears in her eyes as she desperately tried to acquire that one, last embrace before he disappeared over the horizon for months at a time. He had always stopped. He had always made the time to force a smile for her and tell her that it would all be alright. And he had never broken any of those promises. He had always come home. It always had been alright.

"What's wrong?"

Caithlin looked up at X'And.

"Oh... nothing. Come on, we don't want to be late for the admiral."

The two made their way into the circular reception hall and then up the spiral staircase leading to the second floor. The admiral's flag lieutenant – a stout faced youth who Caithlin never managed to remember his name – shot across from the other side of the landing area to open a door for her with a courteous bow. X'And stepped forward and growled down at the portly staff officer, sharp teeth bared in his long, scaly snout. The flag lieutenant immediately backed away, pulling at his collar as his face reddened.

"What was that about?" Caithlin hissed as the two continued along the wood-paneled corridor.

"He treated you differently. Because you are a woman. He should treat you the same."

"He was being a gentleman and opening a door for me," Caithlin glowered up at her first mate, "that's a perfectly polite thing to do."

"He wasn't doing it to be polite. He had other things in mind. You shouldn't be so naive."

"X'And, there are times when a gargantuan reptilian seadog is just what I need for protection. A boy barely out of his adolescent years holding a door open for me is not one of them. I'll let you know when I need you to growl at somebody."

The corridor wound around to finally emerge at a pair of tall, ornately carved double doors. The doors, already propped open, led to a grand staircase of marble that led down into an extravagant hall, furnished with enough rows of highly polished tables and chairs to comfortably dine two hundred people. The ceiling of the hall was painted with a truly masterful panoramic seascape, depicting a fierce naval battle between age-old Basilean warships and the slim, green-hulled vessels of the elven Sea Kindred. Beneath a darkened sky and in rough seas raging higher than a frigate's quarterdeck, the Basilean warships smashed through the elven line, dealing destruction from their smoke-belching broadsides. Caithlin smiled. The Battle of Agor Point. A low point in human-elf relations, but a stunning victory for the Basilean Navy.

At the far side of the dining hall, bathed in long pillars of light shining through tall windows, Caithlin saw Admiral Sir Jerris Pattia amidst a semi-circle of at least a dozen naval and marine officers. She recognized Jaymes; his first lieutenant, Karnon Senne; and Marcellus Dio; but none of the others. Caithlin walked down the carpeted stairs and across the dining hall to where the collection of sailors had gathered around a large, oval table at the north wall. Jaymes greeted her with a friendly smile from the other side of the small crowd. Caithlin returned it. X'And stared across at Jaymes and growled. Caithlin carefully placed her booted foot atop X'And's and applied pressure until he stifled a yelp.

"I told you not to growl at gentlemen on my behalf," she whispered forcefully. "Especially not that one. Now, start behaving, or I'll send you back to the ship without any lunch."

A flushed-looking lieutenant raced down the stairs as the bell tower gonged away above them. Caithlin noticed Zu'Max, senior lieutenant of the frigate *Deliver's Flame*, stood amidst the human sailors. By his side was a shorter, thinner reptilian with smoother skin. An arkosaur, no doubt the *Deliver's Flame's* captain, resplendent in a uniform of red and green, adorned with eye-catching lengths of gold braid hanging from one epaulet. The only uniform to rival its splendor was that of a man stood next to a confident-looking captain; the gold trim of his loose fitting tabard marked him out as a naval battlemage.

X'And saw the salamander and the arkosaur, and suppressed a snigger.

"What?" Caithlin demanded under her breath.

"What?" X'And retorted.

"What's funny?"

"Doesn't matter. An old joke. It loses in the translation."

"Go on, what is it?"

"It... it won't make sense in your language. Besides, it's from a different time and not really appropriate in this day and age. It's not fair on arkosaurs."

Caithlin rolled her eyes and cleared her throat.

"If you and I are going to be the petulant children in this rather formal gathering of professionals, at least tell me the bloody joke."

"Erm... do you think that arkosaur looks at all like he should be selling ship insurance?"

Caithlin looked up.

"No... why?"

"I told you it would lose in the translation. Doesn't matter."

"Right oh!" the admiral began, raising his voice over the polite din of conversation, "Gather round, gather round!"

The assembled officers encircled the oval table. Atop the table were carefully modeled islands, accurately replicating the various island chains and archipelagos to the south of Keretia. Lined up on the northern table edge were a number of beautifully constructed model warships, each no bigger than a fist.

"I've spoken to most of you individually now," Jerris said, "but this is our first meeting as a group. You all represent the command of the vessels making up Orange Squadron, a group assembled to counter the threat of an Ahmunite Fleet that is now confirmed as operating just to the south of our area of responsibility."

Caithlin felt a shudder of fear. Ahmunites? Near here? She took a slow breath. She had faced hurricanes, orcs, pirates... Ahmunites were merely another danger. This was just another day.

"We've had some slightly more reliable reports regarding what we are facing," the admiral continued. "Their flagship is one of the ancient war galleys. Big girl, the war galley, about the size of one of our third-rates. She's protected by three Khopeshii type frigates and an assortment of smaller vessels. So, with Zakery's *Shield Royal* detached from the Grand Fleet, escorted by Marcellus and Jaymes's frigates and our friends from the Three Kings, we're on a pretty even keel to start with."

Caithlin exchanged a look with X'And. Once again, unrated vessels were not really in the equation. The sloops, the brig... not worthy of mention. Certainly, Caithlin mused, the *Martolian Queen* would be turned to driftwood if she tried to stand alongside a Khopeshii in battle, let alone a mighty war galley. But the souls on board were still people and worthy of being referred to as such when lives would likely be lost.

"The problem we have," Jerris leaned over the table, "is finding the bastards. Now, these red markers you see on the map before you are confirmed sightings of the Ahmunites. The yellow markers are suspected sightings. You'll see that there's a pattern already."

Caithlin looked across the markers, immediately noting that, so long as one discounted the yellows as potentially untrue, all of the sightings were close to busy shipping lanes or relatively densely populated colonies.

"All near traffic lanes and settlements," remarked a richly dressed captain Caithlin did not recognize. "If I know the Ahmunites, that means they're looking for live bodies for something."

"But... doesn't that just mean the sightings have occurred where there are people to see and report things?" Jaymes ventured hesitantly. "It's just that... if it's a quiet area of land or sea, there's nobody to see them in the first place and report it in."

"Jaymes Ellias! Rising star turn of the *Pious!*" Jerris grinned. "Oh! That nearly rhymes! I'll make a note of that! I'd imagine that'll get annoying to you extremely quickly! Which is all the more reason to use it! But I digress. On another day, I'd clap you on the shoulder and congratulate you for your lateral thinking! But as it is that we've received confirmed reports that two entire farming colonies have been emptied of every man, woman, and child by the Ahmunite fleet, I'd dare say that Zakery has the weather gauge on you on this one!"

A young lieutenant bellowed out what Caithlin had heard was referred to as a 'career laugh.' She glared at the little shit angrily. The admiral turned to look at where Marcellus had picked up one of the model ships – an Elohi Batch One, no doubt representing his own frigate, the *Veneration*. He looked across at the admiral and smiled apologetically.

"Sorry, sir. Lovely model."

Caithlin had to agree. She had never had the patience to make model ships, but she had an entire shelf of them at home from her childhood. Again, courtesy of her generous and supportive father.

"Well, thank you, Marcellus!" Jerris beamed. "Built it and painted it myself! Fiddly little bastards. I find it especially vexing to get the sails looking half decent. I'm also eternally confused as to why the model makers don't put enough guns on the bloody things to accurately represent the real ships, but I digress. Thank you for the compliment, sir!"

"Admiral Artavius in the capital makes these as well," Zakery added. "Not as good as yours, mind, sir. He... erm... puts the tiny ones, the sloops, two to a base."

"Two to a base!" Jerris thundered, his face twisted in sudden and uncompromising fury. "Ones above! Do ye take me for a madman, sir?! That would look ludicrous, man, ludicrous! Steward, get me a gin! Right, back on course! Your job is to put to sea, proceed south, and scour the entire area of these markers to find the bastards. Then sink them. Closing with the enemy will require the regulation levels of flexibility and aggression expected of all Basilean naval officers once the scenario presents itself, but the search itself? That's what we need to plan here."

The splendidly dressed arkosaur frigate captain chittered

something to Zu'Max in his native tongue. Caithlin looked up at X'And. Before her first mate could translate, the arkosaur spoke to the assembled Basileans in their own tongue.

"If it were a salamander squadron," the arkosaur said, his accent perfect, "we would position our flagship centrally so as to be in the best position to react quickly to the enemy as they are revealed, and to allow a better flow of communication. The frigates would act as escorts, as you have already said, Admiral. That leaves the unrated ships to take position on the flanks for the search which, as providence would have it, also coincides with shallower waters."

Marcellus looked across the table at Jaymes. The younger frigate captain narrowed his eyes and tilted his head before shaking it.

"I'm not sure, sir," Marcellus addressed the admiral, "by tying three frigates to Captain Uwell's *Shield Royal*, we lose an awful lot of search capability."

"Not all three, sir," the arkosaur held up one long, thin finger, "just the two Elohis. My J'Koor'uk can still take part in the search, due to our shallower hull. Your Elohis have always been better suited to deep water operations, but our J'Koor'uks, well, much of our pirate hunting takes place in shallow water. This is where we excel."

Again, Marcellus and Jaymes exchanged disapproving glances. Caithlin folded her arms. Both sides of the disagreement made sense. The arkosaur pointed out a perfectly viable plan. Marcellus and Jaymes knew that it would likely leave them out of most of the fighting until a proper fleet on fleet action materialized. Caithlin leaned across the map.

"Sirs, if I may. The eastern and western extremities of the search area both lay in shallow waters. I agree with, my apologies, sir, I do not know your name..."

"Captain K'Rath, at your service." The arkosaur bowed his head respectfully.

"Captain K'Rath's plan to position on the flanks. If the eastern extremities were divided between all of our sloops, we would cover a lot of seaspace quite quickly. That leaves the Infantosian Islands, over to the southwest. If that area was searched by myself and Captain K'Rath, that would leave the center to be divided between *Shield Royal*, *Veneration*, and *Pious*."

The mutters that spread out through the assembly of officers immediately reminded Caithlin that she was an expert sailor and veteran ship-driver, but an amateur tactician. What was she missing? Again, Marcellus and Jaymes exchanged looks as if the two Elohi captains shared a mental link. Jaymes pointed at the modeled islands in the center of the table.

"Communications would be our problem, sir," he began.

"*Veneration* and *Pious* can operate at some distance, independently, from *Shield Royal*. But we need communications relays beyond line of sight, and that's where the sloops come in. We need a sloop accompanying each frigate to act as a communication relay back to the flagship, and extending out to the flanks. That leaves only a single pair of sloops searching to the southeast, but I think that is still a viable plan given the relative lack of... adversity in those waters."

Diplomatic. Caithlin suppressed a smirk. He was trying to walk the tightrope between supporting her plan and coming up with something that might actually work based upon its foundations.

"And navigating the Infantosians?" K'Rath grumbled. "I offer the *Deliver's Flame* as a shallow water asset, but not *that* shallow. I know that area only by reputation. Shallow waters and infested by pirates – human and orc. According to what you have on the chart here, we could operate but with no margin for error. How confident are you in the fidelity of the water depth on your charts, Admiral?"

"I was part of the expedition that recorded the data, twenty years ago," Jerris smiled dangerously. "If you run aground there due to inaccurate charts rather than poor seamanship, you can bill me personally for the repairs."

The same sloop lieutenant belted out the same career laugh.

"So we have a plan, then?" Jerris looked around at his officers. "*Shield Royal* holds flag centrally. *Veneration* and *Pious* positioned east and west, with a sloop running communications. Two sloops to the east – *Scout* and *Sprinter*. *Deliver's Flame* and the brig to the west, around the Infantosians."

Caithlin bit her lip. 'The brig' had a name. When every last hull capable of carrying a cannon was needed to stop a marauding, manic orc a few weeks ago, the admiral remembered the *Martolian Queen's* name then.

"To logistics," Zakery said, "we need to calculate how far we can extend south, and for how long."

The planning meeting continued for the better part of an hour, with Caithlin easily following the considerations surrounding her part in the plan from a seamanship perspective, but sometimes feeling left behind a little when tactics were discussed over various potential scenarios. At midday, the admiral called a halt to the meeting and invited everybody to be seated at the dinner tables that had been laid behind them by his staff during the morning. Caithlin initially found her place on the seating plan between two sloop lieutenants – including the boisterous career-laugher – but was relieved when, upon the admiral's insistence, she was moved to sit beside him on the top table. Likewise, Jerris demanded that Jaymes sit on the other side. The rather unsubtle maneuver by the admiral was, she thought, rather sweet; but his blunt and blunderous attempts to bring Jaymes and Caithlin together like some sort of nautical matchmaker were perhaps akin to firing an entire broadside into a ship that had already capsized and caught fire. Nonetheless, when she walked back to the *Martolian Queen* early that afternoon, accompanied by X'And and a growing concern over the liver-destroying quantity of alcohol consumed by Basilean Naval officers, a genuine smile tugged at her lips.

So, it was as afternoon was fading to early evening that, when her bosun issued a polite knock on her cabin door, Caithlin found herself surprised to see her father escorted onto her ship. The aging Genezan again looked wistfully across the deck and the rows of guns of the fighting ship before he walked into Caithlin's cabin at the stern of the brig. He wasted no time in stating his intentions.

"I've come to apologize. I've spent so long worrying about you that I forgot to put compassion first and address my anxieties second. That was wrong of me."

From where she sat on the edge of her desk, her arms folded tightly, Caithlin looked across at her father and remembered the embraces and patience before his long voyages, the presents when he came home, the fastidious care in the delivery of instruction as he taught her to sail on Lake Gehr, the money he spent without a word of admonishment when she ran her first sloop aground.

"I'm sorry, too," she said quietly, "I should have shown you more respect. Everything I know is from you."

"Well, perhaps we both should show some more respect," Stefano admitted. "It's hard sometimes to remember that you're a grown woman and a captain in your own right now, when your mother and I so often see you and your siblings still as children. The other two still act like children, admittedly, but still."

"Well, I made a pretty huge mistake to end up in this mess." Caithlin shrugged uncomfortably.

"But an honest mistake. That's the difference. These vultures here, they pounced on you when they knew you knew no better. But I'll sort that out. Things are proceeding well. Your mast will be repaired tomorrow, and you'll be home in no time."

Caithlin swallowed and looked down at the deck beneath her feet. She was sure that in her father's eyes, that was the solution to all of her problems. She glanced out of the stern windows at the row of majestic Basilean frigates alongside the jetty, a short walk away, then back at her father.

"We could go out for dinner," she suggested, "if your schedule allows?"

Stefano's face lit up with a warm smile.

"That would be fantastic. Truly."

"I could invite Jaymes. I think it would be good for you two to meet."

Stefano's smile and warmth instantly disappeared.

"One thing at a time, Caithlin. One thing at a time."

Chapter Seven

Thatraskos Harbor
Keretia
Northeast Infant Sea

"We're stocked well enough, sir," Kennus issued a thin smile, pressing a stubby finger up along the bridge of his broad nose to return his spectacles to their correct place, "for battle, at least. If, however, we were to venture ashore... unless we wait another week for my supplies from the capital, I couldn't guarantee a good stock of cures for diseases native to this part of the world. Or, for that matter, anything our men may contract... socially."

Jaymes glanced around the ship's sickbay – despite its official sounding title, it was actually nothing more than a screened off area of the gundeck with a table and a few hammocks – and watched the surgeon's two mates busily stock taking their supplies.

"But, if we do go ashore and any of the ship's company contract any diseases, that is something you can handle without supplies?" Jaymes asked. "Arcane remedies, I mean?"

The short doctor's smile altered in tone; the gesture now seemed to be one of impatience rather than pleasantness.

"Captain Ellias, we've served together for some time now. Since you were merely the ship's second lieutenant. I would have hoped you had known me well enough after such a time to know that my arcane training is in battle casualty handling. Not in pathology."

Jaymes momentarily considered reminding the surgeon that even when he was merely the second lieutenant, that status outranked a ship's surgeon. But the sole doctor onboard was not an individual to upset.

"But the crew are still fighting fit?" Jaymes asked. "Any change to last week's report? Seven minor injuries with light duties?"

"Six. Nedlee is fine now, I returned him to full duties this morning."

"Very good, Mister Kennus," Jaymes nodded, "carry on."

Muttering a few choice words about the man's arrogance under his breath, Jaymes proceeded to the hatchway leading to the upper deck and clambered up into the sunlight. A line of sailors passed sacks and crates to each other from a supply dump on the jetty, loading the ship with fresh powder, food, water, and other essentials. Karnon glanced over from where he was talking with two of his marines and then walked across the upper deck.

"Sir," he greeted, "how's all the boaty stuff going?"

"We're getting there," Jaymes said, "we're keeping time, at least. We'll be ready to go in two days, but any delays will mean more supplies arriving."

"Also means those Empire of Dust boneships capturing and killing more civilians."

"I know. How long until your lot are ready?"

Karnon raised one eyebrow.

"We're marines, sir. We're always ready."

Jaymes tutted and rolled his eyes.

"Yes, yes. Very good. You're always ready because us stupid bastards in dark blue sort out your food, water, bedding, powder, grog, pay... it's like looking after children, yet you lunge around here as if that's something to be proud of. That's why you're already good to go and we're still prepping for sea."

Karnon replied with a dark smile.

"Like you said, you do all of that boring, mundane crap for us. So who's the winner in this working relationship?"

Before Jaymes could reply, Mayhew Knox walked briskly across to him from the forward end of the upper deck.

"Ammunition is all onboard, sir," the first lieutenant reported. "I'm getting the livestock brought on next."

Jaymes eyed his second-in-command warily.

"And you've got enough ammunition? You haven't done something stupid like take the standard inventory for an Elohi, bearing in mind that those are written for Batch Ones, and *Pious*, being a Batch Two, has more guns?"

"No, sir. I used the Batch Two inventory."

"And the ammunition is already secured for sea?"

"Yes, sir."

"What about ammunition and powder for muskets and pistols?"

"Finished that last night, sir."

Jaymes quickly replayed an entire career of making mistakes with ammunition stock-taking and resupply in his head but found no other memories of his own ineptitude to interrogate Mayhew with.

"Good job. Carry on."

Karnon watched the bearded naval lieutenant return to the gangway before turning to Jaymes.

"You could give him a bit more credit sometimes. He's a good man."

"I know he's a good man!" Jaymes snapped. "That's what's so bloody frustrating! More than half the jobs I give to him, he carries out to a bloody good standard! But when he ballses up – and he always does

– it's out of bone idleness or stupidity! Lazy corner cutting! I promise you this, shipmate, he'll have pissed me off by the end of the day. He'll do something monumentally stupid or lazy, you just wait and see."

The marine captain folded his arms.

"You seemed a lot happier before you were running this show."

Jaymes grumbled and shook his head.

"That's not how I remember it. I remember being miserable and dejected with being treated like a complete arse by a captain who knew far more than I gave him credit for. Now I'm bloody angry at miserable, dejected lieutenants who would do well to give me far more credit. So I'm a bit happier, but a lot angrier. Must come with the job."

"You still worried about that house?"

Jaymes swore, remembering the deadline for the offer he had been given for the house just outside of town. That perfect home that the heart fell in love with but the head reminded him was the first one he had looked at.

"Yes," he admitted quietly.

Karnon exhaled slowly.

"Well, my part of ship is all sorted and my lads are helping store ship. Once that's done, I'll take them for a run around the dockyard for an hour or two. You out this evening?"

Jaymes looked forlornly up the western slope of the bay to where the more upmarket drinking establishments lay.

"Yeah," he replied quietly.

"Is Cathy meeting us?"

"Hopefully."

"Alright. See you later."

Jaymes continued on his informal rounds of the ship, checking in with the bosun, gunners, carpenter, sailing master, and purser to ensure all was in place for putting to sea with a thousand-ton warship and two hundred and eighty sailors and marines, before then finally stopping for lunch. He did, more often than not, invite the officers and warrant officers to the great cabin for both lunch and dinner, but found himself lacking the desire for company; and so elected to dine alone. It was after a tot of rum to chase down his simple lunch, and whilst he was anxiously perusing the details of the quote for the house he was still considering purchasing, that he was disturbed by a short knock on the door to the great cabin.

"Yes?"

Mayhew walked through the door and flashed a friendly smile to the captain.

"Mister Viconti, to see you, sir."

Jaymes froze behind his desk, numbly aware that he may even have let out an audible gasp as a sickening claw grabbed at his gut.

"I beg your pardon?" he whispered.

"Mister Vicon..."

"How did he get onboard?"

The first lieutenant's face dropped and then set to the familiar mask of 'I'm in trouble again.'

"I... he asked for you and..."

"With what credentials, Mayhew?"

"He... he showed me a master trader's certificate, and..."

"And you know how to spot a genuine master trader's certificate? And of course, you checked my schedule to see if he had an appointment?"

The bearded lieutenant's shoulders slumped and his head hung lower.

"Would you like me to escort him off the ship, sir?"

"No, Mister Knox, that would be bloody rude at this juncture. Show him in, and be ready to see me immediately after I've finished with him. Make sure you've got your hat. And to manage your expectations, I shan't be offering you a seat. Or tea."

"Yes, sir."

The admonished lieutenant disappeared from view for a few seconds before reappearing to stand formally to attention at the door again.

"Mister Stefano Viconti for you, sir," he nodded his head before leaving the cabin.

A thin man in his fifties, standing just at average height and with receding hair at his crown paced boldly into the great cabin. He wore a long coat of ruddy brown over high quality breeches and a shirt of similarly rustic colors, the heavy brass buckles of his expensive but practical shoes polished to a shine. Jaymes stood and walked across to meet him, extending his hand.

"Jaymes Ellias, sir."

Stefano clasped his own hands at the small of his back and surveyed Jaymes from head to toe in silence. Jaymes lowered his hand. The older man cleared his throat and then spoke.

"So you're one of the men who has forced my daughter into her rather unenviable predicament."

Jaymes looked away and sighed. He knew well enough that he was not at his best – the pressures of preparing the ship for a potentially long, drawn out patrol followed by a significant engagement all fell squarely on his shoulders. He worried about Caithlin's role in all of this. When he thought about it, he worried about practically everything. He also worried about starting on completely the wrong foot with the father of the woman he had made a serious commitment to. In his sometimes overly sentimental and romantic mind, 'The One.' He opened his mouth to try again at a diplomatic solution, but the withering, aggressive stare of the master trader triggered another response.

"You come barging onto my ship without an appointment, refuse to shake my hand, and then make baseless accusations made on nothing more than assumption? Your manners, sir, are embarrassing. If that's all you've come to say, I'll bid you a good afternoon, as I have a ship to prepare for battle."

The aging trader tilted his head in confusion.

"Are you not always preparing for battle? You say this as if I should see it as a rarity and feel sympathy for you. Those two hundred poor wretches out there under your command, I feel a great deal of sympathy for them. I've watched my best sailors pressed into a dozen navies and torn away from their families and a well paid vocation for forced service. But you? You're an officer. A volunteer. From a wealthy family. You chose battle, it did not choose you."

"You don't know the first thing about my family!" Jaymes scowled.

"Oh. My apologies. So you are an upper yardsmen, then? You joined the navy as a non-commissioned rating and were selected to advance to the officer corps on merit, rather than joining directly as an officer due to your family's wealth and influence?"

Jaymes turned away from the probing stare. Stefano had him there, the bastard. Jaymes's family was only moderately affluent, certainly with no title or significant plot of land, but wealthy enough for their son to join the navy directly as a midshipman. He paced back to the other side of his desk and looked out through the stern windows at the hive of activity along the jetty. He needed to change the tack of this conversation. Sadly, given the negative effect this would undoubtedly have on his relationship with Caithlin once it got back to her, that meant going on the offensive. And making it personal.

"Ye see," Jaymes began, "I think I can hazard a guess at why you're here and what you think is going on. Your daughter, who you love dearly and have taken care of for all of your life, has ended up in a foreign port, her good will taken advantage of by a powerful and aggressive, expansionist power whilst she is forced into battle with no training and not a thought or care for her well-being. Meanwhile, some slick, womanizing bastard has moved in from the flanks to take advantage of her vulnerability to use and abuse her before ditching her for the next best thing, as soon as she arrives. That about right?"

Stefano merely raised his brow and issued a barely perceptible shrug.

"Well, here's my side of the equation," Jaymes continued. "I saw an experienced and fearless sea captain drag a battered vessel into a safe port and come to an arrangement to give her the best chance she has for her own future, and the future of her crew. My personal involvement in that? It would be ungentlemanly to boast, so I'll let her tell you."

Stefano suppressed a slight yawn.

"Suffice to say," Jaymes leaned across his desk, "I'm more than happy to look myself in the mirror when I think of my conduct during that particular week. I also see a grown woman making decisions for herself, never under duress, and from the last time I spoke to her she seemed perfectly happy with our relationship. Her relationship with you? Between you and I, Mister Viconti, I'd be less confident. Far less confident. You come strutting in here, trying to intimidate me over my relationship with your daughter, yet she's perfectly happy with my conduct and she's bloody raging with you! So, a word of advice. Man to man. Eye to eye. I suggest you get your own house in order before you start attacking others."

The aging sailor stared back at Jaymes, the aloof facade now replaced with an even mix of anger and hurt. He opened his mouth to speak, stammered a few syllables, and then turned on his heel to storm from the cabin. Swearing and plunging his face into his hands, Jaymes sank down to sit on the sill of the stern windows. He replayed the conversation in his head a dozen times, realizing all too late the things that he could have articulated far better and far less offensively. He was in trouble. Caithlin would be furious. He needed to fix things now.

There was a light tap at his door.

"Wait!" he snapped.

He needed to dash across to the *Martolian Queen*, now, and fix this. He knew himself well enough to know that he would brood and ruminate on the potential outcomes of this altercation until there was at least some resolution. He stood up and grabbed his hat from its peg. He stopped. No. He had a duty. Preparing the ship for battle was paramount, and of far more importance than his petty concerns. Besides, he knew there was already some gossip about him and Caithlin, and striding across to her ship in broad daylight would not make things any better. But... a trusted friend who knew them both well, perhaps? Karnon could head across to speak to her. At least let her know and arrange a meeting later.

"Lieutenant Knox!"

The door opened and Mayhew marched in to stand to attention rigidly before his desk and then raise his right hand in a smart salute.

"Mayhew," Jaymes said, quickly pulling his jacket on, "you've been a dick again. Don't let random people onto this ship without the proper permissions. Clear? Now go and tell Captain Senne that I need to see him immediately. Then you and I are going to the port surgery to stock up on some... bottles of pathology."

***

"Come on!" Tem urged, quickening his pace along the rickety jetty to keep up with the taller man. "I've got this all figured out! You trusted in me last time and it paid off! Trust in me with this, and I'll bring you back even more spoils!"

The two pirates walked briskly back from the end of the jetty toward the beach, leading up to the motley collection of shattered ships and their adjoining huts and shacks that formed the settlement of Red Skull. Three pirates still remained prone and motionless on the beach from their excesses the previous night, despite it now being mid-afternoon. On the far side of the jetty, a small brig cast off to make its way north toward the Sand Lane. Next to Tem, Cerri Denayo stopped in his tracks and turned to face the younger pirate captain.

"Trust you? Come on, shippers! Don't you think you're letting a little bit of success go to your head?"

Tem clenched his fists and bounced lightly on the pads of his bare feet.

"I know how that sounds, Cerri. But hear me out. You saw something in me, so you trusted me with a good ship. I went out, I brought it back in one piece, I brought you your share of plunder as I promised, and my crew have voted me back in as captain for the next cruise. I've proved myself."

Cerri let out a long laugh which, if not for the context of the conversation, would almost have sounded charming.

"Here's my point of view, shipmate. I let you borrow a ship you could not fail with. You brought it back with a mediocre haul of booty, and you narrowly survived the captain's vote by three. Three votes, mate! That's not a huge amount of confidence! Every time I go out, I get every vote! Every last one!"

Tem gritted his teeth. That was easy to say with a reputation such as Cerri's. Of course nobody ever dared vote against him. It was a formality, a mere nod of respect toward the rules, when a crew voted on one of the three pirate chiefs. And where were Cerri's huge successes? As a younger captain, he was a legend. Now? He would happily leave a full two months between cruises, drinking and whoring his fortune away on the island whilst younger captains sailed out and gave him a one tenth share of everything they earned. Cerri would dart out to the Sand Lane about as often as an elf made a joke, just to keep up the appearance of still being active, then lounge around on the island while others took the risks for him, and paid him for the privilege.

But what other options were there? Every captain in the region – every pirate, for that matter – had to align to one of the three chiefs.

Hector Dunn? An old drunkard who was even less active than Cerri. Andars Taithe? A cruel, sadistic killer who was in the game for blood, not fortune. Cerri was the beggar's pick of a bad haul.

"What is it that you want, Tem?" the tall pirate asked. "What do you actually want?"

Tem folded his arms, watched the brig sail toward the northern horizon, then looked back up at his superior.

"I want to excel. I want to be the best at what I do. If I was a blacksmith, I'd want to be the best. Same if I was... a farmer. But this is the hand that life dealt me. I'm a pirate. So I want to be the best at it."

Cerri nodded slowly, tapping his chin thoughtfully.

"Right... right. Two things. First, if you want to be the best pirate, then you need to start killing. It's part of the job. You can't swan around the Infant Sea, politely taking a few things from people you decide can spare them. There comes a time when you've got to look a crew of sailors in the eye, shrug in apology for their bad luck, and push them all overboard to drown or feed the sharks because you want everything they own. Ship an' all."

Tem sighed and nodded in acceptance.

"And the second thing?" he asked quietly.

"The second thing," Cerri replied, "is that when I asked you what you wanted, I didn't mean out of life. I'm not your pa, shippers. I was asking why you've come and bothered me with this grand plan of yours. What do you want from me?"

Cerri winced. He tapped the fingertips of one hand thoughtfully between the knuckles of the other. Given the complete lack of enthusiasm that Cerri had deflated his confidence with, he could only see one outcome to this request. Still, if you never asked...

"The *Desert Rose*," Tem said. "I want to take the *Desert Rose* out on the next cruise."

Cerri's features hardened. He remained silent. Tem found himself wondering if, in one possibly arrogant and even entitled demand, he had sunk every last iota of good will that he had spent two years building up with the powerful and influential captain.

"One cruise," Tem continued and lowered his voice, "just one. If I don't bring back a decent haul, you've lost nothing."

"Unless the damage inflicted to that ship is more costly to repair than the plunder you bring back. Or, worse and more likely, you end up losing her entirely and dancing with the Neriticans."

"I brought your sloop back without a scratch. And with two more cannons. And a decent haul of plunder because of the extra share from the schooner I captured and sold. I may not have pillaged an entire treasure fleet like the seadogs of old, but I'm sticking to my course and saying that that wasn't a bad first cruise as captain. I didn't let you down."

Cerri kept his dark eyes locked on Tem's. The water lapped away at the moss-covered timbers holding up the jetty. The pirate chief finally spoke.

"The *Desert Rose* is near two hundred tons. Ten guns. And they're nine-pounders. That's enough to make a fighting brig stop to think. Two masts, larger crew. A lot more to think about."

Tem suppressed a grin. That was a yes.

"I won't let you down, Cerri."

The older man's features still did not soften.

"You haven't got a choice. People often say things like... 'come back successful or don't come back at all.' Not coming back isn't an option. Coming back having failed, also not an option. You make this work, Tem. You make this work."

***

The large local musician crouched over the tiny ukiola plucked away on the four strings melodically, his vocals adding to the warm and vibrant song filling the bar, although the meaning of the lyrics was lost on anybody who did not speak the tongue of the indigenous people who populated Keretia long before the arrival of the Basileans. Sabine let out a long laugh and pitched forward over her glass of wine. Opposite from her at the table, Karnon sat conspicuous in his brazen, purple pantaloons. He pulled a dour face which was clearly meant to show offense at the joke made at his expense, but to those who knew him well enough, it was no doubt part of his sullen but humorous facade. A few feet away, sat next to Jaymes at the bar and leaning over her shot of rum, Caithlin nodded slowly as she stared down into the dark, rich liquid.

"Alright," she finally said.

Jaymes coughed up into his metal tankard.

"Alright? I've just told you that I insulted your father and threw him off my ship! I'm assuming this is a trap? This is a trap, correct? You cannot be... alright with what I've just told you."

"Have you been worrying all day about how you were going to tell me this?"

Jaymes spluttered again, his face twisted in disbelief.

"Of course."

Caithlin downed her shot, winced, and smiled across at him.

"Well, then. Look. He did exactly the same to me. Barged his way onto my ship, and I ended up losing my temper and threatening him. It's even more unforgivable on *your* ship as he has no right to be there. How did he even get onboard? Was this that idiotic first lieutenant of yours again? Don't answer. Anyway, I have to be honest in telling you that I'm disappointed that this is how the first meeting between the two most important men in my life has transpired, but... that's his fault and not yours. To be honest, I'm done talking about him. Yes. I've had a few more minutes to think on this, and I'm angry with him. So let's talk about something else before this ruins the evening for us both."

For the second time in as many evenings, Jaymes felt nausea rising within him from the instantaneous release of worry. He needed to get back to sea. Things were so much more simple and so less worrying when avoiding a horrific death for himself and his crew was all he needed to concern himself with.

"Have you given any more thought to buying that house?" Caithlin asked.

"Still thinking."

Jaymes again felt the guilt of talking to her about spending so much money when money was the root of all of Caithlin's problems. He had offered to help her financially. Three times now. Three times she had politely refused.

"It's definitely a good idea, thinking about a home here," Caithlin pondered. "That reminds me – did you know Marcellus has a daughter?"

Jaymes, his seemingly perennial gut ache easing slowly, looked up from his tankard.

"Yes. Kora. He really dotes on her. They're very close. Marcellus is a widower, but he really has sort of built a wall between work and his personal life. But I've met his daughter a good few times. I gave her a compass from that first pirate sloop I captured after taking command of *Pious*. I think it might have started something, unfortunately. As for Marcellus, his wife passed away years before I met him."

Jaymes wondered whether he should have been inviting Marcellus to these evenings in town with Caithlin, Karnon, and Sabine. There was a bit of an age gap, and he certainly came across as a more mature and serious sort, but was always pleasant and friendly. Caithlin smiled and tilted her empty shot glass thoughtfully.

"Well, I pray it works out for them, that must be difficult. Any ideas of when we're finally going to slip and proceed to sea to go look for the Ahmunites?"

"Tomorrow morning," Jaymes replied, "that's what the orders say."

"Yes, I received the same letter from the flag lieutenant, but proceeding 'tomorrow morning' has been the plan for three days now. Yet, there always seems to be something that stands in our way."

"TNB," Karnon said seriously as he appeared next to Jaymes.

"Oh? What's that?" Caithlin asked.

"Typical naval bullshit," Karnon explained, "these sort of

nonsense delays over stupid mistakes are exclusive to you boaty folk. Would never happen in the marines."

"The reason it's never happened in the marines is because, as a corps, you've existed for about five minutes," Caithlin said dryly. "Three months ago, the Basilean Marines had not even been formed."

Jaymes burst out laughing proudly and pointed a finger aggressively at Karnon's resentful face.

"Did you get delays like this in the legion?" Caithlin followed up.

"Never," Karnon folded his arms and shook his head stubbornly.

"I'm going to call bullshit on that," Jaymes interjected as he finished his drink. "And to answer your original question, the normal result in orders to put to sea tomorrow is a succession of small, completely avoidable delays that come in piecemeal for about two weeks until the whole scenario has blown over and we start planning for the next one. But on this occasion, I would estimate that another two days and we'll be heading south."

Caithlin stood up and pushed her pinewood stool back beneath the bar and grabbed Jaymes's hand.

"Come on, then," she flashed a smile, "if we've got another few days of waiting, I intend to spend every minute I can actually having some fun with my life and forcing you to do the same. So we're dancing."

***

It was with a justified, but certainly not arrogant, sense of pride that T'mork watched the construction site of his temple to Shobik, its marble block walls already protruding up above the dense, jungle canopy, fading against the hazy horizon. His plan was well underway now – a combination of a grand demonstration of his loyalty to the God of Death, seamlessly intertwined with a planting of the flag to expand on the Ahmunite empire. His grand war galley, recognizable by its own marble temple atop its after deck, swept northward in the center of his entire fleet. Turning in place to look ahead, his puckered, dry mouth twisted into a grin as his gaze fell upon the dull, bone-cream hued prow of his vessel.

Boneships. That was what the scholar told him that the mortals called the Ahmunite vessels. Boneships of the Empire of Dust. There was an element of truth in that – certainly, constructing ships out of bone was simply a ludicrous idea, given bone's propensity to sink and to break more easily than stout wood. But dry, fleshless bone was one of the most ancient and sacred symbols of Shobik, and adorning Ahmunite vessels with a symbol of worship was of paramount importance. So T'mork, like all Ahmunite naval commanders, covered parts of his ships with bone. In T'mork's case, it was the prow – jutting ahead of the rest of the vessel, carving through water and displacing it to either side, the forward quarter of each of his ships was encased in the magically twisted, stretched, and reformed bone of his sacrificial victims.

There would be more soon. His temple workforce was made up of both captured sailors, but also the working age men of the coastal towns and settlements his fleet had raided. Yes, it would make more sense in many ways to sacrifice them on his war galley's temple altar, as an undead worker was tirelessly efficient and obedient when compared to a live captive. That was why T'mork had already followed that route of efficiency with the old and infirm. But even he, a great and ancient high priest, had his limits of endurance. No, far better to recover and work his captives to death, safe in the knowledge that acts of rebellion would be impossible just so long as he held their wives and children captive. And when they finally tired and fell? T'mork would simply sacrifice them all, bolster the efficiency of his undead workers, and then head out to find fresh mortal blood as he recovered for the next wave of sacrifices. And whilst the cycle continued, his temple grew; and with it, the symbol of his devotion and loyalty to his god.

T'mork cast his eyes across the powerful fleet flanking his formidable flagship. The next settlements would be just over the blurred, hazy horizon.

***

The low, narrow-hulled xebec tilted around in the wind, its aggressive prow and long, tilted bowsprit pointing away from the jetty. The ship was held firm by its sternspring, a rope pointing aft from midships to where it was secured on the jetty bollard. The last of Tem's crew, a new addition named Hoggir, unwound the line and hopped onboard as the wind took the xebec away from the jetty. Stood on the raised quarterdeck and feeling very much the real captain, Tem looked down at the deck of his ship and her assortment of ten cannons. Three fore-and-aft rigged masts propelled the ship – over twice the weight of his previous sloop. His crew were a mixture of old and new, human and sailors from further afield, blooded pirates and new converts to the cause. Eighty men, all in.

"Take her out on the main!" Tem shouted across to the six pirates at the main mast. "Let her out a little more, lads!"

Halladai moved quickly across the quarterdeck to check the vessel was clear of obstructions as she moved smoothly through the flat waters. Flyde barked out commands to the sailors managing the mainmast's slanted yard as another three feet of sail were carefully lowered to catch the cool, evening wind.

The pale-wood hulled, Ophidian-built pirate ship swung about to head out to sea, a dagger-like silhouette against a blood red, evening sky. Tem looked back at the settlement of Red Skull, his eyes straining against the low light of dusk. He saw the three notorious, commanding figures of the pirate chiefs together on the verandah of one of the island settlement's taverns. The rotund, aging shape of the oldest lounged in a chair. The powerful, dark-bearded killer stood next to him. And finally, the tall, graceful figure of the third leader, leaning against the roof post of the verandah, arms folded and eyes fixed on the xebec as it picked up the wind and altered course to the north.

***

"The navy have already ordered a one-hour cease to all civilian shipping movement, so you'll get out of here without any problems," Kassia said as she struggled to keep pace with the taller woman walking along the dockside toward the lines of jetties.

"With this wind, we'll get out into deep water just fine," Caithlin replied, one hand clenched tightly at the scabbard of the saber hanging from her waist as her boot heels thumped rhythmically on the cobblestone path beneath her feet. "It's heading south at any reasonable pace that will be the problem."

"I've already had next month's lists come through," the harbormaster said, "everything you need will be here when you get back."

"Supplies aren't the problem," Caithlin said as she reached the steps leading to the jetty by her brig, "it's skilled sailors. I've had another two fail to report for muster today. Not enough pay, and now an increase in danger."

Kassia stopped. The dusk had a bitter and uncharacteristic chill, cutting through even the thick material of Caithlin's blue jacket.

"Take care," the older woman said, "I have my ear to the ground well enough to have a grasp of what you're off to do. I shouldn't know, but I do. Keep your wits about you, Cathy."

"Aye," Caithlin threw a cavalier wink, shook her friend's hand warmly, and then quickened her pace as she headed down the stone steps to the jetty below.

It was only a few steps until another familiar voice called out to her.

"Cathy?"

Caithlin looked over her shoulder to see Stefano jogging awkwardly over to her. She bit her lip and shook her head.

"This is a military dock, and warships are departing on active operations," she scolded her father. "We've been through this before. You shouldn't be here."

"I know," her father breathed heavily as he reached her, "but I saw the amount of activity going on and that the *Martolian Queen* was storing ship. I know something big is happening. I wanted to see you off. That's all."

Caithlin stopped and looked across at her father. She saw the same man who had lovingly and patiently guided her through all of the trials and tribulations of childhood and adolescence, and those early, dangerous days of the first voyages across the seas. The patient, loving man she had always been proud to call her father.

"I'm sorry for these last few days." Stefano swallowed. "I'm just not at all used to this level of worrying. Facing the perils of the sea is one thing. I've always handled that. No father should ever have to face seeing one of their children go off to war. It's entirely different."

Caithlin nodded slowly. She was still angry at him for the way he had treated Jaymes; it would fall on her at some point to clarify to her father just how serious that relationship was.

"We'll sort all of this out if I come back," she said coolly.

Stefano's face dropped.

"*When* you come back."

Caithlin mentally chastised herself for such a petulant remark. It had been deliberate. It had meant to worry and to cause hurt. She leaned up to kiss Stefano on the cheek.

"Goodbye, father. Ones above willing, I shall see you in a few weeks."

"I'll be waiting here. Ones above protect you. I... do love you."

Caithlin nodded again silently, then turned on her heel as she quickly packed the emotions away out of sight. A bosun's call whistled out a shrill cry to announce her as she stepped off the gangway and onto the deck of her fighting ship. Sixty of her sailors stood neatly at attention in smart imitation of a naval ship's company before a cry from Jonjak, her second mate, dismissed them back to their duties.

"Ready to cast off, Captain," X'And reported formally.

"Straight to it, then," Caithlin confirmed. "How are the rest?"

"*Shield Royal* has already raised anchor in the bay. *Pious* joined her about half an hour ago. *Veneration* has raised her gangway, so I think they're back on track after having to deal with this morning's galley fire. Three of the sloops are already out, one is still alongside. I don't know what has delayed them."

Caithlin looked across the bay as she clambered up onto the quarterdeck, seeing the magnificent site of a Basilean third-rate defender and a Batch Two, three-masted Elohi sailing slowly in company not far to the south.

"No time to waste, then," she said to X'And. "Take her out of the harbor and take position off *Pious's* port quarter."

"Aye, Captain."

***

"Officer of the Watch, sir!" Danne Estrayia, the sailing master, bellowed across from the starboard side of the quarterdeck. "Ship's on station! Two cables off the flag's port quarter!"

"Thank you, Mister Estrayia!" Lieutenant Kaeso Innes acknowledged.

The short lieutenant walked a few paces over to Jaymes and smiled apologetically.

"Captain, sir. We're on station. Two cables from *Shield Royal*. Steady on a course two points west of south, wind's from south of east. Making good five knots."

Jaymes nodded.

"Thank you, Kaeso. You have conduct."

"Aye, sir, I have the con."

Jaymes took a moment to gaze around as the frigate's bow and stern lights were illuminated in the rapidly darkening evening. *Shield Royal*, standing resplendent in her towering, one thousand and eight hundred ton majesty, took center with the two Elohi frigates flanking her. Ahead of each frigate was the familiar shape of a naval sloop – a vessel which, Jaymes thought, no matter how long he spent on frigates, he would always consider himself intertwined with. Another pair of sloops were stationed off to the east – *Scout* and *Sprinter* – now little more than night lights bobbing up and down in the undulating, black sea. To the west, the salamander J'Koor'uk frigate cut through the waves with grace and poise. A little further out, the *Martolian Queen* was just about visible.

Jaymes remained stationary on the steps leading down to the upper deck. In well over a decade of naval service, it was the largest fleet he had ever been a part of. And somehow he found himself in command of the second largest vessel in the fleet – if only the third in terms of seniority of command. For not the first time in recent weeks, he stopped to think of the friends back home who he grew up with. They would never see a sight quite like this. Shivering as a gust of unseasonal chill swept across the deck of the frigate, Jaymes headed aft and to his cabin.

Samus had already drawn the curtains and illuminated the lamps. Jaymes closed the door behind him, hung up his jacket, and untied his neck scarf. His eyes fell on the collection of letters and envelopes on the table in the center of the cabin. His orders. A pamphlet from naval command detailing the capabilities and vulnerabilities of Ahmunite vessels. The deeds to the house he had just finalized the purchase of.

Three letters; a cheerful and upbeat letter from his mother, a heartfelt letter of apology from Stefano Viconti, and the long sentimental letter of love from Caithlin, all of which had arrived just before sailing.

Jaymes changed for bed, blew out the lights in the great cabin, picked up the letters from his mother and Caithlin, and moved across to his night cabin to read them both one last time before sleep.

Chapter Eight

Hegemon's Warship *Pious* (36)
278 souls on board
The Cols, South of the Sand Lane
Northeast Infant Sea

One week. One week of struggling to maintain even eight knots with a light, variable but rarely favorable wind. *Pious* had broken away from *Shield Royal*, as ordered, when the Basilean fleet crossed the Sand Lane on the first day of the patrol. The further south they headed, the quieter the seas became – both in terms of other shipping and the waves themselves. The summer skies were devoid of clouds – for the moment, at least – and provided less wind than was expected at this time of year. But, even though the days were hotter as they sailed further south, the temperatures dropped at night time; and with that came a strange, cool mist that enveloped the ships, sometimes evening thickening to a full fog.

It was in such a thick fog that Jaymes found himself on the quarterdeck, halfway through the First Watch of the seventh day at sea, for once glad of his jacket in the evening coolness. He leaned on the taffrail overlooking the upper deck, straining his eyes to even see the fo'c'sle in the fog, let alone the bowsprit. He heard the muttering of conversation way, way above him from the top men who clung to the yards of the mizzenmast, ready to follow the orders from down below on the quarterdeck. The bow and stern lamps glowed eerily away in the fog, painting flickering yellow spheres of light amidst the dull gray.

"I really didn't think I'd need this," Kaeso Innes remarked from next to Jaymes, gesturing at his full length greatcoat, a status symbol of sorts, as such garments were only required for crews employed in colder seas way to the north.

Jaymes opened his mouth to offer a differing opinion but stopped to ponder. It really was that cold. He had never experienced it in all of his years in the Infant Sea.

"Unseasonal," he said quietly, his eyes straining through the fog as the ship continued to glide through the still waters, "damned unseasonal. You've known me long enough to know I'm less superstitious than most sailors, but this is something else. Fog out here, fine. But the temperature tonight?"

Kaeso offered an inane grin as Karnon Senne walked up to the quarterdeck, blowing into his hands and rubbing them together.

"Some of the chaps have been talking," the second lieutenant shrugged, "as they always do! But I do wonder if there is some truth in the natural order of things being upset by the Ahmunites. If there is a bone fleet just out there, bringing with it its necromancy and what not, I wouldn't bat an eyelid if that was the cause of the fog and cold in summer."

"I've seen stranger," Karnon offered dryly as he stopped by the two naval officers. "I've faced Abyssals, undead, horrors manifest from the nightmares of men... rules of nature don't really apply when those lot are about. Strange things going on. Our lot are very quick to take the piss out of you sailors for your superstitions and silly ghost stories. But, I've noticed the marines onboard are a little less necky at the moment when it comes to that sort of banter."

Down below, a dull chime rang out as the ship's bell was rung to alert any other vessel groping through the fog of their presence. There was no reply from within the thick folds of mist.

"Must we do that?" Karnon asked, his breath appearing as smoke in the cold air in front of his face.

"We weigh up different risks," Jaymes answered. "There *could* be bone ships out there, possibly pirates. But what we know for certain is that ships of our fleet *are* out there, and my top concern at the moment is clattering into a friendly ship rather than alerting an enemy that we're here. That's why we've got the lamps lit, too."

The marine officer let out a grunt which most likely indicated his disagreement but reluctance to argue the point. The frigate plowed on, its deck as still and steady in the flat sea as if it were tied up alongside in port.

"I did hear something that made me chuckle this afternoon!" Kaeso suddenly piped up, a merry grin plastered across his pale face. "Stenssen on the port watch. He's in my division. He told me that one of his lot on the main mast team reckon they saw the previous Old Man! Ha! Imagine that!"

Jaymes's eyes widened.

"Sorry, Kaeso, run that one by me again?" Karnon demanded.

"Stenssen said this fellow – forgotten who it was now – was conducting rounds. Went into the cable locker and saw somebody in there. He challenged him, man turns around, and it's old Captain Ferrus! Ha! We need to water down their grog a little more, I fear!"

Jaymes shivered. Karnon turned around slowly.

"One thing, Kaeso. If the previous captain's ghost was roaming this ship... why on earth would he be in the cable locker?"

"No idea!" Kaeso beamed. "But I do like a good ghost story! Never met a ghost. I do think I've heard *every* nautical ghost story ever uttered, though. Marvelous!"

Karnon looked across at Jaymes.

"Sir? Have your duties as captain ever once taken you to the cable locker?"

Jaymes flashed a grin.

"Can't say that they have, old boy. But it's a dark and spooky place, so if I was a complete bastard – and dead – that might be somewhere I'd consider jumping out at somebody to give them a fright. And Charn Ferrus is both of those things. A complete bastard. And dead. But he was a fantastic captain."

The ship's bell rang out again. Jaymes looked across at the spot on the deck where Charn had fallen, cut down by the broadside of an enormous orc smasher. He remembered their last exchanged words, the dying captain looking wearily up at him.

"...Sorry..."

Bleeding from a head wound and stunned by the battle raging around him, Jaymes had thought he had seen Charn taken up to Mount Kolosu, guided by Elohi to a better place. He wanted to believe what he saw – he certainly believed in the power of the Shining Ones above – but it was far more likely that he imagined it all in his concussed state than being blessed with a chance to see the angels take his captain to the afterlife.

The bell rang out again. There were a few seconds of silence. Then, off to starboard, the low, deep peel of something like a cathedral bell rang out twice in response. All three officers sprang in place to stare out into the fog to starboard.

"Lookouts!" Kaeso yelled. "Eyes to starboard!"

The fog shimmered a light, blue-green. A veritable wall of wood suddenly appeared out of the mist, forming into the shape of an immense ship-of-the-line. Two full gundecks, their ports open and their guns run out, parallelled the course of the smaller frigate. Sails, untethered and shredded, billowed slowly in a wind that simply could not move them to such an extent.

"To port!" Jaymes yelled. "Hard a' port!"

The frigate swung away from the impending collision with the larger vessel. The huge third-rate silently followed. Jaymes looked up at the majestic vessel, goosebumps across his damp skin. The prow was covered in ornate, richly decorated metal. The stern was decorated in tall, stained glass windows – all shattered. The entire ship glowed a faint, light blue.

"Ghost ship!" an alert was screamed from up top.

Panicked cries rippled across the deck and masts above.

"Beat to quarters, Captain?" Kaeso breathed.

Jaymes swallowed and looked up at the majesty of the ship sailing serenely alongside them.

"Beat to quarters?" Kaeso repeated forcefully.

Jaymes turned to shout orders forward to his panicked crew.

"Helm, thus! Maintain course! *Pious* ship's company, ho! Dip the ensign!"

Silence fell across the deck. The frigate rolled out on a steady heading. Kaeso grabbed Jaymes by the arm.

"Sir, are you mad?! Dip the ensign? You want to... salute them?!"

Jaymes threw the younger officer's grip off his arm.

"I said, 'Dip the ensign!'" he yelled.

Dutifully, the blue Basilean ensign fluttering at the stern of the quarterdeck dropped by a few feet and then rose again. Jaymes looked up nervously at the towering ship alongside. A lone figure appeared high up on the quarterdeck. A woman of perhaps thirty years, her slim figure draped in a shredded, flowing greatcoat and her long hair partially covered by a tricorn hat. Jaymes stood to attention and brought his arm up crisply in salute. The solemn-faced, shimmering captain above stared back at him, her pale eyes boring into his. She slowly raised her own arm to return the salute. Besides Jaymes, Kaeso and Karnon immediately followed his example and stood to attention, offering their own salutes.

The ghostly captain slowly turned to look dead ahead again. Without another gesture, the towering ghost ship turned away and was swallowed up by the fog. After only a few seconds, not a sign that the ghost ship was ever there still remained. His breathing ragged, Jaymes lowered his arm. Conversation began to ripple across the deck and in the yards above once more. Kaeso turned to look up at his captain.

"Was that...?"

Jaymes nodded.

"The Light of Holy Blessing," he nodded, "an Abbess-class ship of the sisterhood. Disappeared out here about twenty years ago."

His skin hot and covered in sweat against the cold fog, his heart thumping in his chest, Jaymes leaned over the taffrail and took in a few slow breaths. The frigate carried on through the fog and the smooth seas. The ship's bell rang out again. There was no reply. Kaeso cleared his throat.

"Should... should one of us check the cable locker?"

"Crossbow not me!" Karnon gasped without hesitation.

***

Plumes of mist rolled down the hills from the humid islands, hiding half of the vegetation-covered rocks and sheer cliffs. A fierce, early morning sun blazed down furiously to burn away the moisture and fight the wisps of mist back away from the clear, turquoise waters lapping at the cliff bases of the Lesser Yellow Rocks; an island chain Tem knew well. While it was still Wez Polleri and his sloop, the *Ranger's Revenge*, that commanded the small squadron of pirate ships, it was Tem's *Desert Rose* that brought the firepower. And what a cruise it had been to bring that firepower.

In nine days, the four pirate ships had captured no fewer than seven prizes. Two or three sparsely laden sloops with barely any meat to pick off the bones for starters, but after boarding and sinking a Nyssian brig of a hundred tons, the two merchant ships the brig was escorting were easy pickings. Wez, Tem, Yordan, Jhanzee, and their four crews were only two days from Red Skull now, their ships' holds practically splitting with plunder. The entire cruise was, by anybody's standards, an unmitigated success. But, after Jhanzee's *Blue Rise* had taken a few hits against the Nyssian naval brig, it was necessary to stop off for a few repairs that could not last until Red Skull, and the Lesser Yellow Rocks were the perfect place.

As Tem stood on the quarterdeck, leaning nonchalantly back against the mizzenmast and swilling a tankard of grog thoughtfully in one hand, he saw Halladai wandering up from below deck, silver chains dangling off his neck and wrists from plundering during the cruise. The tall quartermaster flashed a weary, hungover grin at the captain as he walked across the gently pitching deck.

"About time you turned to," Tem remarked dryly, observing the height of the morning sun in the clear sky. "We're not home and dry yet, you know."

"What's the point in pirating if you're not going to enjoy every moment?" Halladai asked. "If I wanted early, sober nights I would have stayed in the merchant service. At least this mist is clearing."

"Aye, that it is," Tem replied, watching a dozen of his crew busily cleaning the xebec's nine-pounder guns as fastidiously as if they were naval sailors. "And we shouldn't be too long here. Just fresh water and mending a few leaks on the *Blue Rise*."

"Is it worth us stopping to careen our hull?" Halladai offered.

Tem shook his head.

"This is Cerri Denayo's ship. He'll snatch her right back off me the moment we're alongside. He can do his own damn careening."

The two pirates shared a quick laugh. But only for a brief moment. Tem's eyes picked up something, a flash of movement off to port. The Lesser Yellow Rocks were nothing more than a series of islands erupting up to sit some fifty to a hundred feet higher than the water; jungle-covered plateaus with steep cliffs, and only one or two spots where a sloop might safely beach herself for repairs. But, off to port, between the cliffs and the mist, Tem had definitely seen something.

"What is it?" Halladai asked, turning to look in the same direction.

In the narrow waterway spanning in between two of the tall islands, half shrouded in the morning mist, Tem made out the unmistakable shape of a ship's stern. Smiling as he saw its windows glinting in the sun, heart hammering in excitement, Tem raised his telescope to his eye. He let out a short laugh. A brig, on the larger side of medium, perhaps even a four hundred tonner. No wonder she was trying to silently slip away.

"I see her," Halladai breathed, "what now?"

"We get the drop, that's what!" Tem answered excitedly before leaning over to shout up to his crew on the masts. "Full sail, lads! Set full sail! Lively, now! Helm, three points a' starboard!"

Halladai stared out at the brig, his dark eyes narrowed.

"The drop?" he said with a cynical wince. "Tem, they've already seen us."

The xebec swung about to starboard, her sleek bows lining up with the comparatively boxy, angular brig, her fore-and-aft rigged sails billowing out to harness full use of the wind.

"Not the drop on the brig, shipmate," Tem grinned, "the drop on those three bastards we're out hunting with! Look at that thing, she's beautiful! I don't care for her cargo, I want that ship for myself! She's a perfect size, and I reckon we could cram near twenty guns onto a filly like that!"

His own words reminding him of the danger he potentially faced, Tem stepped forward to the base of the mainmast and shouted up to his lookout.

"Aloft, there! Brig, on the ship's head! How many guns?"

"Deck's cluttered, Capt'n!" the reply was hollered back down. "I reckon on six? No, eight!"

"What size?"

"Can't tell from here! Four-pounders?"

Tem laughed again as he raised his telescope. The Ones above were indeed shining down on him. Success after success after success. And now this, a perfect ship to take as his own. He recognized the ship's Genezan lines even before he saw the corresponding flag of the same nation – his home nation. A match made in the heavens, a ship from his own homeland, caught alone and with minimal defensive armament. This was easy. There was no other word for it.

"They've seen her, Captain!" Halladai warned. "The others are turning in!"

Tem looked over his shoulder and saw the two sloops and the schooner in company with him racing to catch up. He swore out loud as he gauged their rate of closure. Yordan's schooner was keeping pace. The two sloops were gaining, and fast. Within minutes, Wez's sloop slid past Tem's xebec and smoothly turned to follow the brig into the narrow confines of the passageway between the tall islands. Tem looked across to the sloop as it passed and saw the more experienced captain offer him a wink and a gap-toothed grin.

"Tem," Halladai breathed, "I don't like this…"

"I know! I know!" Tem growled in frustration. "This xebec shirehorse has got nothing left to give! Damn this Ophidian hulk!"

As the *Desert Rose* entered the narrow confines of the waterway, Jhanzee's *Blue Rise* swept nimbly past to take second place in the race for the prize brig.

"That's not what I meant!" Halladai warned. "Tem, for the sake of the Seven Circles, look! We're being drawn in! This doesn't feel right!"

For a second, Tem paused. A faint memory, a recollection of a warning from some weeks ago, a cautionary tale from either Cerri or Hector, he could not remember who, about a Genezan brig. It mattered not. There were many Genezan brigs; his homeland was a key maritime power and trade hub for such a relatively small kingdom. No, what mattered now was taking the prize. Wez and Jhanzee could soften it up, by all means, but Tem and the *Desert Rose* would take it.

"Tem!" Halladai grabbed him by the shoulder. "That brig is shortening sail! The bastards are drawing us in! It's a trap, Tem, we need to stand down!"

With a masterful show of seamanship coupled with a dazzling agility which spoke of masterbuilt steering gear, the brig swung about to port. In the time it took her to come about a quarter turn, her Genezan trading ensign was hauled down from her mast and the blues of Basilea were hoisted up in turn as, not four, but nine guns were run out on her port broadside.

"They're hunters!" Tem screamed. "Pirate hunters! Helm, hard to starboard! Now, man, now!"

The xebec came about to bring her bow back toward the wind channeled through the narrow passage. With a rippling roar like thunder, the fighting brig's broadside fired as one, engulfing the side of the ship with smoke as the boom of the guns echoed along the surrounding cliff faces. Tem watched in horror as cannonballs tore into the *Ranger's Revenge*, raking her from bow to stern, snapping off the top of her single mast and sending hundreds of splinters up into the hot air around her. Within seconds, she was listing to starboard.

"They're not four-pounders, Tem!" Halladai warned.

"I can see that!"

Tem looked down the passage between the yellow cliffs of the islands looming up to either side, back toward where he would need to fight his ship through a headwind to get clear of the brig's trap.

"Tem!" Halladai yelled in terror. "Tem! Look!"

Tem looked back down the waterway toward the open sea, in the direction his quartermaster was frantically pointing. He froze in place on the quarterdeck, bile rising in his dry throat. Up ahead, looming around the corner of the island like a dragon padding into a cave, Tem saw a warship with green sails, twice the size of the brig, easing forward to cut off their escape. The ship's hull was made up of dark red wood, with ornate gold trim and a broadside of huge cannons already lining up for a shot. Her lines were fast and agile – frigate built – and the series of flat-roofed compartments beneath her fan sails marked her out as a salamander warship.

The schooner that Tem had captured on his last cruise, now in the hands of Yordan and his crew, could only continue to desperately claw its way through the water away from the frigate, inch by inch in a pathetic attempt to open up the range. The salamander warship's guns boomed out as one, the sound reverberating along the passageway between the island cliffs. The schooner twisted and tumbled from the impact of the huge projectiles, spitting out debris in every direction, and then suddenly broke in half a'midships, slipping beneath the gentle waves with prow and stern poking up from the warm waters.

"Back around!" Tem shouted. "Reverse course, hard a'port! Get away from that damn frigate!"

Tem looked to the north and south of the channel, quickly assessing his options. No time to panic, he needed a plan. Turning back was certain death – he would face a headwind and point his bows straight into the broadside of a salamander frigate. But the channel was too shallow for the frigate, he hoped, so he could at least open up and get away from the thunderous close range guns. Facing the brig? He had a ten-gun xebec, nimble and fast, facing a sturdier but less agile square-rigged, eighteen-gun brig. He was outmatched in a fair fight, but he could at least slip past and get out to sea at the other end of the channel. Not so much *could* – he *had* to.

"Helm! Come to port! Half a point to the stern of the brig! Full sail!"

Up ahead, he saw the two sloops had come to the same conclusion. Jhanzee's *Blue Rise* had slipped past Wez's *Ranger's Revenge*, the latter now sitting lower in the water and leaning worryingly over to starboard. The *Blue Rise* suddenly swung out to port, lining up its guns on the brig and firing, the trio of light cannons sounding like comical fireworks in comparison to the salamander frigate's murderous broadside. It was a well-aimed maneuver – the light projectiles thumped into the wooden wall flank of the brig. In turn, the brig altered further to port to line up its own guns, and again the nine cannons blasted out, this time lined up on the *Blue Rise*. The little sloop lurched over from the impact of the cannonballs, swinging from side to side as the heavier projectiles slammed into her delicate hull.

From behind, at the upwind end of the channel, the frigate fired again. Tem knew there was only one logical target.

"Down!" he screamed. "On the deck!"

Tem threw himself down on the quarterdeck, frantically curling his legs into his belly and wrapping his arms over the top of his head. He heard the rapid droning of projectiles whooshing overhead, followed by snapping, cracking, and cries of panic. As quickly as he had thrown himself down, Tem sprang to his feet to survey his situation.

Behind him, the small sail of the mizzenmast flapped free in the wind, lines of rigging snaking out from it and lashing out where they had been cut.

"Ash!" Flyde shouted. "With me!"

The two sailors scrambled up the foot pegs of the mizzenmast and edged their way out along the slanting yard to haul in the sail. Behind them, the salamander frigate had turned and was now attempting to pursue the trio of damaged pirate ships through the straights. Tem swore. Surely their draft was not shallow enough to get through, and they would run aground? He looked forward again. The *Blue Rise* was approaching the brig. *Ranger's Revenge* was only a ship's length ahead of his own xebec.

Tem heard shouts from the *Ranger's Revenge*. He ran forward along the starboard waist of his vessel, past the crews lined up by the nine-pounder cannons. He reached the fo'c'sle and looked down to see Wez staring up from the sloop's quarterdeck.

"Tem!" The older pirate captain shouted. "We're not going to make it out of here! Get some lines across to us, for the sake of the Ones!"

Tem looked forward to where the brig was maneuvering to line up another broadside on the *Blue Rise*. That was his only chance. To get past the larger fighting ship as it was reloading. He looked down at Wez.

"I can't stop!" He called back, guilt tearing at his guts. "I'll come back! Swim to the rocks, we'll come back after dark!"

Wez stared up at him as the xebec swept past the wounded sloop, his eyes a blend of abject terror and resentment.

"I can't swim, Tem! If you don't stop for us now, we're all dead! You hear? Dead!"

Closing his eyes, bile half-blocking his throat, Tem turned away. He heard the roar of the brig's guns fire again and looked up to see the *Blue Rise* roll gently, almost serenely over, to capsize and sink beneath the smooth waves. Shouts merged into one around him, from the panicked cries below from Wez's sloop, to the damage repair on the mizzenmast, to warnings of course changes from the enemy brig and frigate.

"Captain!"

Tem realized only now that it was the third time Halladai was shouting at him from only two paces away.

He turned to face him.

"Up ahead! The channel opens out again just up ahead!"

Tem looked across and saw the open sea, just past where the pirate hunter brig had slowed to a near halt to half block the exit of the channel between the two islands. That was his chance. Of course, the captain of the brig would know that fighting his way past was his only option, hence going so far to try to block the exit. But the brig had just enough room aft.

"Helm, steady as she bears!" Tem shouted. "Every last one of you bastards, get on the starboard guns!"

Halladai planted a hand on Tem's shoulder.

"*Starboard* guns, Captain?! There's more space to get out forward of that brig! We'll never get behind her!"

"We will," Tem replied, "and we'll rake her stern on the way past, close enough to spit on them! Helm, hold her steady! Don't show those bastards our hand!"

Tem looked back over his shoulder. The mizzenmast sail was reefed in, held under control by Ash while Flyde spliced the lines. Good. Not long now until they would be back up to speed. Further back, its low, menacing silhouette squeezing through the gap in between the island cliffs, the green-sailed salamander frigate continued to close. With a loud bang, its huge, bronze bow chaser cannon opened fire.

"Down!"

Again, Tem threw himself to the deck and lay low. This time there was no crash of impact, not even the shower of water from a near miss. He drew himself back up to his feet and looked aft to see the *Ranger's Revenge* now on her side, what was left of her single mast touching the water and her sail dragging through the waves. Some sailors were already attempting to swim away from the stricken vessel while others clung desperately and pathetically to the mast and the exposed hull in the hope of a miracle to save them.

Tem looked forward again. No time to mourn any loss, there was one chance at escape. The brig loomed ahead, crawling slowly from left to right across the channel opening, its guns still smoking from the last broadside that finished off the *Blue Rise*. There was only one target left now. Tem and the *Desert Rose*. They were close now, close enough for him to look up to the brig's quarterdeck to see a quartet of figures, one of whom would be their captain – his opposite number.

"Ready on the starboard guns!" Tem shouted to the thirty sailors crouched over the five cannons. "Ready now, lads!"

The brig swung about, bringing her bows to starboard. With

expert seamanship from her captain and crew, the brig saw Tem's move and tacked neatly through the wind to run a parallel course, straight down the xebec's starboard side. Tem swore again. He took in a breath. Not to worry. He would not have his stern rake, but it would be one exchange of broadsides and then he was clear with a good head start, while the brig was left to come about again to pursue. He looked across to Halladai. For the first time in as long as he had known him, he saw genuine fear in the older pirate's stony stare.

The bows of the two vessels drew within a ship's length. Tem heard the shout of orders barked out on the brig. The bows crossed, the brig running near upwind slowly as the xebec streamed past at full sail, nearly close enough to jump from one vessel to the other. The guns lined up.

"Fire!"

Tem's world was obliterated in a mass of smoke-filled, thunderous cacophony as the two ships fired on each other simultaneously. Blinded by fumes, deafened by the high-pitched ringing in his ears, Tem numbly felt unknown objects passing by to either side of him, be they cannonballs, splinters, other parts of ship, or even body parts. His heart jumping up to his mouth, he coughed up a lungful of acidic fumes and looked down through streaming eyes, relieved to see no blood on his clothing.

Then Tem heard the screaming. The smoke began to thin, with streams of sunlight punching through the gray from above to reveal the carnage on the deck. Four cannons were blown off their carriages, scattered across the deck with dead or maimed sailors trapped beneath them in pools of blood and wooden splinters. Back aft, the mizzen sail now flew again, but Flyde hung in the rigging, his eyes wide open in shock at the moment of his death. Ash lay on the quarterdeck beneath him, his entrails scattered out across the boards as he screamed hoarsely in pain.

"Helm! Alter course to port! One point!" Tem yelled.

There was no response from the rudder. Tem turned and saw his helmsman on the deck, a good three or four feet of blood-spattered boards separating the upper and lower halves of his body. Tem sprinted back across the deck and took the helm himself, hauling the wooden wheel around to position the xebec with the wind fully from aft. The battered vessel plunged out of the constraints of the island passageway and into the open sea. Tem looked behind him and saw the brig rapidly wheeling around to pursue, but with his ship propelled by fore-and-aft sails compared to a square-rigger, he knew the brig could never catch him now the wind was dead astern. Behind the brig, the salamander frigate plunged through what was left of the *Ranger's Revenge*, crumpling the crippled sloop's shattered hull into splints.

His xebec strewn with debris and the screams of the wounded and dying, the wind billowing out all three sails as the vessel surged away from the carnage behind it, Tem clung frantically to the wheel and urged the vessel onward to safety.

Chapter Nine

Martolian Queen (18)
Privateer (Converted Trade Brig)
Five Leagues northwest of the Infantosians

Do-You-Require-Assistance

Caithlin lowered her telescope from the view of the signal flags and snapped it shut before turning to her first mate.

"They're asking if we need any help," she called down from the quarterdeck to the hatch leading below. "How's all on the orlop deck?"

The salamander looked up from the hatchway.

"We're pumping out more than we're taking in, but we need to get somewhere to get this repaired properly, Captain."

Caithlin looked back across at the J'Koor'uk frigate. The salamander warship glided serenely through the gentle seas to the port of the fighting brig, perhaps a quarter of a mile away, her emerald green sails elegant in their contrast to the dark red and gold hull. Caithlin took in a breath and exhaled slowly as the wind whipped across the brig's quarterdeck, cutting through the slits in her long sleeves to provide some respite from the heat.

That one close-in broadside from the pirate xebec had caught them on the roll, causing damage below the waterline. Dreadful luck. And to make things worse, the xebec had escaped. Still, two sloops and a schooner full of pirates at the bottom of the Infant Sea, that was a good day's work even if the *Martian Queen* and the *Deliverer's Flame* had stumbled upon them entirely by chance. It was typical. A good number of her cruises had been fruitless, but now while looking for an Ahmunite bone fleet, *now* she encountered four pirate vessels.

Three pirate vessels sunk would, by the terms of her commission, result in a financial reward. That was, perhaps, secondary to the more altruistic achievement of ridding the world of murderous scum, which was now – with some experience beneath her belt – beginning to give Caithlin a sense of achievement and purpose. She had managed to sketch the details of each of the pirate ship's flags so that their captains could be identified back in port. None of them leapt out to her as famous. She had not managed to sink any of the big names like Dunn, Denayo, or Taithe.

But the primary task needed to proceed, even without the

Martian Queen and her role within it. They would put in for repairs and resume their part as soon as they could. At least the wind was favorable for Dennoras's Cay. Caithlin turned to Jonjak, her newly promoted second mate.

"Signal the *Deliver's Flame*. No assistance required. Diverting ashore for repairs. Recommend they continue on task."

"Aye, Captain," the former merchant sailor-turned privateer replied before turning to the pennant locker to begin assembling the message.

Heavy footsteps announced X'And's appearance on the quarterdeck. He walked over to Caithlin and offered an uneasy smile.

"Those bastards hit us good and proper," he winced.

"Not as good as we hit them," Caithlin replied without humor.

"Still, we can't afford to stop on the pumps, even for a minute. She'll hold, though. Still heading for the settlement at Dennoras's Cay?"

Caithlin nodded.

"That's right. That's our closest port for repairs, even if it'll barely hold two sloops."

The corners of X'And's razor-toothed maw turned down.

"That takes us right past the Infantosian Islands. And Red Skull."

"Yes. It does."

"And with that xebec outpacing us, those scum will get ashore and tell all their mates about the privateer bastards on the Genezan fighting brig who killed all of their friends."

Caithlin tapped her telescope pensively.

"Yes. I'd imagine that they will. But that's the best option we have."

***

Jaymes's head shot up from staring down at the chart table as soon as he heard the drums rapidly beaten. Jumping up from his chair, he pulled on his jacket and grabbed his sword and scabbard as hurried footsteps thumped along the decks above him and outside the great cabin. Tying his neckerchief on as he paced quickly to the steps leading up to the quarterdeck, he heard the shouts of orders above as the frigate closed up for battle. The late afternoon sun was low in the cloudless sky as he reached the upper deck.

On the quarterdeck, Jaymes found the officer of the watch – Benn Orellio – stood with the sailing master at the foot of the mizzenmast.

"What's on?" Jaymes asked as he approached.

"I've called for beat to quarters, sir," Benn replied, his tone almost apologetic, "there's a sail to the south, slipping in and out of a bank of mist. Square-rigged, two masts. Frigate built. Very low in her lines, not like one of ours."

Jaymes accepted his third lieutenant's telescope and brought it up to his eye. Sure enough, there was a thin, shallow bank of mist starting perhaps two miles to the south atop the calm, warm sea. Very rare for this time of day in these temperatures. He scanned the telescope across the horizon but saw nothing. Karnon Senne made his way up onto the quarterdeck to join the other officers, followed by Mayhew Knox. Jaymes lowered his telescope.

"Nothing yet," he muttered to himself.

"I definitely saw it, sir," Benn swallowed, "I'm certain. Mister Estrayia saw it, too."

"Aye, sir, there's something out there alright," the sailing master agreed.

Jaymes glanced up at the yards above and the barely visible lanes cut into the sea around them by the wind. Beam on – if there was something out there, neither frigate would have an advantage.

"There, sir," Danne Estrayia pointed back into the mist.

Jaymes raised the telescope again.

There she was. Long, low hull rising up into an aggressively pointed prow, with two squat series of square-rigged sails. An ancient design, but an efficient one. It was an Ahmunite frigate, a Khopeshii. The enemy frigate was altering to starboard to come about toward *Pious*.

"Good job, Benn," Jaymes smiled, "now get to your position. I have conduct. Mister Estrayia, reef the mains for battle and get me the weather gauge. Captain Senne, sharpshooters in the fighting tops and the rest of your lads ready for boarding. Mayhew, stay with me and try not to balls this up for everybody."

Jaymes's direction was relayed rapidly through the chain of command as orders were shouted up to the top men on the yards of the three masts and across to the gunners and marines on the upper deck and fo'c'sle. *Pious* came across to port, slowing a little as the wind came forward of her beam and her sails were taken in. Mayhew looked up at the sails, across at the approaching Khopeshii, and then at his captain.

"Sir, should we..."

"Patience, patience," Jaymes said quietly, "let the bastards come to us. We're in no rush."

The two frigates drew closer, the unnatural bank of mist following the Ahmunite vessel from the south. The air grew chill, and the sky just a little darker. Off the enemy vessel's starboard bow, Jaymes saw another small sail and raised his telescope. A far smaller vessel, single-masted and with banks of oars protruding from its hull, sailed alongside the Khopeshii.

"She has an escort," he announced to his command team on the bridge. "Small, looks like an old coastal galley of some sort. I doubt she'll hit hard, but we need to keep an eye on her."

"Aye, sir," Mayhew replied.

Jaymes shut his telescope and gritted his teeth. An Elohi frigate against a Khopeshii was a close run fight, according to the information he had read about the capabilities of the enemy warship – the Khopeshii having the edge in speed whilst the Elohi hit harder with its greater firepower. That balance was skewed as soon as the Elohi was the bigger, harder hitting Batch Two, like *Pious*. But a second vessel, even one so small as the galley ahead, was another factor in the balance.

Up ahead, the Khopeshii turned to port, abandoning the two frigates' head to head charge early for a more favorable wind and to bring its broadside to bear. The small galley followed closely, not far from the much larger warship's starboard quarter.

"Line up the bow chasers," Jaymes ordered Danne. "Let's give them a shot as soon as we're in range."

"Helm!" Danne shouted. "Two points to starboard! And... thus!"

"Fo'c'sle!" Mayhew yelled up forward. "Bow chasers! Target enemy frigate! Stand by to open fire!"

Benn Orellio was already positioned up on the fo'c'sle to take charge of the bow chasers and the forward guns on the broadsides. The new third lieutenant looked back across the length of the ship to the command team on the quarterdeck.

"On your command, Lieutenant Orellio!" Jaymes shouted.

The young officer saluted to acknowledge the command, an overly formal gesture in Jaymes's eyes. He turned to his gunners.

"Surprised they didn't have a go at us with their own bow chasers, sir," Danne remarked to his captain.

"I think they want to keep their distance from us," Jaymes replied. "They want to keep the initiative with their speed, and they don't want to be within range of our close-in guns. But with this wind, unless they intend to point their stern at our bow guns, they're in for a disappointing afternoon."

Up on the fo'c'sle, just aft of the giant, gold painted figurehead of an Elohi from the heavens above, Benn gave the order.

"Target front! Bow chasers, fire!"

The light nine-pounder guns barked out and jumped back on their carriages, propelling the dark smears of round shot across the sky. Two pillars of water erupted half a ship's length short of the Khopeshii. The bow chaser gun captains were already screaming at their crews to reload and change the elevation of the guns on their quoins. Even from this range, Jaymes heard the snaps of return fire. The gargantuan crossbows shot their own deadly projectiles from the Khopeshii's flanks.

They propelled heavy bolts the length of a ship's longboat, each tipped with a glowing blue point.

"Down!"

Along the upper deck of the Elohi frigate, nearly two hundred sailors and marines dived down to take cover from the impact of the enemy shot, only seconds away. Thunks sounded in the water to the stern of the Basilean frigate, and Jaymes allowed himself an exhalation of relief as he clambered back up to his feet.

"Are we turning to exchange broadsides, sir?" Mayhew asked.

"No," Jaymes shook his head, "we'll weather any shit they can throw at us until we're closer. If we're going broadside to broadside, then it'll be within range of all of our guns, not just some of them."

Near the prow, Benn shouted out an order to fire again. The bow chasers banged off their shots, leaving small plumes of smoke to drift back across the upper deck and quarterdeck of the frigate. A second later, a dull thump sounded from the south, and *Pious's* crew let out a roar of celebration. Jaymes looked across at Karnon and shook his head grimly. Fine – let them have that moment – but hitting a frigate with two nine-pound cannonballs would barely dent her.

"Keep on, right at the bastards!" Jaymes shouted above the din to his helmsman and sailing master. "Right into their damn flank! Get us alongside them!"

The Basilean frigate surged forth through the calm waters, closing the gap as she approached the light wooden hull of the Khopeshii. It was close enough now for Jaymes to make out movement on the upper deck of the enemy vessel as figures scuttled about the line of deadly, arcane-charged crossbows. Stood higher up on the isolated quarterdeck was a single, dark figure. The small galley continued to loyally follow the Khopeshii, and behind them both rolled the mist, twisting and twirling in wispy tendrils that seemed to form skulls and ghostly claws above the water. For a second time, the crossbows lining the Khopeshii twanged and thunked into life as they spat out their deadly bolts.

"Down!"

Jaymes felt the heat of one of the bolts as it shot over the top of the quarterdeck at head height. *Pious* shuddered from an impact up forward, and Jaymes heard the shouts of wounded both above in the rigging and somewhere amidships. He jumped back up to his feet to survey the damage. A ragged hole was torn through the mizzen topsail while a second bolt had plunged through the taffrail of the upper deck, killing two sailors before digging into the oak planks near the main mast. With well-drilled discipline, a quartet of sailors had already sprinted off to recover fire buckets filled with sand to extinguish the arcane fires on the projectile's glowing tip.

"Bring her round, now!" Jaymes ordered. "Alongside! Get us alongside!"

"Hard a' starboard!" Danne yelled. "Four points! Lively, now!"

The Basilean frigate lurched out of the turn, her deck slanting beneath Jaymes's feet as she swung about to bring her own guns to bear. From the quarterdeck through the upper deck and to the fo'c's'le, each gun was run out, loaded and ready, with eight sailors each to crew them. Pious turned tightly, past a parallel course and pointing slightly away from the Khopeshii, to line up all of the guns.

"Port guns! Fire!" Jaymes shouted.

"Fire!" The order was repeated from the three lieutenants at their respective positions.

The familiar, somehow comforting cacophony of Pious's full broadside blasted out as one, enveloping the upper deck with white-gray smoke. Jaymes dashed to the far side of the quarterdeck, leaning out through the smoke to see the extent of the damage. The combined assault of the heavy eighteen-pounders, the lighter nine-pounders, and the utterly murderous thirty-two-pound close-in guns smashed into the Khopeshii. Jaymes watched in wide-eyed amazement as holes were momentarily blown straight through the wooden flank of the vessel, propelling fire out of them spectacularly. Almost instantly, the fire was sucked back in and disappeared before the debris blown into the air around the wounded Ahmunite warship paused in mid-flight, then flew back to quickly and neatly reassemble the wooden side of the ship.

Then, just as remarkably, the small Ahmunite galley exploded into a sea of debris, spitting out wooden planks and splints in every direction before slipping beneath the waves.

"What dark sorcerers is this?" Danne exclaimed.

It did not matter. Whatever necromantic energies linked the sacrificial galley to the fast Khopeshii were now severed and gone, alone with the sinking ship. The enemy frigate had played the trick up its sleeve. It was a fair fight now.

"Keep us opening a little to starboard!" Jaymes called through the smoke to Danne. "Don't get too close or the bastard will turn across our bows!"

Across the upper deck, Pious's sailors rapidly worked through their drills to reload their cannons – loading in the powder charges, ramming home, then the wads, and finally the round shot cannonballs. There was a shout from midships as Kaeso Innes spotted a gunner carrying out the drill incorrectly, and he stepped in to intervene. Jaymes took in a breath. That had been his job only weeks before – second lieutenant, taking charge of the upper deck guns in battle. Now, after filling dead men's shoes twice in as many months, he stood on the quarterdeck with final responsibility for any failure resting solely on his shoulders.

"They're still edging ahead, sir!" Mayhew warned. "They're trying to get across our bows!"

Jaymes looked across at the enemy frigate, now so close that he could see the captain on the quarterdeck – nothing more than a thin figure shrouded in shredded folds of black, whipped out in the wind. He momentarily considered allowing the Khopeshii across in front, give them the bow rake and so *Pious* could then tack through the wind to position behind and rake their stern – a far deadlier maneuver. But that would give the Ahmunites a definite shot while his was based in part on skill and luck. No, far better to play the patient game. Play cautiously. Stay side by side and win in the stronger ship with more guns.

"Keep station!" Jaymes shouted to his sailing master. "Turn with them! Don't let them get ahead!"

"Aye, sir!" Danne shouted above the din of orders from the gun crews.

Jaymes looked up and saw every gun captain now standing ready with a raised hand. He felt a swell of pride in his heart as he realized just how much more quickly his gunners had reloaded than their counterparts on the Khopeshii. He had the better ship and the better crew. He would get a second broadside in before the undead had even finished reloading.

"Port guns! Fire!" Jaymes shouted.

"Fire!" The order was relayed by his three lieutenants.

Pious heaved and rolled with the recoil of the combined broadside of seventeen guns, spewing out their deadly projectiles into the side of the enemy ship.

***

Another deafening blast rocked the ship as the broadside cannons fired again. The lighter guns fired bar shot up into the rigging of the Ahuminte frigate; the heavy cannons blasted round shot into the battered hull; while the deadly, close-in guns spat another salvo of grapeshot across the deck. Karnon leaned across the taffrail in between two of the heavy cannons on the upper deck, peering through the smoke to stare across the short gap at the enemy vessel. Holes were punctured in the light wood of the hull; bones of felled undead crew were scattered across the deck; and, perhaps most notably, the yard of the foremast tipped over to one side with a screech of splintering wood and then hung at an angle, the sail dangling below now flapping uncontrolled and unrestrained in the wind.

Below Karnon, a ragged line of enormous crossbow bolts protruded from the hull of the *Pious*, some having managed to force their way through the thick layers of reinforced wood to plunge inside the gun deck. Smoke still wafted up from a puncture just abaft midships where a fire had briefly broken out but had been rapidly contained and extinguished by the veteran crew. Regardless, a still steady stream of screaming, bleeding casualties were being hauled down to the ship's tiny, makeshift surgery by Karnon's marines.

Shouts were issued through the acrid smoke and baking heat, ordering gun crews to rapidly reload and prepare for another devastating salvo against the Ahmunite warship. An instant later, a series of deep, thudding twangs announced another wave of return shots from the Khopeshii as huge bolts shot across the short gap between the two ships and smashed into the Elohi frigate again. The deck heaved and rolled, knocking Karnon down to one knee. He looked up and saw a bolt crash across the quarterdeck, sending up a shower of twirling wooden splints the size of limbs. Leaping up to his feet, Karnon barged his way through the busy deck and across to the steps leading up to the quarterdeck.

Two wounded sailors screamed out for help from behind one of the quarterdeck guns. Mayhew Knox, the first lieutenant, lay at the foot of the mizzenmast, his head in a pool of blood and his eyes drifting in and out of focus as he raised one shaking hand to a wound above his ear. Karnon only recognised Danne Estrayia, the sailing master, from his coat. His head was gone. Jaymes was crouched on one knee, teeth gritted, face pale, and a hand pressed against a bloody wound below his ribs.

"Francis!" Jaymes called for one of his midshipmen. "Get the first lieutenant to the surgeon! Quickly, now!"

Karnon rushed across to help his friend back up to his feet.

"Sir!" Karnon shouted to Jaymes. "You need to get down below yourself! Get to the surgeon!"

Jaymes shook his head.

"The sailing master is dead and the first lieutenant is incapacitated. I'm needed here to command the ship."

Karnon looked down at Jaymes's wound. He had seen soldiers drop dead from less but carry on fighting with worse.

"Jaymes!" he urged. "Get me alongside those bastards! Get lines across so we can board! Me and my lads will finish this!"

Pious's guns blasted out again, and a cheer erupted from the upper deck in response, no doubt, to some visible damage caused on the Khopeshii.

"No need to risk that," Jaymes coughed, "we've got 'em. They haven't got long left... can't take much more."

"We don't need to lose more men! Their upper deck is carnage! Get me across with my lads! We'll lose less in a boarding action than we will sat here, trading broadsides!"

Jaymes swallowed, coughed again, and nodded. He limped over to the quarterdeck's forward taffrail.

"Helm! Quarter turn to port! Get us alongside! All hands, prepare for boarding!"

"Prepare boarding lines!" Kaeso shouted from the deck below. "Break out pikes, hatchets, and pistols!"

Karnon flashed an encouraging smile to his wounded friend, slapped a hand against his shoulder, and hurtled back down the steps to the upper deck.

"Marines," Karnon bellowed, "form up! Two ranks! Sergeants, take charge!"

Red-jacketed fighting men dashed out from a multitude of duties – casualty handlers, assisting the gunners, moving powder and shot: all marines ceased their secondary duties and formed up into two squads, each two ranks deep with their sergeants at the fore. Boarding pikes, swords, and shields were raised and ready. Up on the fo'c'sle, the first two grapple lines were hurled across to dig into hard points on the enemy frigate's deck as the two fighting ships drew closer.

Muskets cracked from the fighting tops above as sharpshooters targeted undead sailors on the Khopeshii's upper deck and quarterdeck. In return, arrows shot across from the Ahmunite ship to clang into the marines' shield wall and slay two Basilean sailors on the fo'c'sle. *Pious's* bows nudged against the Ahmunite frigate as the lines connecting them were drawn in and secured.

"*Pious* ship's company!" Jaymes yelled, drawing his saber. "On me!"

Karnon swore out loud, noting his friend's bloodied shirt and weary eyes. The idiot would kill himself. Savage cries sounded across *Pious's* deck as the securing lines were drawn taught and the two warships bumped alongside each other.

"Marines!" Karnon yelled, holding his boarding pike aloft. "Attack!"

Jaymes was the first across, leading a rabble of frenzied, disorderly sailors charging onto the enemy vessel's quarterdeck in a ripple of pistol shots and clanging of blades. Orderly, disciplined, and moving as teams, Karnon stepped across and onto the ancient boneship as his two sergeants led their squads behind him, moving quickly forward to set up shield walls with pikes held at the ready. With an ungodly chorus of low, rasping moans, the marines were met by a wave of some fifty skeletal sailors clad in blue and bronze, curved swords held high above fleshless, rictus skulls.

The first semi-ordered line of skeletal sailors crashed into the marine shield wall, hacking and stabbing down with their ancient, pitted blades. Karnon stepped into the attack to puncture the forehead of the first skeletal warrior with his pike and then bat a second to one side with his shield, where the undead warrior was beaten down to the deck and stabbed by his marines. At the right edge of the formation of marines, the skeletal sailors enveloped the shield wall, spilling around the edge of the squad quicker than they could turn to defend. Two marines were cut down before Sergeant Porphio screamed orders to bring the rear rank across to counter, launching violently into the skeletons to overwhelm them.

Karnon slew another skeleton and then looked up to the quarterdeck to see Jaymes and a small number of sailors locked in a bloody melee with a black-robed figure and half a dozen more ornately armored skeletons. With a roar, he barged his way through two of the undead sailors, leading his marines to the steps up to the quarterdeck. Only a few paces ahead, one hand still clamped against the wound on his side, he saw Jaymes locked in a fast paced duel of blades with the dark-robed figure. His feet thumping along the ancient plank steps that led up the gold-plated, ornate quarterdeck, Karnon reached the summit and sprinted over to his friend's side.

The Ahmunite captain raised his long, curved sword, eyes of unholy energy glowing from beneath the dark hood. Jaymes stood ready to counter, but Karnon was quicker. With a guttural roar, the marine captain barged his shield into the Ahmunite commander to knock him back away from the wounded Basilean frigate captain, opening a gap in his guard which he wasted no time in exploiting. Karnon skewered the robed figure with a pike thrust through the ribs. He wrenched the weapon clear and lashed his heavy, angular shield into the ancient warship captain's skull.

The revenant captain dropped to his knees, dark energy swirling up into the hot air from the deep wound punched through his torso. A dry gasp hissed from within the folds of the hood. Karnon thrust the steel tip of the boarding pike through the Ahmunite captain's face, withdrew it, and then kicked the robed figure to the deck. The dark robes fell gently down, and bones scattered across the ancient planks. Karnon turned quickly to Jaymes.

"Get to the surgeon!" he growled. "I can lead a boarding action, but I can't drive a boat if you drop dead!"

Nodding weakly, Jaymes acquiesced and accepted the arm of one of his petty officers who led him back toward the Basilean frigate. Content that the quarterdeck was secure, Karnon rushed back down to the upper deck to join his marines. The red-coated Basileans had already turned to advance up the long, slanted fo'c'sle to sweep the final remnants of the undead crew off the top of their own ship. Behind Karnon, a dark doorway led into the temple-like structure that formed the angular after end of the Ahmunite warship. That dark door seemed to almost twist and turn as Karnon stared at it, hisses and moans echoing from within the blackness to warn him against venturing inside.

The armored marines stopped, murmurs of apprehension breaking out through their ranks as they hesitantly faced the entrance leading inside the boneship. Karnon turned to his soldiers.

"Come on, you bloody milksops!" Karnon spat. "I've heard scarier shit at a sodding country fair!"

Ignoring the otherworldly moans echoing within the ancient ship, Karnon hefted up his boarding pike and led his marines inside.

***

A small crowd, perhaps a hundred pirates and settlers of various professions, had gathered along the jetty and sandy beach by the time Cerri arrived. Even in the calm, evening waters and with only the gentlest of onshore breezes, Cerri could make out that the xebec was listing. The vessel he had loaned to Tem crept closer to the shore, navigating the treacherous lane in the seabed below. The *Desert Rose* picked its way through small wrecks of other vessels that had failed to negotiate the lane, drawing closer to the independent pirate settlement of Red Skull. Muttering and grumbling broke out amongst the assembled crowd as the xebec drew level with a barque at the far end of the first jetty, and the extent of the damage along the length of the ship became clearer.

"Out of the way!" Cerri snapped, forcing his way through the crowd and up onto the jetty.

Pirates, carpenters, tavern workers, and merchants parted to allow the pirate chief through to the front of the jetty. Cerri shook his head, felt inside his black coat to make sure he did have a pistol, and, as he saw the holed hull and blood-stained ravaged deck of his ship, decided that he would kill Tem Mosso.

Two sailors jumped off the deck and onto the jetty with lines to secure to bollards as the ship nudged home with a slight bump. No sooner was the ship partially secured when wounded sailors, their limbs and heads wrapped in blood-stained bandages, began stepping down from the upper deck and onto the jetty. Cerri knew over half of them well enough, but he stopped to look twice when he saw Wez Polleri of the *Ranger's Revenge* in the gaggle of wounded pirates.

"Wez!" he called, striding over to the bloodied buccaneers. "Wez! What happened? Where's the *Ranger's Revenge*?"

The younger captain turned wearily to face the tall pirate chief.

"Gone," he shook his head, "she's gone. So is the *Blue Rise*. Yordan, Jhanzee, they're both dead. Gone. We lost three ships."

His eyes narrowed and fists clenched, Cerri bit back on his first response. He turned away from the battered ship disgorging its bloody half-crew and looked up at the crowd on the jetty and the beach.

"Go!" he growled. "Piss off!"

Those who knew him well did not need a second warning and quickly turned to walk away. Some half of the crowd stared mutely at the scene unfolding around the xebec. Cerri drew his pistol and fired it into the air. The rest of the crowd, and the wounded pirates from the *Desert Rose*, dispersed quickly and headed up to the shipwreck-shanty town looming above the beach. Cerri turned back to Wez.

"Who did this?"

Wez's head sank.

"It was a trap, Cerri. We should have seen it. A brig, maybe four hundred tons. She drew us into a confined waterway in the Lesser Yellow Rocks. As we drew close, she flew her true colors. A pirate hunter, Basilean. Eighteen guns. And she was the small one. There was a J'Koor'uk in the mist behind us, moved in to seal us in. A frigate and a fighting brig, Cerri. We didn't stand a chance."

A sliver, just a hint, of sympathy replaced Cerri's seething anger as the story unfolded. Yes, they did not stand a chance. But they should not have fallen for such an obvious ploy in the first place.

"How did you survive?" Cerri demanded.

"Clung to wreckage. The J'Koor'uk sliced straight through my sloop. Eight of us survived. Tem came back after dark to find us."

As if summoned, Tem Mosso stepped down from his ship and onto the jetty. He looked up at Cerri, any attempt to hide his fear having well and truly failed.

"I can pay for the damage, Cerri," he said quietly, "the hold's full of plunder. I can pay for this, and then some."

Cerri took in a slow, deep breath and nodded. He turned away for a few moments, working through his options and their potential consequences before facing his two subordinate captains again.

"This brig. Was she Genezan? 'Bout four hundred tons, merchant built?"

Tem swallowed and nodded slowly.

"Aye."

Cerri swung a clenched fist into Tem's jaw, connecting with a crack and knocking the younger man down onto the wooden planks of the jetty. Wez instantly stepped across to stand protectively over his fallen comrade. The dozen or so sailors still securing the xebec awkwardly continued with their duties in silence. Cerri flung the folds of his coat to one side, wrapped a hand around the handle of his cutlass and stared down at Wez.

"What? What are you gonna do, shipmate? You're gonna fight

me? Huh? Come on, you bloody coward, go for your blade!"

Wez held his hands out passively to either side, his eyes fearfully locked on Cerri's.

"Come on, Cerri! There was nothing we could have done! We..."

"That ship was the *Martolian Queen*, you pair of damned fools! Gods above! Hector warned you about it! I warned you about it! There's three of our captains, rotting in cages on the rocks outside Thatraskos, who were put there by that damned ship! How were you stupid enough to fall for the same bloody ploy that dragged the others in?! This is not a new and clever trap!"

Tem slowly clambered to his feet, one hand raised to his bleeding lower lip. Wez lowered his arms. Cerri spat out a curse and pointed a finger of accusation at Tem.

"Get this ship repaired, Tem. I hope to the Ones above that you've got enough plunder in that hold to cover the costs, because if you don't, I'll sell you into slavery to the Abyssal Dwarfs myself! Repair my ship and give it back to me as I leant it to you, then get back in your damned sloop and get out there again. You've got a long road ahead of you to make this up to me."

Cerri turned on his heel and stormed back toward the Final Grapeshot to order a drink.

***

Caithlin's bare feet hit the decking, the warm water reaching past her knees. The contents of a few burst crates floated past her in the darkened confines of the hold – food stuffs and empty bags of gunpowder. In the shadows forward of the ladder, she could make out four of her crew members crouching in the flood water, desperately trying to affect an emergency repair against one of the ragged holes beneath the brig's waterline.

"The pumps have had it, Cap'n," winced Oswalt, one of the two dwarfs in her crew who looked almost comical next to her with water up to his chest. "I reckon I might be able to repair 'em, but not without a new chain."

Caithlin felt a twist in her stomach. As a veteran of the sea with over a decade of experience, she was prepared for most eventualities, but she knew well enough that taking on water without a working pump meant disaster.

"How long left?" she asked quietly.

"We're trying to get something... anything over that hole," Oswalt shook his head, "but we've already been trying..."

"How long?" Caithlin repeated.

"Hours. A few hours."

Caithlin nodded. She placed a hand on the thick wooden sparring of the hold and patted the ship affectionately. Of all the places to lose her father's ship... she knew full well where they were on the chart. She would have preferred to take her chances in the water with sharks. At least that would be a quick death. And without malice.

"Do what you can," she ordered Oswalt and then turned to climb the ladder back up to the orlop deck.

X'And waited for her at the top of the ladder.

"How bad is it?" he asked quietly, eyeing four sailors just out of earshot.

"Bad," Caithlin replied. "I'll go double check the chart for our position, but we need to get the boats in the water. We need to abandon ship."

X'And gritted his sharp teeth.

"I... well... Cathy, we're less than twenty miles from Red Skull."

"Yes, the thought had occurred."

"There's absolutely no chance of anybody other than those pirates finding us."

Caithlin fished a gold coin out of her pocket. It was the last coin Jaymes had kept for them the night they met, the night he had been sent to convince her to become a privateer and instead had tried to do the honest thing and convince her of exactly the opposite. What she would have given to trade in her predicament, her demise, to magically transport herself to that evening in the plush, expensive sailing club bar where she thought her world was over, but in actual fact, it was one of the most fortuitous nights of her life. What she would have given...

"Captain?" the grizzled voice said a second time.

Caithlin looked up.

"Not now, man!" X'And growled at the white-haired sailor.

"Beggin' your pardon, ma'am," the old mariner tipped a hand to his forehead as if trying to replicate a naval salute, "but it's important."

Caithlin looked down at the sailor. He was new to the ship, having only signed on for this voyage. Shorter than average, thin, with white hair and gray stubble, dressed in patched clothes, and with tattoos extending up both wiry forearms.

"What is it?" Caithlin demanded.

"Could we talk, Captain? In private, like? In your cabin?"

Caithlin lowered her brow.

"My ship is sinking. There's a fair chance that we'll all be dead in hours. And you think I'll trust a complete stranger to take me to an isolated part of the ship when death is at our door?"

The old sailor's face fell.

"N...no. It's nothing like that, Captain, I swear! Look... bring a pistol, anything. I just... if you hear me out, I think I've got a fix for our problem."

"I'll take a pistol," Caithlin replied, "and a salamander who's twice your size. Just in case. Come on."

The trio of sailors clambered up to the upper deck and then moved back aft to Caithlin's cabin. Satisfied that X'And could protect her from any ill-intent from the strange sailor, Caithlin did not bother following up on her threat of arming herself.

"Well?" she asked as she pulled her stockings and boots back on. "What is this? Mister..?"

"Tomaz, Captain. Ebeener Tomaz."

Ebeener dashed over to the chart table and pointed a thick finger at their location.

"We're here. I know these waters, better than anybody on this ship, I'm sure. I've seen the damage myself. I was one of Oswalt's damage party. I... I know Red Skull, Captain. Very well. I can get us beached, and we can repair the ship once the tide is out."

Caithlin leaned forward and planted her fists on the chart table. X'And folded his powerful arms across his scaly, barrel chest.

"How do you know Red Skull, Mister Tomaz?"

The old sailor's shoulders slumped and he let out a sigh, looking down at the decking beneath his bare feet.

"For exactly the reason you're thinkin', Captain."

Caithlin nodded, her teeth gritted.

"Which leads onto the most obvious of all questions in this line of interrogation. In what world would I trust a pirate?"

Ebeener's head shot up, and he met her stare definitely.

"Ex-pirate, Captain. Ex-pirate! I know these waters! We've got two choices – we either take to the boats and they'll find us, and as soon as they recognize me, they'll cut me open and draw out my guts! But our second choice? We beach the ship. We repair her. It's just a pump. We beach, get some planks across the hole properly, and send somebody ashore to trade. Get ourselves a new pump."

Caithlin looked across at X'And, shaking her head in disbelief. She found herself surprised to see the salamander looking at the ex-pirate intently.

"Where would you run the ship ashore?" X'And demanded.

Ebeener pointed at the browned chart.

"Right there."

Caithlin let out a derisive laugh.

"Right there? In the damned pirate harbor? In plain view of the entire population of Red Skull? And under the guns of the harbor fort? That's your grand plan?"

The short pirate shook his head adamantly and grabbed a stick of charcoal from beside the chart. He quickly drew three curved lines across the harbor.

"There!" Ebeener growled. "There! Three lanes, known only to those who sail them! That's one of the secrets, and they'll kill me when they find out I've told you! After the great quake, the sands shifted. This is how you get in and out now! And here? This is the only way a medium brig can get in, and only within an hour, maybe two o' high tide. Which will be only a little before we arrive if we head there now, like... like the Shining Ones are guarding us from above! We're in *exactly* the right place *and* right time to get in and beach here! And this is the only place that's out o' line o' fire of the fort! We beach her here and we can repair her."

Caithlin looked at X'And again. Her impassive first mate raised a clawed hand to his long maw.

"Why? Why betray your comrades?"

The wiry sailor placed the charcoal down and looked up.

"Because... because when you find out one day that you've got a daughter you never knew about, and... and you think on all the things you've done... you can't undo 'em, but you can damn well try to spend what's left of your life doing the right thing. And signing up to a pirate-hunting warship to rid the seas of the scum you once sailed with? That's what I want to face my makers with on my slop chit."

"And if this doesn't work?" X'And asked. "If we get stuck there and surrounded by pirate sloops?"

Caithlin stood up and folded her arms.

"Then we go out with a bang." She shrugged nonchalantly. "What would you rather? Take to the boats and have them pick us up? Or sail right into their hellhole and, if it goes wrong, face them with eighteen guns and our dignity still intact?"

Chapter Ten

Hegemon's Warship Pious (36)
251 souls on board
East Infant Sea

His blue jacket worn through the left sleeve but only over the right shoulder due to his injury, Jaymes stood silently on the fo'c'sle and stared down at the rows of dead bodies. Twenty-seven of his sailors and marines – just under one in ten of his entire crew – lay motionless and carefully wrapped from head to toe in their own hammocks behind the solemn gaze of their guardian Elohi, the ship's silver and gold painted figurehead. Jaymes knew well enough that the casualties sustained for defeating an enemy frigate were relatively light, but he had seen enemy ships taken without losing a single life. There was always a better way, and that fell onto him.

The problem was that, with guns firing and swords clashing, there was little time to weigh up the pros and cons of different courses of action. A quick decision needed to be made, and with well over a decade at sea, Jaymes knew that the wrong decision was better than no decision at all. Still... could he have done better? If he had decided on a different course of action, could he have prevented even a single death? Prevented one single family from the news that would eventually reach them – your son or husband or father died during the course of their duties, body is buried at sea so you do not even have the relative luxury of a corpse to mourn at a funeral.

"The problem with these bastards is that they don't surrender."

Jaymes looked across from his lonely vigil over his dead shipmates. Karnon stood a few paces away, his heavy features grim.

"The undead," the marine captain continued, "they don't surrender. Well, I suppose they do in their own way, but it takes a lot more. Orcs, demons of the Abyss, they all run away eventually. But undead? You've got to drop their leaders to sever the arcane ties that keep them fighting. That's always a hell of a job. And, sadly, more often than not, it ends up in losing more good people."

Jaymes nodded slowly, a flame of pain briefly flaring up the side of his ribs from the injury he sustained from the flying splinter. Kennus, the ship's surgeon, had remedied the problem very quickly with his divinity powers. Qualified in both conventional surgery and arcane healing, Kennus was an invaluable asset onboard a warship. The wound was healed by his powers of divinity magic, but the aches and pains would remain for some time yet.

Jaymes turned to look back across the deck of his ship. The disarray and chaos of battle was already all but cleaned away, with the ship's carpenter and his mates hard at work with damage repair. Cannons were cleaned and broken lines were spliced as the crew set about their duties in near silence around the rows of their own dead, faces hidden in their hammock coffins. Still secured next to *Pious* was the Ahmunite Khopeshii warship, its crew eliminated and thrown overboard to the deep.

"You shouldn't have boarded that ship."

Jaymes rolled his eyes and turned to face Karnon again.

"No," the marine cut off his response, "no, shut up and listen. You shouldn't have boarded that ship. First off, your job is to lead the crew of this warship into battle, and that's done from the quarterdeck. Not a fist fight on an enemy ship. Second, you were wounded. Without treatment, that could have killed you. You had no idea how far that wound extended inside the body. You shouldn't be playing bloody hero."

"Oh, piss off, Karnon!" Jaymes spat. "You've read a bloody children's book on boats, and now you think you have the right to tell me how to command my own sodding warship!"

"Well, somebody has to, because in your bloody navy, the captain is a god and nobody has the balls to stand up to him! In the legion..."

"But you're not in the legion anymore!" Jaymes snapped. "You're here to support me! But supporting me doesn't extend to becoming a patronizing prick who thinks he can tell the captain of a ship how to do his job! Ones above, man! The previous captain of this ship would have had you flogged! I know you're trying to help, but use your bloody head! Of *course* I was going to join the boarding action! There was no other threat! It was one against one, a single enemy ship, we threw lines across, and we had the initiative in boarding! You think I'm going to stand at the back and watch? Look at these men, stitched into their hammocks! You think I'd stand back and watch them die from the quarterdeck?"

Karnon folded his arms across his chest, his brow low.

"Depends. Is that boneship over there worth dying for?"

Jaymes waved a hand dismissively and turned away.

"That's the job. That's the duty."

"It's not what I asked. You know full well that you joining the boarding party made no difference. I had it covered! I'm the captain of marines! This is *my* job! When you're driving your boat around and firing all your guns, I don't come charging in and demand to be a part of it!"

"That's because you've got a handful of duties," Jaymes

replied, taking the time to ensure his tone was a little calmer and less confrontational. "I'm the captain of the ship. I'm responsible for everything. All of it. There isn't a single eventuality where I can step back and say 'chaps, this isn't my part of ship.' I'm involved with all of it. No, not involved. In command and responsible for all of it. And as much as I think of you as a trusted friend who I admire greatly, when the guns start and it all goes to the fires of the Abyss, you're my subordinate, and you need to do what I bloody well tell you."

Karnon took in a deep breath and then exhaled slowly.

"I know. I know that. I'd hate to be one of those arseholes who thinks that because they're mates with the boss, they think they can be an insubordinate prick. I'm not trying to do that, and if that's what's coming across, I've phrased it wrong and I'm sorry. I'm just saying... I'm saying that when it comes to the boaty boaty stuff, I understand that I know nothing. But when it comes to the swordy swordy stuff, I do know a lot more than you, and even though you have command and I'll follow your orders to the letter, you'd do better to listen to my advice."

Jaymes pondered on the marine's words, stepped over to pat a hand against his shoulder, and nodded.

"Alright. That's more than fair. Alright, mate. I'm sorry, I'll try to do better at listening. But right now, I've got twenty-seven of our lads to bury at sea, and a prize haunted frigate to get back to Thatraskos."

Karnon flashed a smile.

"Best of luck finding a group of idiots to volunteer to sail that bastard ship home."

Jaymes saw all three of his lieutenants on the quarterdeck and made his way quickly over to them. All three men turned to face him as he approached; Mayhew's head in bandages, Kaeso still somehow grinning from ear to ear, and Benn overreaching with formality again and standing to attention.

"I'll cut to the point," Jaymes began, "one of you needs to take command of a prize crew and take that Khopeshii home. I'd do it myself, but my captain of marines has already given me a well-deserved bollocking for failing to delegate. So, which of you is game?"

"Sail a haunted ship? Balls to that. Sir," Mayhew offered.

The first lieutenant's defiant expression immediately changed to that of a chastised puppy in reaction to Jaymes's angry grimace. Before he could speak, Kaeso took a pace forward.

"I'll do it!" the short lieutenant beamed. "Even if just for the dit! First command – undead frigate! Bloody marvelous! Most officers have fairly crap stories of their first command – a sloop, or a merchant brig full of rice or something similar – but a haunted boneship! Sign me up!"

Jaymes let out a laugh.

"Thanks, Kaeso. Sincerely. Get yourself a prize crew of twenty lads. Double share in the prize money for anybody who volunteers. That includes you."

The second lieutenant's grin somehow broadened.

"Awfully charitable of you, sir! Thank you!"

Mayhew's face dropped as he looked down at the less senior lieutenant.

"Hang on! If I knew it was double prize money, I would have volunteered!"

Jaymes flashed a vicious smile of his own.

"As the old saying goes, Mister Knox, fortune favors those with valor. Or, more specifically, if you weren't such a bloody coward, you'd be getting paid as much as Kaeso. Right. Funeral service on the hour. Then we'll head for home."

***

The Green Band sat along the banks of the River Jahees, an area of fertile farmland and lush vegetation that seemed out of place amidst the surrounding barrens of the desert. The town of Mastfra that sat in the center of the Green Band was made up of clay houses, ranging in size from little more than huts and hovels to grand, luxurious compounds. The river itself wound on up to the capital to the northeast, populated by the masts of a handful of trading ships; a main trade route for merchant caravans ran alongside that eventually reached the shores of the High Sea of Barri. It was at the capital that T'mork's future lay, once these last few weeks of trials and tests were complete. His success was assured. At least, that is what his brothers told him. Deep down, hidden behind the veneer of confidence and purpose, T'mork felt anything but guarantees regarding the trials ahead of him.

"You'll still be back here," F'Arza smiled, "from time to time, at least."

From atop the balcony of the temple, sweltering in the midday heat, T'mork looked across at his oldest brother. High priest of his own temple on the outskirts of Ul'Astia, he was already the picture of success by the age of thirty.

"You look worried," F'Arza continued, "so I assume it is concerning your move to the capital. Mother and father will manage without you! And you will be back."

T'mork offered a thin smile. Of course his affluent mother and father would be fine, with their rich compound and acres of farmland. But far better that F'Arza believed that was his concern than the truth of the matter. Self-doubt was the subject of scorn within the ranks of the priesthood. If one doubted oneself, where was the faith and resilience to serve Shobik?

The high priest walked slowly over and rested a hand on his youngest brother's shoulder. The two looked down from the temple at the town square below, where a procession of perhaps thirty slaves were marched off to market. Tall, strong men – Ophidian soldiers who surrendered on the battlefield. Having seen enough of the life of an Ophidian slave, T'mork wondered briefly if the men stumbling in the heat below would have done better to die in battle.

"The fortunate ones will be sacrificed," F'Arza said.

T'mork looked up.

"Fortunate?"

"Yes, fortunate! Have they taught you nothing at the college? Little brother, people fear death too much! Outsiders, foreigners, they look on us with contempt because they fear Shobik. Yes, Shobik should be respected and sometimes feared, but also loved! Death, and the God of Death, are not subjects of fear!"

T'mork looked up at the older man and winced.

"But…but we have no idea what is on the other side of the veil…"

"But we have our faith!" F'Arza smiled warmly, his hands spreading to either side as if embracing the world. "And we have The Writings! Guidance! We know that what we do is just and right. It is what separates us from the accursed refugees off to the north. Even after a life of wrongdoing, of straying from the path, of misusing the powers of necromancy, a man can ascend if he is sacrificed to Shobik. By ending their lives in ritual and worship, we offer forgiveness and another chance beyond the veil. We offer mercy."

Those wise, optimistic words gave T'mork a feign glow of warmth within. That gift of uplifting oration was just one of the many skills that had made F'Arza so successful and admired. T'mork could only hope to be half the man his beloved oldest brother had become. He looked up at him again.

"Thank you, brother," he said, simply and sincerely.

Memories from centuries past half drowned out the cries and wails from the lines of women and children on the shore. The procession of inhabitants force-marched away from the burning settlement by T'mork's skeletal spearmen were loaded onto boats at the water's edge. In turn, they would be rowed across to the anchored warships and taken back to the site of the great temple.

From his vantage point at the stern end of his great war galley, T'mork watched the lines of prisoners shoved and pulled along in the early evening darkness as he twirled one of the rings around his shriveled, lifeless fingers. A black ring, trimmed in dulled silver with a simple symbol atop – Shobik's crook. His brother, F'Arza, had given the ring to him as a gift after he passed the trials and was accepted into the ranks of the priesthood, so many centuries before. T'mork looked down at the ring in silence. F'Arza had been a good man, a better priest, and a peerless brother. He bravely but begrudgingly followed Khephren, Supreme Pharaoh of Ahmun, in that valiant march against the rebels of Ophidia so many centuries ago. F'Arza fell in battle, succumbing to the flames of a towering djinn.

T'mork was brought back to the present by the sound of a sniff behind him. He turned to see the scholar, still bound in cuffs, knelt obediently by the stern taffrail as she watched her fellow mortals herded along the beach with tears in her eyes. T'mork offered something as close to a smile as his dead flesh allowed. He pitied her for her lack of understanding but did not resent her for it.

"Do not weep for them. We offer mercy. All will be well."

***

Chander, an aging sailor from the port of Erahmel, scratched away a jaunty tune on his fiddle from a darkened corner of the tavern. His left leg, amputated after it was pierced and infected by a huge splinter thrown up from a particularly lucky shot from a merchant schooner, was now replaced with a wooden peg. Cerri had seen sailors carry on to do great things with similar injuries, but he had also seen pirates succumb to lesser wounds, so he did not hold anything against Chander for being content to wile away his sunset years in a tavern, drunk, playing a fiddle for the amusement of others.

The sky above Red Skull was bright for such a late hour, illuminated by a near full moon and a picturesque canopy of twinkling stars. Cerri cleared his throat as he looked up out of the window from his corner seat. They were overdue a storm. It was hurricane season, and very little poor weather had presented itself yet. The Final Grapeshot – Cerri's favorite tavern on the island – was relatively quiet, with only perhaps thirty patrons and workers. Cerri sat with his quartermaster and his gunner; Mari DuLane and Torg BlackEye.

Mari DuLane was destined for a life on the wrong side of the law. The orphaned daughter of a Valentican mercenary, she ran away to sea at the age of ten and was onboard a passenger ship that was attacked by pirates on only her first voyage. Just over a decade later, she was well known across the three pirate fleets of Red Skull for her brutality in battle and the freedom of her affections which she used without hesitation to get what she wanted from the men she worked with – Cerri included. Torg, the bald and tattooed sailor from the frozen north, certainly shared Mari's macabre temperament; but outside of battle, Cerri found him to be about as pensive and quiet as a Varangarian was capable of.

Cerri took another mouthful from his battered tankard and glanced across at the far end of the dimly lit bar. Tem Mosso and his Ophidian quartermaster, Halladai, were drinking small glasses of something that appeared to be fierce. Honoring their fallen friends. Ash had been a good sailor and a good fighter, Cerri was sorry to hear of his loss. Flyde he did not know as well, but again, a pirate with a decent reputation in a world where reputation was prime.

"That boy needs to toughen up," Mari remarked as she leant back in her chair, her green eyes narrowed. "This isn't the game to get attached to people."

"Aye," Torg grunted, finishing his wooden tankard of ale.

Cerri remained silent. Yes, Tem was too altruistic for this life and, given the loss of the three ships recently, also perhaps too naive. But he had not been the senior captain – the fault lay with Wez there – and Tem had the backbone to turn back to rescue the crew of a rival ship. That was why Cerri had not shot him on the spot.

"He's a fool, sure enough," Cerri agreed, "but he is loyal. Loyalty matters. You two would do well to remember that."

Mari's face lit up with an amused grin as she shook her head in contempt at the comment. Torg flashed a warning glare at Cerri but quickly backed down when it was reciprocated. Cerri finished his drink and looked across to the bar, attracting the attention of Siaren, one of the tavern workers. Siaren was one of Cerri's go-to girls when the mood took him, but as soon as Mari DuLane entered a tavern, the working girls kept their distance. Siaren nodded an acknowledgement and set about pouring a fresh mug of ale for Cerri.

The door burst open and Jonty, one of Cerri's crew, looked across the dim room and then sprinted over to Cerri and his two officers breathlessly.

"Captain!" he gasped. "There's a brig coming in! A fighting brig! She's already past the cay!"

Cerri sat up and folded his arms.

"Run that one by me again, shippers?"

"A brig, flying Genezan merchant colors!" Jonty pointed to the bay. "A merchant flag, but she's got a deck full of guns, like a fighting ship!"

Cerri stood and barged his way past the gangly pirate, the heels of his expensive boots thudding on the dry wooden planks as he paced over to the tavern's door. He stepped out into the humid night and walked across the verandah. Half a dozen other pirates were already following him out until he turned to face them.

"Back inside!"

Cerri turned again and looked out across the bay. His eyes widened. The brig was a decent size, some four hundred tons, but sitting low in the water. He watched incredulously as the brig effortlessly navigated the western lane as if possessing years of experience of operating from Red Skull, then gently ran herself aground on Dodger's Bank – out of the line of fire of Red Skull's defensive fort but with her guns lined up on the town. Almost immediately, she began lowering two boats into the water. The boats filled up with sailors – perhaps eighty men between the two – and began rowing toward the jetty.

Cerri walked back into the tavern. This was a problem. Andars Taithe was already out on a cruise with four of his ships, and Hector Dunn had passed out from drinking an hour ago. This was all on Cerri as the sole chief, sober and alert, at Red Skull. Tem Mosso intercepted him only two paces into the tavern.

"Is it true?" he demanded. "That Genezan brig is here? Now?"

Cerri flashed him with a warning glare.

"Get out of here, Tem. Go. Halladai, too."

"Those bastards killed Ash and Flyde!"

Cerri leaned in and stared at the younger captain.

"I told you to go. Last chance, Tem."

Trusting in Tem's common sense to follow simple instructions, Cerri walked past him and back to his table.

"Torg – wake up every man-jack who can wield a cutlass. Every last one. Get them ready. There's eighty privateers rowing to our jetty, right now."

Torg stood, grabbed his hatchet, and walked quickly out of the tavern.

"Eighty?" Mari asked. "What in the Abyss is going on? That's not enough to assault this place! Are they suicidal?"

"Perhaps," Cerri said, "but they've just driven a four hundred ton ship through our lanes and beached it perfectly at Dodger's Bank. They know more than they should. So they also probably know that we've got a lot of ships out right now, there aren't many of us here at Red Skull, and those who are will take time to assemble. So let's just stand back and see what they're up to."

In only a few minutes, the two boats were tied up at the jetty, and the small crowd of eighty sailors walked as one toward the main settlement. Cerri watched out of the window as the crowd made its way up the shallow hill and along the main lane, directly toward the Final Grapeshot. Several smaller groups broke away, and by the time the crowd reached the path leading to the tavern, Cerri reckoned that it was half the size. Some twenty sailors, gruff looking, armed men, walked up the path, across the verandah, and into the tavern. Cerri sat down, accepted his drink from Siaren, and watched the crowd of invaders trespass into his favorite drinking den. A huge, hulking mass of a salamander leaned down to squeeze through the doorway and stepped inside. Chander's fiddle stopped. The entire tavern fell silent. His reptilian breath escaping in low, threatening rasps, the salamander looked slowly around the room.

A final figure stepped into the tavern, and Cerri's eyes opened wide. A blonde woman in her mid-twenties, without a doubt the most beautiful woman Cerri had ever laid eyes on, paced boldly across the silent room, a blue jacket with ostentatious gold epaulets worn over a white, silk shirt. She slid a handful of golden coins across the bar.

"Tot of rum for each of my men," she ordered curtly, her accent unmistakably Genezan.

Polle, the tavern's owner, looked across nervously to Cerri. Cerri nodded his approval. Polle set about placing glasses across the bar. The low buzz of conversation tentatively broke out amongst the patrons again and, from the looks on every man's face, the topic of conversation was the stunning Genezan woman. From next to Cerri, Mari swore and paced across the dry boards to the older woman.

"I don't know who the hell you think you are, bitch," Mari scowled, "walking in here like you own the place, but…"

"I'm the one who has just sailed a privateer fighting brig into your harbor without so much as a shot being fired in resistance," the Genezan woman cut her off cooly. "I thought that much was obvious."

Mari rapidly drew a knife and pressed the point against the privateer's throat, leaning in with a snarling grin.

"You think you're funny? That's who you think you are? You'll be leaving this island in *pieces,* you f…"

Mari's speech was cut off as Cerri heard the familiar metal-on-metal click of a pistol cocking. The scarlet-haired quartermaster's face paled, and she took a step back away from the Genezan sailor. The blonde woman stepped with her, a pistol shoved under Mari's jaw.

"I've sailed to a lot of nations, girl," the privateer said coldly, all eyes in the bar following the altercation between the two women, "and I've encountered many cultures. In pretty much every one of them, there is a saying which equates to the same warning. Don't bring a blade to a shooting fight. Now, I'm going to share a drink with my crew without another word from you. If I hear from you again, that ceiling will be decorated with your rather lackluster, witless brains. Do you follow?"

Without a word, Mari slowly sheathed her knife and stepped back away from the Genezan privateer. Cerri planted a hand on the red-headed pirate's shoulder and signaled for her to take her seat in the corner of the tavern. Polle began pouring out the rum, and again, conversation slowly began to fill the dimly lit tavern. Both captivated by the fearlessness and beauty of the woman, and still deeply concerned by the presence of so many armed men in his town, Cerri walked across to stand by her at the bar. He flashed a charming smile to her as she glanced across.

"South dock, Pre Baro," he crooned, "I used to frequent Geneza in another life. I take it that's where you first sailed from?"

The blonde woman took her rum and inspected it with a disapproving raise of one eyebrow.

"I'm supposed to be impressed by you naming a district of my home city?"

Cerri slid across closer, into her personal space.

"You've just landed a small invasion force into my home. I'm being perfectly civil. Cordial, even. I think that should impress you."

The woman took a silent sample of the rum and raised her brow again, this time evidently impressed at its quality.

"I didn't sail in here under a flag of war, so no, I'm not impressed. Besides, we can cut the small talk. I know exactly who you are." She looked up at him.

"And I you," Cerri smirked, "Caithlin Viconti, captain of the *Martolian Queen*. Genezan trader turned Basilean privateer after losing your cargo following an attack from the orc pirate Ghurak."

Caithlin met his gaze but said nothing.

"I know people everywhere," Cerri moved closer still, "including hidden away within the port authorities at Thatraskos. We have mutual friends. So tell me, what in the seven circles of the Abyss is a girl like you doing in a place like this?"

The privateer captain met his stare fearlessly without flinching.

"Getting a drink," she smirked.

Cerri slipped an arm around her waist and leaned in. Before he knew what had happened, he was screaming out in pain as his arm was twisted behind his back with a force like iron, and his head had been slammed into the bar with a loud crack. The huge salamander leaned over him, razor teeth bared and one eye flinching insanely. The scaled monster twisted again, and Cerri screamed out as he felt the ligaments of his shoulder joint only a breath away from snapping.

"You appear to be laboring under the misapprehension that I might be enamored of you." Caithlin swilled her rum around idly in its glass. "That's really not the case. You see, I'm rather taken by handsome, clean cut, prim gentlemen with good personal hygiene and impeccable manners. I've already bagged one of those whom I'm completely committed to and you... well, you have literally none of those qualities. That whole fallacy about women being attracted to bad boys? Not me. My entire life, I've been utterly repulsed by men like you. You understand why I don't reciprocate your interest in me?"

Cerri looked up at the huge salamander as the occupants of the tavern watched in silence. The salamander lifted Cerri's head up and slammed it into the bar again.

"Answer!" the unhinged monster hissed.

"Yes!" Cerri gasped. "Yes... I understand!"

"Now you must be thinking, 'I'm the king of this place and I'll kill her, her unhinged salamander, and her entire crew for this.' Well, you would be insane not to try. The thing is, we were all as good as dead a few hours ago, so this right now is all borrowed time. Coming here, drinking your rum, watching this thing I keep around twist your arms off. If you kill us after this, we at least had a few hours of fun that we never should have had. So it's all a bonus, really. And right now? If I had a choice between drowning a few hours ago, or having one last rum and then blowing a pirate's brains out before I die, I'd call the latter something of a victory. You're still following this?"

Again, the salamander lifted Cerri's head up and slammed it down, splitting open the skin of his forehead and splattering blood across the bar.

"I follow! Call it off!" Cerri pleaded.

A peel of laughter broke out amongst Caithlin's sailors. The salamander leaned in closer, saliva dripping down his teeth and onto Cerri's face. Cerri looked around in agonized desperation at the small number of supposedly loyal pirates in the tavern. It did not matter that more fighters were being mobilized at that very moment, that he was the leader of an entire fleet, and the most dangerous man on the island. What mattered was that at that exact moment, he was outnumbered and outgunned by a dangerous band of privateers who were willing to die.

Caithlin finished her drink and placed her glass down calmly on the bar. The salamander chittered and shook excitedly, looking at her for approval.

"Call it off!" Cerri begged. "Please! Just call that thing off and you can walk away from here! As every seadog in this hole is my witness!"

Caithlin nodded to the salamander. Bile in his throat from pain and fear, Cerri collapsed forward as the mountain of salamander muscle finally released him. Blood dripping into his eyes from his head wound, he rolled over and backed away from the privateer and her salamander. Caithlin stepped after him and leaned in close.

"I'll be seeing you again," she seethed, her eyes narrowed. "Of that, you can be sure. And by the Ones above, I promise you, the next time we meet, I will not be so pleasant to deal with."

Issuing a quick whistle to tell her sailors to finish their drinks, Caithlin flashed one last warning glare at Mari and then paced out of the tavern with her sailors in tow.

***

Her pulse racing, her eyes darting from corner to darkened corner as the group moved back toward the jetty, Caithlin's shaking hand gripped the handle of the pistol tucked into her red sash like a white-knuckled vice. Shadowy figures watched the group of sailors from dark alleyways between shanty huts and tents, and through the windows of the great cabins of beached and broken vessels. More of her sailors silently stepped out to rejoin the main group, each five or six of them who returned to the fold giving her just a little more mental security as they headed back toward the boats.

"Nearly there," X'And whispered encouragingly to her, "nearly done now, Cathy."

A short way out to sea, she saw the *Martolian Queen*, now lying beached, tilted and helpless where she would stay, high and dry, until shortly before the next high tide near sunrise. They had the cover of darkness to make this work, and no more.

At the jetty, their group now back up to the full size of some eighty sailors – well over half of her crew – the final two crew members waited for them. The dwarf brothers, Oswalt and Nudd, both sat on bollards and smiled as nonchalantly as if they were out on a midnight stroll.

"You both sorted?" X'And asked. "You got what you need?"

"And then some." Nudd grinned with a wink.

Within minutes, packed back into one of the boats with her crew heaving on the oars to return her to her ship, only then did Caithlin allow herself to breathe. Wedged between X'And and Nudd in the tightly packed boat, she watched the terrifying setting of the notorious pirate den of Red Skull slowly distancing itself from her. A spark of inspiration, a germ of an idea was growing in her mind. X'And turned to her and grinned.

"Watching this thing I keep around twist your arms off?" he quoted her words from the pirate tavern.

Caithlin looked up and shrugged apologetically.

"I'm sorry, honestly. I think I got a little carried away with the act. It was the best I could think of."

X'And flashed a broad grin.

"I thought it was hilarious! You did well in there, Captain. The plan was to convince those bastards that we're crazy and have nothing to lose, and I think that went as well as it could have."

"Your one-eye-twitching act of lunatic monster was pretty convincing," remarked Cole, one of the *Martolian Queen's* original sailors from her days as a merchant ship.

"Who said it was an act?" X'And beamed, before turning to the two dwarfs. "So what did you get? You managed to find a chain for the pumps?"

Nudd let out a derisive snort and pulled open his bag.

"Chain? Please, X'And, I'm insulted. I stole an entire pump."

Oswalt kicked his own bag.

"Likewise. Just in case. You can never have too many spares."

Caithlin allowed herself a brief laugh, the taste of rum still burning in her mouth. The idea hatching in her mind would not go away. She looked up at her brig again. Sitting far higher in the water now, the hold would be slowly emptying itself of water. Another couple of hours and the damage would be above the waterline and easy enough to repair. As long as nobody assaulted them, they would be afloat and leaving the harbor before first light.

"It'll be a long night," X'And nodded as the longboat continued toward the brig, "but we've got a fighting chance now."

Caithlin turned to X'And.

"I've had an idea."

"Oh?"

She pointed to the jetty, at one of the ships tied securely amidst the array of small vessels.

"That old girl there," Caithlin said, "that gunbrig."

X'And peered out into the darkness.

"That's a sloop, Captain."

"It's a gunbrig. Basilean. You know how funny those lot are about categorizing their ships incorrectly."

"Single mast. Square-rigged. Pretty poor design, really. I'm not sure what it is – I'll stick with sloop – but it's certainly not a brig."

"That doesn't matter!" Caithlin urged. "The point is, she's about the same size as the *Martolian Queen*. From what Ebeener told us, that's the largest ship that can get in and out of this bay. Those things are designed for coastal bombardment, so I'll bet her draught is a little shallower than ours, and she's already aligned in the right direction for the wind and a fast escape."

The salamander first mate looked at the ship, then at Caithlin again as the rows of oarsmen listened intently to the hushed conversation between their two leaders.

"You think they'll come after us with that?" X'And exclaimed. "A deck mortar is a bastard of a thing to aim at a moving ship. Or d'you think they'll attack us with that while we're beached?"

Caithlin shook her head.

"If they had any sense, that would be the first thing they would use whilst we're lying helpless and waiting for the tide. But at this range? Our broadside would blow those bastards to splinters first. No, that's not where I'm going with this. That gunbrig, she's the only former Basilean naval vessel in the harbor... I intend to cut her out."

The salamander looked at his captain incredulously, his

sparkling eyes wide in surprise. His sharp-toothed mouth opened as his eyes narrowed with doubt, reluctance pasted across his scaly features. Then, slowly, his face softened into a grin.

"Yes. That could work. Yes…"

Mark Barber

Chapter Eleven

Red Skull
Infantosian Islands
East Infant Sea

Insects buzzed and small, reptilian creatures croaked repetitively from the surrounding bushes as the group waded silently through the knee-deep swamp water. The first part of the circular route had been unpleasant enough. Hacking through the jungle that had, in fact, only been possible due to how bright the night was beneath the near full moon and stars. The plan was simple enough, but the mile-long route could not have been more indirect. Lower the boats from the *Martolian Queen*, paddle west to the more secluded shoreline – remaining out of line of sight of the improvised fort – and then double all the way around the southern edge of Red Skull, through jungle and swamp, to get to the jetty from the far side. Where an attack would be least expected.

Up ahead, X'And held up a hand to stop the cutting out party. Caithlin froze in place. Something slithered past her knee in the thick, warm water. She looked around in the silence of the early morning darkness but saw nothing save the swamp and the drooping, skeleton-like vegetation sprouting up from its murky waters. For not the first time in the last few months, she wondered how her life had shifted so quickly from captaining a merchant ship in largely safe, well-guarded waters to wading through a swamp, armed to the teeth with weapons she barely knew how to use, leading a party of cutthroats in a sneak attack on a dangerous pirate settlement.

X'And waved his hand to signal the group to move on. The sixty sailors, handpicked for their fighting prowess from a motley crew recruited from merchant mariners, ex-navy, veteran privateers, and landsmen with no experience at sea, continued forward. It was another hour of sneaking stealthily around the back of the settlement, during which Caithlin noticed a worrying number of sentries posted around the town's perimeter. Cerri Denayo had not dragged himself up to the top of the pirate hierarchy in the east Infant Sea by being a fool. No, they were expecting something. Still, with every hour that passed without event, the repairs on the *Martolian Queen* were given more time to progress.

It was perhaps an hour before dawn by the time the sixty sailors had negotiated another length of jungle running around the perimeter of the pirate settlement, to arrive on a small plateau overlooking the eastern end of the bay. The jetty was now a stone throw away, and tied up alongside was the prize. A Basilean gunbrig, its lower hull painted white, the black paint along its sides was a recent addition to the Keretian fleet and showed it to be a relatively new acquisition for the pirates. It looked to be in fine condition with its huge deck mortar positioned neatly fore-and-aft.

Out in the bay, still neatly beached on the sandbank, sadly sat the *Martolian Queen*. There was no flag atop the main mast. That was to be the signal from the crew onboard that the repairs were complete. That did not bode well.

"There are lookouts everywhere," X'And whispered from where he crouched in the dark undergrowth next to Caithlin. "Every ship has a couple, there are more along the jetty... even along the beach."

Caithlin scanned her eyes along the waterfront. She counted at least thirty pirates.

"One thing," she murmured, "they all look rather bored. You notice that? As if a bunch of drunken criminals being ordered last minute to stay up all night, and then nothing happens for hours... well, it's almost as if they're not the most alert or efficient guards."

The salamander grinned.

"Leave this to me. I'll take ten of our best lads. Men who have done this sort of thing before. We'll take out the jetty guards and get the gunbrig secured. You can then come down and join us."

Caithlin looked up at her old friend.

"Absolutely not, X'And. This was my idea, and I've got us into this mess. I'm not hiding up here and dodging the danger whilst you do all of the hard work!"

X'And shook his head with a smile.

"You're not dodging danger. Cathy, if I need a fearless and skilled captain to get a ship through a hurricane, I'll look to you before anybody else I know. But this? You don't know what you're doing. You'll put the rest of us in danger. I know you've killed a couple of bastards now with pistol and sword, but this? It's a bit different, sneaking up to somebody and then not bottling it when you've got to kill them in cold blood. Stay here. When we raise a flag, come join us."

Caithlin watched as X'And and his chosen few sailors slithered down the hill and disappeared into the darkness. She looked up at the horizon. The faintest glimmer of light blue peered over to herald that the rising sun was not far away. She looked back at her own brig. Still no flag. Minutes ticked by. The blue line on the horizon grew brighter. Still no flag. Still nothing happening on the jetty. Caithlin looked down across the beach. Was there one less guard? Were X'And and his band picking them off? She looked across at the brig, and then to the horizon. More minutes ticking by, time running out and still no change.

"Come on," she whispered to her sailors, "let's get closer."

Crawling forward through the undergrowth, every disturbed bush and snapped twig causing her to freeze in terror, Caithlin slowly made her way down the slope toward the edge of the settlement and the jetty. A pirate disappeared from the deck of one of the sloops tied up alongside. Then another was gone from the end of the wooden pier. Caithlin paused and looked across at the *Martolian Queen*. A pennant flew from the mainmast.

"The repairs are complete!" she whispered excitedly to the sailors next to her – Fenn and Nudd.

The message was passed on through the undergrowth. Oswalt's team back on the brig had done their part. Still no sign of any activity on the gunbrig, and the blue line on the horizon was now accompanied by a sliver of orange. Caithlin's hand began to shake again. This was her fault; if she had just remained on the brig, they would be preparing to sail as soon as the tide came in far enough. Instead she was stuck in a bush, with what could be a poisonous snake slithering across her boots, a pistol in each hand, and a small army of pirates standing between her and a prize she did not have to take.

Caithlin stood up. Enough. There was no way that they were getting out without a fight, so might as well start things now. Ignoring the hissed cries of warning from her sailors, Caithlin strode out of cover and onto the jetty. She looked up at the skies above and saw a trio of colored lines dart across the heavens; something that holy writings told her was a sign of favor from the Shining Ones, whilst more modern scientific texts claimed it was movement of astral bodies. Caithlin chose to believe in both, one being caused by the other.

Her soaked, booted feet clumped up onto the boards of the jetty. She stood in plain view, illuminated by the string of flickering torches suspended along the pier between the lines of fast pirate vessels. There was a shout from the far end of the pier. Caithlin looked up and saw a tall, muscular man staring at her. She looked over her shoulder and saw a second pirate walking toward her from the shore end of the jetty. Caithlin walked toward the gunbrig and the pirate who had challenged her, now deeply regretting her impatience and rapidly trying to formulate a plan in her mind where she survived. That plan was simple enough.

The pirate drew closer, his pace picking up, close enough to make out that his arms were covered in tattoos and his belly hung free over his belt, between the folds of an open waistcoat. Caithlin checked over her shoulder. The second pirate was still closing.

"Oi!" the first man yelled. "Who the hell are you, love, and what are you doin'..."

Caithlin raised her pistol, shot the man square in the chest, and then span on her heel to bring up her second pistol and gun down the other pirate. Both men fell down, dead. There was a moment of complete silence.

Shouts sounded out from both ends of the pier. Blades clashed, and the screams of wounded drifted across the night air. Caithlin shoved both of her empty pistols into her sash and drew her sword.

"*Martolian Queen* ship's company! On me!" she yelled and sprinted for the Basilean gunbrig.

With a roar that pierced the warm, stifling air, Caithlin's sailors burst out of the undergrowth and onto the jetty. Caithlin was the first to reach the gunbrig and stepped onboard to see a trio of ragged pirates look up at her in surprise. The first, a bald man with rings in both ears, raised a pistol but was immediately gunned down by one of the sailors behind Caithlin. The remaining two pirates wasted no time in jumping overboard.

"The lines!" Caithlin shouted over her shoulder to Dangar, her bosun. "Cast the lines away!"

Sheathing her sword again, Caithlin leapt up onto the ratline leading up from starboard to the top of the main mast and began climbing. An insect buzzed past her ear. Then a second, only this time it ripped a neat, blackened hole in the reefed sail above her. Not insects – she was being shot at from the shore. Caithlin had no idea why that made her laugh, her limbs light as she sprang up to the yard and set about releasing the sail. Down below, she saw X'And run down the jetty with a wounded sailor over one arm and then jump onto the gunbrig's deck. A second sailor joined Caithlin on the yard and helped release the mainsail.

The mainmast swung out as the gunbrig pushed away from the jetty, leaning into its forespring before that, too, was cast away. To the north, the broadside of the *Martolian Queen* thundered into life, lighting up the night before cannonballs tore across the beach and into the ramshackle pirate settlement. They were answered almost immediately by a return volley from the hill fort to the south, and pillars of black water leapt up around the Basilean gunbrig.

"Bring her starboard!" X'And yelled to Nudd on the helm. "Two points! Head for open water!"

With the mainsail set and two more sailors clambering up to position along the yards, Caithlin sprang back down the ratlines and leapt over to the quarterdeck. The gunbrig picked up speed, while off the port bow, Caithlin saw the *Martolian Queen* slowly nudging itself off the sand bank as the tide continued to rise.

"That was not part of the plan!" X'And yelled across the quarterdeck at Caithlin as a dozen sailors quickly set about loading the gunbrig's meager broadside of six-pounder cannons. "I don't recall us talking through you walking out to this ship all by yourself!"

"Good thing this isn't a bloody democracy, and that you work for me, isn't it?" Caithlin snapped back at her first mate.

The salamander's anger seemed to instantly dissipate, and he hung his head shamefully. The *Martolian Queen* fired off another broadside into the pirate settlement and then turned slowly to starboard to bring her stern to the wind. The guns on the fort spoke again, and this time the gunbrig lurched as a shot plowed through her stern and into the captain's cabin, shaking the quarterdeck violently. Caithlin stepped across to the helm and looked down at Nudd.

"I'll take her from here," Caithlin ordered, grasping the wooden wheel. "That mortar, do you know how one of those things works?"

The gap-toothed dwarf grinned up at her.

"Like I invented it meself, Captain!"

Nudd whistled to attract the attention of a handful of sailors and led them over to the fo'c'sle to load the massive, stumpy mortar. X'And paced across to the helm.

"Begging your pardon, Captain," he said respectfully, "but that's a forward firing weapon. Do we really want to be turning around to point back at the jetty we've just escaped from?"

Caithlin span the wheel a little to port to centralize the rudder, smiling as the ship responded to her touch and gunfire continued to crackle from the shoreline.

"We've got a vessel designed specifically for coastal bombardment." Caithlin smirked. "I think it would be thoroughly rude of us to leave without sending those scum at least one parting shot."

***

The crack of small arms fire woke Cerri in his seat. Cursing himself, wiping at his eyes, he sprang out of the tavern chair and bolted for the door. A gaggle of eight or nine other pirates – who had also, no doubt, fallen asleep in the tavern – followed him out onto the verandah. It was still dark, although the first rays of dawn sunshine were beginning to present themselves over the horizon. The gunfire continued, and Cerri saw muzzle flashes briefly light up the night along the beach.

"Cerri!" Mari called from behind him. "What the hell is going on?"

The privateer brig was still aground on Dodger's Bank, as he had expected given the tidal times. Shouts, gunfire, and the clash of blades sounded from the jetty. Cerri's face dropped.

"No... they wouldn't..."

The harbor lit up as the privateer brig fired a full broadside.

"Down!"

Cerri flung himself to the ground and covered his head with his hands. The earth thudded as cannonballs smashed through wooden huts and beached ships, shaking the ricketty foundations of the tavern and covering Cerri and his pirates with dust and clods of earth. Behind him, he heard the hill fort fire a return salvo. He staggered to his feet and groped around in the dust and the dark.

"The jetty!" he coughed to the others. "Those bastards are cutting out one of our ships!"

Emerging from the cloud of dust and smoke, Cerri heard the cries of the wounded in the decimated huts around the beach. Muskets and pistols were still firing at the bottom of the slope leading to the waterfront.

"Cerri!" a familiar voice called from an alleyway to his left. "What in blazes is going on here?"

Cerri turned and saw Hector Dunn, the oldest of the three pirate chiefs, stagger out into the open with a small band of his own pirates.

"That privateer brig!" Cerri pointed at the Genezan vessel aground on the sandbank. "Her crew is cutting out one of our damned ships!"

"The crew who came ashore, embarrassed you in full view of your own sailors, and then walked away without a challenge?!" the old pirate captain scowled. "You mean *that* crew?"

Footsteps thudded down from the southeast corner, and Cerri looked across to see Tem sprinting over with about twenty of his own crew.

"Cerri!" he gasped. "They're at the jetty! There's at least fifty of the bastards! What do you want us to do?"

Cerri held both of his hands up as more pirates ran past the impromptu gathering in seemingly every direction. His shoulder immediately flared up in pain from where the insane salamander had pinned him hours before.

"We stop bloody panicking for starters," Cerri growled, "and we form up into units to counter whatever it is that they're doing!"

Hector pointed down at the bay.

"It's a bit late for that, you useless bastard!"

Cerri stared through the dark and saw a shape moving away from the jetty. As his eyes adjusted, he made it out to be the Basilean gunbrig that Hector had captured earlier in the year. The ship's mainmast was set, and it turned smoothly toward the bay as muskets continued to fire potshots at it from the jetty and beach.

"That's my ship!" Hector yelled, spittle catching in his gray-white beard. "You bloody fool, Cerri! You've let them take my ship!"

Cerri span around and pointed a finger of accusation at the older pirate chief.

"You slept through all of this, you drunken old sot! Don't you dare try to pin this on me!"

The bay lit up again as the brig's guns fired.

"Down!"

The three groups of pirates dived to the sandy earth as the next wave of cannonballs crashed through the settlement. Again, clouds of choking dust blew through the darkness and splinters of wood dropped down on Cerri's back. Coughing, his eyes streaming, Cerri staggered up to one knee. The hill fort fired again. More wounded men cried out. Panic and confusion reigned once more.

"Come on!" Tem yelled through the darkness. "Let's chase the bastards down!"

"With what, boy?" Hector growled. "They've got an eighteen-gunner out there, and now they've taken *my* gunbrig! Thanks to Cerri, we've gone from being a figure of fear in the entire region to a bloody laughing stock, and an outgunned one at that!"

Cerri flung his arms wildly through the darkness and smoke in a vain attempt to find Hector.

"One more accusation like that, you drunken old bastard, and I'll feed you to the fishes piece by piece!"

The dust cleared away. The crackle of muskets continued. Cerri looked down and saw both the privateer brig and the recently captured, now liberated, Basilean gunbrig easing away from the shoreline and toward open sea. Curiously, the gunbrig was altering course hard to starboard, insanely turning its bows back toward the very danger it had just escaped from. Cerri's jaw dropped open as he realized why.

"Oh shit!"

The hollow thump of a mortar sounded from the bay, followed by the droning wail of an enormous bombshell arcing up into the dawn sky.

"Leg it!" Cerri screamed.

Sprinting for the treeline at the edge of the settlement, Cerri felt panic rise again through his chest as the droning grew louder. The world lit up. Heat washed over his body. An unseen hand picked him up effortlessly and flung him forward through the thin, wooden wall of a merchant hut. His ears ringing, his body bruised, aching, and covered in debris, Cerri staggered to his feet after he did not know how long he had laid numbly in the wrecked hut. Around him, pirates from his own crew as well as Tem's and Hector's limped out of the debris of shattered buildings. The air stank of burning. Black smoke billowed out from a blaze raging where the Final Grapeshot tavern had stood only a minute before.

"The utter, utter bastards," Cerri whispered to himself as he stared at the wreckage of his favorite tavern.

Out in the bay, the brig and the gunbrig sailed away into a rising sun.

"This is all on you!" Hector growled, limping across the wreckage strewn quarter of town. "This is all because…"

Cerri raised his pistol, cocked it, and pointed it at the ancient pirate. Instantly he heard the cocking of more weapons and saw four of Hector's pirates pointing their pistols back at him. More pistols were drawn, and amidst the broken planks of wood and toxic fumes of the fire, two lines of a dozen pirates stood facing each other with weapons drawn – those loyal to Cerri, and those to Hector.

"We don't have time for this!" Cerri growled. "We need to torch this place and leave!"

"Torch this place?!" Hector scoffed. "You bloody coward! We need to rebuild and fortify it! Some bastard has told tales, and now the Basileans know the lanes in and out of here!"

"Exactly, you daft old lemon!" Cerri stared down the barrel of his pistol. "They'll be here with bloody frigates next! Marines! A full sodding invasion! We need to leave!"

"No! No, no, no! We've had a bloody nose and now we need to fix our defenses! Make sure they can't do this again! We need a second fort, possibly a third! Cannons on the west side of the bay, no blind spots!"

Cerri lowered his pistol and turned away from Hector and his pirates. Stood next to him, loyally with their own weapons drawn, were Mari, Torg, Tem, and Halladai. He looked across at Mari.

"Get the lads together. All of them. Every spare hand, seadog, and man jack you can find. I need two hundred sailors. Get to the south side of the island and get the *Dark Siren* ready."

***

Mauriss, the perpetually red-faced and flustered flag lieutenant, closed the doors to the admiral's office behind Jaymes. His hat under one arm and his sword and scabbard carried in his free hand, Jaymes walked tentatively toward the admiral's desk, wondering if he should be marching to then stand to attention, or if this time he was not actually in trouble.

"Rum," Admiral Sir Jerris Pattia beamed from his drinks cabinet as he fetched two glasses, "you're a dark rum man."

Bloody hell. It was not even nine bells in the morning yet.

"Yes, sir. Thank you, sir."

"Take a seat, dear boy."

Jaymes hesitantly placed his bicorn hat on the admiral's desk and slowly sat down, eyeing the senior officer suspiciously. He had already fallen into the kindness trap too many times before and then, with his guard down, been thoroughly reprimanded. Jerris brought over two glasses, slid one across the smooth desk, and then took a seat opposite him, just outside of the fierce sunbeams pouring in from the open balcony behind him.

"Now then!" the admiral began. "I'm normally rather put out by the sort of captain who abandons a patrol early to skulk home for a comfy bed, wine, and women. But... you appear to have brought back a captured frigate. Or at least something we could roughly categorize as a frigate. This makes me happy, Jaymes. Very happy. And when I'm happy, you and your jolly jack tars all get prize money."

Content that this was not, indeed, 'a trap,' Jaymes reached for his rum.

"It is... a boneship, though. So... like a ghost ship, but worse."

Jaymes dragged his hand back again from the tempting, ruby nectar in the glass and looked across at the admiral.

"Yes, sir. We did have some... problems bringing her in. The prize crew complained of all sorts of noises and bizarre goings on onboard, especially at night. The sheets and braces were breaking with annoying regularity. We tried to tow her three times, and the line broke every time, even in calm seas. It was as if she really, really didn't want to come back with us. Then we lost a man. Carried out a search of every deck and space, man overboard procedure, the lot. We figured the ghosts had claimed him. Then... well, we found him."

"Where?" the admiral demanded.

Jaymes pulled at his dark neckerchief.

"Some things are not worth highlighting to an admiral, sir. Suffice to say, the dirty bastard has been appropriately disciplined."

"Oh... oh. I shan't ask any more."

"Thank you, sir."

Jerris took a swig from his whiskey and looked thoughtfully out of the window, across the sea of masts in the sunlit bay.

"Well," the admiral remarked dryly, "we can't use her. Can't have a boneship sort-of-frigate flying a Basilean flag. Wouldn't do, Jaymes, wouldn't do. The practice of selling ships back to their owners after hostilities end isn't really on the table, either. However, I've absolutely no doubt that one of the arcane colleges back in ole Goldie Horn will pay handsomely for her. So rest assured, you'll get your prize money. But we do need to get a crew together and sail her for the capital as soon as possible. I remember a few years ago a prize boneship being brought in. By your previous old man, in fact, Charn Ferrus. Anyway, she was left at anchor out in the bay. Snapped her own anchor cables overnight and drifted off, never to be seen again. As you say, Jaymes, these bloody undead ships don't want to be kept."

Jaymes suppressed a quiet chuckle at the thought of his former captain's inevitable fury upon finding out that a captured prize ship had floated away overnight. He found himself thanking the Ones above that he was not involved in that calamity and the ensuing reprimand.

"More importantly," the admiral continued, "we've given those skull-faced bastards a kick in the nuts or whatever they have instead, by depriving them of two of their warships, including that little galley you sent to the bottom. So, we've lost a sloop for a frigate and a galley. I'd say we're winning."

Jaymes leaned across the desk.

"We lost a sloop, sir?"

Jerris nodded grimly.

"We've had a few progress reports sent in via that sea-mage on the *Shield Royal*. I'm afraid the *Ocean Knight* failed to report back to the *Veneration* some days ago. Doesn't look good."

Jaymes bowed his head and mentally uttered a quick prayer for Lieutenant Dianjlo and his crew.

"Still!" The admiral slammed both hands onto the desk with a force that made Jaymes jump. "You've taken a frigate off of the bony bastards, and the *Martolian Queen* came in last night with one of our gunbrigs in tow, liberated from Red Skull! Can you believe that? I'm seeing Captain Viconti tomorrow about it all."

"Oh... the privateer's back alongside, sir?" Jaymes found himself stammering suspiciously. "I hadn't noticed. I mean... I wasn't looking for it. Just a little brig. Very easy to miss amongst all of the larger vessels in the harbor. Not that I..."

"Alright, Jaymes, alright. You didn't look for the brig and there's definitely nothing going on between you and Captain Viconti. Fully understood. When are you heading back out to rejoin the patrol?"

Jaymes took a swig from his glass of rum and then tapped a fist against his chest as the fierce, surprisingly strong rum flowed down his throat.

"I figured a couple of nights alongside, sir. We need a few repairs after the hits we took, and I need to replace the men I lost."

"Are you forming a press gang?" the admiral asked.

Jaymes shook his head as he took another swig from his rum.

"Not unless I really have to, sir. I'd rather not take pressed men to sea. Not fair on my crew and not fair on them. I'm hoping the talk of bringing in the Khopeshii will generate some real interest in joining my crew. There's always out of work sailors in town, and if I'm bringing in prize money from captured frigates, I'm hoping I'll get enough volunteers. Finding a sailing master of sufficient expertise to replace poor Mister Estrayia, that may prove to be more of a problem."

The admiral drained his glass, half closed one eye in discomfort, and then stood up.

"Grand, Jaymes, grand. Well, good to see you. Sorry about your sailing master. Never met him, but I heard he was a good egg. Do let me know if anything changes with your plans, but if I don't hear from you, then I'll expect to see you departing in two days. Best of Basilean, old boy."

Jaymes finished his rum, winced at its obscene strength, and then stood up.

"Thank you, sir."

After departing the office, Jaymes made his way down the spiral staircase to the main entrance, shaking his head as he did so in a futile attempt to shrug off the effects of what appeared to be triple strength rum, and a double shot at that.

"Captain Ellias?"

Jaymes turned at the door to see Lieutenant Mauriss rushing down the stairs after him, brandishing a piece of paper. The tubby staff officer stopped by Jaymes and took a second to catch his breath.

"I'm... awfully sorry to shout after you like that, sir..."

"It's alright. What news, old chap?"

The flag lieutenant handed the paper over.

"Curious thing, sir. I was assembling quotes for the repairs to your vessel. Coincidentally, just moments ago, I was visited by a representative from a company I haven't worked with before. He said he would repair your vessel, completely free of charge! I've never heard anything like it! I checked his credentials, and they're faultless. Perhaps he's just looking to make a name for himself in a new port?"

His eyes narrowed suspiciously, Jaymes snatched the piece of paper and scanned his eyes over it. The signature block at the end of the paper immediately leapt out.

Stefano Viconti. Master Trader, Master Carpenter.

Jaymes handed the paper back.

"Are you content, sir?" Mauriss asked. "I appreciate that this is highly irregular. Perhaps even worthy of suspicion..."

Jaymes shook his head.

"No, it's alright. I know him. Well, we've met. Let's see what he can do."

"Aye, sir."

Suppressing a chuckle at the thought of the odd apology and thankful for a blast of fresh air in his lungs as soon as he stepped outside, Jaymes pulled his hat back on and headed back to his ship.

Chapter Twelve

Green Cove
Southern Coastal Road
Keretia

With a surprisingly clear and painless head, but no immediate memories of the previous evening in his semi-awake state, Jaymes half opened his eyes. The bed was far too comfortable for his cabin onboard the ship, and he heard the clucking of hens rather than the familiar lapping of waves against the wooden boards of the hull. An arm was draped across his chest. A smile spread across his face as he realized that he had spent his first night in a house he owned, and Caithlin was asleep next to him. Morning rays of sunshine illuminated a vertical line between the thick, blue curtains hanging over the windows. Hens continued to cluck in the courtyard outside.

Feeling a sudden hankering for a hot drink, Jaymes carefully eased himself away from underneath Caithlin's arm. She grumbled something incomprehensible in her sleep and held him in place. He waited a full minute and then carefully tried again.

"No," Caithlin mumbled.

"I'll bring you back a drink?" he offered hopefully.

"...alright."

A few minutes later, clad in comfortable civilian trousers and a short-sleeved shirt, Jaymes made his way back up the stairs of his new home and into the master bedroom with a tray balancing a pot of tea and two cups. He found Caithlin on the now open balcony, clad in one of his uniform shirts as she took in the sun and gazed out across the warm, turquoise waters of the Infant Sea. The house was, in many ways, ideally placed. Not long to take a carriage back into Thatraskos, but just around a corner of a steep cliff face that hid the port from view entirely, giving a peaceful feeling of isolation from the woes of work. The house itself, a relatively grand affair of a main building, walled courtyard, and external stables – without any horses – overlooked a shallow, sandstone cliff and white sand beach.

Jaymes placed the tray down on the balcony table and set about pouring the drinks.

"It provokes thought," Caithlin began with a slight but warm smile, "waking up in a place like this."

"Oh?" Jaymes passed her the first cup.

"Yes. This house, this bed, this view... it puts things in

perspective. A life at sea, living onboard... it's all rather... shit, isn't it?"

Jaymes laughed into his tea.

"I wasn't expecting that! You deriding our life, or you swearing."

Caithlin shrugged.

"I'm a pirate now, me hearty. Or privateer, pirate hunter... I don't really know what. But they all swear. And drink. Anyway, I'm absolutely taken with this place of yours, and now thoroughly regretting my life choices in going to sea."

"Even with your own cabin as captain?"

"Even with that. If I lived here, storms wouldn't possibly kill me, there's no pirates, no sharks... in fact, I'm entirely of a mind to seduce some handsome but stupid frigate captain and spend my days as a lady of leisure, playing the harpsichord and reading poems. There's a lot to be said for a normal life. On land. In a house. That's far safer than cutting out gunbrigs on Pirate Island."

Jaymes's smile faded at the last few words. Caithlin looked up at him, her eyes still full of mischievous merriment until she saw his expression. Her smile faded.

"Please don't worry," she said seriously, "I had it covered. I do take care of myself when we go out into all that."

Jaymes rested a hand on hers and mustered an unconvincing smile. Caithlin bit her lip and then spoke again.

"Speaking of which, Karnon spoke to me last night. He's worried about you, you know."

Jaymes peered into his mug of tea.

"He doesn't need to."

"Well... he told me about your clash with the Ahmunite frigate. More specifically, about you getting hurt. He said that he knows you are besotted with me – his words, not mine, but you don't hide it well – and that you're more likely to listen to me than to him. So... well, you know I'm not particularly affectionate with my words... I'm rather besotted with you, as well. And I agree entirely with Karnon. You shouldn't be taking risks that you don't have to."

Jaymes tilted his head, narrowed his eyes, and chose his words carefully before replying.

"Look... you know you're still new to this whole fighting command thing? Well..."

"No, no," Caithlin cut him off, "I'm new to lining up a broadside and positioning for a stern rake, but I'm not new to the sea, danger, or command. If I was in a storm, I wouldn't climb to the top of the mainmast to affect a repair myself. I'd stay on the quarterdeck to command the ship – my job – and get some other poor bastard of a topman to get on the roof to do his. Karnon should lead the boarding actions, not you. And certainly not when you're hurt, even if you do have some magic-wielding ship's surgeon to fix you up."

Jaymes gnawed on his lip pensively but remained unconvinced.

"I'll take better care," he offered.

"Thank you."

"As long as you take better care and leave cutting ships out to that monster of a first mate of yours."

"Deal. And he likes you, too."

A few minutes passed by in idyllic silence as the two held hands and stared down from the balcony at the sandy beach and the gentle lapping of the waves. A little way out to sea, a pod of dolphins jumped in and out of the water in graceful arcs.

"I nearly forgot," Caithlin suddenly piped up, "I have a present for you. Now, I know you've been awfully good at bringing me flowers and I haven't been very good at reciprocating. So I have something for you. It should be arriving at your ship about now. But it's not very romantic."

Jaymes looked across, his interest piqued by the enigmatic statement.

"Whatever it is, it's very kind of you, I'm sure! Do I have to wait, or are you going to tell me?"

Caithlin grinned broadly.

"It's a matching pair of nine-pound cannons, still on their original carriages, Basilean naval markings and badged up with Dolgarth foundry shields!"

Jaymes's eyes opened wide.

"Have... have you removed those from that gunbrig you captured?"

"I'm not answering that. Besides, it's my prize, and I can do what I want with it. But as far as you're concerned, *Pious* is now a thirty-eight, not a thirty-six. Don't say I never give you anything. Or that romance is dead."

Finding himself inexplicably excited by the thought of that little extra firepower, and the prestige that came with signing ship's paperwork off as being a thirty-eight, Jaymes leaned across to kiss her.

"Thank you!" he beamed. "The admiral will have some questions! But thank you!"

"You're most welcome. I have an appointment with him this afternoon, and I think he'll be most interested in what I have to say. But that's this afternoon. What do you want to do with the morning?"

Jaymes finished his tea and stood up to lean across the rail of the balcony. He stared out to sea, finding himself entirely content and happy with life for the first time in as long as he could remember. Having Caithlin by his side, his new home, and respite from the ship... even the two new guns were disproportionately exciting.

"Cathy... you know we were just talking about how crap life at sea is? And that a normal life on dry land really would be fantastic? Would... would it be terrible of me to suggest that we spend the morning together hiring a little sailing dinghy and pottering around the coast?"

Caithlin glanced out to sea. Her smile faded away and then she looked back.

"You know that when I joke about seducing you for your money, and moving into your house, and stopping work when I have these debts to pay... you know that is a joke, don't you?"

Jaymes moved across and placed an arm around Caithlin's shoulder.

"Of course I know. But that gunbrig you're selling would be worth more if it wasn't missing two guns. And you do know that my offers to help you are sincere?"

"I do. And I do appreciate them. And I'm not turning down your help out of stubbornness or pride – the Ones above know, I need all the help I can get – but what we have, it isn't fair on you to fix my debts. I won't allow that to come into what we have."

The two stood in silence for some time, looking out at the gentle, sparkling waves cascading across the idyllic beach below.

"Come on," Caithlin finally said with a smile, "let's go and take a well-deserved break from sailing by spending the morning together on a little sailing boat! It'll be fantastic!"

***

Caithlin placed her sword and hat on the flag lieutenant's desk as she strode past. Mauriss leapt to his feet and failed to meet her stare.

"Be a good fellow and look after those for me, would you? The admiral is expecting me. I do have an appointment."

Caithlin issued a courtesy knock on the grand double doors, did not wait for a reply, and then walked briskly inside the office. Admiral Sir Jerris Pattia stood on his sweeping, white marble balcony in the early afternoon sun as he stared down across the bay, armed only with a stubby glass of what appeared to be neat gin, eliciting the wonder within the privateer captain's mind of what he actually did for a living.

"Captain Viconti!" he greeted with a grin. "I do appreciate punctuality! What can I get you to drink? You're a white wine lady, if I recall?"

Caithlin paced over to the desk, eyeing the little admiral as he darted over to his drinks cabinet. She mentally chastised herself as she failed to stop him pouring out a glass for her – she needed to stay focused and keep him on the defensive, after all – but she had found herself developing a taste for good wine, and Jerris was known universally for his expensive liquor cabinet.

"Thank you," she said curtly, without a smile, and followed him out onto the balcony.

The admiral winced in the blazing sunshine, rocking on the balls of his feet as he looked down across the forest of ships' masts extending out from the various piers. *Pious* dominated the harbor as the largest warship currently alongside, but both the *Martolian Queen* and Caithlin's prize gunbrig were certainly within the larger half of ships within view, with so many of the Thatraskos Fleet's frigates being currently at sea.

"Mauriss tells me that you're planning on departing tomorrow evening, to resume the patrol to the south," Jerris said.

"Yes, that's right. A few repairs and then we'll be off."

"Jolly good. And on behalf of the Admiralty, sincere thanks are in order to you and your crew for liberating our gunbrig."

And there it was. So it began. Caithlin feigned an overdramatic, almost theatrical blink of confusion.

"I'm terribly sorry, Admiral. *Your* gunbrig? I'm afraid there must be some confusion. It's my prize."

Jerris issued a polite laugh and took a swig from his gin.

"Not at all, not at all! You're still new to privateering, my girl! It's all in your certificate of commission. Any prize you take is given to the Basilean Navy. Standard stuff – we'll pay you nine tenths of the ship's value, as one tenth is forfeit to the Duma. That nine tenths is then split between you, your officers, and your crew at a rate of..."

Caithlin interrupted by producing her commissioning certificate – one of the two papers she had pre-prepared – and unrolled it slowly.

"Oh, I know all of that. The thing is, it says here that prize ships *'may be sold'* to the Basilean Fleet, at a nine tenth value to account for the Duma tithe. May."

The admiral waved a hand to one side.

"I appreciate the confusion! It is rather hard to understand at first. The 'may' is a polite way of saying that..."

"I checked with the harbor master's legal representative. The word 'may' in this context gives me legal authority to choose who I sell the ship to and for how much. So I'm not selling it to you. I'm selling it to the Valentican Navy."

Jerris's smile faded. He placed his glass down on the balcony rail and stood up straight. His eyes narrowed. A scowl formed on his lips.

"I beg your pardon?"

Caithlin would be lying to herself if she did not admit that she found the short man intimidating. A veteran of war, powerful and influential, with a metaphorical share in her very future. But then she remembered what her father had told her about the terms of her commission. Of the inherent dishonesty from the Basilean Admiralty. She met his stare evenly.

"I'm selling the gunbrig to the Valenticans," she repeated with a nonchalant shrug before sampling her expensive wine.

The admiral took a step forward, his face reddening just a little.

"Now, explain to me, why would you do a thing like that?"

"You know full well," Caithlin countered, "because that is a Basilean warship, part of the Keretian Fleet. *Your* fleet. And even though she's not the largest or most dangerous of vessels, she belongs here. And the attack on your national pride, your navy, the humiliation of seeing her flying a Valentican flag... well, I think that would be unacceptable to you, to put it mildly."

Jerris locked one hand inside the other at the small of his back, never removing his eyes from Caithlin's for even a moment.

"By the blood of Bolisean," Jerris hissed, "you would *dare*... You stand there, drinking my wine, threatening me with *that* after all we've done for you..."

"Don't you dare insult my intelligence by pretending you've done me any favors!" Caithlin snapped. "I limped into this port with a sinking ship and dead crew, and you took full advantage of the situation to use my ignorance against me and dupe me into signing for a ten year commitment that legally I shouldn't have! You want to use the wording of commissions and contracts against me? Fine. Two can play at that. I don't have to sell the ship to you. That's the law."

Caithlin produced her second piece of paper and thrust it beneath the admiral's nose.

"Here. *That* is what I'll sell your ship back to you for."

The admiral's eyes shot open. He stared at Caithlin with a mixture of alarm and anger.

"That's three times what she's worth! New!"

"I know that, Admiral, I've done my research. And that, of course, is without factoring in how much you owe me for assisting in the destruction of a further three pirate ships, as well as what I'm going to charge you for a copy of the route through the sand banks to get into Red Skull. But one of two things is going to happen. Either you pay that amount, or you watch one of your warships sail west and fly the flag of a nation state that Basilea is not on good terms with. Not remotely. And I'd imagine you'd need to explain that one to the Duma. If not higher."

"This is bloody preposterous!" Jerris spluttered. "You might as well fly a black flag with a skull on it, you bloody pirate! Yes, that's exactly what you are! I ought to have you arrested for this!"

Caithlin flashed a sly smile.

"Look on the bright side. Any ship I sell, I have to give one tenth of the sale to the Duma. So... if I sell it for three times the price, the Duma effectively gets triple the tithe."

"But we'd be paying ourselves! That's utterly meaningless!"

"I didn't make the rules, Admiral."

Jerris turned away. He paced along the balcony, muttering expletives under his breath as Caithlin took a moment to keep her nerves in check and keep her cool. With a snarl, the admiral dashed over to his desk and produced a certificate of payment and quill.

"This is extortion!" he growled as he scratched the details onto the paper. "You're a bloody pirate!"

Thinking of the proper pay day she would finally reward her crew with, and the chip this would knock off her debt to the Basilean crown, Caithlin fought to suppress a victorious grin. She failed entirely as she accepted the certificate from Jerris.

"Thank you, Admiral."

Turning on her heel, she paced back toward the door.

"Captain Viconti!" the admiral snapped at her, his voice echoing across the cavernous office.

Caithlin turned again to face him. The admiral offered a slight, conspiratory smile.

"Well played, old girl. Well played."

Caithlin smiled again.

"Thank you, Admiral. Good afternoon."

After recovering her sword and hat, Caithlin made her way down the spiral staircase and out of the administration building's main entrance. Craning her neck to look up at the clocktower, Caithlin looked for the time as she remembered her pre-arranged meeting with her father at her ship. She had taken barely a pace when she bumped into a small figure standing a little over her waist height. She looked down and saw the young girl she had seen days before with Captain Marcellus Dio of the *Veneration*. The girl looked up at her in silent awe.

"Hello," Caithlin issued a slight and awkward smile.

"Are you a captain?" the young girl asked quietly. "Your epaulets look like captain's."

"Yes," Caithlin stood to one side to allow a marine officer entry into the administration building, past the awkward conversation she was locked into in front of the main doors.

"Did you come in with one of the ships yesterday?" the child continued timidly.

Caithlin looked around uncomfortably.

"I... I'm afraid we're not really supposed to talk about that sort of thing."

"Oh. It's just that my father was on one of the ships that went out a few days ago, and I've seen two come back. But not my father's ship."

Caithlin dropped instantly to one knee to look across at the girl at her own eye level.

"Oh, no!" She smiled. "I think I've seen you with your father! Captain Dio? I don't know him well, but I do know him, and I know that when my ship headed north, his frigate was absolutely fine! Please don't worry. The two ships you saw only came back in for repairs and to secure prizes. The *Veneration* is fine, as is your father, I'm sure!"

The girl's shoulders rose and fell, and she nodded.

"Thank you."

Caithlin looked around the dockyard.

"Do you have a governess who should be looking after you at the moment?"

"Yes. I ran away when she wasn't looking. I wanted to see if I could find my father."

Caithlin's smile became more sympathetic.

"I really should get you back home. What's your name?"

"Kora," the girl answered, "what's yours? I didn't know the navy had women captains."

Caithlin stood up again and checked in every direction in search of a panicked governess.

"I'm Caithlin. To be honest, I'm not sure if the navy does allow women to captain ships," she replied. "The Sisterhood has women ship captains. In fact, they don't allow men in their ranks at all. Anyway, I'm neither of those, not really. I'm a privateer. I'm only a Basilean Naval Auxiliary captain."

Kora's face lit up with a huge smile.

"You're a pirate?!" she exclaimed with glee. "A real life pirate?!"

"That's the second time somebody has called me that this afternoon," Caithlin sighed.

Kora formed one of her hands up into an impromptu hook and closed one eye.

"Aarrghh, matey!"

"Yes. Quite. Come on, let's get you safely home."

After less than half an hour, a chance encounter with a particularly worried looking governess on the cobbled street leading from the naval dockyard to the town center resulted in Kora being returned home, and Caithlin freed to resume her afternoon. She found her father waiting, with a courtesy she appreciated given his financial share in the ship, at the foot of the gangway leading from the shore up to the *Martolian Queen*. Caithlin nodded for her father to follow her and led him to her great cabin at the after end of the ship where she discarded her sword and hat.

"I'm not sure I'll ever get used to you walking around with

weaponry," Stefano said.

"That makes both of us," Caithlin replied, perching on the sunlit window sill by the stern windows of her cabin.

"I've conducted the repairs on the ship. And that bloody great frigate. I've called in a lot of favors to make that happen so quickly, and at great cost."

"I know," Caithlin said, "Jaymes told me. It's the least you could do after storming onto a warship to pick an argument with the captain. Not your finest forenoon, father."

Stefano folded his arms and glared at his daughter.

"I've written him a letter of apology! And repaired his ship! What more does he want? Ones above, Cathy! Basileans! Basileans and your bloody fragile generation with your hurt feelings!"

Caithlin looked up, her eyes narrowed. She pointed off toward the anchorage to the southwest.

"Did you see the Ahmunite frigate there, just around the corner? About eight hundred tons, bows covered in human bone. That one? Jaymes took that in a boarding action, leading from the front after taking a wooden splinter a foot long across his abdomen. But by all means, you go and tell him that you think he's too fragile."

Her father rolled his eyes and turned away.

"I don't want to argue, Cathy. Not again. It's not why I'm here."

"Then stop looking for problems with Jaymes. Good gosh, I get enough of that nonsense from X'And."

A slight smirk tugged at the corners of Stefano's thin lips.

"X'And is a smart fellow. Fantastic sailor. I've always liked X'And. Grand lot, the croc-backs. I've always liked the way they conduct their business."

Caithlin shook her head and let out a breath. The generation-old slur was, Caithlin was certain, not even remotely welcome to the salamanders, but somehow her father thought it was a compliment. And in his odd way, it was intended as one.

"Have you heard anything back yet?" Caithlin asked. "From the legal people in the capital? I checked in with the harbor law offices yesterday about another matter, but they'd heard nothing."

Stefano's face dropped. He suddenly seemed to age a decade before her very eyes, a thin and gray old man compared to the powerful, sometimes intimidating father she remembered from her childhood. He shook his head slowly.

"Nothing yet. But no news is not bad news. Granted, it's not good news either, but it's a mere frustration rather than anything terminal. And I'm still optimistic. You've known me long enough to know that I say things straight, as they are and without sunbeams, and I'm telling you that I think we will have good news. That ten years, or nine now, that you owe. I think we'll be cutting that in half at worst."

Caithlin nodded again and leaned back against the window. She looked out across the bay at the east end of the harbor, where the civilian merchant ships were tied up alongside or waiting at anchor serenely. The harbor that she first sailed into at the age of seventeen, marveling at the grand Basilean frigates tied up on their piers in an area that she then had no access to. Now, practically trapped in the naval side, she found herself looking longingly back at the freedom that the mercantile half of the bay represented. Then she remembered climbing up the mainmast of the gunbrig as she was cutting her out, with musket balls flying past her. She remembered how much she enjoyed the exhilaration of it.

"I'm sorry about what I've said about your fellow," Stefano suddenly said. "It's just... it's difficult for me. My dealings with the military have always been strained, and my encounters with Basileans have never been particularly friendly. Combine the two, and... well, I find myself jumping to conclusions. I know that isn't fair."

Caithlin glanced across at him, noting the sincerity in his eyes. Again, he looked older than he should. She found that to be more upsetting than she expected. She reached inside her jacket pocket and took the special gold coin that accompanied her everywhere, flicking it up into the air with a ping as her thumbnail caught its edge.

"Would you be open to a mid-afternoon glass of wine?" she offered. "I know a few excellent places around here."

Stefano quickly replaced an accusatory glare with a more even expression.

"It's... a little early for drinking."

"Not for pirates like me," Caithlin countered, stone-faced.

Her father paused, then shrugged.

"Yes. Alright."

Just over a day later, firing their guns in salute as they passed the harbor breakwater, *Hegemon's Warship Pious (38)* and the privateer fighting brig *Martolian Queen (18)* slipped and proceeded together, picking up a wind abaft the starboard beam and sailing out to resume their patrol to the south.

***

The light-wooden hulled xebec cut through the dark, gentle waters. Swirling mists wrapped around the slender hull, white fingers of fog curling and pointing almost supernaturally as they were illuminated in pools of yellow light from the ship's lanterns. On the quarterdeck, Tem folded his arms and stared out across the borrowed ship's bows, trying to stay focused on looking for hazards in the fog but finding his mind wandering to problem after problem every few moments.

Things had been so much more simple until so recently. A boy miner, he had decided after four years of darkness and back-breaking boredom that a life at sea would be far better. A chance encounter in a tavern and a long night of drinking armed him with enough information to join a merchant ship instead of the navy, but after three years of harsh discipline that made him miss the dark depths of the mines, the day Cerri Denayo's crew boarded his ship was the day he volunteered to join a pirate crew.

Tem was snapped back out of his wistful reminiscing as Halladai walked up to the small quarterdeck from the upper deck, the steps creaking beneath his feet. He offered Tem something that appeared to be an attempt at a smile but came out as little more than a lop-sided sneer. Tem attempted to return the gesture, but likewise imagined that he only summoned up enough enthusiasm for a facial tick.

"Quiet night," Halladai remarked, "at least this mist is starting to clear a little."

"Can't sleep?"

The Ophidian nodded. A few long, drawn out minutes of silence followed until the quartermaster spoke again.

"We're lucky, having this ship again. Or perhaps you've just got a gift at talking your way out of things."

Tem looked around at the battered xebec. Cerri had been truly livid when his rushed plan to get a dozen pirate ships to sea had been hatched. Tem knew that he was lucky to be alive; rumors had filtered back to him that the only reason Cerri had not killed him was that he had doubled back to rescue survivors after the ambush by the J'Koor'uk and the privateer brig. He was even luckier that he had been given temporary command of the *Desert Rose* again – Cerri wanted every ship out to hunt for the Genezan woman who had dared to insult him on his own island and then bombard him with one of their own ships. With that in mind, Tem had suggested giving the *Adventure Prize* to another captain whilst he limped on with the still damaged *Desert Rose*. Damaged, but still larger, harder hitting, and more prestigious than a sloop.

"I've lost you again," Halladai said quietly. "You still thinking on Ash and Flyde?"

Tem shook his head and spat out a curse. He had not, in fact, been thinking on his two recently killed friends, but now he was. Stupid, really. It had been a blessed few years with very few close friendships made, and even fewer deaths suffered by his shipmates. It tended to be all or nothing – a cruise was successful, with perhaps a sailor lost in a storm or to an unlucky defensive shot from a merchantman, or ships left Red Skull and were never seen again. Not much in between.

"Yeah," Tem admitted, "a little."

"We'll settle this for them." Halladai nodded with determination. "We'll find that Genezan bitch and cut her in half."

Tem sniffed and nodded. That much, at least, Tem, Halladai, and Cerri were all agreed on. Tem glanced to either side of the xebec. The mist continued to clear. For a brief moment, he thought he saw a yellow lamp off to starboard, but it was gone as soon as it appeared, and tricks of the light in these conditions were common.

"How many ships did Cerri get out in the end?" Halladai asked.

Tem shrugged.

"It looked like about a dozen. He was heading off to the other side of the island to prepare that bloody great frigate of his last I heard, but I didn't see her sail. There's always complications with ships of that size, that's why you need a navy to run them. We're better off swarming over something like a fighting brig with a dozen sloops."

The Ophidian let out a short bark of a laugh.

"This, from the man who traded in his borrowed sloop for a slower xebec!"

Tem turned to face his friend and flash him a grin. He stopped, a chill shooting up his spine as he saw the shape in the clearing mist behind Halladai. His eyes fixed in terror. His throat dried instantly and his hands shook. A wall of ancient wood bobbed gently up and down in the waves, only a few cables from the xebec. Over twice the length, thrice the height, and over five times the displacement of the xebec, the colossal shape loomed closer out of the darkness and the mist. Halladai, clearly picking up on the cues, span in place and swore in his native tongue as his eyes traveled up the full length of the towering, eighteen hundred ton Ahmunite war galley that eased across the waves to intercept the battered xebec.

Chapter Thirteen

In the seas southeast of the fallen Republic of Primovantor
Dedicated to the worship of Shobik, True God of the
Afterlife
That worship carried out onboard 'Purification of Ul'Astia',
a galley of war of one hundred and twenty cubits

Much had changed with the passage of time across the centuries dividing T'mork's mortal life from his now purified existence. The entire world he had lived with was gone, replaced with different land masses, empires, and seas after tumultuous events that he understood but could not imagine. But some things remained the same. For instance, Demelecles, the captain of T'mork's war galley, could still recognize the unmistakable lines and build of an Ophidian ship. Yes, the vessel now secured alongside T'mork's *Purification of Ul'Astia* was modern and a product of this new world the Ahmunite sailors now found themselves in, but the shape – the character – had little evolved, and that – to find Ophidians this far north – was of interest to T'mork. The high priest grimaced. Acknowledging them as 'Ophidians' rather than rebels was giving them status and national identity.

Another static in the development of the world around T'mork and his subordinates – both sentient and otherwise – was magic. The terminology may have changed, but the essence was the same. An individual was trained to manipulate what, in T'mork's mortal days, was known as the wells of sorcery, but now had become the arcane plains. There were spells and incantations that any magic user of any discipline could learn, and then those of certain schools of magic. And, as a necromancer, T'mork did briefly toy with the idea of using these common schools of magic to make a grand and spectacular entrance when he boarded the captured Ophidian ship, but decided against such an ostentatious show of power.

Stepping down from the long ladderway leading to the deck of the much smaller ship, T'mork turned to regard his latest acquisition. The three-masted ship – a xebec, according to Demelecles – was battered in places, showing damage from a recent battle. The crew – some forty men – were gathered together in one large group on the upper deck, surrounded by twenty revenants. Whilst T'mork knew better than most the fighting prowess of revenants, he also knew that a determined band of armed men twice their size had a good chance of fighting them off. It was the powerful war galley and deadly Khopeshii that sailed alongside the xebec, no doubt, that persuaded the crew to surrender without a fight. Besides, another fifty skeletal sailors waited, armed and ready on the upper deck of the war galley. A similar number were poised on the deck of the Khopeshii, running silently alongside the port bows of the xebec.

T'mork paced slowly across the deck, his milky-orb eyes fixing from crew member to crew member as he closed with the band of prisoners. All of them – to a man – regarded him with blatant fear plastered across their doomed faces. Just as it should be. T'mork heard a familiar breath behind him as the captured scholar dropped from the final rung of the ladder. She was useful, skilled, obedient. He was almost tempted to reward her for her service by asking her what her name was. T'mork turned to the scholar. Her dirty face was streaked with tears, as always. Yet, she stood healthy, unhurt, and well fed, but seemed completely unappreciative of that fact.

"Find out who the captain is," T'mork commanded.

The young woman stepped tentatively forward and stammered out a sentence in a language T'mork did not understand. A few seconds passed in silence. She repeated the challenge but was again met with no response from the crowd of captured sailors.

"Very well," T'mork whispered and stepped forward.

He picked out a sailor – a young man barely out of his adolescence, with the fair hair and skin of a man of the north, clad in ragged, striped trousers and a loose fitting shirt.

"Bring that one to me," he ordered two of his revenant sailors.

The young sailor looked terror-stricken from side to side as two of T'mork's revenants grabbed him by the arms, dragging the pleading man across the deck toward T'mork. The scholar began to sob, clearly knowing what was to come. Before T'mork could speak again, a second sailor stepped out from the crowd. Another young man, not old enough to have seen over a quarter of a century, with blond hair and the olive skin tone common of the peoples of the southern Successor Kingdoms, as they were known in this new world. This second sailor, standing tall and confident, stared through his fear at T'mork and spoke.

Barely a second had passed when a third sailor emerged from the crowd. Perhaps a little older, tall and powerfully built, with the darker skin tone often seen amongst the people of the south.

"I..." He pointed at himself. "I be commander."

T'mork narrowed his eyes and leaned forward with interest. The man spoke the tongue of the Ahmunites, or at least something similar enough for the words to be recognizable. But languages evolved over time. Perhaps this was their tongue now? The second sailor, the blond man, rushed forward a pace and pointed at himself again, shouting out in his own language. The darker-skinned man shook his head.

"No. I be commander."

T'mork smiled and pointed at the first man – his would-be victim – and the blond, olive-skinned sailor.

"Throw them back in with their comrades. If they speak again, kill them and the men who stand to either side of them. You – tell them that."

Obediently, the scholar translated T'mork's words into their own language. The two men were dragged back and thrown into the crowd of captured, silent sailors. T'mork turned back to the taller sailor who had stepped forward.

"You are Ahmunite?"

He shook his head.

"Ophidian."

T'mork smiled again. A descendent of the hated, treacherous refugees who shared a common tongue centuries ago. But even within his still, dead heart, T'mork felt that this man could not be held accountable for the sins of his ancestors. Then again, T'mork possessed enough self awareness to know that his empathy and benevolence had always been a little over-developed.

"What are you doing here?" T'mork spoke slowly, clearly knowing that some words would have morphed into something else over the passage of time.

The Ophidian sailor looked confused for a moment and then nodded.

"Pirates. We am pirates."

T'mork let out a brief, quiet laugh. Pirates had seemed so exciting and courageous to him as a child. Then, when he met and fought them, he found only desperate men and women struggling to make enough money to stay alive. He issued a slight shrug of his shoulders.

"Then you, my friend, are out of luck. I have no use for a pirate ship."

The Ophidian darted forward desperately as T'mork turned away.

"Ships of war!" he cried, pointing to the north. "Ships of war, coming! Basileans! Salamanders! Searching!"

T'mork turned back. He leaned in to regard the Ophidian sea captain curiously, wondering if this was the truth or a desperate ploy in an attempt to save his own skin. The pirate failed to meet the high priest's probing stare. T'mork's lipless mouth twisted into a yellow-toothed grin.

"How big?" he demanded. "The salamander warships? What size?"

The Ophidian pointed across to the Khopeshii maintaining

Mark Barber

station off the xebec's port side. He then pointed to the damage cut into the xebec's hull and masts.

"That size. It did this. I... search them. Tell you where they be."

T'mork raised a dry, shriveled finger to tap his chin thoughtfully. On the one hand, another forty slaves for the temple – especially workers who were fit and strong – would be useful. On the other hand, he could find forty slaves nearly anywhere. A ship crewed by mortals that could infiltrate the merchant sea lanes without causing mass panic, and then report back to him? That was a rare opportunity. But the counter to that was that the man was Ophidian. In many ways, that in itself was deserving of death.

Stepping forward again, T'mork leaned down to stare into the man's face, hunting out any signs of dishonest intent. But even if that dishonesty was there – and this was a pirate, so it was a safe assumption – there were ways of forcing loyalty. Fear was probably the most effective of those ways. With his right hand, T'mork fished down into one of the pouches at his waist. With his left, he grabbed the Ophidian by the wrist. The pirate instinctively attempted to drag his arm free, staring fearfully up into the Ahmunite high priest's eyes as he did so. But, perhaps remembering what was at fate, he quickly ceased resisting and allowed his arm to be pulled upward.

T'mork picked out a small, black item from the pouch at his waist and held it up. An ancient, dormant scarab beetle. A symbol of both luck and rebirth to the Ahmunites. Murmuring a simple incantation, his words mumbled in dry rasps as tendrils of magical energy flowed from the arcane plains and into his body, T'mork channeled these unnatural powers into the scarab. The beetle's wings slowly, awkwardly, fluttered open. The Ophidian recoiled, his face twisted in terror and revulsion as he watched the ancient, thumb-sized beetle brought back from the dead.

The pirate screamed in pain as T'mork slammed his hand down onto the mortal's forearm, and the scarab burrowed into his flesh.

"You will search for warships," T'mork commanded him as he yelled out, his arm shaking, "and you will report back to me. If you flee, I will know. With this scarab, I will always be able to find you. If you try to remove it, you will die. You are mine, now. You, your ship, your crew. You are all mine."

***

Wrapping a supportive arm around his quivering friend's shoulders, Tem helped Halladai over to sit down on the upper deck before gently leaning him back against the mainmast. The quartermaster stared, bleary-eyed and pale-faced, at the black scarab which now lay motionless, half buried into the flesh of his shaking forearm. As the xebec drifted on through the night, the flotilla of Ahmunite warships picked up speed and accelerated gently away, leaving their new scout ship pitching and rolling in their wake.

"Water!" Tem shouted across at Hoggir. "Get him some water! The rest of you, get us underway and set a course for west of nor'west!"

With a combination of anxious mutters and terrified silence, Tem's sailors set about carrying out his orders. Tem dropped to one knee by Halladai.

"Why?" he whispered. "Why did you do that? I'm the captain! I'm responsible for this!"

Halladai looked up, his dry, cracked lips forced into a weak smile.

"Ahmunites," he gasped. "We have a... history. I knew I could... make them listen to me. They would have killed you outright, Tem."

Leaning to one side to cough and splutter as nervous air remained trapped in his aching gut, Tem found himself yet again wishing for those simple days of following a captain's orders as another pirate took on the responsibility of command. Those days were easier and, if his darkly clouded memory served, those days only saw the loss of friends very, very rarely. But now? Was this his fault?

Halladai rested a hand lightly on Tem's shoulder.

"Don't look so... worried... shipmate. We're not dead! We have... options..."

Tem tried to match that courageous smile but failed.

"What options?" he whispered desperately.

Halladai shrugged lightly.

"I can leave... they only know where I am. Or... they only know where my... arm is... lesser men have done well at sea... without one arm..."

Tem felt the urge to shout at his friend, to tell him not to suggest such ridiculous ideas. But, being truthful with himself, he had already considered both of those options. And worse.

"It's too early to worry," Tem swallowed, "too much can change. Look, let's head up near those Basilean bastards and see what we can see. If we report back to the Ahmunites and we do a good job, maybe they'll let us go."

Halladai let out a choked laugh at Tem's words. It lacked both humor and optimism.

"This is us... for now..." he whispered, his eyes drifting in and out of focus. "We work for the boneships, for now."

Tem stood up and looked ahead, past the bows at the short, squat Ahmunite vessels clearing away toward the dark horizon. Fortunes changed so quickly. What he would have given to go back merely a single hour, and be in a different place so that the Ahmunites had never found him. What he would have given to have a life so simple that all he needed to fear was an angry pirate chief, rather than the lords of the god of death himself.

***

The frigate's bows rose steeply up the turquoise wall of water before the ship pitched over at the crest of the wave, giving Jaymes a momentary feeling of utter weightlessness before the thousand ton warship nosed over to lunge back down into the next trough. The metal-plated bows carved their way through the foamy waves, sending sheets of warm water smashing across the fo'c'sle and soaking a dozen sailors before it fell back down to either side.

"Do you want extra hands up top, sir?" yelled Grace Bynnio, *Pious's* new sailing master.

Jaymes turned from his position on the heaving quarterdeck to look across at the veteran sailor, on temporary loan from the Sisterhood. The short, middle-aged woman had hawkish eyes which looked as though nothing would escape their attention, with flecks of gray in her auburn hair. Standing out from the ranks of the Basilean Navy, she wore the white leggings and tunic, trimmed with blue, of her order.

Jaymes shook his head and shouted his reply back over the howling wind.

"I don't think so! *Pious* is a tough lady – I don't think anything will start falling off of her just yet!"

Up ahead, the broad sails of the Ahmunite vessels were a blur, a smudge on a drizzly horizon to the south. Only appearing now as a faint, green line across the horizon were the first signs of land – islands of the Leeward Archipelago. His feet wide apart for balance on the rolling boards of the quarterdeck, Jaymes raised his telescope again. The larger of the two sails was clearly another Khopeshii, pretty much identical to the prize ship *Pious* had recently brought back into Thatraskos. Next to her was something shorter and squatter, with a similarly shaped structure on her deck that even from this range could be seen glowing a pale blue. Jaymes also thought he could intermittently see one, no two, much smaller sails flanking the two ships; but from this distance, they could have been the white peaks of large waves. Way off to port – right on the limit of the visibility in the dreary conditions – Jaymes could see a tiny Ahmunite slave galley parallelling *Pious's* track, cautiously remaining at a distance but no doubt following the progress of the Basilean vessel.

"We're closing, I think!" Kaeso Innes shouted from the port side of the quarterdeck, leaning into his own telescope. "It's that oar-driven little fellow next to the frigate! The Khopeshii has reefed some in to let that thing keep up!"

Another huge wave smacked into *Pious's* bows with an audible slap, knocking the frigate up at an angle before she teetered on the peak and then plunged back down toward the white-rippled waters. Even given the severity of their task, Jaymes could not help but smile at the indescribable experience of standing atop a thousand ton ship being tossed around by the elements.

"The center of this weather is heading north, sir!" Sister Grace called across. "I think we'll see the wind back and slack!"

Jaymes looked abaft, back over his frigate's stern. Sure enough, the worst of the rain seemed far away now and, exactly as his new sailing master said, that would likely see the wind dying away and altering off to port a little more. That would likely help them – yes, the Khopeshii would also benefit from the wind change, but the squat, oar-driven ship would not; and as long as the Ahmunite frigate was holding back to stay in company with her, *Pious* would close all the more quickly. Off to port, the slave galley continued to fight against the building waves to keep pace with the Basilean frigate.

Jaymes was interrupted from his pondering by the unsteady thump of booted feet on the steps leading up to the quarterdeck. Jaymes looked across, just about succeeding in suppressing a smile, as he saw Karnon Senne stagger over toward him. The marine captain tentatively took step after step across the heaving, soaked deck like a toddler learning to walk, one hand gripping the forward taffrail with white knuckled intensity whilst the other flew out for balance above his shaking legs. Karnon, green faced and wide-eyed, finally made it over to Jaymes, Grace, and Kaeso.

"Don't you dare puke on me!" Jaymes grinned. "This isn't an issue shirt, I bought this one myself!"

"Officers are supposed to buy all of their own rig!" the pale-faced marine managed between worryingly vocal belches. "Anyway, look over there! Three points starboard of the bows! You see it?"

Jaymes raised his telescope again. Starboard of the bows he could see the mist drizzle atop the vivid green of jungle-covered hills beginning to clear well enough. Then he saw it. A dark smear, a pillar of black. After a few moments to allow his eye to adjust, he could make out two distinct columns of black smoke rising from the water's edge of one of the larger islands in the chain.

"Yes, I see it!" he called to Karnon. "I'll need to head down below and grab a chart, find out what's..."

"Already checked, sir!" Karnon shouted. "It's a colony settlement, at a place called Roe's Spring! It's one of ours!"

Jaymes snapped his telescope shut and ran a hand across

his mouth, his humor of the dire situation immediately deflated. It did not take much to put two and two together when an undead flotilla was running away from a burning settlement full of civilians. He looked across at Kaeso and Grace.

"We need to get marines ashore," he called, "and it needs to be quick! I'm not losing those Ahmunite bastards!"

"In this sea state, sir?" Kaeso smiled uncomfortably. "We can do it... but it won't be fast! And we're carrying on the chase without our marines? What if we need to board?"

"There are Basilean citizens on that island!" Jaymes replied. "They *must* be our priority! We'll have to make do without Captain Senne and his troops! We need to find somewhere to get the sea boats into the water!"

Grace pointed toward the eastern edge of the island.

"Perhaps there, sir? There will be some shelter from the wind from that high ground, and we can resume the pursuit around the western edge of the island!"

Jaymes nodded.

"Looks good! I'm going below to check the chart, to make sure we've got the sea room and the water beneath the keel! Karnon, get your lads ready for a boat transfer ashore, full kit, I'm leaving you behind!"

The mention of leaving Karnon behind on firm land and potentially with a fight on his hands seemed to immediately cure him of his seasickness. He smiled and staggered off to assemble his troop. Jaymes turned to Kaeso.

"Mister Innes! You have the con!"

Jaymes headed below toward his cabin to formulate his plan over a chart.

***

The first of the two boats nudged its prow into the sand with a jolt as a fresh shower of rain swept in across the island. Karnon was the first out of the boat, vaulting over the side to plunge into the warm water up to a little below his waist. His marines followed him from both boats as he waded the short distance to the shore, checking over his shoulder to see both boats paddling around in the surf to then begin rowing back toward the anchored frigate. Forty marines, armed with a motley assortment of spears, swords, crossbows, and muskets waded up through the rain-speckled, blue-green water and onto the beach.

"Sergeant Porphio!" Karnon turned to yell. "First Squad! Form up on my left! Sergeant Juut! Form up Second Squad on my right!"

Both sergeants turned to yell at their marines, each assembling a unit of twenty fighting men in two ranks in the wet sand. Karnon, relieved to have his feet sinking slightly into firm, steady ground, looked up to where the beach gathered into a natural pathway leading up to the settlement atop a trio of hills to the southeast. Further to his right, a small jetty that was once used to load supplies for the colony, and export the sugar grown at the site, was blazing furiously. Even from this distance, Karnon could make out a handful of charred corpses around the fire. He thanked the Ones above that he was not downwind of it.

"First Squad," Karnon ordered. "Take the lead!"

"Pikes! Swords!" Sergeant Porphio bellowed. "Up front! Rank of five! Crossbows and muskets to follow!"

The forty marines made their way up the snaking path to the higher ground as, simultaneously in the small bay, *Pious's* two boats returned to the ship at anchor. Karnon could practically feel Jaymes's frustration from here, delayed in his pursuit of the Ahmunite boneships by committing to the laborious process of dropping anchor to launch and recover his sea boats. Moving his squads up the hill, Karnon was momentarily transported back to a similar series of maneuvers only weeks before when, on his first battle as a marine rather than a soldier of the legion, he led his men ashore to close with a band of marauding orc pirates. Again, human colonists were targeted. The difference this time was that orcs would capture helpless colonists to sell as slaves to the Twilight Kin or Abyssal Dwarfs. The Ahmunites? Treatment at the hands of the Empire of Dust would likely result in eternal slavery amidst the ranks of the undead. Karnon was not sure which was worse.

A familiar and unwelcomingly sickening smell wafted across the hot air as the marines advanced along the pathway weaving between the fields of long grass, blown in patches by a stiffening wind beneath a gray sky. Two further columns of black smoke continued to blossom up in acrid plumes at the end of the dirt road connecting the tiny harbor to the main settlement. From his central position between his two squads, Karnon eyed the sugarcane fields to either side as they advanced on the settlement, but he saw or heard nothing to galvanize him into action.

On the outskirts of the small colony – a collection of wooden huts and storage houses at the bottom of the final hill, the peak of which was dominated by a burning manor house – the marines encountered more bodies. Perhaps a dozen, all fighting age men who lay with improvised weapons not far from where they fell. All had been shot with arrows or cut down with bladed weapons.

"No necromancers in this group, then," Porphio remarked to his captain. "They wouldn't have left bodies behind if they could animate them."

Karnon looked helplessly around the deserted settlement, the crackling of flames accompanying the gentle rushing of wind through the tall grass and sugarcane of the fields. Rounding a cliff face at the northern edge of the colony, Karnon saw *Pious* sailing past, her sails set full as she picked up speed to resume the pursuit of the Ahmunite frigate and her accompanying vessels. Content that there was no enemy to fight, for the moment at least, Karnon turned to his troops.

"Teams of ten – fan out and search the area for survivors."

***

"Ship's steady on a course of sou' by southeast, making good twelve knots," Kaeso reported to Mayhew on the quarterdeck. "Wind from the northeast, sea state has been moderate to rough. Sails are set to full; the captain does not want studding sails. Enemy vessels on the bow, two miles ahead, Ahmunite frigate and something resembling a bomb ship, possibly one of those Soul Hunters. Could be a couple of slave galleys, too, but we didn't get close enough before we put the sea boats in the water to drop off the marines. And we're still being watched by that little bastard off to port, parallelling our course."

The taller lieutenant nodded sagely as he surveyed the horizon to the southeast.

"Understood, Mister Innes. I have the con."

"You have, old boy. I'm off to get my head down."

Content that the watch handover had been conducted thoroughly enough, Jaymes watched his Second Lieutenant walk back down to the upper deck before turning to head down below to his cabin, his four hour watch now complete. Jaymes could, naturally, take conduct of the ship for himself, but he was content for his lieutenants to run things during a simple pursuit, aided by the advice from his new sailing master. He looked up at the heavens, noting a trio of pillars of light where the sun was winning in its fight against the blue-gray, drizzle-bearing clouds, and offered a quick prayer for Danne Estrayia, the role's previous incumbent. He then glanced back over his shoulder at the colony at Roe's Spring, or at least what he imagined was left of it beneath the still rising columns of black smoke as the island retreated over the horizon.

"You alright, sir?"

Jaymes turned back to face his first lieutenant. Mayhew Knox annoyed him. No, that was not fair. Mayhew Knox *frustrated* him. A fundamentally good person and a capable officer, but only when either kept under close supervision or in those golden few days of high performance and motivation which came immediately after Jaymes had shouted at him for doing something lazy, stupid, or both. Only three years Jaymes's junior, Mayhew could have been commanding his own sloop by now. But he lacked the consistency of command performance and the motivation. The potential was there, at least.

"I'm alright," Jaymes flashed a smile, "just keen that we don't lose that Khopeshii. I think that ship, or the smaller ones in company with it, likely have some of the workers and their families onboard. If they're still alive, we're the only chance they have."

"If that is the case, sir," Mayhew continued, scratching at his neat, dark red beard thoughtfully, "I take it we won't fire on them? Can't risk a stray shot breaking through the hull and harming our own citizens. But if we board, we'll get shot up on the way in, and then we're closing for a boarding action with no marines."

Jaymes issued another smile – one which he hoped was encouraging, even confidence-inspiring – but was driven by the common sense thought process vocalized by his first lieutenant.

"If there's any doubt when we catch up, we'll load bar shot and aim high. Everything into their masts and rigging. And if it comes to boarding, we did well enough even before we had a specialized corps of marines. I'd rather have Captain Senne and his lot with us, of course, but we'll do well enough."

Mayhew's face momentarily seemed to portray a sentiment of slightly elevated ease, even confidence. Then his eyes narrowed, his head tilted, and then both eyes widened suddenly as he looked aft, over Jaymes's shoulder. Jaymes span around on his heel and looked back over the after end of the frigate, toward the Leeward Archipelago. His heart froze in his chest as he let out an audible breath before training and experience overcame his natural reaction to freeze in panic.

"Hard about!" Jaymes yelled across the quarterdeck to his helmsman, and up to the topmen along the yards of the three masts. "Hard a' starboard! North, by northwest! Back to the island! Beat to quarters!"

***

Standing atop the rain-soaked cliff, frozen in place, Karnon stared out to sea in utter disbelief. Below the cliffs, only a handful of cables out into the bay, the sea was suddenly disturbed into a swirling vortex of dark, turbulent water. The whirling waves twirled faster, spinning before spewing outward with waters rising to great, foam-tipped crests in all directions. Less than a second later, the bone-colored, ram-tipped prow of a great ship burst up out of the sea. Atop the prow was a weapons platform with a huge catapult secured in place. The entire warship shot up at a diagonal angle, like a great sea monster angrily clawing its way up into the air above. A long, broad hull of light wood followed, topped by two masts fitted with wide, stout yards. A tall stern finally emerged; atop it was a great temple and pillars of white marble, all shedding sheets of sea water as the warship fell forward to plunge down into the sea with a force that Karnon thought must surely break her back.

With the waves still seemingly flying outward from the ship's bows, Karnon saw ant-like figures scrambling across the deck and up the masts and ratlines as skeletal sailors clambered up to the yards. Simultaneously, ancient sea boats packed with skeletal figures were lowered into the water from both sides of the ship. Karnon span in place to address his astounded marines.

"Form up! Get back into squads! Sergeants, take charge! Get everybody back together and get to the hill at the top of that beach!"

Four sea boats were propelled forth through a channel of unnaturally calm water that cut through the crashing waves to either side of the bay. As he led his men in their desperate run toward the beach where the Ahmunite landing party was headed, Karnon reckoned on facing at least double the number of undead soldiers compared to his own unit. The marines sprinted back along the path weaving through the decimated, burning colony and reached the top of the shallow, sandy slopes leading down to the bay's main beach. The four Ahmunite boats were only moments away from reaching the beach themselves, their oars propelling them through the still waters with an eerie show of inhuman discipline to their timing.

Karnon took a few moments to take in the surrounding terrain, looking for areas of cover that gave clear shots at the undead invaders as they moved inland, or hid his troops from sight. He turned to his two sergeants.

"Sergeant Porphio – get your shooters up on that ridgeline to the west. Start firing with the muskets as soon as they're within range. Keep your pikemen and swordsmen closer to the path, and down out of sight. Sergeant Juut – you do the same with that lip of ground atop the cliff, just over there to the east. We'll hit them with a crossfire as they come up the beach and then charge downslope to attack before they've got a proper foothold."

Both sergeants faced their squads to relay their orders, moving their marines into position on either side of the sandy rock faces leading down to the beach. Knowing Porphio was a more experienced sergeant, Karnon elected to follow Juut as the newly promoted sergeant chivvied his marines off to position atop the cliffs. The naval soldiers were not even in position by the time the first Ahmunite boat drove up onto the beach. A trio of cracks sounded from the far side of the cliffs as Porphio's marines opened fire with their muskets, their position given away by puffs of smoke rising above the lush vegetation running around the rim of the natural bowl of the beach. Down below, one of the skeletal oarsman's skulls caved in as a musket ball blew through it, and the undead sailor crumpled forward over its oar.

"Muskets!" Juut yelled. "Targets front! Independent firing! Open fire!"

Six shots snapped out in quick succession, filling the air with the stench of burnt powder. As the first undead sailors jumped out of the boat and onto the beach, one was struck square in the chest and fell back to lie motionless in the surf.

The second boat pushed up onto the beach, and another twenty skeletal sailors, garbed in tattered uniforms of dark blue and gold, leapt out of the boat and formed up into ranks in the wet sand. Another salvo of shots fired down from Porphio's marines on the far side of the beachtop cliffs, dropping another two skeletons where they stood. Almost immediately after, the rumble of cannon fire echoed from the anchored Ahmunite war galley in the bay. It was followed by the low, droning whine of cannonballs flying through the air before the ground shook, and Karnon saw clumps of earth and chips of rock thrown up into the air just behind Porphio's marines.

The musket-armed marines crouched in the clifftop undergrowth around Karnon fired again, but on the beach below, the third and forth sea boats had already arrived, and more skeletons armed with spears and curved blades were assembling in fighting ranks, despite the cracking of muskets slowly thinning their numbers. Again, a deep rumble sounded from the ancient war galley in the bay. This time, however, there was no smoke from the cannons emerging from her flanks.

Gray-black clouds suddenly sprouted up above the huge warship, churning and twisting with unnatural speed. Sparks of yellow flashed from within the bubbling, black cloud as the rumbles intensified. Then, even more suddenly than the dark clouds had appeared, a deafening roar whooshed out from the skies above the ship as jagged bolts of lightning shot across the skies, just the briefest of flashes for a fraction of a moment. The arc of lightning spat out to cut across the clifftops on the far side of the beach, tearing through Sergeant Porphio's squad of marines.

"Sir!" Sergeant Juut shouted to Karnon. "We need to fall back! They outnumber us, they've got guns on the warship for support, and they've got a mage! We need to fall back!"

"No!" Karnon yelled. "No! We close with those bastards down there on the beach! We close with them, and we cut them down! As soon as we're in among them, that ship won't fire on its own troops!"

"They're undead, sir!" Juut urged desperately. "They don't give a damn about knocking their own down! We need to fall back!"

Karnon looked out to sea again, his eyes tracking right to look further to the east. There, emerging from the murk and drizzle, he saw the familiar lines of *Pious*. The frigate pelted toward the bay, rising and falling with the heavy swell and the towering waves, her bow chasers blasting out a series of speculative, long ranged shots at the Ahmunite war galley.

For just a second, Karnon found himself inexplicably thinking about his cabin on the ship. That cozy, wooden walled room, his escape from the nonsense of his working days and nights, his time to retreat into himself and mentally regroup for the next day. He thought of his books, the novel he was so near to the end of. He thought of the pile of letters from his wife that he took everywhere with him, now tantalizingly close enough for him to practically reach out and touch, but barred from him by an ocean of white-tipped waves. What he would have given, at that moment, to be back in that cabin with his books and his letters.

"Alright!" Karnon shouted to Juut and his squad. "We'll fall back to the settlement! We'll regroup there! Come on, let's go!"

Karnon and his marines had taken barely half a dozen steps away from the clifftops when the war galley's broadside boomed out again. Karnon heard the whistling drone of cannonballs, but different this time. The pitch, the rapidly increasing volume; he knew even before the impact that they were the target. The ground beneath his feet was dragged away from him, twisting to a bizarre and unnatural, diagonal angle as his body was wracked with sharp pains. The skies tumbled, the world twirled, the rocky ground rushed up at him, and all faded to black in an instant.

***

The intensity of the waves began to ease as the frigate rounded the corner of the island, the sandstone cliffs shielding the waters from the worst of the wind. Up ahead, the huge Ahmunite war galley still lay at anchor in the bay but had already sprung around her anchor to line up her broadside with the approaching Basilean warship. How in the seven circles had they managed that?! Jaymes had seen Trident Realm creatures emerge suddenly from the depths, but an entire Ahmunite warship, the size of a third-rate? If he had not seen it with his own eyes, he would say that even in seas seemingly capable of anything and everything, it was still impossible.

Spitting out a string of obscenities from his position on the quarterdeck, Jaymes lowered his telescope from his eye. Stood next to him, telescope still raised and scouring the clifftops, Mayhew swallowed uncomfortably.

"They're marching our marines down to their boats. Our lot have surrendered."

"Yes, I can see that!" Jaymes snapped.

"How in the Abyss did that ship manage to..."

"I don't know, Mayhew! I don't bloody know!"

Grace took a few paces across to stand next to the two naval officers.

"Sir. The enemy frigate and her accompanying ships are nearly out of visual range."

Jaymes looked across at the veteran sailing master.

"Plot them. Plot them on our chart. We'll resume the chase when we're done here."

Mayhew looked across at his captain, fear painted plainly on his face, but said nothing. Grace paused, narrowed her eyes, and then spoke.

"When we're done here, sir? Taking a fifth-rate frigate head to head against a ship with the power of the third-rate, without the advantage of surprise, support, or the weather gauge? What state do you expect us to be in when we're done here, sir?"

Jaymes turned to square up with the sailing master, drawing himself up to his full height.

"That's the enemy flagship. That's our marines being taken to her. Our ship's company. Our friends. Our job is to destroy the enemy. Our responsibility is to our shipmates. We will be in a poor state after this is done, but we will do our damned duty! Clear?"

The two great catapults atop the war galley's deck flung their arms up and forward, sending huge projectiles of glowing purple-red arching up through the rain-filled sky. Finding his hands quivering and a clawing sensation ripping between his lungs, Jaymes could only stand and watch the deadly balls of magical fire loop down toward his ship. The first fell well short; the second plunged into the sea much closer and sent a pillar of water up over *Pious's* foremast, the projectile continuing to glow and shimmer as it fell down to sit on the seabed not far below.

Jaymes raised his telescope again. The war galley's sea boats were not far from coming alongside, where they would be hoisted up along with their captives. As Jaymes regarded the larger, more powerful enemy ship, he saw flashes of orange along her flanks. A second later, the boom of the heavy cannons echoed across the bay and the whoosh of cannonballs droned through the air. A trio of water columns splashed up off the starboard bow before the whole ship shuddered as a cannonball clanged against the metal encased prow of the frigate. Jaymes leaned over the quarterdeck's forward taffrail to shout down to the upper deck.

"Get the carpenter up for'ard with his mates! Get that damage checked!"

Before a reply was issued, Jaymes again felt the deck lurch from beneath his feet. There was no impact. No sudden turn. No, the frigate was slowing down. He looked up at the sails above and saw them billowing as the wind suddenly dropped away. He looked to either side of the ship and saw the same, tell-tale windlanes carving through the turbulent waters, but for just a few dozen yards around *Pious,* the wind seemed suddenly calm.

"Haul the sheets in!" Grace called across to the crews on the sails and their sheets. "Lively, now! I don't want to see a single fold up there!"

Mayhew rushed across to stand by Jaymes's side.

"Sir... I... that wind, dropping like that. I know you've seen more of this than I have, but... I think this is sorcery. I think we're being slowed down at precisely the moment we're facing an enemy broadside, and we're out of range of our own bow chasers still. Sir... we're sailing very slowly into the perfect position for a much larger ship to rake our bows."

Jaymes span around to face the younger officer, anger forcing his eyes to narrow into a furious glare. Their duty was clear. It was the enemy flagship, the whole reason for their patrol. It was Karnon and his marines onboard who needed rescuing. It was his duty to his nation, and to his friend. And this incompetent coward was trying to talk him out of it.

Jaymes stopped as soon as he opened his mouth to yell at his first lieutenant. He remembered being in those very shoes, on this very quarterdeck addressing this ship's previous captain. He recalled the frustration of trying to talk sense into a pig-headed, duty-obsessed, glory-seeking fool. A better captain than Jaymes could ever hope to be. But Jaymes could always try to be the better man. He looked forward at the looming Ahmunite ship of war, her guns bristling in readiness. He estimated the range – comfortably within striking distance for the majority of the war galley's weapons, but only just approaching range now for his nine-pounder bow chasers. And for what? To tickle away at a fully alerted enemy ship with twice *Pious's* firepower and a stronger hull? Jaymes looked up at the sails above as the wind eased – exactly as Mayhew said, far too quickly and conveniently to be anything other than dark sorcery from the quarterdeck of the war galley. He looked back at his first lieutenant and clamped a hand against his shoulder.

"Thank you, Mayhew. You're right, we need to be cleverer than this. Bring us around to starboard and get us clear. Head north and get out of range of those guns."

The younger officer nodded.

"Aye, sir. Helm – hard to starboard, northerly heading. Sister Grace – sails set and trimmed, full."

"Aye, sir, full sails," the Sisterhood sailing master acknowledged, relief showing across her weather-beaten face.

The frigate lurched around to starboard, her yards shifting in the changing relative wind as she came about to take the waves on her port beam, leaning her over away from them. As the heavy, eighteen-pounder port guns lined up with the war galley, Jaymes momentarily considered giving the bastards one broadside at long range, but decided against antagonizing them further or risking harming his captured marines. No, a plan was formulating already. A plan that was far, far better than sailing a fifth-rate frigate directly into the broadside of a ship of the line.

The war galley's catapults heaved another pair of huge projectiles at *Pious* as she turned away from the fight, but at such a long range from weapons designed to fire at stationary, shore-based targets, the catapults' flaming munitions again missed their mark. Jaymes rushed over to the port aft quarter of the deck, bringing his telescope up to his left eye. The sea boats were being recovered by the war galley now, and moments later, the huge ship began springing around her anchor to line her bows up with the western side of the bay. Jaymes watched the evolution completed as the boats were recovered, the anchor was weighed, and the sails were set. Sadness and guilt tore at Jaymes's heart as he watched the huge ship make way to the west with his marines onboard. But it was the only way.

Footsteps across the quarterdeck brought Jaymes back from his melancholy spectating of the enemy flagship. He looked across and saw Grace approach.

"Sir."

She pointed off to starboard. Jaymes looked across and saw the Ahmunite slave galley that had been tailing them for some time had now broken away to head off to the southeast.

"Interesting course she's taken up, sir," the sailing master remarked dryly.

Jaymes nodded. He pointed at the war galley.

"That bastard there – that's what I wanted to get a course from. That little shit that's been following us? Seeing where they're off to, that's a bonus. Get fixes off both of them, plot their courses and compare it to where the Khopeshii was heading. With those three on the chart and a bit of luck, I'm hoping we'll have a cocked hat to narrow our search down."

The Sisterhood sailor gave a curt nod.

"Aye, sir, will do. Your plan is a good one, sir, it's the most accurate and empirical way to hunt them down. But I think it'll be just confirmation of a hunch, with a bit of luck. I've been sailing in these waters since you were a boy, sir, and…"

"How young do you think I am? Bloody hell!"

"No offense intended, sir – but I know these waters well. And I think I know where they're all headed. I think I know where our citizens – and our marines – are being taken to."

Chapter Fourteen

Southern Ansares Isles
East Infant Sea

Temples throbbing with dull aches, and sharp pains dancing along his back and legs greeted Karnon as he slowly awoke. The room was all but pitch black; his surroundings were cramped, hot, and filled with the stench of sweat. He could hear hacking coughs and the occasional moan of pain. He patiently awaited for his eyes to adjust to the darkness, noting that his ankles and wrists were shackled. The ground beneath him was dry and dusty. He slowly forced himself up to a seated position. A familiar voice whispered in the dark.

"Sir? You up?"

There was light emitting from somewhere. Not much, but enough for Karnon's eyes to begin to make out rows of shackled men, packed together shoulder to shoulder in the dark room, all seated or lying prone.

"Sir?" Sergeant Porphio asked again.

"Yeah... yeah, I'm up. Where are we? How many of us are here?"

The older marine shifted against his chains from next to Karnon.

"Don't know how many survived, sir. Gilly, Dex, and Smudge are in here with us. I saw Fauster and Lang from a distance last night. They've taken us to an island. They're building a temple. There's hundreds of people here, maybe over a thousand. They're using them all to build this bloody temple. Not just the living, either."

Gritting his teeth, Karnon slowly attempted to shift around where he sat to look down at his chains. Pain rocketed up his back and across his shoulders. He failed to suppress a hiss.

"Might be worth lying still, sir," his sergeant whispered. "I patched you up as best I could after they took us onto their boat."

"Ship," Karnon corrected weakly, faint memories of momentarily regaining consciousness on the enemy flagship slowly returning to his aching head.

Another cough wracked a poor wretch from somewhere on the other side of the blackened prison cell. Not far from that, Karnon thought he could hear somebody sobbing quietly.

"You'll have to work today, sir," Porphio continued. "I bought you as much time as I could. Promised them that you'd be on your feet and good to work. Whatever injuries you're carrying, if you don't work today... well, that'll be that."

Karnon swallowed, his parched throat aching. He rubbed the skin beneath the chains on his wrists and felt dried blood.

"You promised who?" he whispered. "We're dealing with Ahmunites. Most of them aren't sentient, and those who are don't speak our language. As a general rule."

"They've got a translator, sir. Another prisoner. Some poor girl from Ophidia. She gets paraded around with their boss – some high priest. I saw what they did to some of the others. Just... now's not the time for Hegemon and nation, sir. These bastards aren't here to piss about. Any back chat or bravery, and they'll kill us."

Karnon cleared his throat carefully and nodded slowly.

"Alright. Understood. But we still need to find a way out of here."

Porphio shifted suddenly in the darkness, leaning across.

"Find a way out, sir? You'll see when they drag us out to work at dawn. There's no way out. Nothing obvious, at least. They've got hundreds of undead bastards watching us, and we're chained up around the clock. We're in an even worse position than when we surrendered on the beach."

Karnon swore and grunted, unable to hide his disappointment with his old legion comrade.

"If they hadn't knocked me out, we wouldn't have surrendered on the beach, Sergeant. And every day, every hour that goes by from now on, we get weaker. Keep your wits about you and be ready for anything. As soon as I've come up with a plan, we're escaping."

**

It was difficult to mentally justify why, after centuries of dormancy followed by purification for the highest of all callings and an afterlife of meaning and purpose, that T'mork still found some pleasure in the arrival of clement weather. The wind and rain had picked up markedly overnight, but the last storm clouds were now retreating to the east to leave behind skies of clear blue and the burning sun that T'mork remembered so well from his mortal life. Perhaps that was it. Perhaps, lingering beneath that drive, that higher purpose, there was still a part of sentimentality that clung to memories of his youth, of his lost brother, F'Arza, reminded to him every day by the ancient ring on his dry, dead finger.

It mattered not. T'mork knew the seasons well enough to recognize this for what it was – a lull between storms, a brief respite before the winds drove in again to whip the seas up into a fury. But from where he stood, on the wide stretch of beach at the foot of the jungle-covered hills of an island he had not bothered to learn the name of, he could at least look up at the nearest of the peaks and enjoy the pride in his act of worship. The pride in pushing forth the boundaries of Shobik's influence, at the half finished temple that stood as a monument to the God of Death, and to T'mork's leadership and resolve.

The temple's base was built of marble, taken from the hold of his war galley. But there had only been enough to build a prism; a rectangular base and grand stairs leading up to a flat platform. After the resources he had brought with him had all been used, it was down to the crudeness of wood from the island for the temple's main chambers. A temporary measure.

T'mork watched as his hundreds of workers set about their tasks. The unskilled cut down the trees, under the supervision and direction of those skilled with lumber. The lumber was rip cut and then further cut for planks, which were then carried up to the hill and the temple. There, in accordance with the dimensions originally laid down in the Book of Ramillitep – but committed to memory by all priests of Shobik – the temple was constructed. A few workers had also been diverted across to the clifftops to construct a group of catapults to defend the temple from attack from the sea. The entire site was a perfect demonstration of how the living could work alongside the dead – the undead worked tirelessly, all hours, at menial tasks whilst the living conducted those jobs that required skill and initiative.

T'mork had, of course, taken measures to ensure his living workers were cared for well enough. Food and rest, shelter overnight; anything to keep them alive for as long as possible so that his source of skilled workers was adequate. Those who fell from exhaustion or were executed for trying to escape were simply reanimated and carried on as undead workers. T'mork tried to minimize that wherever possible; living workers using their initiative were a commodity – which was why he kept the women and the children hostage to ensure compliance – and every undead worker he needed to keep animated was a tiny drain on his powers. And it all added up. The sentient undead were the ideal solution, but they were even more of a drain and, from experience, raising revenants alongside their still living friends and families was a recipe for disaster.

"Master."

T'mork looked across to regard his addressor, dragged back to the present from his plans.

The Ophidian pirate, the captain of the ship he had captured, stood on the beach before him and gave a courteous bow. T'mork nodded to acknowledge the sign of respect. Good. That respect would keep the captain and his crew alive for longer. The irony of that thought was not lost on T'mork – he offered a painless death followed by a chance at eternal servitude, acknowledged and loved in the eyes of Shobik – yet he knew it took much for a mortal to realize this. He respected that. The ones who served loyally, he allowed them to cling to that ludicrous want and need to remain alive. In the end, they would come around to the true way.

"You did well," T'mork acknowledged. "The Basilean warship was exactly where you reported. Honesty will get you far. Unfortunately they did not have the courage to face me – and I do not blame them for that – but I've taken away some of their crew and sent them away with a bloody nose. So, a minor victory. In part thanks to you and your crew."

The Ophidian captain looked out across the bay, where his three-masted ship waited at anchor, awkwardly between the towering war galley and Khopeshii. T'mork still found some anger bubbling away within him, threatening the discipline he was justifiably proud of as he regarded the two remaining Khopeshii in his fleet. The loss of the third was something not easy to wear.

The pirate captain turned away, looked down at the static scarab burrowed into his forearm, and then back at T'mork. More specifically, his eyes looked *near* T'mork. Close enough to demonstrate some confidence, but still low and avoiding eye contact as an appropriate show of respect and subservience.

"Master, I… my crew ask… to know what… we do to be released. To go home. Whatever we do to serve and prove worth… we do it."

T'mork closed his eyes and hung his head regretfully. They did not understand. They failed to comprehend that if they proved their worth, he would reward them with death and the prize of purification. Even the Ophidian, perhaps. The captain and his crew were petrified of death and what lay beyond, and for what? Something as childish and trivial as the fearful veneer of dead flesh that encompassed the purified soul? Nonsense. To allow them to leave and return to their mundane, pointless existence? That was no reward. He opened his eyes again.

"Allow me be honest with you. You've earned that, at least. It is highly unlikely that any of you will walk away from here alive. Almost impossible. If you fail me or betray me, I will inflict a death more painful than you can imagine. If you serve me well, I will reward you with a gift you cannot yet understand or appreciate. Yes, there is a middle ground somewhere where, perhaps, I may let you leave alive. I understand that you want that. I do not agree with it, but I understand it. Beyond that, I have no more answers for you other than to command you to serve me loyally, and bravely, with all that you have."

The expression painted on the Ophidian sailor's face was neither surprising nor unfamiliar – the standard combination of despair and fear that T'mork was well accustomed to from the mortals he sometimes dealt with, saddened by their innocent ignorance. Yet T'mork, benevolent in his mercy, felt an almost paternal sympathy for them all.

"Back to your duties," he said, almost softly, "one of my scouts has reported enemy activity to the east of here – possibly the Basilean flagship, if the size they have reported is to be believed. Get back onboard and head east, stay close enough to report anything back to me. I shall be slipping anchor myself by sunset."

***

Tem left Hoggir to coordinate hoisting the sea boat back onboard the xebec as soon as he saw Halladai's feet touch the ladder built into the side of the hull. The quartermaster's dour face as the sea boat was rowed alongside the ship already told Tem all he needed to know, yet he found himself mentally demanding confirmation of the turns the conversation with their Ahmunite overlord had taken. The Ophidian pirate heaved himself back onboard, his shoulders slumped and his face heavy with despair. Those of the crew close enough to see him immediately fell silent. Tem gestured for the older sailor to follow him to the far corner of the quarterdeck, out of earshot of the other pirates.

"Dare I ask what happened?"

Halladai met Tem's stare silently. For a moment, a fleeting moment, he thought the veteran pirate might actually burst into tears. Still, he said nothing. Tem found a flash of anger flare up from his gut, but even in his exhausted and anxious state, he knew better than to give it credence.

"You've done enough, shipmate," he said quietly. "Come on, it's time. It's time that undead bastard knows I'm the captain. He can pull that thing out of your arm and put it in mine. Let's..."

"No!" Halladai shouted. "No! He's not going to let us go, Tem! Not now, not ever! Look – we either carry on as slaves to that bastard, or we... or... this *thing* gets thrown into the deep, and my damned arm with it!"

The fire rose again at such a stupid, defeatist, and pointless suggestion.

"Shut up with that stupid idea again, you damn fool! Just... shut up! Let me think!"

Tem span on his heel, running his hands across his sweat-covered face and his fingers through his hair. He took a few long breaths and fought to control his fears, assembling his thoughts into something resembling clarity to come up with a plan. Nothing came. Initially, at least. Then, after spending a few moments eliminating all of the most obvious routes that lay ahead of him and all of their most likely, grizzly ends, a few less obvious threads began to present themselves. Slowly, very slowly, Tem allowed himself a slight smile – the first in several days.

"Halladai, I think I have something. That frigate we found, the Basilean fifth-rate. That's part of something bigger, maybe an entire fleet sent to turn these bastards to matchwood. What if... what if we switched sides?"

Halladai shook his head.

"For what, mate? For what? Use your head! We've got a xebec here, and not a particularly big one! You're talking like we're sailing around in a man o'war! We can't make a difference!"

Tem shook his head.

"No, mate. You're wrong. We *can* make a difference. If we time it well. We can't scratch that war galley, but that Khopeshii? We get right behind her at the right moment, rake her stern from close enough to spit on her? We'll make a difference alright."

Halladai swore in his native tongue and threw his arms to either side.

"And then what? Suppose it's not enough? And the Ahmunites win, and we're traitors? Suppose they lose, and the Basileans grab hold of us? Suppose we escape the whole thing and Cerri finds out we've assisted the same side that sent a captain onto his island, insulted him to his face, cut out a ship, and then bombed his favorite tavern with it? Every one of those outcomes, *every* one ends up with all of us dead!"

Tem gritted his teeth and shook his head again.

"No. No! You think up a better plan for us, I'm all ears. Until then, we carry on with these zombified bastards. We do our job for them. We make ourselves look useful. And all the time we're doing that, we wait for the right time to do some damage. Some real damage."

***

The windward horizon was already orange with the dawn sun, a semi-circle of blood red peering slowly up to dispel the azures of the night. A dark shape was silhouetted against the rising sun; the stern of a ship disappearing off to the north, leaving only an Ahmunite frigate and two slave galleys at anchor in the bay. Day two. Day two of felling trees, sawing logs, and shifting the wood up toward the top of the first hill, where the logs were then turned into planks to be taken on to the temple. Day two of harsh work from before dawn until after dusk, with only the briefest of rests for the most meager of meals. Day two of frantically searching for other marines hidden in the crowds of silent, subservient slaves to their merciless undead masters, looking in passing lines for familiar faces to exchange a meaningful nod with. To warn that action was not far off.

The banging and hammering from atop the main hill was already well underway as Karnon and the line of slaves were marched silently out of their crowded prison and into the hot, dawn air. Karnon looked up and waited for his eyes to adjust to the near darkness, struggling to pick out the ant-like figures of undead workers continuing without pause on hammering the wooden walls into place atop the marble base of the temple to Shobik. There were certainly enough of them – perhaps a hundred reanimated corpses consisting of dwarf sailors, elderly workers who failed to keep up with the cruel pace demanded of them, and younger men who had attempted to escape or simply showed a resistant attitude to their captors. Only a stone throw away was a battery of half a dozen large catapults, their arms and buckets pointing out toward the bay below.

"They might be onto us, sir."

Karnon did not respond to the whisper from behind him in the line. He recognized the voice of Kartrite, one of his older marines and a survivor from Juut's squad.

"I heard one of the workers telling tales to a guard."

Karnon suppressed a curse. Treacherous, weak-willed, civvie bastard. Trading in freedom for the erroneous belief of favor from the captors. Most of the guards were brainless, non-sentient skeletal sailors, but there were a handful of the dangerous ones always on hand. The revenants, the sentient undead who could think; who could understand.

The prisoners filed out in long lines from their cramped huts, waddling in ungainly queues as much as their chained ankles and wrists allowed. Karnon glanced around as they moved forward to the foot of the first hill, always on the lookout for survivors from his two squads of marines. So far he had counted only twelve from forty. Each line – Karnon did not know how many ragged and wretched hundreds were present – was halted. In repetition of the day before, a skeletal guard at the head of each queue gave a bronze key to the lead prisoner, who unshackled their ankle chains before handing the key to the man behind. The wrists remained restrained, always.

As the key was handed back toward him, Karnon saw one of the revenants with an escort of two blue and gold garbed skeletal swordsmen walking along the lines of prisoners. In one of the adjoining rows, an aging, thin worker collapsed to his knees and was quickly dragged back to his feet by the men in front and behind him, most likely saving his life. The key arrived with Karnon, and he quickly unchained his ankles, eyeing the trio of undead sailors cautiously as they drew closer.

The revenant stopped by Karnon. He uttered something in a long dead tongue, and the two mindless skeletons paced over to grab him by his arms.

"Sir!" Kartrite called out.

"Stay in line, man!" Karnon snapped as he was marched away from the hundreds of staring prisoners.

So this was it. His wrists bound, stripped of his weapons, armor, even his uniform jacket, Karnon held his head high as the skeletons dragged him after the revenant toward one of the clifftops overlooking the bay. It was a beautiful sight, looking into the rising sun of some island he knew not where, exactly, within the eastern reaches of the Infant Sea.

A perfect blue sky and warm sunshine, with a gentle breeze rustling through the long grass and palm trees, scattered along the clifftops and surrounding hills. Beautiful birds of a dozen colors sang their morning songs. Insects rattled in the bushes. The ship silhouetted against the rising sun was larger now – Karnon at least had the presence of mind to realize that he was looking at the bows – not the stern as he first thought – as the ship sailed into the bay rather than away. Another of the Ahmunite fleet coming back in. Karnon smiled as he thought of that book he was slowly learning so much from as the two skeletal guards stopped him at the clifftop and drew their swords.

Of course, Karnon would go out with a bang. He would swing his fists, shout and swear, go down fighting as a Basilean marine should. His smile faded for a moment as he thought of his wife, of those few short weeks they had together after he moved her out to Keretia, ostensibly for their long future together at Thatraskos. Still, no need to be sad. Not now. He knew her well enough to know that she, too, would want him to go down with his fists swinging.

The revenant issued another dry, raspy command to the two skeletons. The first raised its sword whilst the second attempted to force Karnon down on his knees. Karnon shrugged the dead, boney hands away and pushed the skeleton back.

"Come on then, you ugly fu..."

Karnon's words stopped dead in his mouth. His eyes narrowed. He stared past his executors and into the sun. Another sail appeared as a second ship swung out from behind the first. A smile spread across the marine's lips. The smile became a laugh. The laugh grew in volume. He pointed at the tall sails of the two fighting ships – too tall to be Ahmunite.

"I think you've got a problem, dickheads!" he laughed at the trio of Ahmunite sailors.

The revenant turned to look down across the bay. Karnon had no idea that the undead were even capable of shock or alarm until that moment. He turned and sprinted back toward the lines of prisoners, screaming at the top of his lungs.

"Run! Run!"

The *Veneration* swung nimbly to port, easing out of the line astern formation from her position behind *Pious* as the four ships sailed toward the island with the sun at their backs. In turn, the *Deliverer's Flame* and the *Martolian Queen* altered to starboard, lining up for the longer length of beach at the far end of the bay. Only now was the tiny slave galley at anchor in the bay beginning to respond, springing about to turn to face the attackers. There was still nothing from the Khopeshii.

Jaymes scanned his telescope across the width of the bay. It was clear enough, now; a pathway led up from the beach to where there was a small jetty, past some long, low huts and up through the trees on the side of a shallow hill to a newly constructed temple. There were figures hard at work on the temple construction – odd, given the early hour – and another, larger group assembled near the clifftops overlooking the beach. Off to the west, further along the clifftops, was a defensive battery. Five... no, six, large catapults had been dug into the clifftops, giving a commanding view of the bay. They were already turning to face the four intruding ships.

"Enemy battery! Clifftops, south of southeast! Mister Turnio, signals!" Jaymes shouted across to his signals midshipman.

"Aye, sir!" the adolescent responded before rapidly attaching the appropriate colored flags onto the signaling halyard.

"Bow chasers! Target a point and a half to port! Clifftop battery!"

The order was relayed across to the fo'c'sle, and the gunners quickly set about aiming the forward facing nine-pounders toward the Ahmunite catapults.

"That little bastard's anchor is up," Mayhew reported, his own telescope lined up with the two enemy ships ahead.

Jaymes brought his own telescope about to regard them.

"Yes... there's movement on the Khopeshii now, too. Bit late, though. Unless that war galley appears from the depths again, I'd say we have them where we want them."

Jaymes looked across to port and saw Marcellus Dio's frigate racing alongside *Pious*, sails full. To starboard, the low, graceful salamander J'Koor'uk easily kept pace, whilst just visible through her emerald sails on the far side was the stout, stocky privateer brig. Behind them, now invisible against the rising sun, was the sloop *HW Scout*, under the command of Joshua Azer.

It was Joshua who had spent two days tirelessly racing between the larger ships of the Basilean force, relaying messages and coordinating orders from Captain Zakery Uwell on the *Shield Royal*. Finding the enemy anchorage was largely down to Jaymes and Grace on the *Pious*; the plan for a dawn attack and amphibious landing lay with Marcellus, but it was Zakery who approved it. However, with a war galley unaccounted for and shallower waters in the bay ahead, the towering *Shield Royal* lay in wait at the end of a chain of three sloops stretched in a communication line beyond visual range.

"They're firing!" Mayhew shouted.

Jaymes brought his telescope up again and saw that the arms of the six clifftop catapults were indeed raised. After a brief check of the skies above, he saw half a dozen glowing projectiles arcing toward them. They were in range now, but the shots were not accurate.

"Shooting, Lieutenant," Jaymes corrected.

"Sir?" Mayhew queried.

"They're not firing; they're shooting. You can't 'fire' a catapult, just like you can't fire a bow. They're not firearms. You shoot them."

"Yes, sir."

"It's a common mistake made by many true idiots, most often on the stages of the theaters of Ol' Goldie Horn, where bad actors scream 'fire' to hundreds of off-stage, imaginary archers. Truly destroying the immersion and suspension of disbelief for anybody in the audience who knows the first bloody thing about the real life military. But not at all appropriate for the quarterdeck of one of the Hegemon's warships."

"No, sir," Mayhew replied as the closest of the magically flaming projectiles slammed into the water between *Pious* and *Veneration*, "and a fantastically odd time for such an extended rant, if I may say so, sir."

Jaymes rapidly lowered his telescope and stared across at his inanely grinning first lieutenant.

"You may, Lieutenant. You may."

A shout was issued from *Pious's* fo'c'sle', then relayed back from midships.

"Approaching range for the bow chasers!" Kaeso Innes yelled from his position near the base of the main mast.

Jaymes looked up forward and saw the two light cannons lined up at the catapults. From off to port, *Veneration* opened fire with her own bow chasers; two brief bangs and a cloud of smoke drifting back across the frigate's upper deck in a sort of anti-climactic show of force that Jaymes had somehow always felt was unbecoming of a mighty frigate.

"Forward guns! Target one and a half points to port! Open fire!"

Pious's two bow chasers exploded into action, leaping back against their restraining ropes. Jaymes raised his telescope and surveyed the enemy battery. Some dust in the air from near misses from both Basilean frigates, but no hits. The six Ahmunite catapults again flung their arms and buckets up and forward, and another salvo of glowing projectiles soared up toward the four warships. Up ahead, the Khopeshii had raised her anchor and was now setting sail to drive out to meet the invaders.

***

Karnon had killed men with his bare hands before. With the ability to bludgeon with fists and elbows – and most importantly, to be able to choke – it was achievable enough to take a life. But what Karnon realized as he rolled around in the dust with the revenant sailor, the chain of his wrist shackles wrapped around his adversary's neck, was that animated corpses did not need to breathe. Panic ensued in every direction around them – slaves ran screaming and shouting for the jungles to the south, revenants charged around the disorderly skeletal guard force in an attempt to assemble units, cannonballs smashed into the catapult battery on the clifftops. Gunfire echoed around the cliffs of the bay while the impact of the shots shook the earth underfoot. And amidst all of it, teeth gritted, arms shaking, Karnon clung tenaciously to a revenant sailor's back and tore through the dead flesh of his throat with the rusted chain of his shackles.

"Sir! Turn the bastard around!"

Fighting to overwhelm the powerful undead warrior, Karnon pivoted in the dust and flung the revenant over his side. Stood above him, brandishing one of the curious, curve-bladed swords of the undead sailors was Tommias, one of the most recent additions to his marine force. His eyes ablaze and a vicious snarl twisting his features, the young marine lunged in with one swipe and beheaded the revenant.

"That'll do it!" Karnon sneered, grabbing the defeated revenant's own dropped blade and jumping to his feet. "Come on! We've got to get the lads all back together!"

"I saw Sergeant Porphio leading the civvies over to the jungle!" Tommias breathed.

"Right," Karnon grinned, "let's get our lot back together and grab ourselves some kit."

Another broadside erupted like thunder in the bay, and the ground shook again as the entire might of a Basilean frigate's starboard guns smashed into the cliffs. Dust, clumps of earth, and chips of rock flew up into the air not far from where the two marines staggered on their feet, and Karnon let out a laugh as he saw an entire segment of cliffside fall away into the sea, taking one of the catapults and its skeletal crew with it.

Down in the bay he saw *Pious*, drifting slowly forward with only her mainsails half-set, her bows hidden beneath the gray smoke of her own guns. *Veneration* had already dropped anchor and lowered her sea boats into the water, which were now being crammed with red-jacketed marines. Further toward the beach and the jetty, a salamander frigate and the *Martolian Queen* had come closer in, dropped anchor, and already had sea boats of their own paddling steadily toward the shore. The two Ahmunite warships that had been at anchor in the bay – Karnon had no idea what they were, a big one and a small one – had cut past *Pious* and were fleeing to the east, positioning to harness the wind for the most expeditious retreat.

Ahmunite sailors hurriedly assembled at the foot of the pathway, just above the beach. Four blocks of twenty skeletons, each four ranks deep, were ushered into place by a blue and gold armored revenant. Front and center ahead of them was a separate unit of twenty of the feared revenants armed with curved-hafted, long-bladed weapons that Karnon recalled grimly from his days in the legion. Shambling down to join them along the pathway leading up to the temple construction site were the undead workers, perhaps a hundred of them, armed with hammers and axes.

"Let's get to the jungle and find our lot," Karnon repeated, "but the way these dumb arseholes are assembling their force, I don't think they'll be much left for us to deal with. Come on, mate."

***

Fortune had been with *Pious* and her crew for sailing into the bay. Now, at anchor and with her broadside lined up on the beach, lowering the sea boats meant either stopping the cannons from firing, or taking the more hazardous option of hoisting the boats down on the windward side of the hull. Jaymes had opted for the latter to keep the supporting fire constant, but now peered over the port taffrail to see one of the boats hanging at a horrific angle due to some vast incompetence on the lines, whilst the bosun was yelling expletives at his team. The second boat was successively in the water and was loading up with sailors handpicked for their eagerness and ability in close quarter fighting.

"Sir!" Mayhew forced his way through the queue of impatient musket and hatchet wielding sailors waiting on the upper deck. "Sir! That Khopeshii is out of range of our guns! If we weigh anchor now, we can still give chase!"

"No," Jaymes shook his head grimly, "we stick to the plan, mate! We've got the most guns – we sit here and we blow the shit out of anything shoreside that doesn't have a pulse! Let them go – the priority is getting our people back from the island!"

The stern of the second sea boat was gently lowered into the waves until it sat at something resembling a safe and acceptable angle in the water. Mayhew moved closer until he was out of earshot of the sailors on the crowded deck.

"I still think I should go, sir," he urged. "It's typically the first lieutenant's job to lead the shore party, not the captain."

"But we're atypical, you and I!" Jaymes grinned. "I've seen you trying to waft a sword around, and I know I'm a double-hard bastard! Even if I don't look it! Keep the guns lined up on that beach – as soon as they start moving down the pass, blow them all back to their graves. If you don't have a clear shot or you have *any* concerns about hitting our own people, shift target and blow up that pissy little temple of theirs. Understood?"

Mayhew winced uncomfortably and then nodded.

"Aye, sir. Understood."

Jaymes looked down the side of his ship and saw the first boat, packed with sailors under the command of Benn Orellio, push clear of *Pious's* hull and lower its sweeps into the water. Jaymes looked up through his telescope again to survey the bay – two boats from the salamander J'Koor'uk were moments away from the beach, with two more from the *Martolian Queen* not far behind. Above them, the undead defenders were already marching down toward the beach. Only two units remained atop the cliffs. Good. They had few ranged weapons – a serious oversight from their commander.

Pious lurched again as her powerful broadside spoke, belching out acrid smoke and sending a wave of cannonballs toward the shore. A sailor halfway down the ladder steps built into the midships of the frigate's hull let out a cry as he lost his grip and slipped to plunge into the water, re-emerging a second later amidst laughs, jeers, and sarcastic applause from the ship's company.

"Belay that!" Grace yelled from the quarterdeck. "Bosun! Take charge of that debacle before I have you flogged!"

"Aye, ma'am! Listen in, you bunch of f..."

Jaymes took one last look at the beach and shook his head in despair as he saw how far off the mark his gunners were. He handed his telescope to Mayhew, pulled on his blue jacket, clipped his sword to his belt, and swung over the taffrail to lower himself down into the boat. Within moments, shoulder to shoulder amidst forty of his sailors, the boat pushed clear, and his men began paddling toward the shore. Once clear of the *Pious,* he looked to the east and saw the Khopeshii and slave galley fleeing at full sail. A moment later, his world exploded into a deafening roar as his ship's entire broadside erupted from behind and above him, spitting out fire, smoke, and possibly brimstone from the depths of the Abyss as round shot whooshed over the heads of the sailors crammed into the sea boats.

His ears ringing painfully, Jaymes watched with morbid fascination as, combined with the firepower of the *Veneration* – which had fired simultaneously with the *Pious* – the broadside smashed into the shore. The combined might of the two frigates' guns swept over the top of the sea boats of the *Deliverer's Flame* and *Martolian Queen* to tear into the cliffs and beach. Entire segments of land twirled up into the skies amidst the carnage – even from this distance, Jaymes swore he could see skeletal bodies flung up toward the heavens, disintegrating spectacularly midair. The beach disappeared behind a bank of dust and smoke. Moments later, when the first salamander boat drove up onto the sandy beach, the tough warriors it disgorged met next to no resistance.

Chapter Fifteen

Southern Ansares Isles
East Infant Sea

Twenty-eight marines stood smartly in ranks, despite their injuries, stubble, and ragged clothes as the captain of their ship, together with the third lieutenant, walked across to greet them. Karnon snapped to attention.

"Marines! 'Shun!"

The three ranks of marines brought their bare feet down – without the normal crunch of boots – and stood rigidly to attention. Karnon brought his looted, ancient, and bizarre Ahmunite sword up to salute. Jaymes brought his own blade up to return the salute, his face baffled and amused. He stood in front of his friend and offered a silent smile as the ship's companies of *Pious*, *Veneration*, the *Deliverer's Flame* and the *Martolian Queen* all carefully escorted the lines of freed slaves down to the beach jetty and the awaiting sea boats.

"At ease, Captain. You... err... you're still not dead, then?" Jaymes greeted.

"No, sir," Karnon replied rigidly, "two days of light lifting and shifting to help out a local faith group with their place of worship. Charitable stuff, but I'd still recommend docking two days' pay from the lads here, the bunch of loafing bastards."

Barely stifled sniggers broke out along the ranks of disheveled marines. Jaymes let out a brief laugh.

"Glad to see so many of you still in one piece. I'm sorry for the men who didn't make it through."

Karnon felt his face twist into a grimace.

"We'll give them a decent burial. On Basilean soil. They'd all be content with that."

"We'll make sure of it," Jaymes agreed, nodding at the lines of workers, merchant sailors, spouses, and children being marched down to the sea boats at the jetty, "but we've got to clear out of here and get these civilians somewhere safe before we go to battle against that war galley and finish this once and for all. Fall your men out and get them back onboard."

Karnon snapped back to attention and turned about to face his troops.

"Marines! Turning right! Dismissed!"

His unit turned smartly as one and took a pace forward before hurrying off to help with the island's evacuation. Karnon looked up at the smoking ruins of the destroyed temple with grim satisfaction before half-smiling uncomfortably at his friend, now they were left alone.

"Thanks. Thanks for coming back for us."

"I'm a bit disappointed," Jaymes shrugged, "I was expecting something as least as dramatic as a volcano island."

"Well. Regardless. Thanks for getting us out of this mess."

Jaymes smiled.

"Through thick and thin, old boy."

Karnon narrowed his eyes.

"What?"

Jaymes's smile instantly faded away.

"Come on. You've been onboard long enough to know what that means."

Karnon shook his head. Jaymes folded his arms.

"Really? Bollocks."

"Eyebrows," Karnon admitted, escalating the stakes to the age-old challenge to a dubious claim that, in the event of later being discovered to be a lie, would result in the liar's eyebrows being shaved off.

Jaymes shook his head in disgust.

"Bloody hell. It means... you know what? It doesn't matter what it means. One day people will all be saying it, and they'll all know that the phrase's noble origins lie in the glorious days of sailing warships."

"I doubt that, mate. Very much."

Jaymes grumbled something under his breath.

"Just... get your sorry carcass back on my boat. We're leaving."

***

Captain Henneus remained still, seemingly frozen in place on one knee before the grand doors of the *Purification of Ul'Astia's* after deck temple. The revenant frigate captain's decomposed face was hidden behind the hood of his black cloak, his head bowed in reverence. Demelecles watched the exchange from the port side of the after deck, his arms folded across his chest as he sneered down at the rival warship captain. For T'mork, that age old rivalry was meaningless now. At that moment, at that precise second, all was meaningless. All was failure.

"They did... what?" he asked slowly, towering over the kneeling sea captain.

"They arrived at dawn, Master," the Khopeshii captain said, his gravelly voice low and filled with regret, "they outnumbered us greatly. They sent forces ashore. They... destroyed the temple."

It could only have been a reflex reaction, something still buried deep within T'mork's consciousness from his days as a mortal, but he found himself half pivoting on the spot and clutching at his chest. The temple? The temple was gone? Destroyed? Desecrated...

"How?" T'mork demanded, the cool evening breeze whipping across the deck and rustling his blue skirts. "How did they do it? It matters, Captain. It matters to me deeply. Tell me – briefly now, for I do not wish to dwell on the details of sacrilege – how did they desecrate the temple to almighty Shobik?"

The rigid revenant captain, still hidden beneath the dark folds of his cloak and hood, remained still with the discipline of centuries of servitude.

"Cannon fire, Master. They desecrated the temple with cannon fire from their warships."

T'mork clenched his fists and nodded slowly. For some reason, that was not as bad as he had expected. Certainly, his disciplined emotions were ravaged from one side by the utter shame of his failure, the failure of his duty to Shobik that he alone must shoulder as high priest and master. On the other side, his mind was assaulted with mental images, his rage-filled imagination running as wild as a child's when he thought of that desecration, that vile sacrilege to the god of death himself. But knowing the sacred temple was destroyed by cannon fire was somehow less of a blow, less of an insult to his name and his legacy than if the non-believers had dared set foot within the temple to destroy it.

"The scholar," T'mork whispered, "bring her to me. She is still on your ship?"

"I regret, Master, but no. She was ashore, with the slaves working on the temple. She was taken away on one of the Basilean ships."

T'mork turned again.

"Taken away? How many of the slaves did they recover?"

Henneus continued to stare down at the deck, immovable on one knee.

"When I last saw them, they were loading slaves onto boats. It must have been all of them, Master. Every last one. There was nothing to stop them. They have destroyed our temple. They have taken our workers, our people. They... I... betrayed almighty Shobik. It was I who ran. I offer myself humbly and willingly for sacrifice, Master."

T'mork grunted and hissed.

"Nonsense. Do not waste my time with trivial gestures, Captain. You were faced with overwhelming opposition. You stood no chance. I need your warship. I need you in command of her. You did the right thing by retreating. The burden of blame falls onto me. But now is not the time for despair. Now is the time for vengeance for Shobik, and all he stands for. Now is the time to close with our enemy with all of our force."

The Khopeshii captain slowly raised his head. The shadow of his dead features, the dry skin stretched across the skull beneath the hood, stared up at the high priest.

"North, my Master. They must have headed north. They would want to take the workers to safety. The closer they are to Keretia and the security of more warships and soldiers, the more confident they will feel of providing safety to those they call their own."

T'mork looked across at Demelecles. The captain of the war galley issued a single, simple nod of the head. T'mork wrapped the fingers of one hand around the clenched fist made of the other.

"North of the temple it is, then. I shall converse with every ship captain we have. We shall sail through the night. I shall exhaust myself to the point of expiration, if I must, to bend the elements to my will, to drive our righteous fleet straight into the defilers. Back to your warship, Captain. There is much to be done."

***

The salty scent of the sea fought with the sweet aromas of the jungle as the three men walked slowly along the overgrown pathway, the midday sun beating down on their backs. A little way offshore, the waters were alive with activity – three frigates and a brig lay at anchor whilst a constant precision of sea boats, their oarsmen no doubt fatigued by their seemingly endless efforts – ferried personnel to the lush island. Sir Laval Curzon, the owner of Roe's Spring colony, clasped his hands at the small of his back. His thin, wrinkled face was now at least clean shaven and he wore loose, ill-fitting clothing donated to him by Marcellus Dio that was, at least, more befitting of his title and status.

The tall colony administrator looked down at the old, disused jetty as another boat of freed colony workers was rowed ashore, this time by one of the red boats from the salamander J'Koor'uk. He then turned to look uphill at the decrepit, half-collapsed collection of wooden huts and houses, overgrown with twirling vines and thick, shining leaves of the local vegetation. Another overgrown path led away from the ghost town toward a half-collapsed, stone ventilation tower near the top of the closest peak.

"I imagine this will be for no more than a week, sir," Marcellus offered, glancing downslope to watch as a detachment of his marines carefully escorted another boatload of workers, spouses, and children up the hill. "I'm so very sorry that this is our only viable solution. For now."

Laval offered a smile.

"Not at all, Captain. This is merely a minor inconvenience compared to what you have delivered us all from. No, no. Your priority *must* be to end the threat posed by these Ahmunites to all innocent people in this region. You cannot allow us to slow you down any further."

Jaymes looked across at the older man, finding himself admiring his courage. Yes, it was little more than sleeping in huts for a week. But these people had never signed on for that. For many, it would be an ordeal.

"We will make do here for as long as is necessary," Laval continued, "but time is not on our side. I remember this mine closing down. There was still enough gold down there, but the entire operation was not financially viable. And that was because of the costs of keeping this little town supplied. The only thing here in abundance is fresh water at the creek to the north."

"Once we've moved everybody ashore, we will send across all of the food we can spare," Jaymes added, "and the Ones above willing, sir, we will be back to ferry you all home once the enemy is dealt with."

The older man's eyes narrowed a little, sorrowfully, as he looked across at the two captains.

"Home. But what state is home in? I fear it is not much better than what we have here. But, as I said, it is still far better than what you have both saved us from. So on behalf of the six hundred of us who you have safely delivered here, please accept my sincere gratitude. Our job now is to merely survive until we are taken away again."

Jaymes looked to the north. Only a couple of days sail back to Roe's Spring, but then that would be straight into rebuilding after the destruction brought down by the Ahmunites. And then it would be another trip for those taken from other settlements.

"I'm hoping that you will have assistance sooner than you think, sir," Marcellus said. "I've sent one of our sloops back to Thatraskos to inform Governor Ecclio about our situation. Supply ships will be sent quickly, I have no doubt."

"And if the sloop fails to reach Keretia?" Laval asked carefully. "What then of all of us, marooned here in a site abandoned for its vulnerability to pirate attacks and complications in resupplying?"

"The sloop is a secondary means of ensuring your safety. We are still your primary route home. We will be rejoining Captain Uwell and the *Shield Royal* as soon as we have delivered enough supplies to you. I would not be fearful of pirates in these waters, merely due to practicalities. As you've said, the mine was closed years ago. There is nothing for them to gain financially by attacking you here. The plan remains as we discussed – we will depart here, form up our fleet, hunt and destroy the Ahmunites, and then return to bring you home."

Laval took another few steps uphill, looked up at the settlement that nature had reclaimed the better part of a decade ago, and then turned to force another smile.

"Of course. Captains, thank you again. We will make do here. Your task is far more hazardous than ours. Allow me to offer you my best wishes and my prayers once you are gone."

Marcellus and Jaymes both accepted and shook the hand offered to them by the once wealthy colony owner and then began the walk back down toward the crumbling jetty. Another two boats of workers were making their way across from the two Elohi-class frigates while a team of stout salamanders rowed their own sea boat back toward the J'Koor'uk. A team of sailors from the *Veneration* met the first boat and set about helping the half-starved occupants toward the path and the line of escorting marines.

"Grand job on tracking these poor people down," Marcellus said to Jaymes as they walked toward the jetty, "but we will hopefully have this dealt with soon enough. This was all about that temple for the Ahmunites. They'll be back here, and soon. I don't think it will be long until we see a signal."

The older captain nodded toward the western horizon, where a single Basilean sloop bobbed gently in the blue-green waves. That sloop was one of a two-ship chain leading across to the *Shield Royal*, well beyond the horizon – the three ships between them formed a net which the Ahmunites could not pass without raising an alarm.

"I'll get myself back onboard and be ready to go," Jaymes said. "Best of Basilean luck to you, Marcellus. See you back home."

The older captain smiled softly and shook Jaymes's hand.

"And to you, old boy. And to you."

Jaymes made his way carefully back down the path toward the jetty and the line of sea boats, threading his way through the endless procession of freed slaves struggling up the path. Some were in tears, others smiled and made jokes. Some offered him thanks and shook his hand as he passed; others flashed venomous glares as if he were somehow to blame for their plight.

Jaymes reached the jetty and the small collection of the remains of wooden buildings long ago destroyed by storms. He glanced down the small strip of sandy beach and saw a lone figure sat on the rocks, back facing him, looking out to the northwest. Jaymes stopped in place. So many of his friends had told him that he was a sappy, overly sentimental, and romantic fool. That was why he had tried so hard to push all thoughts of Caithlin away whilst he had a job to do. He had, of course, failed miserably, but he liked to think at least that those sentimental thoughts were well-timed, when it did not interfere with the execution of his duties. But now, seeing her, he found his heart pining like the subject of one of those terrible romantic poems that were in vogue a decade ago while he was being schooled in literature as a midshipman. He made his way across the beach toward her.

The noise of the line of freed captives and the boats being brought alongside gradually faded behind him. The waves lapped across the hot sand. Gulls squawked noisily in the blue sky above. The gentle breeze rustled the vegetation emerging from the gaps in the dry, sandstone rocks to his right. A dangerous foe lay perhaps only hours away, but if one had to die, then the eastern reaches of the Infant Sea were a paradise in which to lay down one's life.

Jaymes stopped as a bulky figure stepped out from the rocks to his right to stride across toward him. He swore and shook his head. The huge salamander sailor looked him dead in the eye as he paced across the burning sand, fists clenched purposefully. Suddenly feeling the fatigue of the previous days, Jaymes folded his arms and met the salamander's glare without flinching until the huge sailor stood in front of him, towering over him.

"She doesn't want to be disturbed," X'And's gravelly voice challenged.

"She can speak for herself well enough," Jaymes replied. "So I'll ask her myself. If she doesn't want my company, then I'll respect that and I'll leave."

"She told me that she wants some time alone," the salamander leaned in, his glinting eyes narrowing. "Which part of that are you struggling to understand?"

Jaymes wrapped a fist around the handle of his sword and stepped in to stare up at the privateer first mate. He knew, of course, that if fisticuffs were to ensue, the salamander would tear him apart; possibly even fatally. But if this ridiculous clash of characters that had bubbled away for weeks now were to ever become violent, Jaymes was happy to draw his sword. And if it came to that, he was confident enough that he would win.

"Have I ever treated Caithlin with anything other than respect?" he snarled up at the salamander.

X'And remained silent.

"Which part of my question are you struggling to understand?" Jaymes snapped. "I said: have I ever treated Caithlin with anything other than respect?"

His nostrils quivering, his huge arms folded across his scaled, barrel-like chest, X'And's mouth curled up to reveal rows of sharp teeth.

"I know what humans think is beautiful in a woman. And I know how human sailors treat women. I know what they all want from somebody who looks like my captain. My friend. I also know that beyond all of that, she is... a beautiful soul. That's why I stop people like you from getting to her."

The words had no aggression, no danger in their tone. Instead, a real sincerity. As if the monstrous first mate was opening up rather than threatening. Jaymes took a step back and took his hand away from his saber.

"And that... that's why I love her," he said quietly.

The salamander stared at him in silence for a few long moments. His features softened. He took a step to one side, half turned, and gestured to his captain.

"Go on."

Jaymes let out a long breath, thought quickly of a few things he could say to try to build some sort of bridge between himself and X'And, but realized almost instantly that all sounded fairly terrible. He nodded his gratitude and walked up to the rocks overlooking the other side of the bay.

Caithlin sat atop a low, yellow rock, one in a family of about a dozen that led down like stepping stones toward the sea. Jaymes knew her well enough to detect her sadness, even before she looked over her shoulder as he approached. She wiped away at her red-rimmed eyes with the heels of her hands and attempted a smile.

"I can go, if you'd rather be alone," Jaymes offered.

"No," she shook her head, "I'd rather avoid most people at the moment. But not you. I'm glad you're here."

Jaymes stepped across the jagged, yellow-hued stones and sat down next to her. She immediately rested her head on his shoulder, so he placed an arm around her.

"Have you got any stories from your past?" Caithlin asked quietly. "Something funny. Anything. Something to take us away from here."

Immediately put on that spot, Jaymes frantically searched for some dim and distant memory that might force a laugh. He found nothing.

"I... err... nothing is leaping to mind."

"Anything. First thing you think of."

Jaymes thought of something. He realized too late that he had started talking and was committed to finishing the tale, despite not wanting to.

"Alright. My nineteenth birthday. There was an administrative delay on me taking my lieutenant's board, so I'd only been promoted a few months before and had just joined a new sloop. *HW Wave Dasher*. Anyhow, I was far more serious back then, very career-minded and wanted to go places. I met the ship in the capital, alongside at Royal Dock. I accidentally let slip that it was my nineteenth birthday the next day, so a rather large group of the chaps insisted on taking me on a run ashore. Unfortunately, the decision was made to take me to an area known for its houses of ill repute."

Caithlin raised an eyebrow. Jaymes held up his hands.

"So... so... you know I'm a man of faith, but perhaps not as much as I should be. I wasn't only far more serious and career-minded back then, I was also a lot more religious. So I told the chaps that I wasn't going near any of the women, as I was – and very much still am – only going to commit to something physical with a lady who means a great deal to me. But I realized that was boring for everybody else, so I offered to down every pint of ale that touched my hand, in one, for the entire day. I was drunk by lunchtime, plastered by mid-afternoon and – I'm reliably informed – that when I passed out at ten bells after a rather heroic effort, I'd projectile vomited seven times. Which, I think, was the only thing that saved me from having to see a doctor. They found me just before I passed out, picking a fight with two on duty militia guards, telling them to get a proper uniform. Fortunately, the militia fellows just laughed at me. Then I fell over. I... find myself immediately regretting having told you that story."

Caithlin laughed warmly for a few seconds and then fell silent. The mirth in her eyes was gone a moment later. She looked out to sea, her eyes no doubt not by coincidence looking in the direction of Geneza.

"I'm glad that you did. I wish I had a story like that. I was always the serious one, certainly compared to my younger sister. I never got drunk. Before I met you, at least. You're a terrible influence. There's this... story, I suppose, from a few years ago. Stuck in my mind. It came up soon after we arrived here, and now it won't leave. And it has me in tears, like an idiot."

Jaymes rested his head on hers and remained silent. He remembered advice from his mother – good advice. Do not try to fix things. Just listen.

"I was nineteen, too," Caithlin said, "it was supposed to be an easy run. A shipment of cotton from Geneza to Spartha. The *Island Spirit*, a two hundred ton brigantine belonging to my father. The son of one of his partners – now a full partner himself – Jense, he was captain. Only his third run. It was my first run as first mate. There was a young man – Edgen. He was seventeen, had worked in a mill but decided it wasn't for him. He'd only just shaken off the title of landsman. He was sweet on me. A lot of them were. I didn't reciprocate with any of them. But I tried to be as pleasant, polite, and proper as I could be."

Jaymes felt her shoulders shake. He bit his lip and remained silent.

"We hit a storm. It came out of nowhere. I'm sure you've seen the sort around the Martolian Sound. Edgen was up top, right up on the yard of the top gallant. He shouldn't have been, but he was trying to work up to becoming a top man, just far too quickly. The ship rolled in the storm, and he fell. He went into the water, sank like a stone for a second, then appeared. I was midships, securing a broken ratline. He... looked right up at me, from the water. He let out this terrified cry. His eyes said everything. What he wouldn't have given to be back on that heaving, soaked, sickening deck with me. Just a couple of feet away. He couldn't swim. He just... one moment, this terrified cry. And he was gone."

Jaymes let out a breath. It was a tale that, tragically, he could empathize with.

"I'm so sorry," he said quietly.

"I... could have jumped in. I was a decent swimmer, back then. I'm a very good swimmer now, far better. When I stop and think of the conditions that night, well, if I tried to swim in them now, I'd probably be dead. Back then? Seven years ago? I wouldn't last five seconds."

"There's nothing you could have done," Jaymes offered, immediately regretting the rather trite choice of words.

"I know. Thank you. But I know. I know one is supposed to anguish over what one should have done. That's the done thing. But in moments of clarity, I know there was nothing anybody could do. But the thing is... when we returned, my father insisted that it was me who went to tell Edgen's mother. It was me that walked to that tiny cottage and told a widow that her only child was dead. I'll never forget those cries. The disbelief. The grab of my arm, the pleading to tell me that there was still a chance. I... hated my father for days after that. I fully understand why he did it now. I... even appreciate it. I thank him for it, because I needed to know how to deal with that. What to say and how to say it. The thing is... that was the most saddening thing I ever saw in my life. Until today."

Jaymes turned and dropped down to one knee to face her, holding one of her hands. His chest ached from seeing the pain the memory caused, but again, no wise words of consolation presented themselves.

"I'm sorry," he repeated again, uselessly, "I'm... sure that whole tragic experience will better place you to really help somebody who needs you, one day."

"But that day is today," Caithlin said, her voice steady, her stare stony. "I've never seen six hundred people with their lives shattered. Mothers, fathers, sons, daughters, dead. Killed by those bastards. And for what? Innocent people worked to death in front of their own families. The things some of them told me! Jaymes, I... I'm not sad. I'm angry. I'm furious. I thought I was angry with the pirates on Red Skull that I told you about, but this?"

Jaymes looked past Caithlin to the south. Dark clouds of blue-gray had already smeared out the horizon, diagonal lines swiped down from them where rain fell down miles out to sea. He looked back at Caithlin. She stared up at him with grim resolve.

"We've got to send these murdering scum to the bottom," she hissed, "the Ahmunites, the pirates, all of them. Anybody who would hurt helpless people. It's why the Ones put me in this position. It's why I've got a ship packed with guns instead of crates of cotton now. We've got to take the war to all of them."

Jaymes nodded.

"Yes. Yes, we do. That's why we're here."

Caithlin squeezed his hand a little tighter. She met his gaze, her expression seemingly an equal blend of anger, sorrow, and gratitude.

"Thank you," she said quietly.

For what, he was not sure. Then a flutter, a tiny flash of color to the southwest, attracted Jaymes's attention. He looked out and saw a sloop – HW Scout, he believed – flying an amber pennant. Jaymes slowly raised himself to his feet. Still holding his hand, Caithlin stood and turned to look southwest, past the storms and to the little sloop.

"That's it," Jaymes exhaled, "that's the signal. They've found them."

"It's like the Ones above just listened to every word I said," Caithlin whispered. "Time we were off. Time we took the fight to them."

Caithlin stared at the sloop in silence for several moments and then pulled Jaymes in for a kiss. She grabbed her sword and hat. Both captains paced along the beach toward the jetty and the sea boats waiting to take them to their warships.

Chapter Sixteen

Martolian Queen (18)
Privateer (Converted Trade Brig)

Only scant gaps of blue shone through the bulbous, white clouds propelled across the early evening sky. What started as a stiff breeze from beam on was now a strong wind, whipping up the seas and causing even the mighty third-rate – the *Shield Royal* – to pitch up and down as her prow rose and fell with the swell. The fleet was lined up in something akin to an arrowhead, with the *Shield Royal* at the point. To her port, the salamander J'Koor'uk kept pace easily with the *Martolian Queen* tucked in to her side. To starboard, holding the weather gauge and clearly signaling the Basilean fleet's intent to strike with her Elohi frigates, *Pious* and *Veneration* sped onward with two tiny sloops windward of them. Up ahead, strung across the darkening southern horizon, like bone beads on a necklace, was the Ahmunite fleet.

On the quarterdeck of the *Martolian Queen*, Caithlin and X'And surveyed the enemy with their telescopes. Caithlin felt cramps and spasms of pain in her abdomen as she picked out two enemy frigates – Khopeshii, if she correctly recalled – holding center. Two slightly smaller ships with single masts flanked the frigates, with a ship to leeward which was a similar size to Caithlin's fighting brig. Windward, opposite the Basilean sloops, were two oar-driven galleys of similar size and tonnage.

"Those Khopeshii," Caithlin asked as her knees bent beneath her with the rise and fall of the quarterdeck in the heavy seas, "what sort of cannons are we facing?"

"Crossbows," the salamander first mate replied, "giant crossbows. We need to keep our distance. And from the Soul Hunter, too. I think the most useful thing we can reasonably do is engage the leeward Dust Chaser on the bow."

Caithlin brought her telescope left. She felt the slightest sensation of relief, just from taking her eyes off the Khopeshii, as if they would not attack her if she did not dare look at them. Aside from one nightmarish engagement with an orc smasher, they were the largest enemy ships she had ever faced. But she knew, from what *Pious* had encountered, that something far, far worse was yet to come.

"Is that the Soul Hunter? The one without sails? With... that thing on its upper deck?"

"Yes, that's the one," X'And replied, "and we'd do well to steer clear of it."

An explosion sounded to starboard, and both Caithlin and X'And lowered their telescopes to look off to their right. Caithlin felt a wave of exhilaration as she saw a colorless wave of energy pulse out from the *Veneration*. The figurehead, a delicately carved Elohi on the bow, now had real, tangible flames of blue flickering from the top of her staff where only a wooden representation of that holy fire had been seconds before. A second explosion echoed across the wind as a blue flame whooshed up from *Pious's* figurehead. Small, neat lines of blue fire danced along *Shield Royal's* bowsprit as the mighty vessel carved through the turbulent waters. Caithlin could not help but smile. It was a magical, uplifting sight that she had only witnessed once before. Excited chatter rippled through the gun crews along the upper deck of the *Martolian Queen*. Even from this distance, Caithlin could hear the crew of the *Shield Royal* brought together in worship as a hymn drifted across the wind.

"They're with us," she whispered, "the Shining Ones have sent their Elohi to watch over us."

X'And exchanged a brief smile with her and then raised his telescope again.

"Well, well," he said suddenly, "have a look at the very lee of their line. Look who's just come out of that rain shower."

Caithlin brought up her telescope again. She tutted thoughtfully as she saw a familiar sail emerge from the gray murk of the rain clouds to the south of southwest. It was the pirate xebec who had escaped them at the Lesser Yellow Rocks.

"Well, well indeed," she repeated, fighting to ignore the cramping of terror threatening to rise up from the pit of her stomach.

She lowered her telescope, clamped one shaking hand onto the handle of her sword, and grasped the coin in her pocket with the other. If X'And had noticed the fear she was fighting to ignore, he was polite enough not to say anything about it.

"Where's that war galley?" She found herself snapping suddenly as an unpleasant, corkscrewing motion swept over the *Martolian Queen* as she began to roll as well as pitch with the wind and waves.

Before X'And could reply, a shimmering ball of purple flame spat up from the Soul Hunter and flew across the cloudy sky before dropping like a comet into the sea between the *Shield Royal* and the *Veneration*. The battle had begun.

***

The line of Basilean warships thundered down from the north, the figureheads and bowsprits of the three largest fighting vessels ablaze with blue fire. Bowchasers blasted from the fo'c'sles of the giant third-rate ship of the line, the Elohi-class frigates, and the salamander J'Koor'uk. His chest tight with fear, his breathing short and uneven, Tem stared wide-eyed at the fleet of warships opposing him. His feet remained seemingly rooted to the spot on the quarterdeck of the xebec, his white-knuckled grip clinging to the taffrail in front of him. He had seen huge warships before, when visiting foreign ports in his days as a merchant sailor – but never had he opposed warships of such size, and in such numbers.

"Captain!"

Tem jumped and looked over his shoulder.

He realized now that it was the third time he had been addressed.

"Captain!" Halladai grabbed him by the shoulder. "Out there! Windward end of their line! Look!"

Tem jumped again as cannonballs from the Basilean bow chasers thudded into the prow of the closest of the two Khopeshii, sending shards of bone and splinters of wood flying up into the air. Cursing himself internally for his lack of courage, Tem lowered a shaking hand to recover his telescope. Round shot whooshed toward the Ahmunite frigates, and another hit was scored. Down on the xebec's upper deck, Tem saw one of his crew – Hann, an old salt of fifteen years experience – depart his station by his gun and rush back toward the quarterdeck.

"Captain!" Hann screamed up at him. "Captain, we need to run! We're not for this! We're not a ship of war! We're in a bloody battle, a full battle, and we're in a merchant ship! We can't..."

Tem half-expected one of his more rugged, violent pirates to dash across and club Hann down for his cowardice. Instead, Hoggir rushed across from his own cannon.

"He's right!" the northerner yelled. "That's a Basilean battleship out there! What in the seven circles are we doing here? We attack small traders, not battleships! Enough of this! I call for..."

Halladai's feet thunked down the steps to the upper deck, a pistol raised in each hand, one pointed at each of the pirates who had deserted their station.

"You know the rules!" he hissed, before turning to look at the rest of the crew who stared, pale-faced at the altercation near the quarterdeck. "You all know the rules! You want to vote the captain out? Choose your damned moment! We're in battle now, you dogs! And the rules are that the captain's word is final in battle! And any man-jack of you that wants to break the rules? I'll break your skull with a pistol shot! We all savvy, me hearties?"

Jeffi stepped away from his gun and grabbed Hann by his shoulder.

"Come on! Get it in one sock and get back to your gun!"

Halladai kept his pistols aimed at the two men until they reluctantly returned to their guns across the heaving deck. He then returned to the quarterdeck, backward, his eyes on the would-be deserters and mutineers. Tem nodded in gratitude to him as he returned before finally raising his telescope. After only a brief scan of the horizon, he saw the ship that his quartermaster was calling his attention to.

The Genezan fighting brig. The privateer that had killed Ash and Flyde. She was there, at the end of the Basilean line. Tem snarled out a string of obscenities and lowered his telescope in a steady, clenched fist. He span around to Halladai as the Basilean guns blasted out again. Halladai silently nodded. He pointed at the scarab buried in his forearm.

"That's not going anywhere, shipmate," he murmured to Tem. "We've got time to fix that. Those bastards on that brig? We might not get another chance."

Tem nodded and turned to the helm.

"One point to starboard! Get me to that damned brig!"

***

The two bow chasers barked out again, leaping back on their four-wheel wooden carriages until their restraining ropes held them in place. Stood to one side of the second gun, his telescope to his eye, Jaymes watched as both shots pelted into the prow of the nearer Khopeshii. Splints flew up from the points of impact, but even from this distance, Jaymes knew that the fire of two light nine-pounder guns was more symbolic than actually causing significant damage. Above the guns, the blue flame atop the Elohi figurehead's staff continued to blaze bravely, and an air of courage and purpose seemed to flow down from it.

"Load!" the two bow chaser gun captains yelled, nearly in unison.

"Good shot!" Jaymes shouted. "Fine shooting!"

The words of encouragement elicited one or two grins from younger members of the gun crews, but the old hands knew that this was merely an opening insult to the Ahmunites. The real fight was yet to come.

At each gun, a crew member stepped across to place a gloved thumb over the vent holes to ensure no air entered the weapons during the reloading procedure. Another two sailors moved quickly around to the muzzles of each of the cannons, one using a wadhook to clear any debris from the previous firing while the other used a sponge — a sheepskin covered block of wood on the end of a pole, soaked in water — to extinguish any burning embers inside the cannon before the loading took place.

Content that his gunners were working rapidly and safely, Jaymes headed back across the upper deck and then up to the quarterdeck, where the captain belonged in battle.

"How's *Shield Royal* looking?" Jaymes asked Mayhew as he arrived.

"Seems fine, sir," the first lieutenant replied, "just a lucky shot from those bastards. The *Shield* is still closing at battle sail and engaging with her bow chasers – no sign of a signal for assistance with repairs."

"Right," Jaymes bit his lip, "I'm sure that shot just looked worse than it was."

Jaymes paced over to the port side of the quarterdeck, looking nervously down into the churning waters. It was no use – they were in deep water, well away from the islands; and with the evening gloom approaching, it was impossible to see even a foot beneath the surface of the waves. That bastard war galley was still out there somewhere. And if Jaymes had not seen it appear from the deep before – in a shallow bay at that – with his own eyes, he doubted very much that he would have believed it possible from anything outside of the Trident Realm.

"I think they may jibe soon, sir," Grace offered from a few paces behind Jaymes, where she stood by one of the quarterdeck thirty-two pound close-in guns and its four-man crew.

Jaymes looked ahead again. Yes, the Ahmunites may come about soon, the frigates using their superior speed to rake the bows of the Basilean warships. But if they did, the Basileans need only continue on course to rake the sterns of the Ahmunites, if they were not quick enough to come back around again. With this neutral wind blowing from nearly dead on midships to both fleets as they approached each other from north and south, it really was a case of who would lose their nerve first.

"Stay dead on course!" Jaymes growled at his helmsman through gritted teeth. "If they turn, we'll take their shots and then hit them back harder!"

Along the crowded deck of the thirty-eight gun frigate, Jaymes saw sailors waiting by their guns in their teams, marines already formed up in boarding parties, and spare hands ready and eager to deliver powder and shot from below, or drag the wounded down to the surgeon. Some two hundred and seventy sailors and marines, poised and ready for when the real action began.

And then, just as the optimism and grit flowing down from the blue flame on his ship's figurehead seemed to have peaked in its effect across his crew, Jaymes saw the very thing he was fearing out of the corner of his eye. He turned and looked back to the north, eyes widening and jaw dropping as the bone-covered prow of the immense, ancient war galley thrust up through the crashing, churning waves directly behind the *Shield Royal*.

***

In a dim, distant, past life there was no doubt a time where the experience of underwater travel would have been exhilarating. Now, stood before the after deck temple of the *Purification of Ul'Astia*, bubbles of air rushing past in the warm dark of the water, T'mork stood with his arms outstretched, eyes set dead ahead in concentration. To move an entire, eighteen hundred ton ship beneath the surface of the waves was not merely an impressive show of arcane mastery; it was practically a miracle of sorcery. The great war galley rushed forth, the tip of her main mast barely ten cubits beneath the surface of the water, T'mork's magic dragging her at nearly twice the speed she was capable of under sail.

Pain ripped at T'mork's very core; not the center of his physical body, but the heart of his entire essence; his soul, if such a thing still existed. His cracked, yellow teeth gritted and his pale, orb eyes narrowed, he looked ahead in the gloom of the underwater world he exploited to position his flagship. Yes, there was some necromancy at work, but to successfully carry out such a show of arcane mastery was, in this case, hydromancy. T'mork was, like all Ahmunite high priests, a necromancer above all else; but decades of study had given him a rule over the arcane aspects of water that most would never even witness, let alone feel and control.

But there was necromancy. As the war galley plunged through the warm waters, T'mork felt out with tendrils of energy, searching for life. It was here, there, crammed together in pockets, grouped in dozens or even hundreds. Lives, souls, huddled together on their wooden platforms above the waves, in their mind braving the cruel elements; but in actuality, merely highlighting themselves as targets for defeat. Above all others, the life energy emitted from one of these collective pockets was strong, vast. Six hundred – possibly even seven hundred souls packed together. The Basilean flagship – directly ahead.

A hiss, a hum of pain that was audible even in the dense depths, now escalated to a shout of agony. Limbs shaking from exertion, T'mork kept his ship on course and concentrated on his target. There – a sensation of just a little relative movement. An obtuse angle. Enough for T'mork to feel, to reach out beyond the excruciating pain and calculate what heading the enemy ship was on. And with that, where her stern was. T'mork was no admiral, but when his sea captains told him that lining up a broadside directly at the stern of an enemy ship was optimum, that was a simple enough feat to comprehend.

The *Purification of Ul'Astia* shot beneath the Basilean flagship. Then, with great lines of pain tearing across T'mork like razors cutting past his body and across his spirit, the ancient high priest dragged his ship into a turn. He had done all he could. The position was perfect. Exhausted, agonized, crushed by crippling pain and fatigue, he dropped to one knee. The bows of the war galley lifted with one, final effort. The water grew lighter. The sound of cannon fire was faintly audible. Then, in the space of a single heartbeat, the dull whooshes and crumps of the depths were replaced with the sharp, clear sounds of the surface as the eighteen hundred ton war galley burst up into the air.

The great ship's bows hung stationary for a moment until the entire ship crashed down and sent towering waves spewing out from her bows. Demelecles wasted no time in sending silent commands to his sailors – skeletal seamen were scrambling up masts and ratlines before the war galley had even settled in the water. Sails were lowered from the yards of the two great masts. Weapons were readied. Oars were pushed into place in the water from lines of hundreds of skeletal slaves, chained to their benches in the darkness of the war galley's black interior. Collapsed to one knee, fists clenched in pain and exhaustion, T'mork pushed through the agony to reach out to the arcane plains for energy, fighting past the barriers and hurdles placed by a lesser sorcerer on the Basilean flagship. Battling against his opponent – and winning – T'mork reached out with an arcane hand and dragged the wind around to suit his own fleet. The war galley surged forward under the power of both wind and oar, her terrible broadside lining up with the stern of the Basilean flagship.

* * *

The sheer noise of the broadside of the Defender-class battleship dominated the seascape. Two full decks of heavy guns burst into life simultaneously, illuminating the early evening sky like lightning and hiding the mighty third-rate's hull behind a wall of smoke. Debris flew up from the Ahmunite war galley, parts torn off her flanks and prow from the ferocious cannonfire. The Ahmunite flagship responded almost immediately, pouring a combination of cannonfire, catapult shots, and immense crossbow bolts into the quarter of the *Shield Royal*, pelting her from midships to stern.

"Ones above..." Jaymes exhaled.

Smoke wafted up from the *Shield Royal's* quarterdeck. The flickering, orange tongues of flames licked up from open gunports..

"Captain!" Grace yelled from the far side of *Pious's* quarterdeck. "What orders, sir?"

Jaymes looked ahead as his frigate continued to close with the

Khopeshii. There were no new orders from the *Shield Royal* since the ungodly arrival of the war galley from the depths. Yes, he could alter course and attempt to hurtle across to the *Shield Royal's* aid, plastered by every Ahmunite warship as he did so. Or he could carry on with the plan. He could trust Zakery to lead the *Shield Royal* to victory and fight his own battles.

"Stay on the Khopeshii!" Jaymes shouted back. "Be ready to alter course with her!"

Across the deck of his frigate, Jaymes saw over a hundred men standing ready by their guns, still waiting anxiously to spring into action as soon as their warship's broadsides were lined up on the enemy. Then, up ahead, the Khopeshii finally made her move.

"Hard a' port!" Jaymes shouted in alarm as the Ahmunite warship altered into wind against all expectations. "Bring her through the wind, lads!"

"Helm! Up top! Stand by to tack!" Grace called.

The two frigates turned in, gracefully carving through the rise and the fall of the green-gray waves as if to meet in the middle. The Khopeshii drove ahead, clearly eager to rush in to attack the *Shield Royal* – a good enough plan, to eliminate the greatest threat and then pick off the weaker one by one. But *Pious* was no weak warship. After the two opposing flagships, she reigned supreme in the battle in terms of firepower and raw strength.

"Starboard guns!" Jaymes called down to his second and third lieutenants, as well as their gun captains. "On my command!"

Only five hundred yards separated the two frigates as they arced around to run parallel to each other, stepping out together to starboard to avoid sailing dead into wind. Jaymes saw his opposite number – a gaunt figure in ragged black – stood on the quarterdeck of the frigate boneship. The deadly, giant crossbows of the Khopeshii lined up slowly with the larger Basilean frigate. Along the flank of the Elohi, stoic defenders of Basilea's waters stood ready by the lines of long-barreled cannons. The time was now.

"Starboard guns! Fire!"

The world vanished in clouds of acidic, gray smoke as the volcano-like eruption of the broadside boomed out of *Pious's* side. The ship lurched and rolled out of the blast, the high-pitched whining of temporarily damaged eardrums going some way to dull out the cacophony. A second later, *Pious* rolled again as three huge thuds sounded in quick succession, knocking Jaymes off his feet. Splinters of wood twirled and danced through the smoke and, over the tinny whining, Jaymes heard the screams of wounded sailors and orders shouted to casualty bearers. He staggered back to his feet, raising one hand to the hairline just forward of his left ear and feeling the sting of a wound and the wetness of blood.

"Load 'em!" Jaymes shouted down to the upper deck. "Gun captains! Take charge! Load 'em! Hit the bastards again!"

The smoke from the first tempestuous broadside drifted aft, clearing the view of the deck. Perhaps five or six sailors lay dead around the smoking cannons; some so obviously so that their shipmates were already dragging the corpses clear to throw overboard. Jaymes offered a genuinely sorrowful and regretful prayer for them, still surprised after several battles just how much blood could wash over the decks from comparatively few casualties.

Already, the first hands were leaping up from the gun crews to signify cannons ready. Jaymes looked starboard at the Khopeshii that sailed almost serenely parallel to his own warship, skeletal sailors hurriedly and emotionlessly loading their crossbows. He allowed himself a grim, vicious grin as he saw the damage inflicted to the Khopeshii's hull from *Pious's* guns.

"Starboard guns, ready!" Kaeso Innes called up from below.

"Fire!" Jaymes roared.

***

The ship's bell sounded out the hour, causing Karnon to spin on his heel on the fo'c'sle. He stared incredulously at the young sailor who sounded the bell in a series of double rings, amazed at the combination of both raw courage and dedication to duty, and petty, seemingly pointless adherence to trivia in the heat of battle. A second later, the *Shield Royal's* guns blasted out again, their cannonballs smashing into the Ahmunite war galley in a spectacular show of firepower. These were but two momentary distractions from the far closer matter in hand; the Ahmunite frigate that sailed off *Pious's* bow, as if closed in to exchange pleasantries and news, the distance was so close now.

"Starboard guns, ready!" Kaeso yelled from back aft, somewhere near midships on the upper deck.

An acknowledgement was called back from the quarterdeck, the order rippling down from officers to gun captains.

"Fire!"

The fo'c'sle lit up with muzzle flashes as cannons leapt back on their wooden trolleys like jumping warhorses. His ears ringing, his lungs aching from breathing in the fumes, Karnon wiped away tears from his stinging eyes and stared through the smoke. The solitary yard on the enemy frigate's foremast hung at an angle, the sail flapping near uselessly in the wind as the ancient ship continued to rise and fall in the heavy seas. Gunfire continued to ripple from all directions, carried back to Karnon across the wind as he waited, frustrated and useless, for a boarding action to come his way.

Then the Ahmunite frigate spoke her reply. With deep, thudding twangs of rope let go from restraints, her broadside crossbows flung their deadly cargo into the Basilean frigate.

"Down!"

Karnon flung himself to the deck, hands over the back of his head and eyes closed as he waited for the deadly, inevitable splinters to fly out from the points of impact. The Ahmunites did not disappoint. *Pious* shuddered and rolled away from the damage, the whine of wooden boards stretching to break and ropes snapping echoing across the upper deck. Then the screams, always the screams, as razor sharp splinters of oak found their home in soft bodies. Karnon staggered back up to his feet, the action made thrice as difficult as the frigate soared up a wave to seemingly try to push him back down into the deck.

Chaos reigned. Sailors, some covered in blood from their own wounds or caught in the macabre spatter of their shipmates' violent demises, continued to reload the cannons in time to the shouts of their gun captains. Six sailors to each gun on the fo'c'sle now – normally four if both broadsides were operated simultaneously, doubled up to eight if the action was only on the one side – now at half a dozen due to casualties. Two ship's boys – lads of no more than ten years of age – staggered across the deck to throw buckets of sand over fresh patches of blood and entrails to keep the decks from becoming slippery. Spare hands hurried in pairs to throw corpses overboard and drag the wounded down below for medical attention, shouting the names of the casualties to the bosun as they passed. The bosun – an aging rating with graying hair – recorded the details of the battle as they occurred, writing names, courses, and orders in the ship's log as calmly as if he were writing a poem.

Then Karnon heard a shout from down below. At first a single syllable, repeated three times. The call was taken up by a second voice, relayed along the gun deck. It reached the hatchway leading to the upper deck. Karnon froze in place. He stared, shame-faced at the two boys who fearlessly and obediently continued with their little job as Karnon's limbs refused to respond to his brain's commands. The call from the hatchway had made sure of that. Words that, on the battlefields of his past, he dealt with well enough. But here – trapped on a floating tomb of oak, having once heard from two miles inshore the sound of a ship's magazine exploding – Karnon's courage gave out.

"Fire, fire, fire! Fire on the gun deck!"

***

"Starboard guns! Reload!" screamed Jonjak, the brig's second mate.

Gasping for breath, Caithlin staggered out of the gunsmoke to the port side of the quarterdeck. She wiped a palm across her brow and saw black, sooty sweat. With a clearer view of the battle, she took stock of the situation. In the center, *Shield Royal* stood alongside the war galley, both great ships trading broadsides. Smoke wafted up in plumes from the Basilean Defender-class ship of the line, but she remained alongside the enemy, pouring cannon fire out of her flank.

As for Caithlin's vessel, they eased to starboard alongside a single-masted Ahmunite Dust Chaser, blasting the larger, slower vessel whilst return shots came from a great crossbow at midships and a more modern pair of light cannons beneath the quarterdeck. The exchange of firepower was roughly equal, but Caithlin could already see that the *Martolian Queen* was not as robust as the larger vessel. She looked further around, ahead and to stern. The *Veneration* was locked in combat with a Khopeshii, the two vessels almost serenely sailing alongside each other in the rise and fall of the waves, the evening sky lighting up with yellow flashes from the Basilean guns. Closer in, the salamander *J'Koor'uk* fired a last broadside into the second Dust Chaser, rewarded for their accuracy when the Ahmunite warship's sole mast snapped and collapsed forward over her bows.

Caithlin's eyes scanned further westward. Her jaw dropped and she let out a breath. She could see the flames rising up from *Pious*, even from here. Flickering orange fires streamed out of the gun ports along her side, blackening the hull. The frigate peeled away from its clash with the second Khopeshii, a line of signal pennants rapidly hoisted up the side of the main mast.

Request - Assistance

"Helm!" Caithlin yelled. "Hard a' starboard! Bring us around, two points south of westward!"

"Belay! Belay!" X'And shouted, rushing across the quarterdeck to Caithlin's side.

She shot a furious look at her first mate.

"What in blazes do you mean by..."

The salamander sailor held up his hands passively.

"Captain! I don't mean to try to override your orders! Those signals, they're not for us! They're not asking for help in the fight; they're asking for help with damage control!"

Caithlin gritted her teeth and swore in frustration as she wiped tears from her eyes from the relentless cannon smoke.

"What in the Abyss..."

X'And pointed out to the west.

"Their sloops, Captain! The Basilean sloops are trained in damage control for friendly ships! That's the help they want, not us!"

"We've still got guns!" Caithlin hissed through gritted teeth. "We can still shoot the bastards next to them! We can do that, can't we?"

X'And looked over Caithlin's shoulder, his eyes wide in surprise. Caithlin span in place and looked out to see, incredulously, the pirate xebec they had engaged before their attack on Red Skull, easing in behind the Dust Chaser off their starboard quarter.

"Down!" Caithlin yelled, hurling herself to the deck.

The ripple of light cannons echoed out from her right, and the *Martolian Queen* shook and shuddered. Yells of pain came from forward of the quarterdeck. Debris flew over Caithlin's back; something fell down on her. Coughing, shrugging off the obstruction laying across her and wincing in pain at the bruises across her shoulders, Caithlin staggered back to her feet.

"Starboard guns!" she yelled. "Target that pirate bastard! Helm, starboard! Get us alongside!"

Caithlin saw a shape out of the corner of her eye. She turned and looked down. Crumpled next to her, curled up in a fetal position in a pool of blood, X'And let out a child-like whimper, then something akin to a cry of despair, and lay still.

Chapter Seventeen

Hegemon's Warship Pious (38)
278 souls on board

"Sister Grace!" Jaymes shouted back toward the base of the mizzenmast. "Put sea room between us and that Khopeshii! Whatever you have to do, whatever measures you need to take, get this ship out of the battle until we have the fire under control!"

"Aye, sir!" the veteran sailing master replied before turning to shout out orders to the helm.

Jaymes felt the blazing heat wafting up from below as he hurried down the steps to the upper deck. Smoke poured up out of the open hatchways leading down to the gun deck, from both the after hatch near the quarterdeck steps and the forward hatch at the fo'c'sle. It was joined by more black plumes sweeping up from the open gunports on both sides of the ship. Up forward, the bosun had already collared six sailors and was leading them down into the inferno below to help fight the fire. Orders were screamed from the smokey darkness on the gun deck. Jaymes had seen three fires at sea. None like this. He turned to the signals midshipman.

"Mister Turnio! Signal for assistance!"

"Aye, sir!"

Pious leaned into the turn as she peeled away from the Ahmunite frigate hugging her bow. Jaymes turned to the lines of dozens of anxious gunners crouched over their cannons, staring back at him in anticipation.

"Ship's company!" Jaymes yelled. "Form up into damage control parties! Lieutenants, take charge! Able seamen, front and center! I need two teams of six down below! On the pumps, and one for getting casualties up here to fresh air!"

"Dennio, Tratterli, Vomas, Scareli, Aran, Scarre!" Kaeso Innes called. "On me! After hatch!"

A similar shout for names was made up forward by Benn Orellio. The nominated sailors hurried over to the scuttlebutt, removed their bandannas, soaked them in the water, and then tied them around their mouths and noses. Karnon rushed over to where Jaymes stood near the after hatchway.

"Captain!" he breathed, eyes wide and face pale. "I... I can lead a party down there!"

Jaymes looked across at his friend.

"Stay up here, Captain Senne. I need experienced hands taking charge down there. Kaeso and Benn will cycle the men through."

The marines captain grabbed Jaymes's arm with a tight grip.

"I... need to go down there, Jaymes!"

The two parties of sailors quickly formed up by their hatchways. Under the orders of the lieutenants, the sailors began the climb down through the smoke-belching hatchways to assist with the inferno below deck. Jaymes turned to frown at Karnon.

"This is bigger than your need to prove yourself, mate! I need to save this ship, and I need people who know what they're doing! Stand down and wait for my bloody orders!"

Before Karnon could respond, a single word was screamed from the quarterdeck.

"Down!"

Jaymes heard the whoosh of Ahmunite crossbows as he flung himself down, moments before the shots landed. Huge bolts plunged into the water off *Pious's* bow and sent columns of seawater skyward. A single shot smacked into the frigate's hull, just aft of midships, sending razor sharp splinters hurling across the deck. Jaymes staggered back up to his feet. He let out a breath and a one-word prayer as his eyes fell on the nearest casualty.

Kaeso Innes, his perpetually optimistic second lieutenant, lay on his back, eyes wide open and staring unfocused at the clouds above, atop a blood-soaked deck.

"Mister Knox!" Jaymes yelled up to the quarterdeck. "Take charge of the after hatchway!"

He rushed over to pull the short lieutenant's body away from the hatch, quickly but carefully laying him down by the side of the quarterdeck steps.

"Sorry, Kaeso," he whispered hurriedly as he dragged him across. "I'm... sorry."

Mayhew Knox hurried down the steps and stopped dead in his tracks as he saw Kaeso's body.

"Mayhew!" Jaymes snapped. "Keep it together! After hatch, first party is already down! Get the casualties up and in fresh air; keep cycling teams down there to work the pumps for the hoses!"

"Aye, sir!"

Jaymes turned to check on the progress of the Khopeshii. *Pious* was opening out, slower than the Ahmunite frigate but driven by a better crew. Knox assembled a second party to enter the fray of the burning gun deck. Jaymes saw Karnon had forced himself into the party. Off to port, a sloop was approaching rapidly. It was the *Scout*; Jaymes could see that Joshua Azer already had hoses rigged on the upper deck, ready to spray the hull of the burning frigate to cool the boundary of the fire. On the horizon behind the valiant sloop, Marcellus Dio's

Veneration was giving hell to the battered, second Khopeshii. Jaymes felt a surge, just a hint of optimism despite the blazing hot air spewing out of the hatchway a few paces away. Then another call came from the quarterdeck.

"Captain, sir!" Grace called down. "The *Shield Royal*! It's the *Shield*!"

Jaymes turned to look out to port.

"Oh, gods..."

The towering, noble flagship listed slowly to starboard, the Basilean flag flying in tatters from her stern as the Ahmunite war galley fired another volley into the decimated warship. Sailors leapt from her decks into the raging seas below as the Defender-class ship of the line began to sink slowly beneath the waves.

***

"Captain!"

Ears ringing, vision blurred, another impact and another sea of wooden splinters flung across the deck at head height, missing by inches and providence alone.

"Captain!"

A hand on the shoulder and a rough shake. Caithlin let out a gasp, unsure of how long she had held her breath as she knelt next to the fallen body of her friend. X'And lay crumpled before her, eyes shut and mouth slowly opening and closing with each weak, gasping breath. Oswalt pushed past her, dropping down next to the bloodied salamander and heaving him over to inspect the wound. A huge shard of broken wood emerged from his chest. The dwarf sailor pulled off his bandanna and pressed it against the wound before turning to Caithlin.

"Captain, I'll do what I can!"

Caithlin nodded mutely, forcing herself back up to her feet but still unable to drag her eyes away from her friend. The guns of her own ship blasted into life again; a seemingly ill-disciplined ripple of shots to-ing and fro-ing between stem and stern in comparison to the orderly, coordinated broadsides of the naval vessels around them. Caithlin looked up, past the smoke of the guns. *Pious* blazed, two sloops rushing toward her. *Shield Royal* sat low in the water, rolling lazily to one side, her angle indicative of a vessel that had only minutes to live. So this was it. This was what it felt like to lose. To die at sea.

No. There was always hope. There was always a way. *Veneration* pounded one of the Ahmunite frigates with another salvo, tearing open holes in her shattered hull. The salamanders' *Deliverer's Flame* let loose another broadside into one of the Ahmunite Dust Chasers. The smaller vessel exploded cataclysmically, lighting up the evening sky with a roaring fireball that replaced the entire warship. Caithlin narrowed her eyes.

"Prepare to tack!" she shouted down to the upper deck. "Alter starboard! Westward! We're closing to the center of this mess!"

Responding to her command, a handful of sailors left their guns to scramble up into the rigging to alter the sails.

***

His breastplate and pauldrons removed and placed on the deck, Karnon eyed the smoke wafting up out of the after hatchway. He waited with five other sailors by the hatch as a hundred gunners were cajoled back to their cannons. *Shield Royal* was doomed, her fo'c'sle now under water and her entire rudder clear of the waves as more sailors lined up on her quarterdeck to jump. The salamander frigate had sped over after destroying one of the smaller Ahmunite vessels and was now toe to toe with the enemy frigate whose shots had ignited *Pious's* gun deck. That, at least, gave some reprieve. One of the Basilean force's sloops had managed to close with *Pious* and now sailed close off the port bow, a hose on her deck spraying up against the frigate's hull. Karnon leaned over and scowled in disapproval.

"Bloody fools! Aim straight! Get it through the damn gun ports and into the fire!"

"That's not their job," Mayhew Knox breathed from a few paces away as his knees buckled and straightened with the pitching of the deck in the heavy seas. "They're not fighting the fire. They're cooling the hull to stop the fire spreading. Containing it so our lot can put the thing out. They'd never have the accuracy to fight the fire through a gun port from down there."

Unconvinced by the explanation, Karnon paced impatiently by the smoking hatchway. He did not have to wait for long. Shouts came from the deck below, and seconds later, a grime-covered sailor emerged into the fresh air, eyes and nose streaming as a hacking cough wracked his lungs. Karnon shot across to help the man out; Thole, a petty officer he recalled reprimanding a few weeks earlier for poor standards of dress.

"More coming, sir!" the sailor managed between coughs. Karnon and a gunner from the port battery helped a procession of four more men up from the fire below.

"Two more needed for the pumps!" the last man spluttered.

Karnon looked across at Mayhew. The first lieutenant nodded.

"Khanda, Captain Senne, if you please."

Khanda, the gunner next to Karnon, pulled his wetted bandanna over his mouth and lowered himself down the hatchway, immediately disappearing into the dense smoke. Knowing well from previous experience the dangers of hesitating, Karnon swung a leg over to the top rung of the ladder. Mayhew clamped a hand on his shoulder.

"Wait! Ladder's not clear! Wait for the kick!"

A few seconds passed before Karnon felt a double thump at the base of the ladder. Mayhew issued him a raised thumb. His inner monologue filled with cusses and curses, Karnon lowered himself into the smoke. The evening light was extinguished, he was plunged into darkness, and, as his eyes streamed and violent coughs forced their way through his lips, he suspected that the wetted bandannas over the mouth and nose were completely ineffectual. His white-knuckled hands clung tightly to the edge of the ladder as his feet groped around, slowly one by one in the darkness below him.

The rungs never seemed to end. The heat built up. The darkness was all engulfing, until suddenly the world was illuminated with a raging yellow behind him, the heat painful across his back. Still more rungs. Then, suddenly, a foot hit solid deck. Karnon kicked the base of the ladder twice and turned to face the fire. Seemingly, the entirety of the gun deck was engulfed with a blazing yellow inferno, licking up against the underside of the upper deck. Karnon grimaced as he saw two blackened corpses at the edge of the fire. Two sailors knelt down low beneath the worst of the fumes, crouched over a hose pipe that sprayed a constant stream of sea water into the blaze.

"Sir!" Khanda shouted over the roar of the fire. "Hold onto the line! Don't let go!"

Khanda grabbed onto a thin line of rope tied to the base of the ladder and followed it, disappearing into the smoke once more. Crouching down, not far off crawling on his hands and knees to avoid the worst of the smoke, Karnon clutched onto the guideline and followed the sailor ahead of him. The two made torturously slow progress back aft from the ladder, the familiar scenes of the passageway leading to the officers' accomodation and Karnon's own cabin now seeming surreal and twisted in the fumes and flickering light from the fire. Even though it was a path he knew well, Karnon still found himself lightheaded, disoriented, and confused by the short transit in the hot, dark air to the next hatchway, and down to the orlop deck.

In the comparatively cool, smoke-free orlop deck, Khanda and Karnon quickly found the pumps. Another petty officer took charge of two parties working the two pumps. Hoses led out of each – one forward and one aft to snake up to the gun deck and attack the fire simultaneously from two sides.

"'Ere!" the petty officer shouted to the two new arrivals. "On this pump! Dennio! Arran! Get back up topside!"

Karnon took his place on the metal-handled pump, still coughing from the inhalation of fumes on the transit down into the frigate's dark, stench-ridden bowels as two exhausted, sweat-covered sailors grabbed the guideline and disappeared back up toward the blaze on the deck above.

***

Looking back over the stern of the great war galley, T'mork watched as more Basilean sailors leapt from their stricken flagship. Some plunged beneath the waves and did not resurface, others floundered for a short while before sinking; others still somehow managed to remain afloat despite the heavy seas. A shame – a waste. All would have proven useful to him. T'mork did not consider himself to be a vengeful or petty individual – after all, this entire confrontation was about justice and honoring his god, rather than a childish act of revenge – but the irony would not have been lost on him if he had used the reanimated, purified corpses of those who destroyed his temple to Shobik to then rebuild it.

"Master," Demelecles bowed as he approached the high priest, the second syllable of the word cut off as the cannons, crossbows, and catapults of the towering war galley shot out again. "Captain Henneus... he founders."

T'mork looked off to the west and saw Henneus's Khopeshii, locked in a close quarter exchange of shot with the smaller of the two Basilean frigates. The Basilean was beyond possessing a clear upper hand; Henneus's ship had lost one mast, and even from this range, T'mork could see the upper deck crossbows were half shattered. A frustration, even a disappointment, but not a worry. The Basilean flagship was gone, and the larger of the two frigates was still blazing. Captain M'orbb's Khopeshii – the warship responsible for crippling the large, three-masted enemy frigate – was now locked in battle alongside the lone salamander warship.

T'mork smiled grimly, the dead flesh of his mouth pulled tight over his dry, holed gums. He could feel it even from here, the presence of divinity magic surging out from the two Basilean frigates. He sensed it from their flagship – a divine presence, an immortal force from above, overshadowing the amateur sorcery of the mortal aeromancer onboard the Basilean man o'war – before his own arcane powers dominated the magical theater of the battle. Easily dispelling anything the Basilean mage attempted, and punching through the weak attempts to dispel his own powers, T'mork added his considerable might to the weapons of the *Purification of Ul'Astia* to wear down and defeat the enemy capital ship. Now, admittedly exhausted and reeling from his exertions, T'mork needed a new target. The next in the pecking order of his enemy.

"Captain Demelecles," he wheezed, "the large enemy frigate, the one still burning. Place us alongside her and engage her."

"Yes, Master," the war galley's revenant captain bowed and then turned to head along the ship's waist to the front of the sprawling after deck.

T'mork narrowed his eyes. Across the arcane plains, just as quickly as he sensed it depart and fly away from the doomed Basilean man o'war, he felt the flare up of divinity power from the heart of the burning enemy frigate.

***

"Stay with her!" Tem yelled as the xebec was tossed down into the trough of another wave. "Helm to port... and thus! Midships there!"

The lithe, three-masted xebec eased in toward the privateer brig as gunners in groups of threes crouched over their nine-pounder cannons, sponging out the smoking barrels in preparation for reloading. To port, the fighting brig drifted in closer, close enough now for Tem to make out details on the crew peering over the gunwales – angry, determined-looking sailors whose motley clothing rig made them completely indistinguishable from Tem's pirates.

An order was shouted out from the brig's quarterdeck.

"Down!" Tem shouted.

The brig's guns snapped out a response to Tem's last broadside, accompanied seemingly immediately with the thunking and slamming of impact against the xebec's port bow. Laying on his quarterdeck, hands over his head, Tem knew not whether the sudden list to starboard was from the impact, a sudden flood, or the violence of the waves. Men screamed out. There was a heavy crash from somewhere behind him. Tem forced himself back up to his feet.

Debris and detritus lay strewn across the ship's deck. Another two men lay dead; another three bleeding and wounded. Behind him, the yard of the mizzenmast had detached entirely and the long, wooden boom – complete with sail – balanced precariously against the starboard taffrail. Tem looked ahead – his guns still were not reloaded. He stared out to port. The brig cut in aggressively toward them. Privateers appeared above the gunwales, armed with muskets and pistols. On the quarterdeck of the fighting brig, Tem saw the blonde woman from the bar on Red Skull, her face contorted in rage, a pistol in each hand.

Another order was shouted out, and the muskets and pistols fired. Hoggir fell to the deck, his throat ripped out by a musket ball. Halladai let out a cry, a stream of crimson erupting from his shoulder as he was span around. Sailors on the brig rushed to the waist with lines and grapple hooks. The bastards were preparing to board.

"Hard a starboard!" Tem screamed. "Helm! Hard a starboard!"

He looked over and saw Halladai, teeth gritted in pain, hauling the ship's wheel around as he stood over the dead helmsman. The nimble pirate ship swung about, her bows cutting away from the brig. Whilst her speed was reduced with the damage to the mizzenmast, Tem knew he could bring her closer to the wind than the brig captain would dare with her own ship; the advantages of a fore-and-aft rigger compared to a square-rigged brig.

"Tem!" Halladai shouted from behind the wheel. "What course?"

Tem skittered across the pitching and rolling deck to the helm.

"Get distance from her, and then south! Enough of this! Get south, get clear! The night will be here to hide us soon enough!"

One sleeve soaked with fresh blood, his breathing labored, the quartermaster turned to his captain.

"Get clear?!" he snarled. "We're running? Tem! Those bastards killed our mates! And we've got something out of a damned nightmare watching our every move! And you've bottled it?!"

With a vicious curse, Tem grabbed the back of the older man's head and swung his eyes about to stare down at the deck.

"Look, you fool! Look! Half of our boys are dead! That brig outguns us by nearly double! I'm a pirate, not a bloody hero! And I'm getting us out of here whilst we've got the best chance we've had yet!"

Halladai flung Tem's hand off him, his eyes ablaze with fury.

"And then what?! Huh?! What then, you yellow bastard?! You want me to saw my damn arm off?! The Ahmunites will find us!"

Tem stared back up at the larger pirate. Yes, if necessary, he would have his arm. If necessary, he would have his head. He was not dying or becoming a slave to the Empire of Dust for a man he had only known for three years.

"Look forward, Halladai!" Tem snarled. "Look at your shipmates! You think this is about you? Think of them, damn you! I'm not killing them all for you! Now get us away from that damned brig and clear to the south! I'll find a way to free us from that... thing on the war galley! I'll find a way!"

The xebec continued onward, easing away from the brig with the wind just a few points off the ship's head where a square-rigger could not hope to pursue her. Halladai looked forward across the battered, blood-soaked deck at his shipmates. His features eased from anger to sorrow. His shoulders slumped and his head hung low.

"Aye, Captain. Aye. Let's get our lads out of this."

Tem folded his arms and looked back at the brig. Yes, he was running to save his own skin. Yes, he had used his crew as a bargaining chip to lie to his own quartermaster about his motivations. There was some guilt – some – but not much.

***

His face red and glistening with sweat, Mayhew rushed across the quarterdeck and over to Jaymes. Blinking sweat and smoke from his eyes, he presented himself formally by standing to attention momentarily.

"The fire's contained, sir," he gasped, "but not out. The pumps are holding, and we've got everybody up top and out of the smoke, except for the pump parties and the surgeon's party. Kennus refuses to leave his station. So do the surgeon's mates. We're still trying to get the worst casualties down to them."

His jaw clenched, Jaymes narrowed his eyes and nodded. That was where they were. His ship was on fire, with every spare hand tackling the blaze and moving casualties. They may succeed in fighting the fire back in a minute; it might take an hour. Every moment they concentrated on fighting the fire was more time they failed to support the rest of the Basilean fleet, and with *Shield Royal* now consisting only of the tips of her masts protruding from the water with survivors desperately clinging to them, the battle was well on course to being lost. But if Jaymes gave the order to turn back in to fight, he needed parts of his crew back on the sails and the guns. He needed to remove crew from the pumps, hoses, sand buckets, casualty handling... all of it. He needed to risk the fire spreading cataclysmically, possibly even to the powder magazine.

So that was that. Do nothing and stay alive, or risk every soul onboard to rejoin the fight. Jaymes looked quickly around the quarterdeck at the surrounding battle. Marcellus Dio's *Veneration* raced fearlessly toward the enemy flagship, a sinking Khopeshii frigate in her wake. The salamander J'Koor'uk was now alongside the second Khopeshii – the Ahmunite warship that had set *Pious* ablaze – and was trading shots. Caithlin's *Martolian Queen* was rising and falling with the seas, hurtling across toward *Pious* with a Dust Chaser and a Soul Hunter in pursuit. In and around the larger vessels, Basilean sloops and Ahmunite slave galleys flitted in and out, exchanging fire in their own private fights or valiantly supporting their larger, sister warships.

Jaymes looked across at Grace. The Sisterhood sailing master walked briskly across the deck to join him and the first lieutenant.

"Get the top men back on the yards," Jaymes ordered, "we're going back in."

Mayhew's mouth opened and closed twice, and for a moment, Jaymes thought he was going to argue against the order.

"Aye, sir," he said quietly.

"Sister Grace, get us right into the wreck of the *Shield*. We'll recover every survivor that we can."

The veteran sailing master raised her brows, like an elderly schooling teacher who was disappointed with a student's answer to a simple question.

"Sir... if I may. I recommend we either fight the fire, or we fight the enemy. Those men out there... they're already dead."

Jaymes narrowed his eyes.

"There are over six hundred and fifty sailors on that ship. *Our* people. You get this ship in there, and we recover survivors. Both of the enemy's remaining *real* warships are engaged, and the *Shield* lies directly in our path back into the fight. This is the only chance to recover those sailors. If that war galley comes for us while we're dead in the water, then Captain Dio will rake her all the way to the Mount. If they try to engage us, we'll shoot back. We'll blow our survivors' eardrums out as we recover them, but by the Ones above, we will shoot back and those men will be happy to be deaf but alive. Get this ship to the *Shield Royal*. Now."

Grace exhaled and looked away.

"Aye, sir."

Jaymes paced off to the edge of the quarterdeck and leaned over the taffrail. Below, still skillfully keeping station just off the port bow, the sloop *Scout* was pumping sea water against *Pious's* hull. On the small ship's quarterdeck, Joshua Azer and his lieutenant looked up at Jaymes.

"We're altering to starboard!" Jaymes yelled down. "We're going in to recover as many men as we can from the *Shield*! Can you keep station and keep cooling our hull?"

Joshua raised a hand and shouted back up as his sloop was tossed and rolled by the waves in the failing evening light, the rumble of gunfire still echoing from every horizon.

"Aye, sir!"

Orders were relayed along the smoldering frigate's deck. Blue and white clad sailors flung themselves back up the ratlines toward the yards of the three masts above, ready to adjust the sails.

"Helm!" Grace shouted. "Four points to starboard! Easy, now! Up top, trim the fore, course, and top! Altering to starboard!"

Pious's bows swung through the waves, carving a path through the rough waters, black smoke still trailing from her gunports. Jaymes looked aft and saw the *Martolian Queen* still closing, leaving the slower Ahmunite Soul Hunter and Dust Chaser behind but targeted by their weapons. Jaymes recognized in himself at that moment the desire to bring his entire warship back around to help the woman he loved. But he had a responsibility, a duty, and if a single life was lost due to his own reckless prioritization of personal life over that duty, then he was not fit for the job. He was not fit to stand beneath the Basilean flag.

The thought had barely escaped his mind when the sails suddenly billowed out with a crack above him. Up forward, at the bowsprit, the blue flames from the Elohi figurehead flared up to illuminate the darkening, cloudy sky. For just a few moments, the gunfire seemed to fall silent, or at least nearly so. The wind rushed. The sea swept past the wood and iron hull. A feeling of calmness, of serenity, washed over the quarterdeck. A fresh, cooling wind howled gently across the ship.

The fire extinguished.

Jaymes looked up to the heavens, whispered a prayer, and then sprinted to the fore end of the quarterdeck to shout down to the upper deck.

"Mister Knox! Get all hands back to their stations! Get the guns crewed up, roundly now! Mister Turnio! Signal for the *Scout* to follow us in and recover survivors!"

Chapter Eighteen

Hegemon's Warship Pious (38)

The frigate's bows came to rest as close to wind as her sailing master dared, her sails all but completely furled. To drop anchor would be insanity; instead, the still smoking warship pitched and rolled with the swell, as stationary as it was possible to keep her. Off to starboard, the war galley continued to exchange fire with *Veneration*; further aft, off the starboard quarter, the salamander *Deliverer's Flame* sent another punishing broadside into the final Khopeshii. But *Veneration* could not stand against the Ahmunite flagship for long.

"Lines!" Jaymes shouted from his position a'midships, staring down into the tragic wreckage of what was a great warship of the Basilean navy only minutes before. "Get the lines down!"

There was no time to drop anchor; there was no time to lower sea boats into the water to affect a proper rescue. Just moments few to give the strong swimmers a chance at life and leave the other poor souls in the hands of the Shining Ones until the battle was over. Jaymes was first over the taffrail, quickly clambering down the steps built into the waist of the frigate toward the waterline. The wreckage of *Shield Royal* – a few feet of her stern, her bowsprit, and the top of her main mast still protruding from the crashing waves – was only perhaps a hundred feet from *Pious*.

Survivors were already leaping off the last remnants of the ship to swim across; others were already in the water, clinging to wreckage and paddling for all they were worth. The guns continued to boom away between the surrounding combatants as the first few crewmen from the *Shield Royal* reached *Pious's* hull. An aging sailor, white-haired and bloodied, clung to the lowest step built into *Pious's* hull with wiry hands. Jaymes reached down.

"Come on!"

The poor wretch looked up at Jaymes with exhausted, terrified eyes. Jaymes grabbed him by one forearm and hauled him up and clear.

"Quickly! Up on deck! Clear the ladder!"

At those words, the old mariner seemingly found a new lease of motivation and sprung up the steps with the vigor of a sailor half his age.

"Thank you, sir!" he gasped as he passed Jaymes.

Two more of *Pious's* ship's company clambered down to help

their captain at the waterline as other survivors reached the frigate, some still possessing the strength to clamber up the lines secured to the taffrail far above. Simultaneously, with an admirable show of precision seamanship, *Scout* drifted past *Pious* to tuck in close to the stern of the sunken ship of the line, swinging to port to then nudge her waist with a small thump into the sad remains of the *Shield Royal*. Lines were quickly – and hazardously – thrown across and secured, and survivors who could not swim, consigned to their fate on the sinking flagship, began jumping down onto the little sloop by the dozen.

"Jaymes!"

Jaymes heard a gargled shout from the water, bringing his attention back to the task in hand.

"Jaymes! Help me here!"

He looked down and saw the *Shield Royal's* captain, Zakery Uwell, swimming across with a half-conscious boy of perhaps ten years of age clinging to his back. Jaymes shot down until he was half in the water, dragging the poor boy from the senior captain's back. The terrified child clung onto Jaymes, sobbing as blood flowed from a head wound.

"I've got him! Zakery, I've got him! Come on!"

The older captain remained in the water and shook his head.

"No! There's more back there! Still more! I have to go back!"

"Zakery!"

"Ones bless you, Jaymes! I have to help them!"

Zakery pivoted, pressed a bare foot against the hull of *Pious,* and pushed himself off to swim back across the heavy seas toward the wreckage of his ship. Jaymes dragged himself back up the steps toward the upper deck, the sobbing child clinging tightly to his neck.

"Nearly there, son!" Jaymes managed.

He stopped at the halfway point and turned to look back down. There were no more swimmers. The only other survivors were a handful more men jumping down onto the *Scout*. Perhaps a hundred sailors rescued, all in. Jaymes climbed one more step. He stopped again and turned to stare at the rolling waves. He cast his eyes across the foaming peaks for long, long seconds. Zakery was gone.

***

Sweat covering every inch of skin, his breathing ragged, Karnon dragged himself back up out of the hatch and to the fresh air of the upper deck. Above him, all three masts had their sails set for battle. The upper deck itself was flooded with sailors – perhaps sixty or seventy more than he would have expected, men who Karnon did not recognize.

"*Shield Royal* ship's company!" Mayhew shouted above the din.

"If you're fit to fight, get on the guns! If you can work wood, report to the carpenter's repair party! Wounded, down below and proceed for'ard for the surgeon!"

Wiping the sweat from his eyes, Karnon made his way quickly across to where he had left his armor and set about buckling on his breastplate. Cannon fire thumped from the surrounding horizons, and Karnon saw the *Veneration* alongside the enemy flagship, while the salamander frigate aggressively attacked the final, heavily damaged Ahmunite Khopeshii. *Pious* gun captains waded into the sea of new arrivals, soaked and exhausted-looking sailors recovered from the sunken Defender-class ship of the line, shouting and cajoling men to their new stations by the upper deck and fo'c'sle gun carriages.

Grabbing his boarding pike and helmet, Karnon jogged quickly up the steps leading to the quarterdeck. He saw Jaymes, Grace, and the quarterdeck gun crews standing by. Jaymes flashed him an unconvincing smile as he approached. Over Jaymes's shoulder, Karnon saw Caithlin's fighting brig approaching from the northwest.

"Did you feel that?" Karnon exhaled. "Up here? The lads down below on the hoses said the fire was contained, but the way it suddenly went out... it could only have been..."

"Yes, we felt it," Jaymes's smile was more sincere this time. "And we've recovered as many survivors as we could from the *Shield*. I'm afraid Zakery didn't make it. Joshua has the *Scout* there still, doing what he can. Look, our fortunes have turned a bit, and I think we're back in this. We have a chance. The salamanders are knocking seven shades of shit out of that Khopeshii, but Marcellus and the *Veneration* can't last long against that war galley. But the wind has veered, which is in our favor. That's why I'm signaling to double."

Karnon looked up at the colorful signal pennants hoisted up along the main mast. He had, as with so many nautical skills vital to truly understanding his new role, attempted to learn the complex and seemingly variable meaning of the flags, but failed to comprehend the line of pennants.

"It's in code," Jaymes explained, no doubt detecting the marine's confusion, "and we change the code every three months to keep our enemies guessing, so never bother trying to learn it. I've requested Marcellus prepare to drop back and turn in. He can rake the bastard's stern from close enough to spit, whilst we sail right across her prow and rake her bow. They'll react, of course; but whilst they're trying to defend against one of us, the other will get the optimal firing position. Up to them, really. They either defend against us with our greater firepower, or Marcellus with his better positioning. Either way, we're ganging up on him and kicking him square in the bollocks."

Karnon exhaled slowly, glad of the fresh air and comparatively bright lights of the evening sky after exerting himself for so long on the pump on the orlop deck.

"Chances of us boarding them?" he asked.

Jaymes met his stare.

"Better than average. With the ship's companies of two frigates boarding from both sides simultaneously, we'll have the bastards. Just so long as *Veneration* can hold on until we catch up."

"Understood," Karnon replied, "I'll get my marines assembled and ready. I'll lead the boarding action, sir. Just a reminder."

Jaymes raised one eyebrow.

"Not a chance, mate. Not a chance. I'll lead the show."

***

Pious's bowchasers erupted, spitting out roundshot toward the towering war galley. The noise of the cannons somehow lifted a weight from Jaymes's shoulders. They were back in the fight now, free of the terror of a fire onboard and now, thanks to *Veneration* sinking one of the Khopeshii, the odds were once again balanced. From his position on the quarterdeck, Jaymes raised his telescope and looked forward across the bows.

The enemy war galley's weapons bristled along her flank. Atop the upper deck were the age old but deadly crossbows, augmented by pivot-mounted catapults. However, ornate gun ports were carved into the wood of her hull where modern cannons, most likely looted from defeated enemy vessels, were positioned and pointed at *Veneration*. With a low rumble, the cannons fired alongside the more traditional Ahmunite armaments. *Veneration* visibly leaned away from the impact, holes punched in her hull and her foremast leaning over as her rigging was severed in several places. Within seconds, a familiar set of signaling pennants ran up her main mast.

Request - Assistance

"I know, mate, I know," Jaymes whispered to himself, "we'll be there as quickly as we can."

Jaymes snapped his telescope shut and rushed to the forward end of the quarterdeck, leaning over the taffrail to shout commands down to his signals midshipman.

"Francis! Signal our sloops to close with *Veneration* to assist with repairs if she breaks away. And tell... no, *request* the *Martolian Queen* drop back and engage the those Ahmunite slave galleys."

"Aye, sir."

The low clouds shot by overhead, whipped across the top of

the frigate's trio of tall masts in the whistling wind. The green seas rose and fell as gunfire continued from every direction. Orders were shouted from the fo'c'sle as the bow chasers were sponged and reloaded. Back aft, the salamander J'Koor'uk turned nimbly to simultaneously fight off the attacks of the final Khopeshii and the last Dust Chaser that had abandoned the pursuit of the faster privateer brig. The fo'c'sle guns fired again, and Jaymes saw impact on the stern of the towering enemy war galley. A couple of nine-pounders would not do much, but at least the bastards knew that a new threat was coming and *Veneration* was not alone.

"Sir!" Midshipman Turnio called from the upper deck. "Reply from the *Martolian Queen*."

Jaymes turned to look out across the port quarter. Joshua's nimble sloop was racing towards *Veneration*, as ordered. A single signal pennant fluttered from the main mast of Caithlin's brig.

Negative

Jaymes swore out loud and paced over to the after end of the quarterdeck, staring back at the fighting brig. The eighteen-gunner remained stoically on station off the port quarter, rising and falling with the fierce waves, her deck littered with debris from damage taken earlier in the battle. His teeth gritted, Jaymes strode across to the stairs leading down to the upper deck.

"Samus?"

The gray-haired steward appeared at the foot of the steps.

"Sir," he responded gruffly.

"Fetch me a pistol."

"And your jacket and hat, sir," the old sailor nodded with a sneer.

Jaymes threw a clenched fist up to either side.

"Confound it, man! We're about to board an enemy flagship, and you think this is the time for formality and ensuring I'm in the correct headgear?!"

The veteran steward stared up at him without flinching.

"Now more than ever, sir."

Jaymes frantically searched for a witty riposte. He found none.

"Alright. I'll meet you halfway. Pistol and jacket."

The steward ambled off.

"And hat, sir," he mumbled under his breath.

"I'm not wearing a bloody hat in this wind!" he called after Samus. "I'm sure you won't offer to dive in and rescue it once the wind decides to float test it!"

Muttering to himself, Jaymes turned and saw Grace had appeared stealthily behind him.

"We need to trim for the wind again, sir," the sailing master announced. "We obviously don't want to rake the war galley's bows at the same time as *Veneration* has her stern. Do you want us to hold back a little, or forge ahead?"

"Forge ahead," Jaymes answered immediately, "don't hold anything back. Get us straight across her prow so we can kick her in the teeth, then hard to port to close for boarding."

***

"Confound them," T'mork hissed, careful to keep his voice low, lest any of his revenants should overhear and form an opinion of their own. "What does it take to sink them?"

The ropes and winches of the *Purification of Ul'Astia's* crossbows and catapults whined under strain as they were wound in and took tension; the smoke from the accursed dwarf cannons slowly cleared to reveal the Basilean frigate still sailing. The forward of her two masts was battered, splintered, and bent, but still the captain stood tall on the quarterdeck with his officers and gunners.

It should have been so easy. It should have been over by now. Once T'mork had used his unique powers to move his flagship beneath the waves to engage the enemy's largest warship – and, thanks to his vastly superior arcane mastery, to fight and win – it should have been a case of picking off the smaller ships one by one. Yet the enemy frigate off his starboard bow had destroyed one of the Khopeshii, the second Khopeshii commanded by Captain Henneus was struggling to fight back against the salamander ally of the Basileans, and now the larger of the two enemy frigates was hurtling across to join the first.

From his vantage point in front of the grand entrance to his ship's temple, T'mork stared at the approaching frigate. Slightly larger than the one he currently engaged, this was the warship that Henneus had managed to set fire to. Now it raced toward T'mork's war galley, metal-encased bows slicing through the waves, her angelic figurehead holding a torch tilted forward and blazing with blue fire. T'mork could feel the presence of his enemy's heavenly guardians even from here; the figurehead seemed to stare directly at him as the Basilean frigate punched through the heavy seas on a direct path to engage, bow chasers blazing. For a moment, just a brief moment, confronted with such a noble and valiant spectacle, T'mork wondered if he actually was the villain of this whole piece.

"Eventualities and options," he turned to bark at Demelecles. "What may happen, and what options are open to me?"

The black-robed, ancient sea captain turned to face his high priest.

"They will attempt to divide our weapons, Master," Demelecles said as a group of five skeletal sailors rushed past them to replace weapons operators on the forecastle who had been returned to the grave by Basilean cannons. "The quickest way would be for the larger frigate to approach us from our port bows. That way, they will envelop us from both sides simultaneously. If so, I believe they will then attempt to board us."

T'mork narrowed his pale eyes.

"If so? You believe they may try something else?"

"Yes, Master. If they are truly reckless and wish for a higher risk approach which could yield more effect, they may try to attack us from forward and aft simultaneously, instead of both sides. A far more difficult feat of seamanship to line up their weapons, but if they were to achieve, then we will be raked."

T'mork folded his arms across his bare, dead chest.

"Our best option to counter such a maneuver?"

The winds whipped at Demelecles's dark hood, hiding his features.

"We turn with the smaller frigate. Cut off her approach. And we concentrate all of our weaponry there. We refuse to let them divide our attention."

T'mork clenched one fist and wrapped the fingers of his other hand around it. Would the Basileans take the most solid, dependable approach and attack from both sides? No. That way they would both suffer the devastating broadsides of the *Purification of Ul'Astia* simultaneously. That, and something about the speed with which the second frigate approached, it seemed too... reckless for the safe tactical option. They would try the raking fire, T'mork believed. And they would expect T'mork to do all that he could to destroy the smaller frigate before the three-master arrived. Which, at its current pace, was only minutes away. No. No, he would not do what they would expect.

"Captain, break off our attack. Turn in to face the larger frigate. Destroy that warship."

Demelecles bowed his hooded head.

"Yes, Master."

***

Jaymes was close enough now to make out Marcellus's distinctive figure on the quarterdeck of the *Veneration*. For a moment, he feared more than anything else for his friend's safety – not for his own sake, but for his daughter's – but quickly packed away and shoved the sentiment down to keep his mind on the task in hand. With the prevailing wind still some way south of westerly, *Pious's* sails seemingly caught every last fistful of air to propel her toward the Ahmunite flagship. Fleshless sailors, clad in faded blue and pitted bronze, scrambled across the upper deck to crew the huge crossbows, while on the forward weapon platform, the giant catapult was laboriously turned in place to line up with the approaching Basilean frigate.

Veneration brought in sail on both of her masts and slowly dropped back, allowing the war galley to pull ahead. To port, the *Martolian Queen* raced past *Pious*, the fighting brig overtaking the frigate as she in turn overtook the Ahmunite war galley. *Pious's* prow swept past the war galley's stern, close enough for a perfect shot as the smaller ship overtook from port.

"Steady!" Jaymes shouted down to the dozens of sailors standing by the warship's broadside of eighteen guns. "Hold fire 'til we cross their bows!"

Pious surged past the war galley. Jaymes looked up onto the enemy quarterdeck and saw only two figures – a hooded sailor clad in the black robes of an Ahmunite captain, and a tall, powerfully built man whose ornate robes and appendages marked him out as important. With a colossal, almost feral roar, the cannons on the war galley fired, blasting into *Pious* as she swept past. The valiant frigate shook from the impact as debris flew back from the fo'c'sle, screams of the wounded emanating from the hidden impact point and nine-pounder cannons flung up into the air off their carriages. A huge crossbow bolt thudded into *Pious's* hull near the midship's position, penetrating the thick wood and cutting through the gun deck below. The prow catapult flung a flaming projectile up at the Basilean warship, but at this speed, it failed to hit, even at such a short range. Shaken, battered, and her fo'c'sle awash with blood, *Pious* swept past.

"Now!" Jaymes shouted. "Turn in across her!"

"Helm! Hard a' starboard!" Grace ordered.

Pious lurched off to the right, rolling out of the turn in the heavy seas.

"Signals!" Jaymes called down to the base of the main mast. "Now! Hoist the signals!"

Colored pennants shot up the side of the main mast.

Veneration - Request - Attack - Stern

The war galley turned starboard with *Pious* in an attempt to maintain station with her, preventing a clear opportunity for a bow rake. Jaymes smiled grimly. He had lost his perfect shot, but it did not matter. Marcellus had responded to the signal flags. With a flawless display of seamanship, *Veneration* altered course violently to port to race across the war galley's stern at a perpendicular angle, close enough practically to jump onto the enemy ship. Jaymes took one last look, assessed the closing angle, and realized that *Pious* did not have the speed to position for the bow rake. Now was as good a shot as ever.

"Starboard guns! Fire!" Jaymes shouted.

Pious's side was lit up with the combined blast of her ferocious broadside, spewing out roundshot into the bone ship's hull. A moment later, *Veneration* fired, blasting her own shot straight through the war galley's vulnerable stern.

***

The second enemy frigate closed rapidly from the port quarter, her flanks still blackened from her earlier fire, and her Elohi figurehead staring forward with determination, torch blazing blue flames. T'mork watched the enemy ship draw closer, his mouth twisted in a confident smirk having dispatched the enemy flagship, pushing thoughts of the damage his vessel had already suffered to oneside. The first Basilean frigate remained off the starboard bow, dropping back steadily. T'mork could have laughed. The ploy was bold, he would give them that, but obvious. The lead would attempt to rake and then both would try to grapple and board. No matter. He was outnumbered now and knew he may suffer the wrath of a raking shot from one ship if he was unwary – but not from both.

"Captain," he turned to Demelecles, "attack on your discretion as they pass by our port bow. As soon as they attempt to turn in for the bow rake, turn with them. Keep the crews divided between weapons on both sides."

"Yes, Master."

Demelecles paced forward to take charge of the port weapons as the Basilean frigate streamed past. T'mork stood tall on his after deck, before the ship's temple to Shobik, arms folded as he watched the smaller enemy ship. Up forward, the combined might of the *Purification of Ul'Astia's* crossbows, catapults, and those distasteful cannons erupted into the frigate. Clouds of smoke blossomed out at the front of the ship, with storms of wooden splints flying back into the exposed crew. T'mork's smile grew broader. Crossbow bolts smashed through the frigate's hull. Then the Basilean warship turned in. Up forward, Demelecles turned to face the two skeletal sailors clinging to the ship's heavy wheel, an unspoken mental command was passed to them, and the mighty war galley turned to starboard only an instant after the more agile Basilean frigate.

"Good," T'mork muttered to himself.

Now to only weather their fire, and their advantage was spent.

A line of signal flags shot up the frigate's main mast. T'mork narrowed his eyes, the dead flesh of his face twisting over his age-old bones. He turned to look back at the first, smaller frigate as the mighty war galley eased over to starboard to deny the larger Basilean warship from raking the bows. T'mork's jaw opened just a little.

"Bastards..." he whispered.

The two-masted frigate was hurled to port by an aggressive turn of her wheel and expert handling of her sails. The warship came almost full about, seeming to pivot on the spot and carve directly through the *Purification of Ul'Astia's* wake. Then the deadly guns of the frigate passed by the stern. Then they fired.

T'mork was thrown forward, hurtling through the air in, what he could only assume in his dazed state, was a deeply ungracious somersault. He landed with a series of cracks on the hard, unforgiving deck, his world lost in a cloud of dust and smoke. He felt pain race across his torso, unlike anything he had felt since his mortal life. Limbs refused to obey his mind's commands. Up ahead of him, bones and debris were scattered across the deck. He felt sunlight against his back when he knew he should not have. With shaking hands and a sense of panic rising through his core, he struggled to turn to see what his sacrilegious foes had dared to do to his ship's temple. Then the broadside of the three-masted frigate hit the port bows.

His senses still dazed and his mind addled with weariness from arcane exertion and the concussive force of the blasts, T'mork could only look up from his prone position to see the forward weapon platform torn clear off his ship, sending the mighty bow catapult flying up in into the air in pieces. Skeletal crewmen flew back with it, breaking apart in midair amid a sea of wooden splinters and shards of bone from the broken segments of bow. T'mork opened his mouth to shout out for Demelecles, but nothing came. He tried to calm his mind to reach out across the arcane plains, grasping at the consciousnesses of his subordinates through invisible links unfathomable to the mortals who dared assault his temple, but again there was nothing.

With pain ravaging his broken body, T'mork managed slowly, after trying and failing several times, to turn in place. Twisting painfully over on his side, he tilted his head to look back aft.

"No. No..."

The walls of the glorious temple to Shobik still stood, but the entire roof had collapsed in on itself from the force of the Basilean guns, allowing sunlight to light up the upper deck of the war galley through gaps where that temple stood only moments before. Flames licked up from the heart of the temple, blackening the white, marble walls as chunks of masonry fell from the ruins in the ship's turn, plummeting over the side of the after deck to drop into the seas below, never to be recovered.

"No!" T'mork screamed, an unstoppable will surging through his shattered, splinter-punctured body. "No!"

Limbs shaking, the ancient high priest forced himself up onto one knee. To port, the larger Basilean frigate swung in as if to ram the noble Ahmunite war galley as the second frigate eased to starboard toward her sister warship. His senses flooded with pain, anger, insult, and confusion, T'mork lifted a shivering, deformed hand and channeled his powers from his core to the environment surrounding him. He pushed past the mastery of necromancy, probing down through his understanding of the essence of the waters around him and the force locked within. Clenching a fist of broken fingers, yellowed teeth gritted in agony as he willed every last drop of his being, T'mork summoned the surrounding seas to wash up over his stricken vessel and eradicate the insult to his beloved god.

Yelling out in agony and exhaustion, T'mork held one arm outstretched as green waters surged up in massive, wall-like waves to wash over the flaming remains of his sacred temple. The fire was gone in seconds. T'mork collapsed back down, offering silent prayers to beg forgiveness to Shobik for his failure. The defiling flames extinguished, T'mork fell back down to his hands and knees.

"Master!"

He opened his eyes again.

"Master!"

T'mork looked up. Whether he had been lost to the plains for seconds, minutes, or hours he did not know. The sky above was still bright with the last of the evening sunshine, forcing its way past the low, billowing white clouds. Demelecles stood over him, an arm outstretched. T'mork took it, forcing himself back up to his feet with a cracking of bones.

"Master, they are on us! They have lines across!"

T'mork stared out across the port bow. The three-masted Basilean frigate was up against his war galley, lines and grapples holding the two ships firmly together. A young, dark-haired naval officer in a uniform of dark blue jumped across onto the *Purification of Ul'Astia's* deck, pistol blazing as he gunned down a revenant sailor, saber held high in his other hand. Behind him, adding to the sacrilege of the war galley's sacred deck came two dozen sailors, roaring and screaming as they attacked, their ranks bolstered by fighting men in armor with pikes and shields. A second later, a beautiful woman in white, a red sash around her waist, clambered up over the prow and flung herself forward with pistol and sword, her features twisted in fury as a wave of attackers followed her from lines hanging down the side of the ship.

With a yell of insurmountable rage at the disrespect paid to Shobik by the attackers, T'mork held his staff aloft and surged forward to attack.

Chapter Nineteen

Martolian Queen (18)
Privateer (Converted Trade Brig)

The brig surged across the heaving waves, pitching up past the horizon before diving down in between the next peaks. Off the starboard quarter, *Pious* charged forward to overtake the huge boneship war galley, screams still sounding from her fo'c'sle after the withering fire from the enemy flagship. On the brig's quarterdeck, Caithlin looked up at the two mighty vessels off to starboard. She remembered limping into harbor and looking up to see *Pious* for the first time, her ship shattered from that fateful encounter with orc pirates. A Batch Two Elohi-class frigate had seemed overwhelming at the time, towering over her four hundred tonner; now, next to the war galley which sat at nearly twice the tonnage of the frigate, *Pious* seemed almost toy-like in comparison.

"Another point starboard!" Caithlin shouted across to the helmsman. "Tight in alongside! Tight!"

The *Martolian Queen* leaned across and closed the gap with the Basilean frigate. Then, behind them, *Veneration* suddenly swept across the Ahmunite warship's stern, her guns firing directly into the aft of the quarterdeck as she passed. A cheer went up from Caithlin's crew of a hundred sailors as fire and smoke leapt up from the after end of the enemy ship, its macabre temple collapsing in on itself. A moment later, the guns from *Pious* blasted away, but whatever damage they caused was hidden from view on the far side of the frigate.

"Come on!" Caithlin urged as her fighting brig overtook the frigate in the turn. "Come on, now!"

A stone throw away, high up on the deck of *Pious*, Caithlin heard orders shouted out. Sail was taken in. Her turn to starboard tightened. The thirty-eight gun frigate suddenly slowed.

"They're boarding her!" shouted Jonjak from where he stood to supervise the starboard cannons. "By the Ones above, they're boarding her!"

Caithlin swore. Boarding a war galley with the remaining crew of a battered frigate. She looked aft at the *Veneration*. Marcellus's ship swept behind them both, altering to starboard to re-enter the fight but still far too far to assist in boarding.

"All hands!" Caithlin yelled above the howling wind. "Prepare for boarding!"

Dozens of pairs of eyes turned to face her, pale-faced and incredulous.

"You heard the cap'n!" Nudd hollered. "Get yerself a pistol and an axe each, yer bunch o'bastards!"

The *Martolian Queen* swept past *Pious*, and Caithlin looked across to see boarding lines were already secure. A volley of arrows shot across the gap from the Ahmunite vessel, tearing into the upper deck of the Basilean frigate. As the scores of sailors busied themselves around her – some readying hooks and lines, other weapons, others up top to prepare to tack through the wind – Caithlin turned to Oswalt.

"Whatever happens when we board," Caithlin urged, "you get X'And onboard *Pious* – understood? Whatever it takes, get him to their surgeon!"

The wrinkled dwarf nodded seriously.

"Aye, Captain, you can trust me with that."

Caithlin looked out to starboard, assessing her brig's rate of turn against the wind and sea state, visualizing her course back into the two warships.

"Helm, starboard!" she shouted. "Full wheel! Up top, stand by to tack!"

The brig came about nimbly, taking the wind on the beam. She slowed rapidly as the wind came toward her head, and Caithlin gritted her teeth as she heard the masts and rigging straining with the maneuver. There was enough momentum. But not enough time or sea room to stop.

"Brace!" Caithlin shouted. "Brace for impact! Helm, drive us right between them!"

The war galley and the frigate were pulled in tight now, but a small gap remained between the bows of the two towering warships. It was not enough, but it would have to do. Caithlin rushed down from the quarterdeck and between her gun crews toward the fo'c'sle. Above her, the fore mast leaned back dangerously in the head wind, its restraining lines squealing in protest.

"Get the lines across!" Caithlin yelled to her sailors.

Four men stepped up with lines and hooks, swinging them up to find purchase on the deck of the ancient Ahmunite vessel. There was no point in waiting for impact. Caithlin dreaded to think of the damage the *Queen* would suffer from such a reckless maneuver. She paced forward, grabbed one of the lines from a crewman, and stood on the taffrail. The gap ahead between the war galley and the frigate was gone. Even with the headwind slowing them to a near standstill, there would be a crash. But the line in her hand was steady, secured to the enemy vessel. It was time.

"*Martolian Queen*, ship's company!" Caithlin yelled. "On me!"

Propelling herself off the taffrail, Caithlin swung across the narrow gap between the ships and over the raging seas below until her

feet slammed into the bone-covered hull of the
war galley. A second later, she heard the crash of impact behind her,
and the splintering and cracking of snapping wood and lines. Her teeth
gritted, her eyes set in determination on the lip of the deck above,
Caithlin clambered up the rope toward the fight. The muscles in her
arms ached, the sound of musket fire and twang of bows above drew
nearer. Shouts echoed from below from her crew as they followed her
up the four lines.

The lip of the deck drew closer. Caithlin almost paused.
Monstrosities, the stuff of nightmares, undead warriors lay in wait. And
here she was, nothing more than a merchant sailor...

No. That was in the past now. Caithlin was a privateer. She
had faced orcs and pirates, and won. With a snarl, she clambered up
the last few feet and then hurled herself over the taffrail and onto the
Ahmunite upper deck. Ahead of her stood two ranks of skeletal sailors,
the first armed with curved blades and the second with bows – at least
fifty of them, all in. To her right side, she was numbly aware of Jaymes
leading a charge from the deck of *Pious*, pistol and sword in hand.

With an angry shout, Caithlin drew her pistol and sword. She
raised her pistol and shot the nearest skeleton in the head, cracking
open the skull. Without hesitating, her battle cry growing louder, Caithlin
sprinted forward into the line of undead. She batted aside a sword strike
from the first adversary to create an opening, and then beat the undead
sailor down to the deck with a frenzied blow to the temple from her
pistol butt.

***

Jaymes was first across onto the enemy ship, greeted with a
line of at least two dozen undead sailors as soon as his foot touched
the ancient deck. The front rank stood ready with curved blades whilst
the second rank notched arrows to their bows; the same warriors
who had shot salvos of arrows into *Pious's* upper deck as she drew
alongside to board. A taller, more ornately armored sailor stood at the
far end of the two ranks; dead, rotting flesh marking him out from the
bare bones of his ranks of subordinates. With a snarl, Jaymes raised
his pistol and shot the leader in the chest before charging forward with
his saber raised.

A great cry echoed out from behind him as his sailors and marines
followed him across the enemy deck, pistols, muskets, and crossbows
shooting into the front rank of enemy sailors as they charged. A return
volley of arrows shot directly into the Basilean force as they surged
across the deck; by providence or divine intervention alone, Jaymes
thought in the briefest of moments, he escaped injury as he felt the

wind rush by from either side as arrows pelted past him.

With a silent, eerie show of orchestrated discipline, the front rank of blue and gold clad skeletons charged out to meet *Pious's* ship's company. A roar came from behind Jaymes, and he was barged out of the way as Karnon swept past him, impaling the first skeleton with his boarding pike before sweeping the skewered enemy sailor around to knock down a second undead mariner. Jaymes lunged forward to his friend's side, beheading another of the undead sailors to cut open a gap in their ranks and then lead the charge through to attack the skeletal bowmen. Jaymes hacked down a second adversary as another attack was spearheaded through the Ahmunite ranks. His eyes widened in surprise as he saw Caithlin leading that second charge.

There was no time to recover from his alarm. An invisible wave swept across the deck to knock combatants from both sides hammering down against the wooden planks. His vision blurred and his back bruised from the sudden attack, Jaymes recovered his sword and staggered back up to his feet. Standing at the after end of the upper deck, Jaymes saw the black-robed figure of the war galley's captain, five spectacularly armored undead guards, and, ahead of them, the tall and powerful high priest he had seen earlier on the flagship's quarterdeck. With a dry, raspy howl, the high priest held his long staff aloft, and a bolt of lightning lanced out into the nearest Basilean sailor, blowing a blackened hole through the hapless man's guts before instantly emerging from the other side to chain a deadly impact into another two sailors.

With their battle cries merged together, Jaymes, Karnon, and Caithlin sprinted headlong at the enemy commanders.

***

The neat lines of the two opposing forces were gone, merged into one mass of anarchy as the upper deck to the *Purification of Ul'Astia* was awash with bitter combat. More skeletal sailors attempted to rush up from the cannon positions and oar benches below, but the chaos of the fighting across the top of the warship blocked any clear route into the action. His rotten fingers closed around the haft of his staff, T'mork watched the fighting unfold before him as he fought to regain his strength. Even with the losses sustained from the combined onslaught of the guns of the Basilean ship of the line and two frigates, his remaining crew outnumbered the boarders. However, the sheer ferocity of their initial attack marked them out as veterans; enough to concern him. Then, seemingly from nowhere – and he had only himself to blame for ignoring the second ship as too small to be of consequence – the brig that swept in to join the action now left his crew both outnumbered and outmatched in ferocity. Without his input into the fight, they would lose. He would lose.

Fighting off the weariness that ravaged his body, T'mork closed his eyes and once again concentrated to draw deeply from the arcane plains. Holding out a fist, his mind's eye visualizing the endless seas of purple-blue energy that only one who had mastered the arcane arts could ever gaze upon, he drew in from the endless well around him. He focused the energy he had harnessed, shaping and twisting it into something more conventional, yet also more deadly. Opening his eyes, T'mork let out a cry of exertion as he opened his hand to emit a jagged bolt of lightning to strike down the closest enemy sailor. The raw, magical energy jumped from man to man, killing three of the Basilean boarders and forcing their closest comrades to flee back away from the edge of the after deck.

The marginal, much localized turning of the tide in T'mork's favor was reversed almost instantly as a Basilean warrior, clad in armor and bearing a pike and shield, barged his way forward. The soldier lanced the end of the polearm through the first of T'mork's elite guard, making a mockery of the ancient warrior's skills, before resuming his charge to slam his shield into a second revenant and, with a rage-filled cry, barge him backward and over the edge of the deck to plummet into the sea below. The gap carved into T'mork's defenses was instantly exploited by both Basilean ship's captains who hurtled through, their sabers held high.

Demelecles stepped in to face the female captain of the brig, sweeping his curved khopesh blade at her abdomen and forcing her to jump back away from the savage strike. Two more of T'mork's guards pounced onto the frigate captain who skilfully parried the strike of the first revenant before riposting with a heavy strike that severed the warrior's hand above the wrist. With only a single guard remaining by his side, T'mork turned to face the renewed onslaught of the armored warrior, who was already charging back into the fray.

***

Karnon raised his shield to block the revenant's first attack with a resounding clang. With a skill that seemed almost uncanny in a reanimated corpse, the guard stepped in to follow up with a second strike, forcing the Basilean marine back another step toward the edge of the deck. From around the edge of his shield, Karnon saw the tall high priest lunge into the fight with a wide-eyed, teeth-baring sneer, sweeping his staff around toward Karnon's legs. The marine lowered his shield to block the attack and then leaned across to face his first assailant, thrusting his pike forward to force the metal tip through the revenant's shoulder. The undead warrior fell back, giving Karnon the opening he needed to step in to lance his pike at the high priest.

The towering undead leader effortlessly batted the strike away, and in an instant, the wounded revenant was back on Karnon, bearing down with his curved khopesh. Karnon blocked a series of well-executed strikes, holding his ground as he defended with shield and the haft of his pike alike.

***

Her eyes set grimly on her adversary, her feet planted far apart for balance, Caithlin stared down her opponent. A slim figure wrapped in long, ragged robes of midnight black, the war galley captain's faceless void met her stare from somewhere beneath the dark hood. The figure swept forward to strike, scything down from above with an overhead attack. Caithlin raised her own saber to deflect the blow with a ring of metal on metal before stepping to the left and dropping her shoulder to avoid the follow up attack.

Tirelessly, each strike aimed for a different part of her body, the Ahmunite captain forced her back step by step. Caithlin looked around for help, for somebody who could step in and stand by her side against this ancient, merciless foe. She was no sword fighter; that much she realized at that moment. Three months before, she did not even know how to hold a sword properly, let alone attack with one. Now, the shouts and screams of angry attacks and agonizing injuries echoing around her, she desperately defended herself with a series of what felt like wild swings rather than the disciplined, calm, and precise parries she had been taught. The undead captain continued to advance. Then, arrogant even in undeath, the captain carelessly swung down at her and lost his balance. His arm followed his blade past Caithlin, and she saw an opening.

Striking out with one foot, Caithlin kicked the undead captain in the side of the knee, buckling the leg. The Ahmunite sailor's khopesh dropped down, and Caithlin swung in, digging the vicious edge of her saber into the revenant's shoulder. The limb was half severed, yet the captain silently swapped his blade to his other hand and barged in to attack her again. Perhaps emboldened by her one successful strike, Caithlin parried correctly and bounced her saber of her adversary's khopesh, straight into a riposte. The point of the saber ripped through dark robes and sliced across the undead captain's chest. He staggered back a pace but again leaned forward to attack, only this time more slowly, carefully, and with greater deliberation.

***

Facing two revenant guards at once, Jaymes nimbly stepped across the deck to keep both enemy swordsmen in a line in an attempt to always block one from attacking him. The two ancient guards picked their way through the surging crowd of fighting men and undead around them, trying to encircle the Basilean frigate captain. To his left, Caithlin was locked in a duel with the war galley's captain; to his right, Karnon faced another guard and the high priest himself. The numbers needed evening up, and quickly.

Jaymes darted around counter-clockwise, again placing his two adversaries in something akin to a line astern formation to prevent the second from reaching him. The first revenant brought his khopesh slicing around at Jaymes's throat. He stepped back with one foot, leaning as far back as he dared, and felt the air part beneath his chin. Determined not to let the revenant capitalize on the opening, Jaymes leaned forward again and struck out with his saber. He hacked into the revenant's back but only succeeding in producing a loud clang as the straight edge of his blade slammed into the undead sailor's bronze breastplate.

The second revenant was around and on him, but with a carelessness that seemed almost mortal – human, even – he raised his sword high above his head to strike. Jaymes saw the opening and lunged forward with his leading foot, thrusting his saber into the revenant's face. The tip of the blade punctured the undead sailor's throat, sliced up through his neck, and came to a stop inside his skull. The revenant's limbs sagged down, the khopesh fell from limp fingers, and the sailor cluttered down to the deck. Jaymes withdrew his blade and brought it instantly back up on guard, just quick enough to defend himself from his sole remaining adversary.

Glancing across at Caithlin and desperately formulating a plan to close by her side as he saw her struggle against the war galley captain, Jaymes dodged and parried a series of attacks before forcing an opening into the revenant's defense and taking the initiative back.

***

The human warrior was good, that much T'mork granted him. But skill was no excuse for sacrilege. For destroying his temple ashore, and now for desecrating the place of worship built on the *Purification of Ul'Astria's* after deck. It was inexcusable. The fight continued to swarm around them, with Demelecles gaining the upper hand against the female captain, whilst the male frigate captain had succeeded in defeating another of T'mork's guards. No matter. They could be resurrected at best, replaced at worst.

Ahead of him, the armored human with the pike and shield bore down on one of T'mork's two remaining personal guards, battering the revenant across the side of the head with the edge of his shield. T'mork briefly considered drawing from the well of arcane power once more, but the thought of tapping that reserve yet again left him weary to the point of a tangible, almost mortal nausea. Brushing aside his fatigue, T'mork threw himself into the fight and swung his staff around in a wide arc at the armored human. He connected heavily with the Basilean's shield but did not move him even an inch.

The revenant attacked again, forcing the human's shield back across to his left. T'mork saw the smallest of openings and swung again, this time battering the shield further across. The revenant leaned in to exploit the opening, but the human blocked another attack with his pike. Pike and shield both across the left side of his body to counter the revenant, T'mork saw the opening widen. He swept his staff around to smash into the Basilean warrior's lower legs, pulling them out from beneath him and sending him clattering down to the deck on his back. With a victorious snarl, T'mork raised his staff to finish off his bold adversary.

**

The sheer stench of the revenant's rotting flesh threatening to overpower Jaymes as he struggled in a deadly embrace, both swordsmen pressed together face to face by the surging crowds of the boarding action across the upper deck. There was a scream behind Jaymes and a body thunked down onto the wooden deck; now with just a little room to maneuver, he took a half step back and raised his sword, smashing the gold-plated basket hilt into the undead sailor's face three times in quick succession. The revenant's head snapped back with each punch, the second rewarded with a shower of broken teeth and the third by detaching one side of the jawbone entirely.

The undead guard staggered back, and Jaymes stepped in to follow, piercing his adversary's spine with a thrust of his saber before twisting it and withdrawing. The blue and gold clad sailor clattered down to the deck and remained motionless. Jaymes looked up quickly.

Only a few paces away, Caithlin was locked in battle with the black-robed captain of the war galley, both of them taking turns to advance and retreat in front of the ruined temple atop the quarterdeck. Jaymes barged his way past one of Karnon's marines to reach the combatants, shouting out as he saw the revenant captain swipe out at neck height. Caithlin's quick reactions only narrowly saved her from decapitation from the vicious strike. Jaymes arrived only a second later and lunged forward to strike at the captain's side. The ancient seafarer twisted on the spot and blocked the blow. Jaymes bounced his sword lightly off the khopesh and into a riposte, lancing his saber through the side of the captain's chest. No longer needing lungs to breathe, the undead captain merely jumped back away from him and raised his sword once more.

The war galley captain leapt forward, ragged robes trailing behind him as he attacked. Jaymes held his ground with parries, ducks, and dodges. After seconds of furious clashes of blades, the clang of metal upon metal ringing across the upper deck, Jaymes saw the captain overextend and lean too far in to attack. He reached across to clamp a hand around the undead captain's boney wrist, yanked him stumbling across in front of him, and brought his own saber sweeping down to hack off the revenant's head. The hooded head bounced twice across the ancient wooden boards and came to a rest. The fight swarmed forth around Jaymes, but Caithlin was already out of sight.

***

With a determined grunt, Karnon pushed himself back up off the deck and onto one knee, taking another hammer-blow into his shield from the undead high priest. The final, persistent revenant guard leaned in, rotting lips curled back to reveal broken, brown teeth as the nightmare figure loomed over the marine captain with curved khopesh held high. Karnon saw the most fleeting of all opportunities and took it, hurling himself forward to lash out with his heavy shield. The rim of the shield caught the revenant under the neck, snapping his entire head back with an audible crunch of bones. Karnon followed up with a strike from the haft of his pike, but before he could finish his adversary off, he felt a slam into the back of his leg and was again knocked down to one knee, pain flaring up his thigh.

Karnon looked up to see the wild-eyed, twisted features of the Ahmunite high priest stood over him, glowing staff raised for the killing blow. Karnon again attempted to raise his pike and shield in time, but saw in a desperate near slow motion, as if watching the vain act from outside of his own body, that he would be too slow to defend himself.

Seemingly from nowhere, Caithlin dived across from the high priest's left side and swung the butt of her pistol into the Ahmunite's face. Karnon heard the cheekbone break and saw the towering sorcerer stagger back from the blow. Leaping to his feet, Karnon thrust the razor-sharp tip of his pike into the last, wounded revenant guard's gut. The undead sailor fell to the deck, and Karnon stepped forward to stand side by side with Caithlin, his pike and shield raised as the two faced the Ahmunite commander. The two became three a moment later as Jaymes stepped across to join them, saber raised.

***

Practically feeling the eyes of Shobik upon him, watching him as he had this one last chance to avenge the sacrilege wrought on two temples, T'mork leapt forward to strike. The armored marine blocked his staff and immediately countered with his pike. T'mork was faster and swiped the pike to one side, but then let out a hiss of pain as the frigate captain's saber plunged in between his ribs. With a snarl fueled with a fury he knew to be righteous, T'mork swung his staff at the frigate captain regardless, advancing on him in an attempt to push him back away from the sacred temple, crumbled across his warship's after deck.

T'mork let out another cry of pain as the female captain slashed her own saber across his bare back, parting rotten flesh to the bone. Refusing to yield an inch, he raised his staff above his head. The marine plunged his pike into T'mork's gut whilst the dark-haired frigate captain swung his saber up to sever one of T'mork's hands at the wrist. A knee buckled beneath him. His staff clattered to the deck. Down on one knee, his one remaining hand pressed over the stump of his severed wrist, T'mork looked across the deck of the *Purifiaction of Ul'Astia*.

Demelecles's body lay motionless only a few paces away, his head gone. Basilean sailors and marines flooded the deck, locked in a bitter and bloody fight against the ship's undead defenders. Off the starboard bow, the second Basilean frigate moved in to board and complete the encapsulation of T'mork's flagship. Aft, behind the fight, the salamander frigate increased speed as it closed with the war galley, the fleet's final Khopeshii slipping beneath the waves behind it.

All was lost.

No. T'mork closed his eyes and hung his head. There was never an excuse to give up. To despair. To abandon faith in Shobik and his cause. Clenching his one remaining fist, fumbling blindly within the well that was the very last of his arcane energy, T'mork grasped onto his final gambit.

***

Looking down on the broken, crumpled wreck of the high priest, Jaymes almost pitied the defeated monster knelt before him. Around him, the combined force of sailors, marines, and privateers continued to sweep across the deck. The battle remained hung in the balance, but with Marcellus's *Veneration* closing from the starboard bow to board with her own ship's company, victory was now close at hand. Jaymes raised a battered, bruised arm up and held his saber high to deliver the final blow.

The high priest's head jerked up. His orb-like eyes opened. The undead monstrosity smiled a broken-toothed grin, his white eyes flashing with determination. He raised a clenched fist and then opened his hand. With a blinding flash, Jaymes was thrown back across the deck. Winds howled around him, pushing him tumbling back toward the fo'c'sle. The whining gale tugged at his flapping clothes, pinning him to the deck as he struggled to raise himself to one knee. Caithlin and Karnon were pinned to either side of him, teeth gritted as they struggled against the hurricane force.

Behind them, a line snapped. Then another. Jaymes looked over his shoulder. Only two of the lines connecting *Pious* to the war galley remained unbroken as the high priest's tempestuous magic pushed the ancient ship and the Basilean frigate apart from each other, threatening to trap the Basilean sailors on board the Ahmunite bone ship.

"Fall back!" he yelled above the roaring wind. "Fall back to *Pious*! Ship's company, fall back!"

Dozens of sailors and marines struggled to lean against the howling wind all around Jaymes, Karnon, and Caithlin. The undead sailors cut men down, completely unaffected by their master's magic. A third line snapped, leaving only one.

"Fall back!" Jaymes shouted again.

Men from *Pious* and the *Martolian Queen* alike turned and sprinted away with the wind on their backs, running and jumping back to the Basilean frigate. Jaymes struggled to remain in place, shouting warnings to his men and trying to raise his saber again as he locked his eyes on the wild-eyed, snarling high priest. A hand wrapped firmly around each of his arms – one from Karnon, the other from Caithlin – and he was dragged back toward his own ship. The final line parted with a loud crack. The final few sailors and marines ran and jumped across, leaving only Jaymes, Karnon, and Caithlin onboard the towering boneship.

The war galley drifted away from *Pious* and the *Martolian Queen*, propelled to safety by the unnatural, unholy winds.

"Come on!" Caithlin urged. "Jump!"

She turned on her heel and sprinted away, jumping off the bows of the bone ship and swan diving elegantly into the raging waters between the three warships. Jaymes turned to Karnon as a line of undead sailors sprinted toward them.

"Go!" he roared above the howling winds. "Jump!"

Karnon quickly unbuckled his heavy breastplate and let it fall to the deck, tore off his helmet, and dropped his shield. With that, the two men hurtled across the final few feet of ancient, accursed deck and flung themselves into the evening sky, hearts in mouths as they plummeted down into the sea below.

The violent sea zoomed up toward Jaymes as he thrust out his arms and extended his hands to transform his fall into a dive in the last moments of his descent. The warm waters accepted him and plunged up over him; in the comparative darkness, he heard something like a rock falling to his right and saw a dark shape surrounded by scores of bubbles. Jaymes swam down after the plummeting shape, wrapped his hands around Karnon's armpits, and kicked for all he was worth to drag his friend up to the surface.

Gasping for air, the two men burst free atop a foam-covered, green wave. Guns rumbled again all around them. The unholy, magical hurricane winds pushed the Ahmunite war galley free and clear of her assaulting frigate and brig, past the *Veneration*. Within seconds, Caithlin swam over to meet them in the crashing waves between the ships.

"G...get me on a boat! Now!" Karnon gasped.

"Have you got him?" Caithlin asked, her head turning and her eyes darting around the towering waves.

Jaymes wrapped one arm around Karnon's torso and leaned back, holding his friend across his chest.

"I've got him!"

Kicking with his legs and throwing one arm around to propel himself backward, Jaymes swam himself and his panicked captain of marines back across the towering waves, the short distance to his frigate. Unhindered by a survivor to rescue, Caithlin broke away and swam quickly across the darkening seas, reaching the *Martolian Queen* before Jaymes and Karnon made it to the midships steps built into *Pious's* sturdy hull. As soon as Karnon's hands reached the wooden steps, he scrambled up the side of the warship like a rat up a drainpipe, never pausing to look back down below.

Jaymes followed, looking up to see dozens of pairs of eyes peering over the starboard taffrail, down at the two officers as they clambered back up toward the upper deck. Above them, the sails of all three of *Pious's* masts crumpled and flapped in the wind as it turned to oppose them, keeping the frigate all but dead in the water.

Jaymes reached the safety of the upper deck, accepting a hand from Mayhew to help him over the final step. He looked out across the darkening skies and saw that *Pious, Veneration,* and the *Martolian Queen* were all pitching and rolling in the heavy seas, the wind now dead against them. Against the blurred, darkening horizon of dusk, the Ahmunite war galley tore away through the waves, the winds perfectly aligned off her port quarter to propel her at a speed simply not possible for a vessel of her size to achieve without dark, unnatural assistance.

Dripping wet, exhausted, disappointed at victory being wrenched from his grasp, Jaymes made his way through the crowds of surviving sailors and marines to walk back to the quarterdeck. He looked across and saw Grace, armed with a flail from her part in the boarding action.

"Sister Grace," Jaymes gasped, "get us out of this unholy wind and give chase to those bastards. If it takes all night, we'll find them."

The Sisterhood sailing master flashed an encouraging, determined smile that was completely at odds with the lack of hope in her cool eyes.

"Aye, sir. Right away."

Chapter Twenty

Hegemon's Warship Pious (38)

It was with no small amount of relief that, as the first light of dawn finally appeared above the horizon, Jaymes managed to make out every last ship of the fleet in the surrounding waters. All had survived the night's bitter, relentless storm. *Veneration* surged through the choppy waves to the east, northward bound on a course for the Roe's Spring colony survivors. Half way between the two frigates, the *Martolian Queen* slid down into the trough of a surging wave, her fore topsail torn and ragged, sailors venturing up into the rigging to attempt repairs from the aftermath of the night's violent winds. Ahead of them were the two surviving sloops – *Scout* and *Sprinter* – somehow still afloat having spent an entire night dealing with waves as large as themselves. Finally, off to port and closest to *Pious* was the *Deliverer's Flame*.

As the dawn sun rose, the seas were gentler than overnight but still refusing to truly rest. A line of signal flags shot up the outside of the *Martolian Queen's* main mast.

Pious - Request - Close - Exchange - Crew

Jaymes stood on the quarterdeck with Benn Orellio, now effectively promoted to second lieutenant – only days after passing his lieutenancy exams – with the tragic loss of Kaeso Innes. Another figure, a stranger to the quarterdeck of a Basilean frigate, hunkered over in the morning drizzle by the sternlight, with Jaymes's permission. After the better part of an hour at the hands of Surgeon Kennus, X'And limped across to look over at his ship's signals.

Jaymes turned to Benn.

"Go find out who is on signals duty and tell them to hoist an affirm to the *Martolian Queen*."

Benn nodded.

"Aye, sir."

Off the port bow, the salamander J'Koor'uk swept around to head in closer to *Pious*. Jaymes raised his telescope and peered through the dawn murk at the salmanader frigate's quarterdeck. He smiled as he saw Zu'Max, the salamander first lieutenant who had exchanged some friendly words with him after the admiral's briefing, standing on watch by the mizzenmast. A line of colored flags was hoisted up the J'Koor'uk's own main mast.

Heading - Home - Deliverer - Bless - Basilea - Thank - You - All

Jaymes momentarily considered ordering his guns to be fired to salute the courageous crew of the salamander frigate, but thought that in the dim light of dawn, it might easily cause panic or confusion. He walked over to the forward taffrail and shouted down to Benn and one of his young midshipmen.

"Signal the *Deliver's Flame*. Tell them... Shining Ones bless the warriors of the Three Kings."

"Aye, sir."

Jaymes watched as the two separate signals he had ordered were bent onto halyards and then hoisted up to either side of the main mast. The *Martolian Queen* sailed closer. The *Deliver's Flame* came about through the wind and set course for the south. Jaymes watched the elegant fighting ship depart, sorry to see her go but glad for her crew to be able to return home to their families.

"She has seen much for a young ship."

Jaymes turned around to face the gruff speaker behind him. X'And looked down at a collection of hastily repaired holes in the hull at the side of the quarterdeck, his clawed hands running softly across the battle damage. Jaymes watched the older sailor for a moment, noting the sympathy evident in the reptilian's yellow eyes. The salamander looked up and blinked.

"My first time on a Basilean frigate. I have seen them up close many times – the Elohis, the older phoenix class frigates – but I've never set foot onboard one."

Again, Jaymes found himself at a loss for words. The salamander continued, regardless.

"I see why my people hold your navy in such high regard. It is an honor to stand on your quarterdeck, Captain."

Jaymes nodded curtly in response to the compliment.

"The salamanders stand first and foremost among all races of Pannithor as the greatest of seafarers. The honor is ours."

The lumbering salmander's mouth twisted into the faintest of smiles. He brought his clawed hand up to his eye in imitation of a human salute, and then walked to the steps leading down to the upper deck.

Jaymes watched X'And head back down to stand with the other members of the *Martolian Queen's* ship's company who jumped onto *Pious* as the enemy war galley was wrenching free to escape. Jaymes swore to himself as he remembered his failure. So close to ending the threat of the undead high priest. But so close was still a failure.

"Captain?"

Jaymes turned to face Benn as his second lieutenant

approached.

"Are you happy to lower the longboat into the water for a personnel transfer in this sea state?"

Jaymes looked out across the starboard bow at the heavy swell. White foam lined the tops of the waves, but the wind was not so strong that the foam detached and flew off as spray. That had always been a good indicator to him of when the seas were too rough for certain things.

"Yes, Benn. Happy. Make sure you've got a good coxswain for the boat in this swell, though. Make sure it's an old hand."

"Aye, sir."

The young lieutenant turned and walked back toward the steps leading down from the quarterdeck.

"Lieutenant Orellio?" Jaymes called after him.

The younger officer stopped and turned again. Jaymes walked briskly over. He stopped by the shorter man and looked down. It felt patronizing, in his own mind at least, for a man of twenty-six to be looking at a man just eight years younger and feeling a paternal pride. No. That was not it. He just... saw himself not so long ago.

"Everything alright, sir?" Benn asked.

"Yes. Just... grand job yesterday. Running the guns, leading your division, taking the fore on the boarding action. All of it. Kaeso Innes was a fine fellow, and I'll miss him sorely. He was very popular with the ship's company, far more so than I am. He's nearly impossible to replace. But in the short time you've been here, you've shown us all what you're made of, and I knew Kaeso well enough to know he'd be happy with me saying that you are up to the job of standing in his shoes."

Benn looked down and gave a short nod before looking back up again.

"Thank you, sir. This is all a lot more difficult than I thought it would be. I'm like a lot of people here. Petrified of getting it wrong. So... thank you."

Jaymes watched as Benn gathered a team together to lower the longboat – the largest of the frigate's three sea boats – down into the choppy waters and then begin embarking the privateer crewmen to return to their brig. X'And was the last off. He stood to attention by the ship's waist, turned to face the Basilean flag fluttering from aft of the driver sail, and saluted smartly before lowering himself into the boat.

As the longboat's sweeps heaved her away to cross the short distance between the frigate and the brig, Jaymes found himself contemplating his own words to Benn. *Very popular with the ship's company, far more so than I am.* That had not always been the case. Jaymes knew well enough that as an adolescent midshipman, he was cold, ambitious, and so single-minded in his pursuit of advancement that he was a nightmare to work with. But after just one year as a lieutenant on coastal sloops, he had seen the error of his ways. There was so much truth in all of the old sayings about living your life first and working so that a life could be lived. Advancement meant nothing in the grand scheme of things; certainly a lot less in the sloop driving community. Friendships were struck within the crew of the sloop, irrespective of barriers such as rank, age, experience, and social standing. Jaymes missed those days.

But joining *Pious* as the second lieutenant, he had brought that mentality across with him. He knew the ship's company liked him well enough. He was approachable, treated all with respect, and was quick to defend his division. His expectations of bearing and discipline were low, which made him liked by his subordinates but despised by his captain. Jaymes chuckled at the memory of his old captain as the longboat reached the brig and the first line was thrown across. Charn Ferrus. What a bastard. Hated and feared by the whole ship – but the ship ran like clockwork. The ship was formidable. The foundations Ferrus laid were still visible on *Pious* now, and the crew that Ferrus forged was in many ways what defeated the enemy war galley.

Perhaps that was the only way – to be a complete bastard once one was in a position of command. Jaymes let out a quiet laugh and shook his head. No. The crew of *Veneration* loved Marcellus Dio, and he was an absolute gentleman. Then again, his first lieutenant was a complete and utter bastard who made Charn Ferrus look like a puppy in comparison. It was easy to be a nice fellow when your deputy was a man like that.

Jaymes watched the privateers clamber back up onto the brig and then cast away *Pious's* longboat so it could return to the frigate. Over thinking his approach to command was a complete waste of time, Jaymes returned to pondering. He was who he was, possibly forged into the captain he had become by Charn Ferrus along with the other veterans of that previous captain's era. But there was undoubtedly ample room to be more pleasant in his dealing with both his ratings and his junior officers. That was something he was determined to remedy.

The longboat was hoisted back up onto *Pious's* upper deck without incident and safely stowed away once more. As soon as that was done, Brooke, the ship's bosun, walked to the steps leading to the quarterdeck and waited, looking up at Jaymes expectantly. Jaymes waved him up, and the short sailor walked across, saluting as he arrived. He held out a sealed letter.

"Captain Viconti of the *Martolian Queen* asked me to bring this back across to you, sir."

Feeling more than just a pang of sentimentality in his chest,

Jaymes accepted the letter.

"Thank you, Sam. How's your wife doing? Fully recovered now, I hope?"

"Yes, thank you, sir. Still a bit of a limp, but she's back at work at the mill now."

"Glad to hear. Good job with the boat transfer. Looks about as choppy as a longboat can handle."

The bosun smiled broadly and shook his head.

"Naw, sir! Piece of piss!"

Jaymes laughed as the veteran sailor walked back down to the upper deck. He looked at the letter in his hand and again felt himself swept away with romantic notions and plans for their return to Thatraskos. He looked across to the fighting brig's quarterdeck and saw Caithlin. She raised a hand to wave at him. He returned the gesture with a broad smile and watched as the brig broke away from her position in line abreast. They had failed to eliminate their foe, yes, but they had stopped him at least. There was some achievement in that.

Jaymes looked ahead to the northern horizon and where home lay waiting. A thick bank of fog was forming ahead of the line of warships.

***

Hopping over the side of the boat before its five other occupants did the same, Tem's legs plunged into the water up to the thighs. Keeping their hands clamped on the side of the boat, the six sailors ran the craft up through the surf until its shallow keel dug into the soft sand of the shore. The island was relatively small – perhaps only a hundred acres – most of which sloped up to a low trio of sandy hills, sparsely topped with a thin collection of palm trees and other bright vegetation. The mid-morning sky above was completely overcast with a homogeneous mass of white clouds, preventing the sun's rays from shining down but keeping the close, thick heat trapped beneath.

Two cables off the shore, two ships lay at anchor in the still waters. Tem's battered *Desert Rose*, her hull crumpled in places and her rigging knotted and uneven from a series of hasty repairs, waited in the shadow of a larger ship. The *Dark Siren* was a captured sixth-rate frigate; once a Genezan naval warship, she was now the most powerful and valuable of all of Cerri Denayo's ships, and consequently, rarely seen out of her secret anchorage on the far side of Red Skull. She lay in resplendent wait in the calm waters, six hundred tons and carrying twenty-six guns, ship-rigged with three tall masts. A little way past the two pirate ships, a quartet of pirate sloops slowly sailed past.

"Wait here," Tem commanded four of his sailors.

He trudged up the beach with the final sailor – Halladai. Waiting up ahead, not far from their own sea boat, was Cerri with eight of his own sailors, including his sneering quartermaster Mari DuLane. The tall pirate chief issued a brief hand signal to his own oarsmen and then walked down the beach to meet Tem and Halladai. Colorful birds sang from the jungle trees running along the top of the beach as the waves rustled over the smooth sand at their feet.

Cerri stopped in front of Tem and Halladai.

"You've been missing for days now."

Tem glanced across at his quartermaster, and then up at the older pirate captain.

"We ran into more trouble."

"I know. It's my business to know everything around here."

Tem wearily rested a hand on the pommel of the cutlass by his waist, no longer caring if that might be seen as an aggressive act to his pirate superior. He let out an exhausted sigh, his eyes aching from lack of sleep.

"We were…"

"I know," Cerri repeated, "I know you were dragged into service with an Ahmunite bone fleet. I know you ended up in a full blown fleet battle between the Ahmunites and the Basileans, which a pirate has no place in. I know what's been happening, Tem. Cargo and gold aren't the only treasures in a prize ship. So is information."

Halladai took a step forward and pulled his sleeve up to reveal the scarab still burrowed into the reddened flesh of his arm.

"If you know everything, Captain, tell me: do you know how to get rid of that?"

Cerri's eyes flicked down to the horrific parasite in the Ophidian pirate's forearm.

"I know people who can fix that," he shrugged nonchalantly, "of that, I'm sure. But that'll have to wait, lads. Because you're still in my ship, and I've got a job for you."

His eyes stinging, his throat dry, and his shoulders aching, Tem repressed a sarcastic response and let out a long sigh. The pirate chief continued regardless.

"We're still after that brig. The Genezan privateer. The one who embarrassed me and killed your mates."

"I know," Tem planted his fists on his hips, "we saw her at the battle. Put a couple of broadsides into her."

"And she into you, by the look of it," Cerri replied, nodding at the battered xebec at anchor behind them. "But regardless of that, shipmates, I've information about where she is now. The Basileans were scattered by the storm after the battle. Then there was the fog. It's still out there now – and the gods alone know how and why – in patches all over the place. Point is, the Basileans are scattered. And I've stopped two ships now who say they've seen that fighting brig alone. Separated. So now's our chance, me hearties."

His interest rekindled, Tem smirked as the veteran corsair continued.

"The *Desert Rose* won't take her alone, but with a couple of sloops, I reckon you will. I'll head east of here, or at least a couple of points north of that. Toward the Driftwood Passage. You take the *Baron's Revenge* and the *Highwayman* with you, and you head north of west. There's a fog bank about five leagues out, or at least there was at dawn. If I don't find the brig in the Driftwood Passage, I reckon you'll find her trying to get through the fogbank. Meet back at Red Skull after that, and we'll see about getting Halladai's arm fixed up."

Tem folded his arms across his chest.

"Alright," he replied simply.

It was a solid enough plan, knowing the local geography as he did. If a ship was trying to return to Thatraskos, then the Driftwood Passage was the most direct route – if not, then it would be via the open seas to the west of Shark Cay. Tem looked up at Halladai. The quartermaster's features softened as he turned back to Cerri.

"We'll tear the very seas apart if we need to. You can rely on us, Captain. And... thank you."

Cerri waved a hand to one side and shrugged. Tem swallowed. Halladai was right. They did owe Cerri their thanks. They had shattered his ship, failed to bring much loot his way, lost good sailors, and now had even been violently strong-armed into serving an Ahmunite necromancer. Yet here Cerri was, in possession of the facts but still willing to move past all of these problems, pitfalls, and failures to still make best use of Tem, Halladai, and the survivors of their crew.

"Leave it with us," Tem said, "we'll find her. If she's gone west around Shark Cay, we'll find her and we'll gut her entire crew."

Cerri's face broke into a grin. He offered a brief wink.

"Aye, matey. That's the spirit. No more of this gentleman sea bandit talk, and making heroes out of the likes of Black Davey Krax, Ginny Morrs, and Black Bob Reynault. They were soft bastards, the lot of them. Follow me and I'll make you rich. Follow their examples, and they'll make you dead. Got it, shippers?"

Tem nodded.

"Aye. Got it."

Cerri reached out with both arms and clapped his hands against the shoulders of the two *Desert Rose* pirates.

"Alright, then! See you at Red Skull. Sink that brig, mateys. If you can bring her captain to me in one piece, all the better. If not? I'll settle for news of her death. Go on, sling your hook, the pair of you."

Cerri turned and walked back to his own sea boat and crew. Tem and Halladai trudged through the wet sand in the opposite direction.

"Well now," Tem beamed, "that could have gone a lot worse! I reckon we just got him at a bad time, last time we clashed. And I can understand that, after what happened at Red Skull. No, he's alright, is Cerri. Out of the three of them, I reckon we picked the right sea dog to back."

Halladai kept pace with Tem, his eyes fixed ahead on the *Desert Rose's* sea boat. His face remained stern, impassive. He said nothing in response to Tem's words.

***

The masterbuilt hull of the light frigate *Dark Siren* practically glided across the near still water, her sails somehow finding a way to harness what little wind there was to propel her forward. Defying both the laws of nature and the local weather effects that Cerri knew so well, the fog had spread throughout the morning to encompass a vast area of seaspace. But Cerri had faced the horrors of the undead before, and while there were perhaps some learned men and women of science somewhere who could explain it all better, in his mind it was simple. For whatever reason, the unholy use of necromancy brought cold with it. And when the air chilled and was already humid, fog was created. Nothing more sinister or terrifying than that. And with the amount of Ahmunite activity in the area in recent times, fog was merely a harmless byproduct.

As Cerri paced across the quarterdeck of the captured frigate, he continued to muse on the thought. Of course, his superstitious sailors were already muttering and murmuring about the fog being made of the tortured souls of seafarers confined to the deep without a proper burial or blessing, desperately trying to claw their way back to the surface so that the Shining Ones might see them and send the Elohi down to guide them to Mount Kolosu. Cerri scoffed at the thought. There had been an unseasonal chill, and the air was moist. So there was fog. That was that.

But it did, at least, help his plan. With a combination of scouts and information gleaned from passing merchant ships – volunteered or extracted – Cerri had a good idea what had happened. The Basileans had defeated the Ahmunites in a sea battle. Good. Looking at the bigger picture, it was better to deal with the known rather than be forced to try to understand a new world where the Ahmunites had control of this area of the Infant Sea. During the battle, the Basileans were severely weakened. They had lost a third-rate ship of the line. Even better. Cerri had warned Tem about that – a pirate had no place in a fleet engagement. Better for everybody else to blow chunks out of each other whilst the independent, enterprising pirates stayed well away and were left facing – or evading, at least – a weakened victor.

Cerri shook his head. Tem... an idealistic fool. Cerri had thought twice before lying to him about the Basilean fleet's location and sending Tem and his crew to their deaths, but he had outgrown his usefulness, seemed incapable of obedience, and that old xebec was fairly rotten with woodworm anyway.

"Captain?"

Cerri turned to face his quartermaster. Mari's vivid, scarlet hair fell down from beneath a battered tricorn hat. Her hand rested on the sharkskin handle of a curved cutlass at her side.

"What is it?" Cerri whispered, mindful to keep an ear out for any sign of another ship fumbling through the fog around them.

Mari glanced over both of her shoulders. Another eight sailors shared the quarterdeck with them, ready by the cannons. The upper deck housed the majority of the ship's armaments, and with it, the majority of the one hundred and twenty strong crew. Cerri tutted at the thought. One hundred and twenty. This time two years ago, with his reputation, if he had put out word that he needed a crew for something special, he would have had closer to two hundred cutthroats swarm to his banner.

"The lads," Mari said quietly, "they're not happy. They're not happy with this fog, and they're not happy that we're out here hunting down a single brig that is carrying guns instead of gold and cargo. They're nervous about this fog, and they know there isn't much loot in this cruise."

Cerri let out a choked half-laugh and folded his arms, his eyes still scouring the fog enveloping the frigate.

"Do these pissed up bilge rats know how much a four hundred ton brig sells for? They think there's no money in this? By the seven circles, Mari! You're the quartermaster! Sort this out! Just get Franj, Lukke, and G'Hanno onside. If those three are content, the others will all fall in line. So whatever you have to do – nice Mari or cruel Mari – you get this sorted out. Got it?"

Mari's eyes narrowed and sparkled with a malevolent glint.

"Aye. I'll sort those three out, Cerri..."

Cerri's hand shot up to silence her. Eyes and ears straining, he moved his head slowly from side to side as he concentrated on the sights and sounds of the sea all around. Mari stared venomously at the nearest cannon crew to silence their idle banter. The world was silent in a field of white, save the creaking of the deck and the billowing of sailcloth above. Then he heard it. Off to starboard, there was something. An order called or a shout for assistance... it mattered not. There was another ship there, three points off the starboard bow. Silently, Cerri crept over to the ship's wheel and took it from the helmsman, gently steering the nimble frigate on a course to intercept the sound he had heard.

***

Plous's metal-plated bows cleaved through the calm, turquoise waters, sailors across the quarterdeck, upper deck, and fo'c'sle all tightening her sheets to keep her sails taut in the light winds. Wispy tendrils of fog continued to drift past, transforming the noble Elohi figurehead into a misty blur even from the quarterdeck. Jaymes stood with the officer of the watch – Mayhew, now that they had lost Kaeso – and stared from horizon to horizon as the ship continued to trudge slowly northward. Around him, the men continued with their normal activities, but in complete silence on Jaymes's orders. Visions of the ghostly Sisterhood ship they had seen on their transit south formed in his mind. He wondered how long it would be until sightings of *Pious's* ghost captain were reported once more from the lower decks.

"I'll go mark our progress on the chart, sir," Mayhew murmured quietly.

Jaymes nodded. Good. He remembered a time when Mayhew had told him that, until there was a sighting of land or a clear view of the stars with which to make an accurate plot of their progress, there was not really much point in updating the ship's position on the chart. Jaymes had nearly shot him there and then.

The ship continued onward, each minute bringing them all slowly closer to home. The thought of home brought a warmth to Jaymes, particularly so as he remembered the kind and thoughtful words in the letter Caithlin had sent across to him in the sea boat the previous day. But home was still some way away, and the thick blanket of white all around them was making accurate navigation impossible.

The fog, if anything, seemed to thicken. The air grew colder. Jaymes looked from side to side – a vain act, given the limits to visibility – wondering how far out *Veneration* was. *Scout* and *Sprinter* had swept ahead and would be halfway home by now. The *Martolian Queen* had been separated in the howling winds and mountainous seas of the previous night, and was last seen at first light altering course to the northeast to take the Driftwood Passage route home, leaving the two Elohi frigates in the open sea route.

Mayhew returned a few minutes later with two cups of coffee. He wordlessly offered one to Jaymes.

"Thank you," he said quietly with a smile as he accepted the steaming cup.

"We've barely moved, I'm afraid," Mayhew said, his voice

hushed. "We're only making four knots. It'll be a while in this wind."

"Good thing we're not in any rush," Jaymes offered, "other than getting out of this damned fog, at least. I've never seen anything like it. Not at these latitudes and this time of the year."

"I'm sure the ghost stories will be starting again soon, sir." Mayhew grinned.

Jaymes smiled and then turned back to continue his fruitless vigil of the surrounding fog. It did seem to be thinning, perhaps. The sky above was lighter, indicative of the sun working its way through to burn off the moisture-laden air below. Minutes dragged by. The fo'c'sle was clear now, a sure sign that the worst of the fog was behind them. The wind was beginning to freshen a little, pushing the frigate forward with a pleasing amount of force to increase her speed. Jaymes brought his cup of coffee up to his lips.

He stopped dead and stared ahead into the thinning mist. He narrowed his eyes and concentrated.

"Mayhew?"

"Sir?"

"Don't beat to quarters. Not yet. Go down below and silently get everybody awake and ready. I think there's some bastard out there."

***

A third knock at the door awoke Caithlin from a deep sleep. She instantly transitioned from that awkward, hazy state of semi-consciousness when caught mid-way between dreaming and reality to being fully alert. She sat up in her rather decedent, broad bed in the brig's great cabin, one of the few luxuries she allowed herself at sea, and checked to ensure the loaded pistol she kept lashed to her bedside table was within reach. Light poured in between the gaps in the curtains across the stern windows, but other than telling her that she had slept from dawn until some point during the day, she had no idea what time it was or where the ship was.

"Yes?" she called out.

"Begin your pardon, captain," Jonjak's voice was muffled behind the thick, teak door, "X'And sent me down to wake you. Says he needs you on the quarterdeck."

"Right," Caithlin sighed, "I'll be right up."

Being summoned to the quarterdeck and roused from her sleep was fine; it was a regular enough occurrence. But X'And was supposed to be recovering from his injuries, not standing watch. Caithlin dressed herself quickly, grabbed her pistol and sword belt, and headed up to the quarterdeck. She winced as soon as she set foot on the upper deck; the daylight was blinding in comparison to the dim light of her cabin, despite the thick fog that had returned.

Caithlin exchanged a few courteous nods with members of her ship's company as she walked across to the starboard waist and then up to the quarterdeck, where she found both X'And and Jonjak. She stopped by them both, her fists on her hips.

"You're supposed to be in your bunk, recovering."

The salamander shook his head.

"Not in this. I've spent enough time patrolling the waters of the South Infant Sea to know a *Gherotion*. That's what we call this type of unseasonal fog. This sort of thing is often a sort of hangover from the presence of the Ahmunites and their accursed magic, but... well, that war galley and a couple of the smaller ships did escape. I doubt they would be stupid enough to head north, but you never know."

Caithlin looked around the ship. The fog was in patches, with areas where visibility was good for perhaps half a mile and others where an entire island could be hidden, ready to dash the brig to pieces.

"I know you're a... matter-of-fact woman, Captain, and not open to tall tales of the sea..."

"That was before I boarded a giant turtle with a coral fortress built onto its back, but go on."

"My kind put a lot of faith in what you Genezans call *seseno*. Sixth sense. Perhaps it's nothing but... I've already posted extra lookouts for rocks, and I've taken in a little sail to give us more time to react to anything in the water ahead. I'm still not content. It's hard to explain."

Caithlin shrugged.

"No. I can see why you're concerned."

She turned to her second mate.

"Jonjak, if you end up in a situation like this in future – on watch in a passage between island chains in thick fog – then wake me up sooner."

"Yes, ma'am. Sorry, ma'am."

Caithlin stared out ahead as one of the clearer patches eased across in front of the ship.

"Go and get some rest, X'And," she murmured quietly.

A dark shape appeared in the mist to the port side of the ship's head. Tall, thin. For a split second, Caithlin's heart raced as the shape seemed to take on the form of cliffs, but then it loomed out to form a hull and masts.

"Captain!"

The vessel was larger than her brig, heading straight toward them, becoming clearer as it drew closer. Ship-rigged with three masts, race-built with an aggressive cut to her jib. A warship. Caithlin's eyes widened. She was a San Andrea-class light frigate; a Genezan Navy sixth-rate.

"What in the seven circles is she doing there?"

The frigate bore down toward the brig, her top sails set and her courses furled. The wind was perfectly positioned off her starboard quarter. Her guns were run out and ready for action. Caithlin's jaw dropped as the Genezan flag was quickly run down from her flagstaff.

"Beat to quarters!" Caithlin yelled.

The drum roll sounded, and the deck of the brig exploded into action. A wave of what felt like ice washed across Caithlin's skin as a red flag ran up the frigate's flagstaff, bearing an image of a skeletal demon bearing crossed swords above its head. The pirate frigate's bow chasers exploded into life.

"Hard a' starboard!" Caithlin called. "Get the wind off the starboard quarter and set full sail!"

The brig swung about as sailors scrambled up the ratlines to set the sails in an attempt to outrun the more powerful vessel. But they had the weather gauge and were already making good speed. Even from here, it was obvious to Caithlin that she could not outrun the frigate. She stared back at the rapidly closing pirates, her heart heavy as she recognized every line, every angle, and every last curve of the Genezan frigate.

Caithlin flung herself on her bed, tears streaming from her eyes. It could have been mere minutes or long hours. However long it was, the point was that it was not fair. She had done the right thing. Or at least tried to. Why was she in trouble for that? The arguing downstairs had stopped now. Heavy footsteps thunked up the staircase, and the door to her bedroom creaked open.

"Caithlin?"

Caithlin buried her head in her pillow and remained quiet. Her bed dipped a little as her father sat down next to her. She looked up, her vision blurred with tears.

"It's not fair!" Caithlin sobbed. "They're just clothes! They'll wash!"

Stefano smiled sadly and patted her on the shoulder.

"Your mother is upset because they are your new clothes. And she told you not to wear them for sailing."

"I didn't know I'd end up in the water!"

"You jumped in."

"To rescue a puppy!"

"But it wasn't a puppy. It was just a bunch of twigs and branches floating in the water. I told you that at the time."

"It looked like a puppy!"

Caithlin sat up slowly, throwing her small arms out to either side and looking up at her father desperately. The thin sailor leaned in to embrace her warmly. Caithlin carried on weeping into her father's shoulder as he patiently held her in silence. After a while, he eased her gently away.

"Look. You did really well today. Up until you jumped out of the boat. You know your sheets from your braces and your tacking from your jibing. That's more than most nine-year-olds know! So… I bought something for you. Just don't tell your mother, alright?"

Caithlin dabbed pathetically at her eyes as her father disappeared back out of her room. He returned only a few moments later. His face was lit up with a smile as he presented a model ship to her, the size of his forearm. Despite her woes, Caithlin could not help but beam from ear to ear at the beautiful ship. She had seen one of them – for real – at the Genezan naval harbor. Race-built, full ship rig, brand new design, only two of them in the whole world, with another two being built in the royal shipyards.

A San Andrea-class sixth-rate frigate. She had seen the model at the little stall Aldo was permitted to set up once a week at the tavern on the shores of Lake Gehr, next to the sailing school. It had taken the kindly old ex-sailor two months to build it; she had begged her father for the model for her ninth birthday, but it was too expensive and her mother objected to a warship with guns being added to Caithlin's collection of model ships. Still beaming, she reached out hesitantly for the ship as if moving too fast would make the dream evaporate. She looked up at her father as she held the model.

"Thank you, Father! Thank you! Thank you!"

The model of the San Andrea-class frigate had pride of place on her shelf throughout her childhood, her adolescence, and her early years as a sailor and then merchant captain. It was still on a dusty shelf in her old bedroom back home on the day she brought her battered, sinking brig into the harbor at Thatraskos, past the row of frigates, and looked up into the kindly eyes of a young Basilean lieutenant on the quarterdeck of Pious, *watching her and her crew sympathetically.*

"Captain!" X'And yelled. "They've got sails set and the weather gauge on us! We may have a couple of knots on her, but by the time we've got the wind off the quarter and the sails set, she'll be on us!"

Caithlin looked back at the charging light frigate. Her paint was chipped, crude black stripes were painted along her once beautiful hull, and her figurehead was vandalized; the wooden effigy of San Alessandra had its eyes gouged out, and a crude, metal strip nailed across her lips. That image alone filled Caithlin's heart with sadness. The frigate drew closer, her deck packed with cutlass-wielding pirates, some of whom were already positioning with lines and grapples to board. Caithlin stared up for a moment of despair, estimating the number of sailors the frigate had onboard. Her crew did not stand a chance. She whipped her head around to face X'And.

"Alright… alright! Bring us back around! Let's face the bastards! We'll give them a broadside right in their damned face as they get to us, and then fight to the last! If this is how we're going to go out, let's make a hell of a noise and go down swinging!"

The salamander sailor looked down at her with a sad, but resolute smile. He gave a slight nod.

"Yes. Alright, old friend. Down swinging we go."

X'And paced across to the main mast to shout orders up into the rigging as more sailors rushed to the upper deck from down below. Caithlin reached into her pocket and produced the coin she had kept from her first encounter with Jaymes. She closed her eyes, kissed it, and muttered a brief prayer for the Shining Ones to watch over Jaymes and her father after she was gone. With that, Caithlin placed the coin away, gritted her teeth, and drew two pistols from her sash as the brig swung about to face the frigate, and her doom.

A cool, calming wind blew across the brig's deck seemingly from nowhere, and blue flames flickered along the edge of the fo'c'sle as the Basilean flag fluttered above the crew of the *Martolian Queen*.

***

The xebec plunged out of the fog, the intermittent bank of moisture stopping abruptly before open sea spread from horizon to horizon. The first of the two sloops, the *Highwayman,* was a good four cables ahead, sails set to full as she skipped across the smooth waters. In any other circumstances, the little sloop on the sun-kissed waters might even have looked pretty, if lives were not on the line. On the quarterdeck of the xebec, Tem stood at the very stern with his fingers wrapped tightly around the taffrail, looking back in desperation for the third ship in his group.

The *Baron's Revenge* appeared a second later, the light sloop frantically clawing for wind in her sails as she rose and fell with the waves. A dark shadow appeared in the fog behind her, looming high over her like a dragon chasing a terrified deer. The shape smashed out of the fog and into the sunlight – a three-masted, Batch Two Elohi-class frigate. The thousand ton warship punched through the waves that tossed and pitched the *Baron's Revenge*, immovable seemingly even by nature.

With shouts of commands to her crew drifting across to Tem and the xebec on the southerly winds, the fifth-rate frigate turned with remarkable agility to line up her broadside on the stern of the *Baron's*

Revenge. The guns fired as one, the hull of the Basilean frigate lit up and then blurred behind a wall of smoke. The *Baron's Revenge* exploded in a ball of wooden splinters, the entire mast spinning away like a child's discarded toy, sixty men killed instantly as the ship was torn apart.

Across the deck of the xebec, crewmen shouted and swore in panic, some looking up at the sails as if trying to will them to push the ship further and faster from the wooden-walled killer chasing them down, others sinking to their knees in despair. The frigate's bows curved around again, and the bow chasers fired. With a dull whoosh and a snapping of wood, two spinning bar-shots tore through the rigging above. The yard of the main mast snapped a quarter of the way from the tip, falling to tear down part of the mainsail. One of Tem's pirates took a running jump off the ship and plunged into the water, appearing a second later and paddling furiously for the open sea.

His heart aching, his lungs burning, Tem stared in desperation from the Basilean frigate, to Halladai, to his damaged rigging above, and to the elusive freedom of the horizon to the north, too far ahead to be of any use yet close enough to provide an entire world of wanting and desperation.

"We've got to go back!" Halladai yelled. "We've got to get back into the fog!"

Tem looked back at the mist behind them, still dissipating, still breaking up as sunlight burnt huge holes through the field of moisture.

"What fog?" Tem cried. "There's nothing left! There's nowhere to hide!"

Halladai sprinted over to Tem.

"Then what? What's left?"

Tem looked up at the main mast above, and then down at his quartermaster.

"We strike the colors!"

"No! We're not surrendering! They'll hang us! Every last one of us!"

Tem swore and wiped the back of his sleeve over his mouth. His head pounded. His skin itched. His gut clenched in agony. So this was it. This was what it felt like to be certain of death. At that moment, he would have given anything and everything to travel back to that day when he decided to jump ship and run to become a pirate. He would have given his soul to become a simple merchant sailor once more. He looked up at the main mast again, and then across at a crewman by the base.

"Strike the colors!" he commanded. "Raise the white flag!"

"Belay that order!" Halladai screamed. "No white flag!"

Tem shoved the mutinous quartermaster with both hands, but the effort was as futile as trying to push a mountain.

"Don't you dare belay my orders! I'm in command here!"

Halladai grabbed him by the collar with both hands and pulled him in, his eyes scrunched up in fury and his face contorted.

"If this is it, then we die! I'm not dancing on a gibbet for you!"

Tem shoved his arms up between Halladai's hands and wrenched them open to force himself free of the iron grasp.

"Some of these poor bastards are new to this! They'll get a pardon, Halladai! Some might live! You and me; we're dead either way! We're striking the colors!"

Behind them, the frigate executed the same maneuver she had used to bring her guns to bear on the *Baron's Revenge*. She swung about rapidly to line up her broadside. The lines of black cannons – longer and more deadly than any of the small guns Tem had ever seen on a pirate vessel – pointed directly at the xebec's stern. Tem turned to bark out an order to his helmsman to turn out of angle for a stern rake. He was too slow.

The towering frigate's guns bellowed again. An invisible hand wrenched Tem up from the deck, into the hot air, and then threw him forward across the upper deck in a storm of wooden splinters. His hearing was replaced with an incessant, high-pitched whine. The air stank of burning and tasted of smoke. His body felt as though it was broken and burned from head to toe. He landed on the deck and slid forward, the sharp lip of a broken plank tearing open a wound in his thigh.

Tem did not know how long he lay still for. Men ran seemingly in every direction, but he heard nothing, save the high-pitched whining. The sun was blotted out as the frigate bore in, looming over the little xebec. Jeffi fell down to his knees next to Tem, a red hole in his chest marking out the deadly accuracy of a marine sharpshooter in the frigate's fighting tops.

Struggling back up to his feet, Tem limped and staggered across the pitching deck toward the pennant locker. Musket and crossbow shots ripped across the xebec, killing men from stem to stern. His bloodied, shaking hands finding the white flag, Tem attached it to the halyard and, urging his pained arms into action, began hauling the white up the side of the main mast for all he was worth.

It made no sense at all to Tem's addled mind when he realized that he was up to his knees in warm water. He looked from side to side in a daze and saw only the quarterdeck, masts, and fo'c'sle were still dry. The upper deck was gone. The xebec rolled to port violently, the yard of the mainmast dipping into the sea. Tem looked down. Halladai floated past him, face up. His friend's eyes flickered over to look at Tem. He offered a weak but warm smile, then rolled over face down and sank beneath the water in a pool of red.

Tem looked up again. The frigate was alongside them, lines of guns pointing down at the doomed xebec. Immense, eighteen-pounders as well as short, stubby close-in weapons from the towering quarterdeck. A broadside of nearly twenty guns – more than double what was required to destroy the crippled, sinking xebec. As Tem's eyes swam across the frigate's quarterdeck, they stopped at a lone figure. A dark-haired man in his mid-twenties, the very picture of the handsome, dashing frigate captain of Basilean news sheets. His white shirt and gold epaulets were stained black with gunsmoke. The two captains locked eyes for a brief moment. Tem saw no mercy in his opposite number; only anger and grim determination. The Basilean captain opened his mouth to shout out a single word to his crew.

Fire.

Chapter Twenty-One

Thatraskos Harbor
Keretia
Northeast Infant Sea

A disheveled, despondent group of perhaps twenty stevedores paused in their work on the quay to watch the frigate silently drift across the harbor and toward the jetty. Rain fell down from a bumpy, uneven canopy of low, gray clouds, pitter-pattering off the green water of the harbor and the thick leaves of the surrounding vegetation. What repairs could have been carried out at sea had already been completed; yet, despite the hours of care and hard work, large parts of the HW *Pious* were still blackened and burnt from the fire she had suffered several days before. Once the dockyard workers had morbidly observed the extent of the damage to the frigate, they continued hauling a series of heavy boxes onto a light, two-hundred ton trading brig bound for the west.

Pious nudged gently alongside the jetty, neatly lined up with the frigates *Devotion, Encounter,* and *Veneration.* After clearing the lower decks of all of his sailors and addressing them on the upper deck, thanking them for their courage and tireless work, and awarding them a cheer-rousing pay bonus, Jaymes headed ashore to the naval administration building. The low rumble of thunder from the south could be heard as Jaymes was presented to the admiral by his flag lieutenant.

"Take a seat," Admiral Jerris Pattia offered a slight smile.

Jaymes obliged and watched as the short admiral poured out two small glasses of rum and sat opposite him, pushing one glass across the long desk. Behind him, through the closed doors of the balcony, the southern horizon silently lit up with a flicker of lightning.

"I trust you received my letter, sir?" Jaymes began.

The admiral sampled his rum and then nodded.

"Yes. It arrived here four days ago. Thank you for keeping me informed. And thank you for staying out there on station to assist with escorting those South Manticamen after the *Duty* ran into trouble. She made it back here in one piece. But it was a good show of initiative to stay out there for longer, especially after the losses you took against the Ahmunites."

Jaymes let out a quiet sigh. Hundreds dead. First and foremost to Jaymes was Kaeso. He would have to visit Kaeso's mother to talk to her. He owed his lieutenant that much.

"I'm sorry we didn't get the bastard, sir," Jaymes offered.

Jerris offered a slight, barely perceptible shrug.

"I employ winners, Jaymes. I only ask that you win. You, Marcellus, and Zakery, bless his soul – you all won. It wasn't a crushing victory worthy of sonnet, but you sank most of their fleet and you rescued our citizens who were taken. Sir Laval Curzon wrote to me to ask me to convey his gratitude to you and Marcellus on behalf of the people of Roe's Spring. And you sent an enemy commander home with his tail between his legs. We even recovered his translator, too, which will result in some solid information about our enemy. That's still a solid victory. You all did what was demanded of you, to a good standard."

Jaymes looked across the desk at the older officer. Whilst his words certainly seemed to express positivity, his tone did not. Jaymes found himself bracing for the inevitable surprise reprimand, but it did not come. In fact, Jaymes observed with no small amount of curiosity that the admiral failed to look him in the eye.

"I'll get you another lieutenant," Jerris continued. "I'm ever so sorry about Kaeso. I knew his father. Good family."

"Yes, sir."

Again, the admiral looked away. He cleared his throat and tugged on his neckerchief.

"Damn shame about the *Shield Royal*. I gather that between you and Lieutenant Azer, you both managed to rescue every last sailor who made it off the wreckage. I'm sure Zakery would be thankful for that."

Jaymes swallowed, downed his rum in one, and carefully placed the glass down on the desk. Images of Zakery looking up at him from the surging water before jumping back into the sea to try to swim back for more survivors flooded into Jaymes's mind's eye.

"Captain Uwell actually survived, sir. He brought one of the ship's boys to *Pious* and then tried to head back to help more survivors. That was when we lost him."

Jerris raised his eyebrows and then ran one hand across his mouth.

"I didn't know him. Not before he came out here with the *Shield*. A good friend of mine at the Admiralty sent me a letter of introduction. Glowing report, really. It rather sounds like Zakery Uwell went out exactly as he lived. A selfless, bloody hero. Little consolation to his family, of course. It never is."

Jaymes looked down into his empty glass, and then back up.

"Shall I pour us both another, sir?"

The admiral blinked twice, slowly.

"Yes. Yes, please. Good idea."

Jaymes walked over to the drinks cabinet by the balcony doors, found the rum, and then walked back to the desk to pour out two more glasses. He sat down again and took another drink.

"Jaymes..." the admiral began hesitantly, staring down at the base of the bottle of rum on his desk. "I'm afraid... the *Martolian Queen* didn't make it back."

Jaymes's head shot up, his eyes wide. He turned to stare out of the rain-streaked windows of the balcony doors. That was impossible. He had seen the *Martolian Queen* only minutes before, as they sailed across the harbor. She was right there! He stood up and paced quickly across to the balcony. Only a gunbrig at the *Queen's* normal berth. That was not it – he would never confuse two so dissimilar ships. It must have been her secondary berth. He looked out. Empty. He stopped, and turned again. He had seen her on the way in! Had he not? No. He hadn't.

"I... it's been..."

Jerris stood and placed a hand on Jaymes's shoulder.

"She's overdue by a week. Should have come in with *Veneration*. Marcellus said he lost her in the fog. I'm afraid she hasn't been seen since. I... I'm terribly sorry, Jaymes. So very sorry."

Jaymes span around again to stare down at the harbor, his eyes scanning rapidly from berth to berth to find the distinctive Genezan fighting brig. Jerris appeared by his side and offered him his glass of rum.

"Take a couple of weeks off, Jaymes. You've had a hell of a time with the battle against that orc smasher, and then all of this Ahmunite business. In fact, why don't you take a month so you've time to travel. Head home. See your parents in the capital. You won't miss much here."

Jaymes shook his head. He looked down at the rum, out across the bay, then back at the admiral.

"I... a month... the repairs. I... just a week, I think, sir. I can be back on patrol in a week. I..."

Jerris shook his head.

"Take some time off. The *Loyalty's* refit has had some problems. Old Harry is tearing his hair out. He can look after *Pious* for you for a while, while he's waiting for his own chariot to get fixed up again. Go home, Jaymes. I'll see you in a month."

Jaymes stopped again. Home. He had not seen his parents in so long. Had not seen his sister or her family. He could go home. Make some sense of this madness. Think it all through. He looked up again suddenly.

"I saw her! Alongside! When we came in! I bloody swear it, I know it! She was right there! Excuse me, please, sir."

Rushing out of the building, sprinting for the main gate of the naval base, running aimlessly through the driving rain for hour after hour, Jaymes checked every berth and every jetty again and again until darkness fell over Thatraskos. But the *Martolian Queen* was gone.

***

The ukiola player plucked carefully at the four strings of the tiny instrument, flashing a smile to a couple of local girls as they walked into the Palm Spring bar. Outside, the storms and their bands of showers had finally seemed to pass, and the night sky was alive with stars above, and a complete absence of wind, allowing the dry heat from the day to linger. The lights of Thatraskos at night – the colored lamps outside every home and bar surrounding the beautiful bay that the population took such pride in – seemed a perfect accompaniment to the merry music of the ukiola and the perfect weather of the hot night.

Propping up the bar alone, Jaymes stared down into his glass of rum. It was only his second, and already he was utterly sick of the bittersweet liquid. He looked up at his own reflection in the mirror behind the bar. At least he avoided the string of cliches associated with despair. Three nights of drinking alone, yet he had not overdone it once. Three days since arriving back at Thatraskos, yet he presented himself for duty punctually every day, clean-shaven and in a smartly pressed uniform to oversee the repairs to *Pious*. He had visited Kaeso Innes's mother, which went about as well as such an occasion could.

Jaymes looked back down away from the mirror. Still, washed and clean-shaven though he was, even he could see the red in his eyes in his reflection.

"Another of the same, Jaymes?"

Tarance, the barman, risked a sympathetic smile. Jaymes shook his head.

"No. Thank you."

The ukiola player finished his song and then began a local favorite in the tongue of the indigenous islanders, a slow song about Thatraskos's myths and legends that was supposed to be uplifting and relaxing, yet at that moment sounded dour and miserable to Jaymes. He finished his rum, wincing at the taste and deciding he would avoid dwarf spirits in the future.

"You open for company?"

Jaymes looked up. Stefano leaned over the bar next to him. Jaymes shrugged and nodded. Stefano pulled up a stool and held two fingers up at the barman to order a pair of drinks.

"Repairs are coming along well," Jaymes offered, "thank you. You didn't need to stay here for that."

Stefano let out a brief, bitter laugh.

"It's just to keep my mind occupied while I wait for other things."

Other things. Of course, Jaymes held out hope that Caithlin would somehow, miraculously sail into harbor at some point. Or a sloop would come in, saying the *Martolian Queen* was damaged and holed up at one of the colony settlements. But those avenues had already been explored. The fighting brig had simply vanished. No reports from merchant ships or patrols coming in from the area. Nothing.

"She sent me a letter," Jaymes found himself saying out loud, "when we last saw each other. I sent a boat across to her ship to return some of her crew who ended up on mine. It came back with a letter from her."

Jaymes pulled the crumpled letter, read a thousand times over the past few days, from his pocket and placed it on the bar.

"I was always sending letters to her, you see. She told me that I didn't need to. Very kindly. Very gently for such a matter-of-fact, sometimes even blunt woman. So I took the hint and stopped with my overly sentimental love letters. Then, at the time I should have written one for her, with all we were dealing with, she sent one to me, and I had nothing for her. Just a boatload of her crew and that bloody salamander she put up with."

"Puts up with," Stefano corrected quietly, "and... well... no, that's not at all like her. I've spent years watching an endless precision of my subordinates and workers fall in love with her and receive her rather blunt, business-like rejections. Always had her mind on the job. She never wrote a letter to a man. Never spoke about anybody the way she spoke about you. So... repairing your ship while I wait is the least I can do."

Jaymes carefully folded the letter and envelope and placed it back in his pocket as two tankards of ale were pushed across the bar in front of the two men. Stefano wrapped his thin fingers around the handle of his tankard and pulled it toward him. Jaymes shot a hand out and placed it over the top of the tankard.

"Careful. Always check your tankard around here. In case some bastard puts a coin in it. You'll end up in the bloody navy if you don't keep your wits about you."

Stefano's dour face cracked into a smile at the joke. He took a swig from his ale and placed it back down. A few moments passed in silence between the two men as the song continued from the small stage near the main entrance, much to the pleasure of the two local girls sat at the closest table. Stefano turned to look at Jaymes.

"You must think I'm mad. Holding out hope."

Jaymes shook his head.

"No. Maybe. If you are, so am I. I've put my new house up for sale. I've got somebody coming to look at it tomorrow. If they buy it, I'll have enough money to buy a pinnace and hire a crew. Then I'm going to go out and search every last island north of the Infantosians. I know these waters and I know what the chances are. They're nearly nothing. But only *nearly*. When I try to sleep, I see images of her clinging to wreckage, or stranded on a beach. So I have to try."

Stefano placed an arm around the younger man's shoulders.

"Don't sell your house. And certainly don't go out into the open sea in a damn pinnace. Give it another few days. I've got a ship from my company on the way here, with a crew. A two hundred tonner with a handful of guns. Come with me. We'll search together."

Jaymes looked up from his ale.

"You know the chances are..."

"I know," Stefano stared straight ahead, across the bar, "I know. But it doesn't stop men like you and I. So we'll go. Odds mean little to me. It's what brought me out here. When Caithlin was duped into this ludicrous privateering contract to pay off a debt that legally she never should have owned. No... no... she told me. You were the one good man who tried to help her. I know that. But I've hired the best law man I know of and I've fought this with everything I have. I've sunk a fortune into travel, legal fees, audiences with the South Mantica Company, and your bloody admiralty. I've done... I've done what any father would do for his daughter. Everything, without stopping, without a shred of remorse for all it has cost me. Because she is worth it a thousand times over."

For a moment, Jaymes thought the stubborn, stern old man might break down in tears. But after the short tremor of the shoulders, he raised his tankard and then continued.

"I'd actually done as well as I could. She had a ten year debt, as you know. That whole business with the orc fleet and then a few early victories, and she'd managed to chip a year off that. All of my work – arguing improper and immoral use of maritime law versus ignorance of the law being no excuse, the incorrect charging of the cargo that was later recovered versus the legally binding signature she made as a captain with full capacity for her actions... long story short, I brought the bastards down by another six years. She only had three years to serve out. We could have done that."

"Still can," Jaymes whispered, forcing a insincere smile that married up with the lack of faith he had in his own words.

Whether Stefano picked up on the noble lie or not, he smiled in return.

"Yes. Thank you, Jaymes. For everything."

"There's nothing to thank me for. I've spent the last few days feeling sorry for myself. But I know that I only knew Cathy briefly. Just a quick flash on the timeline. You were there when she was born and have been there every day since. I know this is far harder for you, and it isn't about me. And I'm really, truly sorry for what you are going through."

The older man looked forward again, his brow furrowed in concentration. He looked like he might say something but remained silent, and then threw Jaymes a slight smile and raised his tankard as if to toast him.

The two men brought their tankards to their lips. Cannon fire erupted from the bay, forcing Jaymes to spit out his ale and jump to his feet. Two other men in the bar, clearly also with naval connections, jumped up and dashed for the main entrance. Jaymes was first out, bursting into the hot night and looking down across the bar's colorful entrance garden, past the west harbor fort and out to sea.

Illuminated in the full moon, south of the harbor and sailing north at full sail, was the unmistakable silhouette of a light frigate. Sixth-rate, foreign.

"That's one of ours!" Stefano yelled as he appeared next to Jaymes. "That frigate! She's Genezan! Why's she firing?"

Jaymes's eyes widened.

"Pirates... it's a bloody pirate ship! Why isn't the fort attacking? I... I've got to get to *Pious*!"

Jaymes sprinted down the hill toward the naval dockyard as another series of bangs and explosions echoed toward the harbor from the south. His feet echoing through the narrow, cobbled streets, Jaymes ran past families appearing at the doors of their homes to see what the commotion was so late at night. Then, halfway down the hill, he stopped dead in his tracks.

The night lit up with gaudy reds, yellows, and whites. Stars whooshed and whizzed across the top of Thatraskos. Lights sparkled and fizzed. It was not cannon fire. It was fireworks, blasted up from the frigate approaching the harbor. A few seconds later, Stefano staggered down to stop next to Jaymes, wheezing and panting. Again, Jaymes thought the older man was crying for a moment. Then he realized that it was laughter. Bent over double, Stefano held out a small, pocket telescope to the frigate captain.

"Look... Jaymes... look!"

Jaymes took the telescope, unfolded it, and raised it to his eye. He stared incredulously out into the bay as the Genezan frigate reached the breakwater between the harbor's two forts. Another salvo of fireworks shot up from something ahead of the warship. Atop the frigate's main mast was a white flag of surrender. In front of her, hidden and overshadowed by the larger vessel, was a two-masted, square-rigger. A brig. Flying the Basilean flag, spitting out fireworks from both sides, came the *Martolian Queen*.

Jaymes and Stefano hurtled down toward the dockyard as

both ships entered the harbor, the entire town rudely roused from their slumber as both fighting brig and frigate alike fired their broadsides in salute of the admiral's flag flying from atop the naval administration building. Crowds of townsfolk had flocked to the waterfront by the time Jaymes and Stefano arrived to see both ships bringing in sail and preparing to come alongside one of the empty jetties in the mercantile eastern half of the harbor. His chest light with excitement, laughter interrupting his breathing and slowing his pace, Jaymes ran along the waterfront alongside the brig, threading through the crowds of townsfolk and dock workers.

The crews of both ships stood on the upper decks. Jaymes saw a familiar figure at the very front of the brig. Music blared out from the privateer ship as a fiddler frantically played the Genezan national anthem from her fo'c'sle, the tempo far quicker than the norm. Stood acrobatically on the bowsprit of the *Martolian Queen* in a remarkable show of balance, a bottle of rum in one hand and the flag of a defeated pirate held high in the other, Caithlin smiled in victory and shouted out in response to the cheers from the crowds along the waterfront.

The battered brig nudged in her bow, and one of her crew jumped ashore to tie a forespring before the stern swung in to line up with the jetty. Stood on the bowsprit, Caithlin jumped down to straddle the long pole before wrapping one arm around it, swinging once around the bowsprit and then jumping the gap to land with a thud on the jetty, bottle of rum and pirate flag still held high. Jaymes and Stefano pushed their way through the excited crowd to reach her at the jetty. Caithlin bowed to the crowd, unsteadily turned to face Jaymes and Stefano, opened her mouth to say something, and then lost her balance and staggered two paces to one side with an amused yelp and a giggle.

"I'm back!" Caithlin beamed. "And... and I got one! Got one of the bastards! A famous one, too! Got him in irons in his own bloody ship!"

Jaymes stared incredulously up at the battered, holed brig and the frigate behind her as the music continued from the fo'c'sle and a rogue firework exploded, late, from the quarterdeck. His eyes locked onto Caithlin's and both of them smiled warmly. Stefano stepped forward.

"Are you drunk?" the old merchant sailor demanded.

"I... well... perhaps a little..." Caithlin slurred merrily, before rushing forward to embrace both men.

***

Her head still throbbing faintly, her face flushed red with embarrassment as a trio of dockworkers laughed as she passed –

clearly remembering her ostentatious arrival in the harbor shortly before midnight of the previous night – Caithlin walked slowly along the jetty. The damage to the *Martolian Queen* perhaps looked worse than it was; makeshift repairs to the rigging carried out at sea could now be resolved properly, although the harm to the hull itself would take more time. And more money. The perennial problem.

"You're looking better than I thought you would after your performance last night."

Caithlin glanced up to see her father striding across from the steps leading down from the harbor master's office. She flashed a smile.

"I don't feel that bad, honestly. Luckily enough, I threw up quite a lot last night, so there's not much left in my system. That really takes the sting out of a hangover, it turns out."

Stefano's jaw dropped a little and his eyes narrowed.

"That's a level of detail that a father never really needs to hear from his daughter."

"I had reason to celebrate," Caithlin shrugged, "I was attacked by a rated warship. My crew took her, without us losing a single life, and then with my crew split in two to sail two ships, we made it home through two storms, one major flood, a lost yard, two torn sails, and a brief whiff of an interested sea monster. Arriving here after all of that was worth a bottle of rum."

"And waking up an entire town, including children, with fireworks and guns?"

"Yes, father. That too. Y'see, I've rid the Infant Sea of one of the most notorious pirates of a generation. What we did out there... we've saved lives. I don't know how many, but it'll be a lot. Even if it were only one, then we did something good."

Stefano's features softened. He paced past the fighting brig, surveying the damage with a keen eye.

"You know that you don't have to do this anymore? With the prize money from that frigate and with what I can raise by selling most of my shares, well, you could come home. You've done it. A couple of months as a privateer. You've survived it. It's something you can tell your grandchildren about one day. But it's done now, and you can come home."

Caithlin leaned across and placed an affectionate hand on the wooden boards of the *Martolian Queen's* flank. Stefano was entirely correct with his earlier comment. There were some things a father should never hear his daughter say. Stefano did not need to know that she had raised pistols and looked men in the eyes as she had gunned them down. That she had seen the light of life fade from a man's eye as she wrenched her saber back out of his chest. And that she regretted none of it. Every life she had taken, every sailor she had killed, they were all pirates. All murderers and cutthroats who preyed on those who could not defend themselves, all for something as crude as money. Every life her crew took made the world a better place for good, honest people.

"Daddy," Caithlin said quietly, "this is me now. This is who I am. This is what I want to do."

Stefano stepped in and kissed the top of her head.

"I know," he said quietly, "I know. Come on, let's look at this prize of yours."

The father and daughter walked up the gangway to the captured frigate, past the two marines who the admiral had deigned to post on guard duty at the warship's waist. Caithlin paced along the upper deck, casting her eyes across the rows of nine-pounder cannons sat low on their wooden carriages. The deck was a shambles, littered with debris and bearing the scars of years of neglect.

"I think she is the *San Alessandra*, judging by the figurehead," Caithlin said. "They called her the *Dark Siren,* but I've already had that name removed. They... defaced her. I had my carpenter do the best he could to restore her, but you know how difficult that is to do when the sea is anything other than flat calm."

Stefano ran a hand along the frigate's taffrail.

"I *know* she is the *San Alessandra*," he said. "I was up early this morning. I did some research in the naval archives here. She went missing four years ago, about eighty leagues to the southwest of here. Anti-piracy patrol. She needs a bit of work, Caithlin, but if I hire some skilled men and women locally, I think I can get her perfect again. I'll need a proper look around, though, to see how badly neglected she is. Then she can go home, back to our navy."

Caithlin winced. *Our navy.* She looked over her shoulder at where the Basilean flag hung from the stern of the *Martolian Queen*. She remembered the flickers of blue flames dancing along the ship's bow as the pirate frigate charged them down to board. She recalled the whoosh of blazing, blue fire engulfing the brig's bowsprit as the pirates boarded them, the feeling of calmness washing across the deck. The look of abject terror in the eyes of the boarders as they stared into space, looking up toward the heavens at things invisible to Caithlin but real enough to them that forty men jumped off the ship to face drowning rather than stand against whatever it was that they saw. The same number again surrendered without a fight, so fearful were they to oppose the celestial force that chose to bless and favor Caithlin and her crew at that moment. Because they flew the Basilean flag. That was her navy.

"You want to keep her."

Stefano said it as a statement rather than a question. Caithlin narrowed one eye and shrugged.

"I'd like an Elohi-class to sail across Lake Gehr to show off to all my peers who were horrible to me as a child. It doesn't mean that it will ever happen. I can't afford to keep her. I need the money to pay my debts and to repair the *Queen*."

"Why? You've just said that you're staying out here. You don't need to pay the debt off quickly, if that's the case. You've got one hundred idiots willing to follow you. You could crew this ship with a hundred decent hands."

"Not if I want to operate a broadside of a dozen nine-pounders at peak efficiency," Caithlin countered.

"Well, I'll bow to your superior experience there, and I say that without a hint of sarcasm. But you could run this ship. Sell the *Queen* instead."

Caithlin turned around and looked aft to where her faithful, ever-dependent brig lay against the jetty, forlorn and silent with her damaged hull and torn rigging. Half a year ago, Caithlin would have sneered at any sailor foolish enough to feel sentimentality for a ship. Now, she found her vision blurred with a tear in her eye.

"I couldn't do that," she whispered, "not after all we've been through. Not after everything that ship has done for me."

Stefano dropped to one knee and inspected the state of the deck.

"Well, you've got time to think. I've got three ships to work on now – *Pious*, the *Martolian Queen,* and the *San Alessandra*. I'll work *Pious* at a good rate out of respect for Jaymes, but I'm not working at cost after what that admiral tried to pull on you. Depending on how many skilled workers I can find, I can work one of these two here simultaneously. There's a fair bit to do here. I might even move your mother out here for a few weeks. And your little sister. Although she'll probably try to poach your man from you."

"She can try!" Caithlin laughed. "But if she does, then I'll run the bitch through myself with my saber."

"Caithlin! Language!"

"Sorry, Daddy."

Failing to suppress a smile, Stefano headed down the upper deck's aft hatchway to the gundeck below. Caithlin remained on the upper deck in the morning sun, looking forward to the frigate's stem and allowing herself a few seconds of idle fantasy as she was, once more, nine years old again and holding up the model San Andrea-class frigate her father bought for her, pretending that one day she could be her captain.

Guttural voices roused him from his dazed, semi-conscious slumber. Harsh hands grabbed aching, scabbed limbs rubbed raw by salt-water soaked clothes for he did not know now how many days. Days of clinging to a pair of barrels, hidden beneath a shred of torn sail cloth that provided the only respite from the blazing sun. Days of staring out from horizon to horizon, praying for a glimpse of land or a sail. Days of crippling cramp, dizziness, hunger, and struggling with the self-discipline required to ration the few mouthfuls of fresh water within one of the barrels.

The first few days had perhaps been the worst. There were other survivors in the water. Two, maybe three different voices scattered amidst the wreckage. One had simply stopped calling out. Sharks took another. By the third day, Tem was completely alone. But as dehydration set in, so too did delirium, which in a twisted sort of way at least seemed to pass the time. Every day Tem would wake, amazed that he had managed to stay atop the barrels in his sleep or confusion. Days of sorrow, boredom, anger, confusion, contemplation, and eventually wishing for death.

Did he deserve this? Was life as a pirate so wrong? His time as a merchant sailor had seen long, harsh days; lashes across his back for innocent mistakes; being cheated out of his meager wages by corrupt, greedy captains; and seeing his shipmates killed in storms. Piracy was his chance to take what he had earned, and from those who owed him. It was never supposed to be stealing from the innocent or hurting anybody. Things... just got out of hand sometimes.

Tem was dragged up onto a deck by strong, unforgiving hands. He looked up through blurred eyes at the hulking figures surrounding him as he was hauled up onto his feet. His legs immediately buckled, and he plummeted back down to the deck. A sea of deep voices came together to laugh at him and spit insults down at him. Tem looked up and saw muscular, green limbs and piggish snouts. Orcs. He found himself laughing at his misfortune. Good. At least they would kill him quickly. Bizarrely, he found himself thankful to the brutish monsters for one last chance to be out of the water.

"What d'you want to do with that?" one voice growled.

"Just kill it and throw it back in."

Again the hands grabbed him by his arms, and he was yanked painfully up to his feet. A blade was held to his throat. His dehydrated, addled mind only saw blurred figures and the blazing corona of the sun high above. His mind drifted to that final conversation on the beach with his chief, where he had been duped into sailing right into a pair of frigates.

"Cerri..." he whispered. "Cerri... you bastard..."

"Wait!"

A commanding voice thundered out, and the whole deck fell silent. Tem heard the distinctive click and thump of a figure with a peg-leg striding over.

"He said something about Cerri, Admrul."

"I know. I heard."

The new arrival towered over Tem. His eyes swam into focus intermittently, just long enough to make out the figure of a truly immense, gargantuan orc in a red great coat and wearing a powdered wig of white curls. The orc leaned in.

"You know Cerri, boy?"

"Y...yes... bastard betrayed me... sent me... the wrong way... Basilean frigate... sank us... killed my crew..."

The huge orc grunted. Then spat. Then let out a long, chilling laugh.

"Cerri Denayo betrayed you and fed you to a Basilean frigate? You're in good company, boyo. So I think I'll keep you. I'll make use of you. You may get your revenge yet, when I find him..."

Epilogue

Thatraskos Harbor
Keretia
Northeast Infant Sea

Beneath a sky painted in azure and sprinkled with stars, Jaymes and Karnon walked up the familiar network of roads and pathways leading from Thatraskos's main market square to the more affluent northwest quartile. Townsfolk appeared periodically in their gardens, lighting their colored lamps to play their small, individual parts in creating the port town's famed night time atmosphere. Music drifted down from the top of the hill, from the more expensive bars and inns. The walk had been largely in silence and, for just a moment, Jaymes pondered on whether tonight would finally be the night that he would challenge and, if necessary, verbally assault Karnon over his ludicrous choice of trousers. That night's selection was a banana yellow.

"I've bought another book..."

"Ones above," Jaymes rolled his eyes, "here we go..."

"As I was saying, I've bought another book. I'm aware that makes me part of a select, tiny minority, if not being alone and completely unique, in that I am a marine who owns *two* books, but I bought it nonetheless. Anyway, this book is on the origins of phrases we use in our modern language. Do you remember what you said to me when you picked me up off that island full of skeletons?"

The two reached a corner halfway up the hill and turned, looking down at the picturesque bay below where work still progressed on repairing *Pious*.

"No," Jaymes yawned. "Go on. What did I say?"

"You said: Through thick and thin, old boy. It's a phrase with glorious origins in boaty stuff. Or something like that."

"Alright. What's your point?"

"Well, according to my book..."

"Here we go..."

"...According to my academically referenced, critically acclaimed book, the origin of the phrase is in the rural term, through thicket and thin wood."

Jaymes stopped dead and turned to face the younger man.

"Bollocks."

"Eyebrows. Buffer in a foulie."

"No, no, no! It's a reference to using both a thick rope and a thin rope in hoisting sails. We were taught that in our most basic sail training. That's been passed down for hundreds, if not over a thousand years. That beats your bloody book, mate."

The two began walking up the hill again, Karnon beaming broadly.

"Not what my book says. It's a rural term referring to facing the hardships of cross country travel. Which makes a lot more sense than your shit rope dit. So no, through thick and thin is not a naval phrase."

"Avast on your bullshit, me hearty. We were using that phrase long before it was commandeered by bloody farmers walking through a field. It's 'thick,' not 'thicket.' You can't just add a syllable and then fabricate some nonsense about idle perambulations through a sodding cabbage patch! It's about pulling ropes through blocks!"

"Agree to disagree."

"No! You're part of the naval service now! Where's your bloody loyalty?"

"Not what my book says. And that's written by a proper author, not some bloody naval officer just making shit up."

The two reached the familiar setting of the Palm Spring and followed the sound of merry music and laughter as they threaded their way through the outside garden, overlooking the bay far below. Jaymes and Karnon were greeted with cheers as they entered the crowded bar and saw a long table against the far wall, packed with their friends.

"You're late!" Sabine called.

"We're so sorry!" Jaymes called back across the bar. "It was *all* Karnon's fault! Again!"

Grumbling under his breath, Karnon paced across the bar to pull up a seat next to his wife. Jaymes found himself more than a little surprised to see X'And was the first on the table to rush out to meet him. The stern-faced salamander held out a small glass.

"Cathy told me you like rum. There was only one bottle of rum from the Three Kings here, and I've never tried this particular distillery, but I thought I'd share it with you."

Jaymes accepted the glass.

"Thank you. Honestly… thank you."

The salamander tilted his head and looked down at the shorter sailor expectantly. Jaymes shrugged and downed the shot. There was certainly a kick – and a hint of something not dissimilar to vanilla – but it was sweet, viscous, and easy to work with.

"This is certainly a lot more sympathetic to the palette than the dwarf stuff."

X'And narrowed his eyes and winced.

"That means it's good."

"Excellent. I shall get you another."

The salamander snatched the glass back.

"X'And," Jaymes stopped him, "thank you for always keeping an eye on Caithlin. I know she doesn't need help with most things, but she does with the stabbing and the shooting. We all do, sooner or later. So, thank you."

"We'll make a hellcat out of her yet," X'And replied. "She's getting a lot better. Particularly with pistols."

"I hear it was you who took down Cerri Denayo during the boarding. There are rumors going around that you bit his leg off."

The burly salamander threw his head back and let out a loud, long laugh.

"I didn't bite his leg off!"

His face then grew deadly serious, and he raised one razor-clawed thumb.

"But I did gouge out the bastard's eye. Still, they're hanging him in two weeks, so he won't need it. I'll go get you another rum."

Jaymes watched the salamander return to the bar with an almost comical, happy-go-lucky scuttle that seemed odd to him given the nature of their conversation. Caithlin walked over and sat perched on the end of the window sill in the bay window by the bar entrance. Jaymes sat down next to her.

"Thanks for trying with him," she nodded at X'And, "he's always been a good friend to me, but I know he can be difficult with some people."

"So can I," Jaymes shrugged, "and the effort has all been on his part, to be fair to him. How did it go today? Have you made a decision?"

Caithlin hugged one knee to her chest and looked out of the window, past the ornamental garden and down to the bay. A pair of Gur Panther brigs drifted gently out past the breakwater and into the moonlit Infant Sea.

"Yes," Caithlin said, biting her lower lip thoughtfully, "my father and I worked through the numbers. A whole afternoon of rather dry mathematics, but we're there now, I think. He's done wonders with this maritime law man of his, with calling in favors and with being a complete bastard to the South Mantica Company. The upshot is that we could sell both the *Martolian Queen* and the *San Alessandra*, and I could go home tomorrow."

Jaymes would be lying to himself if he ignored his heart growing heavy at the thought, but he also knew that it was best for her, and that they would make it work somehow.

"Stop looking so sad. I'm not doing that. I'm staying here."

Jaymes looked across at her.

"Why? You can go home. I know we're in this for the long haul, and I'll get across to Geneza every chance I get."

Caithlin smiled.

"I know you would. But I want to stay here. With you. And if I'm honest, after a lot of soul searching, I've come to something of a realization. An epiphany. It turns out that I'm really rather fond of blowing shit up."

Jaymes could not help but laugh. Caithlin leaned in to rest her head on his shoulder and held his hand.

"I'm not criticizing what my father has done with his life. He's a self-made man who built that company from nothing, and that's an incredible achievement. But I don't want to spend my life trading and working in commerce. I've realized that I want to make the world a better place. And by staying here and doing this, I genuinely believe that I can do that."

Jaymes wrapped an arm around her shoulder. X'And caught his eye and gestured pointedly at his bottle of rum and two glasses.

"Which ship will you keep?" Jaymes asked.

"Well, that was the hard part. The *San Alessandra* is the *Queen's* better in every respect as a fighting ship and is the right choice. But she should go home, where she belongs. And I've grown more attached to the *Queen* than I ever thought I would. I could never sell her."

"So you're keeping her?"

Caithlin shook her head.

"I'm keeping both. I'm sending the *Queen* home with father. I'm selling her guns back to the navy, and she'll be re-roled back for trade. What she was designed for, where she belongs. I've written a letter to the Genezan Admiralty and asked for permission to fly the *San Alessandra's* original commissioning pennant, alongside a Basilean ensign. If I'm going back to war against pirates, I'd be a fool not to take a sixth-rate if I had the chance."

"That's the best of both worlds in most ways," Jaymes agreed, "but financially... that's the worst option you had. You're not going to pay off that part of the debt your father couldn't write off. Not like this."

Caithlin shrugged.

"I know. And it doesn't bother me one bit. Just like at the start of summer, when you faced your choice and you decided to stay here with me. I don't care about the money. We both belong here. We're both in the right place."

Jaymes leaned back against the window and looked to the far end of the bar at the table, scanning his eyes slowly from left to right across the assembly of his friends.

Karnon looked back at Jaymes, grinned, and held a hand up to offer an ancient and particularly rude gesture. His wife immediately whacked him on the shoulder. X'And pointed frantically at the bottle of rum and glasses in front of him. Marcellus, his first evening with the group, raised a glass of wine to Jaymes and Caithlin with a smile.

Sat next to him, his daughter, Kora, waved enthusiastically at Jaymes and then formed her hand into a makeshift hook, closed one eye, and growled at Caithlin. Caithlin returned the gesture with a wink. At the end of the table, Stefano looked at Jaymes and his daughter, offered Jaymes the warmest smile he had seen from the man, and gave him a slight nod.

Jaymes was in the right place.

***

One week later, against the backdrop of a setting sun and a fiery, orange-yellow sky, *Hegemon's Warship Veneration* slipped her mooring and sailed past the breakwater toward the Sand Lane for her first anti-piracy patrol since her repairs and replenishment. She was followed by the heavier *Pious,* who eased out to take position off her starboard quarter. The last frigate past the breakwater, and the diminutive admiral raising a glass to them all from his balcony, was the privateer frigate *San Alessandra*, on her first voyage since her restoration to her original fit and hull colors.

The arrowhead of frigates set a southerly course together to make the world a better place.

About the Author

Mark Barber writes in the military history and wargaming genres. He has written military aviation titles for Osprey Publishing and spent several years working with Gaijin Entertainment's record breaking 'War Thunder' software package, acting as a historical consultant, in-game content writer and article writer. He has also written several titles for Warlord Games' 'Bolt Action' tabletop game, and has written fiction for the 'Infinity' and 'Kings of War' franchises.

Look for more books from Winged Hussar Publishing, LLC – E-books, paperbacks and Limited-Edition hardcovers. The best in history, science fiction and fantasy at:
https://https://www.whpsupplyroom.com
or follow us on Facebook at:
Winged Hussar Publishing LLC
Or on twitter at:
WingHusPubLLC
For information and upcoming publications

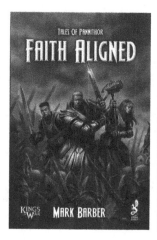